The Conquest of Andalusia

Novels of Islamic History in Translation Series

The Conquest of Andalusia

A historical novel describing the history of Spain and its circumstances before the Muslim conquest, the conquest itself under the command of Tariq ibn Ziyad, and the death of Roderic, the king of the Visigoths

---

Jurji Zaidan

translated from the Arabic
with an Afterword and Study Guide by
Roger Allen

Sponsored and with an Introduction by the Zaidan Foundation

The Zaidan Foundation
For Intercultural Understanding, Inc.

7007 Longwood Drive
Bethesda, MD 20817
Email: GCZaidan@aol.com
Website: www.zaidanfoundation.org
Tel: (301) 469-8131
Fax: (301) 469-8132

Table of Contents

The Conquest of Andalusia

Introduction

About the Novel[1]

The events in this novel take place just before and during the conquest of Spain—or Al-Andalus to the Arabs—in 710-711 AD (91-92 AH). This led to an Arab presence of almost eight centuries in the Iberian Peninsula until the last piece of Spanish territory under Islamic rule (Granada) was reconquered in 1492. Soon after the Umayyads assumed the Islamic Caliphate in 661 AD (41 AH), they established their capital in Damascus. By this time, the Islamic conquests had reached as far east as India and China, while in the west, most of North Africa had been conquered. The native Berber tribes converted to Islam, but the Christian Byzantines still retained most of the ports. The major unfulfilled goal of the Umayyads was to conquer Constantinople and destroy the Byzantine Empire—a feat they attempted three times without success during their almost one-hundred-year reign. The conquest of Andalusia was of lower priority—and it seems to have happened more as a result of local North African initiatives than of any centralized plan. It was, after all, undertaken with local resources and limited Arab material support. The commander of a joint Berber-Arab army, Tariq ibn Ziyad, was himself a Berber[2].

The story opens on Christmas Day 710 AD in Toledo, the capital of Spain at the time, and ends in 711 AD at the conclusion of the battle in Andalusia, in which an Berber-Arab invasion, commanded by Tariq ibn

---

1 First published in 1903 in Arabic as *Fath al-Andalus aw Tariq Ibn Ziyad*.

2 In this novel, Jurji Zaidan uses the Arabic term barbari to describe the indigenous peoples of North Africa, which has been translated as Berber. More recently, however, that term has come to be regarded with disfavor by the people whom it describes, the preferred term being the one by which they describe themselves: Amazigh (plural: Imazighen).

Ziyad, defeated King Roderic and the Visigoth army and cleared the way for the Arab conquest of the Iberian Peninsula. Two centuries earlier the Visigoth rulers had conquered that same land and had been converted to Christianity by Arian bishops. Later, when Arians were declared heretics, the Visigoths submitted to the Roman Catholic church. When the novel opens, the Council of Bishops has forced the Jews, who held predominant positions in trade, crafts, and professional services, to either convert or be banished. Meanwhile, the Visigoth dukes and counts ruled the provinces under an elected king, exploiting the indigenous population and slaves to farm the land and supply menial and military services. This socio-political context sets the stage for conflict and conspiracy between the Visigoth aristocracy and the king, between Christians and Jews, between Catholics and Arians.

The novel depicts the political climate and social mores of Spain at that time. The fast-paced narrative presents many surprises on the way to its appointed end. But one of the more distinctive attributes of Zaidan's approach is the continuous and perceptive commentary and reflection on political and social organization and particularly on human behavior, sentiments, and motivations under varying external conditions. Comments on the nature of a failing state and the impossibility of permanent internal reform, even at the hands of honest politicians or statesmen, are as illuminating as the author's perceptive remarks on the loss of personal identity when people abandon their ethnic characteristics—in this case, implying the Visigoths' abandonment of Arianism. Zaidan also analyzes the power of a common religion or language in unifying people from different cultures—a theme found in many of his other works. Last but not least is the depiction of the Jewish role in aiding the Arab invasion. Jews under Islamic rule were able to preserve their religious heritage and thrive in exchange for a tax at a time when Jews in Visigoth lands were being forced to convert to Christianity. Those who did not do so were faced with either expulsion or execution. Their hopes and expectations were to be borne out in the period after the Arab invasion and until the thirteenth and fourteenth centuries, a period that proved to be a golden age of tolerance and achievement for the various communities living in Spain until the Christian reconquest of Spain, an event that led to the Inquisition and the expulsion of both Jews and Muslims.

Jurji Zaidan—The Historical Novelist

Jurji Zaidan (1861-1914) was a prolific writer who at the dawn of the twentieth century sought to inform and educate his Arab contemporaries about the modern world and the heritage of the Arabs. He is considered one of the most prominent intellectual leaders who laid the foundation for a pan-Arab secular national identity. Pioneering new forms of literature and style in Arabic, he founded in 1892 one of the first—and to this day most successful—monthly journals, *al-Hilal*, a magazine that is still popular today in its 119th year. The *Dar al-Hilal* publishing house in Cairo remains one of the largest in the Arab world. It is a fitting tribute to Zaidan's legacy that new studies reassessing his contributions, and translations of many of his novels—this one among them—are being published one hundred years after his death.

Zaidan was one of the pioneers in the composition of historical novels within the modern Arabic literary tradition and in their serialization in magazines. New editions of the entire series of novels are still being published almost every decade and widely distributed throughout the Arab world—a testament to their lasting popularity. Zaidan's novels were not just for entertainment; national education was his primary goal. The twenty-two historical novels he wrote cover extensive periods of Arab history, from the rise of Islam in the seventh century until the decline of the Ottoman Empire in the nineteenth. The stories depicted in these novels are grounded in the major historical events of various epochs. The particular manners, lifestyles, beliefs, and social mores of those periods, as well as political events, provided the context into which Zaidan weaved adventure and romance, deception and excitement. They were therefore as much "historical" as "novels," reminiscent of the historical novels of Alexandre Dumas in France and Sir Walter Scott in Britain, though Jurji Zaidan's novels more closely reflect actual historical events and developments.

Over the last hundred years, Zaidan's historical novels have been translated into many languages; every novel has been translated at least once, many into four or more languages. To our knowledge there are almost one hundred translations of individual novels in twelve different languages, most in Persian, Turkish/Ottoman, Javanese and Uighur (in China), Azeri, and Urdu, but several also in French, Spanish, German, and Russian. What is noticeable, however, is that not a single one has been translated into English until the present time.

The Zaidan Foundation has so far commissioned the translation into English of five of Jurji Zaidan's historical novels, and more are being planned. The *Conquest of Andalusia*, written by Jurji Zaidan and first published in 1903, is the first of these; the events that it recounts occur before any of the others. Two translations of the novel in Persian and one in Javanese have been done. The Foundation has also commissioned the translation of a second novel: *The Battle of Poitiers—Charles Martel and 'Abd al-Rahman (Sharl wa 'Abd al-Rahman)*, first published in Cairo in 1904 and due to appear shortly. It is set in France at the beginning of the eighth century and describes the Arab invasion of France and how the Franks, under the leadership of Charles Martel, united to stop their advance in Europe. Two other novels cover the 'Abbasid period, during and after the reign of Harun Al-Rashid, best known to the Western world as the caliph whose court is described in the *Arabian Nights* during the zenith of Arab and Islamic power and civilization: *The Caliph's Sister— Harun al-Rashid and the Fall of the Persians (al-'Abbasa Ukht al-Rashid*, 1906) and *The Caliph's Heirs—Brothers at War: The Fall of Baghdad (al-Amin wa'l-Ma'mun*, 1907). The fifth novel, *Saladin and the Assassins (Salah ad-din al-Ayyubi*, 1913), takes place at the time of the Crusades.

The Zaidan Foundation[3]

The Zaidan Foundation, Inc. was established in 2009. Its mission is to enhance understanding between cultures. To this end, the Foundation's principal objective is the international dissemination of the secular and progressive view of the Arab and Islamic heritage. Its first program is the study and translation of the works of Jurji Zaidan. Its audience is the broader English-speaking world: the United States, England, and Canada, to be sure, but also English-speaking Muslim populations with little or no knowledge of Arabic, such as Bangladesh, India, and Pakistan. To achieve its objectives, the Foundation supports directly or through educational or other institutions the translation and publication of historical, literary, and other works, research, scholarships, conferences, seminars, student exchanges, documentaries, films, and other activities.

3 More information about the Zaidan Foundation and its activities can be found on the Foundation's website at www.zaidanfoundation.org

Acknowledgements and Thanks

The Zaidan Foundation was fortunate to have Professor Roger Allen, a noted scholar and teacher of Arabic literature and experienced translator of many Arab literary works, undertake the translation of this novel and provide an illuminating analysis of Zaidan as a historical novelist in his Afterword, as well prepare a Study Guide. He is the Sascha Jane Patterson Harvie Professor of Social Thought and Comparative Ethics, School of Arts & Sciences, Professor of Arabic & Comparative Literature, and Chair, Department of Near Eastern Languages and Civilizations, University of Pennsylvania. He has also served as President of the Middle East Studies Association of North America in 2009-2010.

Many people have generously contributed their time and energy to the Zaidan Foundation, helping to craft its mission and goals, designing and advising on the implementation of its programs and reviewing studies and translations. Foremost among these are Ambassador Hussein A. Hassouna, Ambassador of the Arab League to the United States, Ambassador Clovis F. Maksoud, Professor of International Relations and Director of the Center of the Global South at American University, as well as Edmond Asfour and Bassem Abdallah—all members of the Foundation's Advisory Council. Professor Thomas Philipp was instrumental in helping launch the Jurji Zaidan project following a fortuitous meeting after several decades. Thanks are also due to Said Hitti, who read several manuscripts of the translated novels. Last but not least, my greatest debt is to my wife Hada Zaidan and our son George S. Zaidan for their support of all aspects of this project. The original idea of the Jurji Zaidan program came from Hada, who had more than a marital interest in this project, as her grandfather, Jabr Dumit, was one of Jurji Zaidan's closest friends. In addition to their general and unstinting support, both she and George, Jr. helped design the program and made detailed reviews and many suggestions on the products sponsored by the Foundation.

George C. Zaidan
President
The Zaidan Foundation

Washington, DC
October 2011

Dramatis Personae

RODERIC	king of the Visigoths
ALFONSO	son of Witiza, king of Spain, engaged to Florinda
FLORINDA	daughter of Count Julian, governor of Sabta, engaged to Alfonso
COUNT JULIAN	governor of Sabta, father of Florinda
TARIQ IBN ZIYAD	governor of Tangier and commander of the Muslim armies
FATHER MARTIN	retainer of King Roderic
BISHOP OPPAS	uncle of Alfonso
YA'QUB	servant of Alfonso
SULAYMAN	one of Count Julian's retainers
BARBARA	Florinda's aunt and governess

Sources Used

The author has relied on the following authors and sourceworks in composing the novel and depicting its historical events:

Charles Romey (1804-74), History of Spain (*Histoire de l'Espagne*)
Encyclopaedia Britannica
François Guizot, *History of European Civilization*
Reinhart Dozy, *Analectes sur l'histoire et la littérature des Arabes d'Espagne* (1855)
History of Islamic Civilization
Charles-Louis de Secondat, Baron de Montesquieu
Ibn Khallikan
Ibn al-Athir
Al-Maqqari, *Nafh al-Tib*
Al-Taqwim al-'amm
'Ilm al-farasa al-hadith
Edward Gibbon, *Decline and Fall of the Roman Empire*

Note: All footnotes in the text are those of the author except those designated as *"Translator's Note."*

Chapter 1
Andalus, the Goths, and Toledo

Al-Andalus is one of the provinces of Spain. Its name was originally Wandalusia, a name derived from Al-Wandal or Al-Fandal. It was later colonized by the Romans. When the Arabs conquered the region, they called it Al-Andalus. Thereafter they used the same name to describe the whole of Spain.

Spain as a whole was the Western Roman Kingdom until the fifth century AD. Its rulers were the Goths, a Germanic tribe that had traveled from upper India to Europe in quest of pasturage and livelihood. They resided in the desert regions of Europe just as the Arabs did in those of Syria and Iraq. They took over the Western Roman Kingdom a few centuries before the Arabs gained control of the Eastern kingdom. From there they established kingdoms in France, Germany, England, and elsewhere, all of which still survive in Europe.

This particular tribe of Goths, the Visigoths, gained control of Spain in the fifth century AD and cut off relations with the Romans. They created a Gothic state in the region that only came to an end with the Muslim conquest in the year 92 AH (711 AD) at the hands of Tariq ibn Ziyad, the famous Berber[4] commander.

At that time, the capital of the Gothic Kingdom in Spain was Toledo, on the banks of the river Tagus in central Spain. It was a well-populated city, with fortresses, palaces, castles, churches, and monasteries;

---

4 In this novel, Jurji Zaidan uses the Arabic term barbari to describe the indigenous peoples of North Africa. We have thus translated it as Berber. More recently. however, that term has come to be regarded with disfavor by the people whom it describes, the preferred term being the one by which they describe themselves: Amazigh (plural: Imazighen). *Translator's Note.*

1

it was indeed a center of both religion and politics. Every year there was a gathering of bishops in the city to discuss matters of public interest.

At the time of the Muslim conquests, the king of Spain was Roderic, whom the Arabs call Ludhriq. Of Gothic origins, he became king in 709 AD. In fact, he was not a member of the royal family, but usurped the throne, leaving the sons of King Witiza vowing vengeance against him. In those days Spain was divided into provinces or dukedoms, each one being ruled by either a duke or count. The source of their authority was always the king, who resided in Toledo.

The city of Toledo is situated on an outcrop of hills, completely surrounded by the river Tagus except on the north side, exactly like a horseshoe. Beyond the river to the east, west, and south are mountain-chains that prevent the people of Toledo from seeing the horizon; they are covered with olive and vine plantations, along with oak and pine forests. Right in the center of the city is the cathedral that the Muslims converted into a mosque after the conquest; it is a magnificent and imposing building. Anyone looking at Toledo's buildings from above would recognize a mixture of styles, both Roman and Gothic. Fringing the city to the north, as well as on the far bank of the river in other directions, there are also fruit orchards and other types of trees. Anyone looking out of the windows of his house can take in the entire scene.

Chapter 2

Florinda

One of King Roderic's palaces was situated to the east of the city on a hill overlooking the river. All around the palace different types of trees and flowers were scattered across the hillsides, intersected by several streams, whose random courses only enhanced the beauty of the scene. These gardens covered a very wide area, and, except on the river side, they were enclosed by a wall patrolled by guards for whom houses had been built alongside the garden gates.

Alongside the royal palace was another, smaller one, connected to the larger one by a pathway. The smaller palace had its own separate gate, which gave on to the gardens from another side. And, if that were not enough, all around the gardens were various other mansions, some reserved for the king's retinue, others for princes. The whole ensemble included a further large palace, where, according to the custom of the Goths at this period, the sons of dukes and counts who were provincial governors would be housed. It was their custom to gather all the sons and daughters of governors in the royal court in Toledo where they could consort with each other, grow up in the king's favor, be trained in his service, and then get married.[5]

On the morning of December 25, 711 AD, the people of Toledo were busy celebrating Christmas. They flocked to churches and monasteries, offering each other Christmas greetings. The most crowded church of all was Toledo Cathedral because the archbishop celebrated there and King Roderic attended the mass in person, accompanied by his retinue and senior ministers. In spite of its size the cathedral was

---

5 Ibn al-Athir, part 4, and other Arab historians.

packed, and the cathedral square and surrounding streets and roads were crammed with people of all sorts and ages. They were all hoping to catch a glimpse of the royal procession and the king himself. What made them all particularly keen to see him was that he was relatively new to the throne; until now the people of Toledo had rarely set eyes on him, let alone other people living in the neighboring regions. For that reason, they were seizing this opportunity and rushing to get a glimpse of the man who had stolen the throne from his predecessor, Ghitsha.[6]

Not a single woman stayed at home, if not to actually witness the mass, then certainly to get a look at King Roderic. However, there was one young girl at the king's court who made use of the preoccupation of the king and his courtiers with the feast day to spend some time on her own and consider her situation. She was the daughter of a count, one of the king's governors, and she resided, along with all the other children, in the palace next to the king's own residence. A few days before, the king had had her transferred to the small palace directly connected to his own; it was a distinct honor for her, but it had aroused the intense jealousy of all her male and female companions. As a result, this honor was largely responsible for the miserable state she was in.

When the king, his retinue, and all the other courtiers had left to attend the mass in the cathedral, she had excused herself, saying that she did not feel well. It was a beautiful day, something of a rarity during the winter months. With the royal palace at the center of the scene, the brilliant sunshine was reflected in the river Tagus and the gardens on the other banks, causing the dew on the leaves and flowers to evaporate. It was just the kind of day when people would leave their homes and take a stroll around the orchards to bask in the sunlight and enjoy the beauties that nature had to offer.

The young woman took advantage of the absence of the king and his retinue, left the palace, and walked around the gardens. Over her dress she was wearing a red silk cloak lined with fur as protection against the cold. It managed to cover her shoulders and most of her body, except for the hem of her purple dress with its brocade embroidery; it glistened in the sunlight and trailed delicately behind her. Her head was covered in a white silk mantilla, which brought her golden hair together

---

6 This is the name the Arabs gave him. In Europe, it was Witiza. *Translator's Note.*

in a single cluster and allowed it to cascade down her back untrammeled as though she had just emerged from the bathhouse. It was the way that Roman women wore their hair, and the Goths of this period were following their example. Her golden hair glistened through the mantilla, most especially when the sunlight shone on her as she strolled among the trees. Even so, the fact that she was wearing the cloak could not hide her lovely appearance and the exquisite poise with which she walked. Her complexion was delicately pale, with the slightest tinge of red; the total effect was made that much more strikingly lovely by how distraught and ill at ease she seemed. Her eyes were bright and sharp; they were blue, but not quite. Only a magician would be able to provide a perfect description. Her tiny mouth would break into a smile, but only ever in a respectful and duly modest fashion.

As she walked around the garden, the trees were all stripped of leaves and the plants had no blossoms, almost as though they shared her depression. However, the ground was covered in green grass embossed with some flowers that bloomed in the wintertime. She paid no attention to the branches that hung over the path, so occasionally one would brush her shoulder or strike her in the chest or head. An old woman was fussing around her, keeping an eye on her movements and clearing obstacles from in front of her. In fact, she seemed no less worried than her young charge, but time had trained her well, and life's experiences had taught her that nothing lasts.

The girl kept looking back toward the palace while she walked, but then looked through the trees at the gardens in the distance that overlooked this orchard. Above the gardens snow-capped mountains were visible, and in the reflected sunlight they looked as if they were made of silver. Sometimes the girl went down into a valley, then climbed up a hillock; all the while the old woman kept picking her a flower here and a piece of fruit there. The girl took them without saying a word, almost as if she was condemned to stay silent and talking had become some kind of crime.

After she had been walking for a while, she reached a wide field overlooking the river. It was covered in short grass, which made it look like an embroidered carpet. As the sunlight fell on it, little flecks of dew kept flying off. The girl decided to sit down on the grass in the sunshine, eager to enjoy the warmth and the lovely pure blue sky above.

She turned toward the old woman. "What do you think, Auntie?" she asked, her voice cracking a little because she had been silent for so long. "Shall we sit in this meadow and enjoy the beautiful weather?"

The old woman fussed with her head scarf, which she had been using to cover her head and ears as protection against the cold.

"Sit wherever you like, my dear," she said. She then bustled over to a wooden bench on one of the garden paths and brought it over.

"I'd rather sit on the grass," the girl replied. "It's nice today."

With that, she sat down, and the old woman joined her, sitting in front of her and still keeping a close eye on her precious charge's movements. She took in the surroundings and was delighted that her young charge seemed to be so enamored of the natural beauty all around her. She had to appreciate the overlook to the river and the hills beyond it covered in oak, pine, and olive-tree forests. It was all like staring at an enlarged painting.

"Just look at this lovely scene, Florinda," she said, "and your heart will lighten. Leave all your worries behind you!"

The old woman's attempts at distracting Florinda only managed to make her feel sad again.

"You've just reminded me, Auntie, of what I was trying to forget. How can my heart possibly lighten as you suggest, when, as you well know, I'm very worried and scared? Now that I've been transferred to the palace, I'm even more worried than ever."

"Why has moving to the palace made you so worried? Now you're even closer to the king's palace and have a much loftier status..."

Florinda stared off into the distance as far as she could—as though she were staring at a boat far away. "It's precisely the fact that I've been moved that scares me. If only he'd moved me to the city's outskirts or sent me back to my father!"

That said, tears welled up in her eyes. Her thoughts were brought back from the boat in the distance by worries about her father and the fact that he was so far away and by the danger she could sense.

Chapter 3

Alfonso

The old woman was actually Florinda's great aunt. She had looked after her since she was a baby and brought her up in her father's house. Then, following custom, she had been brought to the royal court, and her father had charged the aunt to stay with his daughter. Thus far, she had looked after her for some ten years; during that time she had only grown to love her even more, since Florinda was naturally beautiful and kind. Whenever she saw the girl crying, her heart would break.

"There's no reason why you can't go back to your father," she said. "But I don't see why you can't stay here, especially because of Alfonso."

As soon as the old woman mentioned Alfonso's name, the young girl sat up with a jolt, as though she had been dozing and had suddenly woken up. Her heart started pounding, and the color rose on her cheeks, instantly dispelling their pallor. She gave a deep sigh.

"Don't talk to me about Alfonso," she said, looking at the old woman. "He's partially responsible for my miseries. As you know, I used to think he was what made me so happy. Oh, dear me! Let me cry…"

"How is it that I see you here imagining yourself surrounded by misery? You're one of the luckiest people alive. How can you say that Alfonso is responsible for your misery? He's your fiancé, and he'll do anything to make you happy."

"I'm well aware of that," Florinda replied, "and that's what makes me even more miserable. I love him and he does me, but what's the point? It's all your fault, Auntie! I was feeling quite happy by myself and without a care in the world. But it was you who pushed me to get to know him. May God forgive you!"

7

"I have no regrets whatsoever," the old woman replied, "in making the efforts I did to bring your two hearts together; you're suited to each other in every way. You come from the same family. When I made a point of bringing the two of you together, he was the crown prince of this expansive kingdom. When you got engaged, I thought I had done something that would make you supremely happy. After all, Alfonso was about to become king of the whole of Spain, and you would be queen of the Visigoths. It never occurred to me that events would take the course that they did, a revolution mounted by malicious people who killed his father, wrested the monarchy from his hands, and placed it in that of one of his own commanders."

As she said that, she lowered her voice and looked around to make sure no one could hear her. "So," she went on, "if it's the loss of the monarchy that's making you feel so unhappy, I can't blame you."

"No, no!" Florinda interrupted her. "That's not what is making me feel so sad. It's that Alfonso can no longer come and see me. It's been months since I've set eyes on him. Now that I've been moved to the palace, I don't think I'm going to see him for years. God protect me from the consequences of this move! My heart tells me that nothing good can come of it. That's why I've not been well ever since I moved and feel so miserable..."

"My dear girl," the old woman replied, "that's silly. There's plenty in this palace to keep you amused. It's your love for Alfonso that's making you so sad, and I can't blame you for that. But you have to forgive him for staying away. The king's well aware of what he's taken away from Alfonso, so he's keeping a close eye on everything he does and where he stays."

The little boat that Florinda had been watching on the river had now disappeared behind some rocks, but then it reappeared quite close to the palace garden where they were sitting. When Florinda took another look at it, her heart started racing. In it she had spotted Alfonso in person, along with two of his men. She did not know what to say, so she made do with giving him a wave. He gestured to the two men; one of them got out of the boat and went in another direction, while the second stayed with the boat. When Alfonso set eyes on Florinda, he hurried over. He was wearing the official guard's uniform: short puffy trousers, fur-lined down to the knees; front-fitting armor on his chest over which he wore a purple cloak; around his waist a thick leather belt; on his head a two-sided hat sporting an ostrich feather. Underneath the hat his black hair flowed down to his shoulders. Alfonso was twenty years old, but his beard and moustache had yet to grow long. He had a pale complexion and black eyes; when he looked at people, they got the clear impression of love and modesty, both bound to an innate nobility, with no trace of malice. He had been engaged to Florinda ever since his father had been king; at the time he had been crown prince because he was the eldest of his brothers. Florinda had doubted that she would ever be his wife, but her aunt had been very close to his mother, the queen, and had arranged the whole thing with her. Alfonso had fallen deeply in love with Florinda and would go to sit with her every day. But, when his father was murdered, he saw his own hopes dashed and found himself kept apart from her. Roderic was now king of Spain and used spies and informers to keep an eye on him. Alfonso was afraid to come and visit her, but he kept looking for chances to see her and ask after her health and well-being. Then he heard that she had been moved from the old palace to the one next to the king's own and was living there on her own. That made him very jealous, and he could no longer wait to see her; he was longing to gaze into her eyes and find out what she was thinking. Although things were no longer the same, he wanted to move the marriage forward. He told himself that she had been avoiding him now that the throne had slipped from his grasp.

Just at that time, the people of Toledo were celebrating Christmas. The king went to the cathedral in a huge procession, with Alfonso as a member of his official retinue of guards. As he was riding in the procession, it suddenly occurred to him that he could steal away and go to see Florinda. News had reached him that she was not well; he assumed that, for that reason, she would not be going to the mass that day. He decided to go by boat, so that no one in any of the city markets would notice him, and took two of his own men with him. When he landed, he sent one of them to bring his horse so that he could ride back into the city and rejoin the procession just before the king left the mass celebration, while the other one stayed on board the boat in case it was needed again. Once he had given orders to his men, he turned round and spotted Florinda. He rushed toward her, leaping and bounding over the hundred meters or so that separated them.

Chapter 4

The Language of Love

Florinda was astonished to see Alfonso approaching, and it showed in her expression. Her heart started pounding, and her knees were quivering. She wanted to stand up to greet him, but she was so overcome that she found it impossible. As she watched him approach, she still could not believe that it was actually him. As Alfonso drew close and noticed that she was not standing up to welcome him, he felt sure his assumption that she had grown tired of him was correct. He had been rushing to meet her with all the passion of a lover, but now he slowed down and even began to regret coming and intruding on her. However, he noticed that the old woman was rushing toward him, almost tripping over her gown as she did so.

"A hearty welcome to our beloved Alfonso," she said.

That made him relax a bit, but he still felt uneasy. He walked over to where Florinda was, but she stayed sitting. She was wrapped in a cloak and kept her hands tucked inside it. When he was finally standing right in front of her, she lifted her eyes and gave him a look that cut him to the quick; if the things she managed to include in that look of hers could have been written down, it would have been sufficient to fill any number of pages: rebuke and censure, passionate devotion, love and longing, sympathy and understanding—they were all there. The only way he could think of responding to the entire cluster of messages was to get down on his knees on the lush green grass.

"Warmest greetings to you, dear Florinda!" he said with all the passion of one deeply in love. With that he held out his hand and lowered his head, as though begging for charity.

Florinda stayed where she was, with her hands firmly tucked inside her cloak. The two of them stayed where they were, their eyes sharing a silent conversation of understanding, but then Florinda could not restrain her tears any longer and closed her eyes. Alfonso's face disappeared from her view, and she took one hand out of her cloak so she could wipe away her tears. But Alfonso anticipated her by taking out his handkerchief and wiping her eyes. He then used it to wipe his own face; inhaling her scent, he gave a deep sigh. He held his hand out to Florinda again, but she did not reciprocate. He realized that she was doing it deliberately, playing the flirt and scolding him at the same time. He could wait no longer. Holding out his hand yet again, he grabbed hold of hers. The sheer contact gave them both a jolt, as though they had both come into contact with a strong electric current at the same time.

The two of them spent some time conversing with looks, since their ability to read each other's thoughts made any talk unnecessary. The old woman left them alone and went to pick some flowers and disappear amid the tree branches. Being well aware of the emotions they were both feeling, she wanted to close her eyes to whatever might happen in such circumstances. Alfonso remained silent, having decided to be patient and let Florinda be the first to speak. They spent a while hand in hand, eye locked on eye. Their hearts were both pounding in unison, and their eyes glistened with tears that were the most obvious signs of their shared passion.

"So what has brought you here, Alfonso?" said Florinda, opening the conversation in a tone of voice that combined coquetry and rebuke.

"My beloved," Alfonso replied, "I have no idea what has brought me here. Do you have any idea? All I know is that the love I have for you keeps me a prisoner; I live for your approval, and will die if you reject me. My darling Florinda, do you have the same feelings as I do? I know that you used to love me, but do you still—or at least a little bit? Or have the changes that have occurred and the way our hopes and dreams have been thwarted managed to change you as well?"

She realized that he was referring to the loss of his father's kingdom. Withdrawing her fingers from his, she made as if to look away, although her gaze was still firmly fixed on his. It was as though she wanted to say to him: "Is that all you know about love and lovers' feelings?"

Alfonso realized full well what her look implied. "I've never doubted the sincerity of your love as our two hearts blended into one. But I was afraid that my bad luck had changed you. I also suspected that, in addition to losing my father and the kingdom, my dire fate had led me to lose the one thing that is far more precious to me than the entire world."

As he said that, his eyes glistened and his features relaxed. He was still looking at her and waiting to hear what she would say.

She fell silent again and wrapped herself in her cloak. Turning to look at the river, she listened to the sound of its rippling waters. The only sound to be heard in the garden was the river's ripples and chirping birds.

When the silence had gone on for a while, Alfonso got up to look for the old woman. She came toward them with a posy of flowers in her hands.

"Come over here, Auntie!" he yelled to her. "Please talk to Florinda. I'm hoping she'll tell me something that will give me some comfort and provide some soothing balm for my passionate love."

Chapter 5

Lovers are Forever Doubtful

By this time, the old woman had come back to the spot where the two young people were sitting. She gave Florinda the posy of flowers, then looked at Alfonso.

"If you can't understand things without words being spoken," she told him, "then you're no lover. Do you think it's appropriate for young girls to express their passionate love the way young men can?"

She now turned and spoke to Florinda. "So here's Alfonso," she said. "Talk to him, ask him. I've heard you wondering if he still loves you. I told you that he was totally committed to you, so are you convinced now that I was right?"

Florinda looked up at Alfonso. By this time her real feelings were abundantly clear in the distracted gleam in her eye. As she stared straight at him for an instant, his very gaze was almost enough to whisk her away. The fact that he had lost the kingdom and his own rights of succession was now completely forgotten. He realized that he had to do whatever it took to make Florinda happy, even if it meant losing the entire world.

While these thoughts were racing through his mind, Florinda asked him a question.

"Did you really ever doubt my love for you, Alfonso?"

"Yes, my beloved," he replied, "I did. Lovers are forever doubtful."

"You are right," she said looking down. "I had the very same doubts as you, as my aunt has told you. But..."

"I don't think you've any reason to doubt my love," Alfonso interrupted. "You know full well that I'm a willing prisoner of my love for you. But it's reasonable for me to wonder whether you will keep your pledge to me now that my own fate has taken a turn for the worse. I used to be the crown prince, but now I'm just like everyone else..."

When Florinda heard him say that, she rushed to respond before he had a chance to finish what he was saying.

"My dear beloved," she told him, "when I fell in love with you, it was Alfonso that I loved, not someone who was crown prince. Love is not bothered about status and ranks. When human hearts make a pact and come together, Alfonso, my love, they neither observe, nor assess, nor weigh the pros and cons in the balance. Recommendations and pleasantries play no part in bringing them together; they make no distinction between rights and obligations. The human heart does not recognize symbols of honor; it has no respect for crowns and no fear of scepters. What the human heart loves, my beloved, is another human heart."

As she spoke these words, her cheeks blushed and her expression showed how serious she was. She looked down for a moment and fell silent, although it was clear that she had more to say. Alfonso did not want to interrupt her thoughts, so he simply gave her a look that told her he wanted to hear the rest of her thoughts. Florinda noticed that he was waiting for her to finish saying what was on her mind.

"Even so," she went on, "I'm sorry that you've lost the kingdom, not because I want to be queen, but..."

At this point she was overcome by feelings of both shyness and anger. Her cheeks grew redder still, and she frowned. Looking back at the palace as though she was afraid she was being watched, she fell silent. That bothered Alfsonso, who was able to guess part of what she wanted to say. Even so, he pretended not to understand.

"But what, Florinda?" he asked. "Tell me, beloved. Explain it to me..."

"If it weren't for the revolution," she went on, keeping her voice down, "I wouldn't be suffering these hardships, feeling myself trapped in a lion's claws, and my guardian angel somehow far away." Her voice choked for a moment, but then she went on. "If your father, Witiza, were still on the throne or he'd passed it on to you, I'd be able to feel more at ease. This usurper would not have been able to cause me such distress."

Alfonso interrupted her again, looking shocked.

"So what is causing you such distress?" he asked, his voice tinged with envy. "Has he even spoken to you? Has he done you any harm? Tell me, please…"

"No," Florinda replied, "he hasn't done anything. But I still don't feel safe, particularly now he's moved me to the palace. I don't understand what that means. It's just that I would have been happier if the kingdom had remained in your hands. That's all."

Alfonso was well aware of what she was implying, even though it was couched in the pleasant tones of hyperbole; she was actually blaming him for not demanding his own rights.

At this point he was still kneeling in front of her. When he heard her say this, he felt as though she had poured boiling water all over his body. Emotions now got the better of him, and he was anxious to do whatever he could to make her happy.

"You're right to blame me, Florinda!" he exclaimed as he stood up. "I have indeed fallen short on that matter. But, as the old saying has it, everything comes in its own time. I'd decided not to visit you until I'd managed to achieve the goal of your desires. I've been trying for some time but have yet to succeed. But then I couldn't stand staying away any longer. I was scared your feelings for me had turned cold. Now I've seen for myself that your love is steadfast. That gives me strength in my quest. You should realize, Florinda, that the parties affiliated with Rome that this usurper is relying on are extremely weak. The bishops were only able to appoint him king out of a desire to serve Rome.[7] The other parties in the kingdom all oppose him, including the Visigoths, Jews, and everyone else who hates tyranny. That isn't the entire story, but I'm prepared to swear to you on the head of my own father—dead though he may be—that this Roderic will soon be deposed, and the monarchy will be restored to its rightful owners…"

As he was talking, Florinda kept looking at one of the winter roses that her aunt had brought for her. As she listened to Alfonso talking, she was scattering the petals around. When he reached the words, "the monarchy will be restored to its rightful owners," she threw away all the

---

7 See *The History of Spain* by Romey, part 2.

petals still in her hands. Looking up at him, she seemed to be asking him to confirm the veracity of what he had been saying. He realized what she was asking, and that made him depict the situation with even greater intensity. His own passion made him think that he could do anything. Lifting his hand, he pulled at his hair that stretched down to his shoulders.

"If you don't believe that I'm telling the truth," he said, "then I hereby vow to myself and also to your aunt here that, should I fail to fulfill my promise, I will not keep any hair on my head."[8]

Florinda realized that he was absolutely serious about this pledge, but at the same time she was well aware of how many obstacles stood in the way of his hopes. She was anxious to minimize the pressure that his pledge put on him.

"We don't need pledges like this," she told him. "Don't expose yourself to danger simply because of a throne. It's all empty glory. Our goal should be to live in peace and security, out of the reach of people who hate us. That might even require that we live in a hut built for the slaves who toil in the fields and pastures."

---

8 For the Goths, letting hair grow was a sign of nobility. Only slaves shaved or cut their hair. *Translator's Note.*

Chapter 6

The King's Procession

Alfonso really wanted to respond, but just then he heard a bugle call. That gave him a start. When he listened carefully, he could hear the sound of drums and the jingling of bridles, which told him that the king's procession was returning to the palace from the cathedral. While he was still busy talking to Florinda, it had actually already reached the palace. He regretted not having gone back sooner and realized that Roderic would inevitably disapprove of his actions. Florinda noticed that he was looking shocked and heard the same sounds as he did. Knowing full well that he was late in rejoining the festivities, she told him to leave.

"It's time for you to say farewell," she told him. "May God be with you!"

Clutching her hand, he said good-bye. "Pray for me," he asked her. "You're an angel, and your prayers will be answered. Include me in your intercessions in the hope that I may be able to win your approval."

Her response was to flutter her eyelashes at him.

He took off back toward the boat so as to steer clear of the rest of the garden, then mounted his horse and took another route back. Florinda stayed standing where she was, watching him ride away until he disappeared. With the old woman at her side, she started thinking again about the various issues she had been mulling over before Alfonso arrived. They both turned round and headed back to the palace, although Florinda was so overwhelmed by the conversation she had just had with Alfonso that she did not say a single word. She regretted talking so forthrightly about the king and worried that it might cause her beloved Alfonso some harm.

That morning, as King Roderic led the procession to the cathedral, he had been somewhat concerned about Alfonso. He had expected to see him in the procession along with the rest of his retinue. In anticipation of the king's visit, the cathedral had been beautifully decorated with sweet-smelling flowers; candles had been lit, and censers of incense wafted their scents over everyone close to the great church. The voices of cantors and prayer leaders echoed around the church and could be heard from a considerable distance. People gathered in crowds to get a glimpse of the king's procession, so much so that they almost crushed each other. Those who were looking down from roofs and windows even outnumbered people standing in the marketplaces.

When the king's procession reached the cathedral, the bishops came out to greet him, accompanied by priests and monks carrying candlesticks; one of them was carrying the cross, another the communion cup, and a third various Christian emblems. The king dismounted at a distance and so did his retinue. The first person to greet the king was the archbishop, and the king responded with his own greeting. The king bent low and kissed the archbishop's hand and the embossed cross on his ring. They all walked across the cathedral courtyard, preceded by the other bishops and members of the clergy, who proceeded toward the west end of the church and entered through the door. Actually, the entrance consisted of three doors, the central one being the largest. Its highest point was shaped like a triangular bridge, with carved portraits representing angels and a selection of saints and prophets.

The king was wearing a golden crown in the Roman style. Beneath it his hair reached down below his shoulders to the middle of his back, while his beard and moustache were long enough to touch his chest. In front of him walked the kingdom's nobility, with their long hair and matching headwear. They could all sense the pomp of this festive occasion, and it made them all proud. As they entered the church, they found themselves surrounded by eighty superb columns made of different kinds of marble, arranged in three rows from west to east. From the floor to the top of the dome, the cathedral's height was forty-six meters, and from east to west its length was a hundred meters. On this particular day, the magnificence of the building had been enhanced by the addition of flower displays illuminated by colored candles and oil lamps placed in front of the portraits on the walls. As the clouds of incense wafted upward, the choristers' voices were drowned out by the noise of the congregation in spite of all the efforts the priests were making to keep them quiet.

The king continued his procession till he reached a special chair reserved for him beside the altar. Making the sign of the cross, the rest of his retinue took their seats in the church. The king followed suit, although his eyes were fixed on his own retinue as if he were searching for something that was missing. By his side sat a priest who was always with him; he lodged in the palace and conducted morning and evening prayers with him, serving as his counselor and guide. The king never attended any function without him and never broached any topic without seeking his advice.

The priest's name was Father Martin. He was an elderly man with grey hair. By now his bones were somewhat brittle, and his face was wrinkled by age. His eyes were sunken, and the effect was only amplified by the long hairs of the eyebrows over them. All his teeth had fallen out, and his lips sagged so much that his mouth looked like a valley between two mountains. In his youth and middle age he had been very loquacious, but, once his teeth had fallen out, he had started mumbling, to such a degree that it was often difficult to tell what he was actually saying. He was fiercely devoted to the Roman rite because that was the one in which he himself had been brought up; in his latter years he was definitely a staunch supporter of the church and its goals. He did not like the Goths at all, which explained why he had played a large part in getting Roderic appointed as king.

Chapter 7

Romans and Goths

The mutual antipathy that the Romans and Goths felt for each other was perfectly natural. When the Goths conquered Spain in the fifth century AD, the country was Roman in its beliefs and aspirations. All its nobles and senior officials belonged to the same faith. Even though the Goths ruled the country for over two centuries, there was never a meeting of hearts and minds nor any agreement about aspirations and goals. The Goths spoke one language and the Romans another. In fact, the Goths may have had more reason to learn Roman (i.e., Latin) than vice versa because Latin was the official language of the Roman kingdoms, Spain being a client territory. So, even though the Goths conquered Spain, they were unable to substitute their own language for Latin (as the Arabs managed to do when they conquered the Roman kingdoms in the Middle East). In their conquests of former Roman kingdoms, the Goths and Arabs shared a lot in common: the Goths came from the north, the Arabs from the south. Both were tough desert tribes who were thus able to overrun the countries involved. Each tribe managed to take possession of a large segment of the Roman territories, but it was the Arabs who managed to achieve something that the Goths did not: building on the vestiges of Roman civilization, they managed to erect a new one that was uniquely their own. Over the course of the ensuing centuries, they managed to mold the various peoples with whom they came into contact into a single community that spoke the same language. The Goths, on the other hand, had spent over two hundred years in Spain, but then had departed without leaving a trace, or at least nothing significant.

In addition, when the Goths conquered Spain, they were adherents to the Arianism sect, named after Arius, a well-known Christian heretic.[9] When the propagators of this belief were suppressed and met with opposition from the patriarchs themselves, they abandoned the Roman kingdom, scattered to both north and south, and started spreading their faith among tribes in different regions. The Germans in northern Europe numbered among those tribes, and the Goths were a segment of the group. When the Goths conquered Spain, Arianism was their creed, and they adhered to it for over a century. During the same period, other sects appeared, and some Spaniards and Goths joined them. One such was the notorious Nestorian sect, another that of the Bashinsiyus, and others as well.

At the end of the sixth century AD, a Gothic king named Reccared assumed the throne. In 587 AD he joined the Catholic faith, and he was followed first by the bishops and then by the people. Spain thus rejoined the Catholic Communion. Most of the bishops were Romans, and they stipulated that, from now on, the king of Spain had to be a Catholic Goth.

However, it was not very long before the Goths realized the mistake they had made in abandoning their own faith and language. They realized that the decision would severely disrupt the state they ruled. The monarch who was most aware of this problem was Witiza, the father of Alfonso. He decided to rid himself of these chains, but the bishops were well aware of his intentions and decided to act. They joined the country's nobility, who were members of the Roman Catholic community, in deposing Witiza and choosing Roderic as king. Some reports suggest that they only did so after Witiza's death. At any rate, that is how the monarchy fell out of the hands of Witiza's family and into those of Roderic and the clergy from his own party. Witiza's supporters believed that Roderic was not actually a Goth and thus considered him to be an interloper.

Father Martin was one of those who worked hard to place Roderic on the throne. He had a special hatred for Witiza and his sons because the former king had hated the priest's fanaticism for Rome and its church. Father Martin played a large part in deposing Witiza and passing the monarchy to Roderic, and that is why Roderic never made any decision

---

9 Romey, *History of Spain*, part 2, p. 252.

without first consulting the priest. Among the things that Father Martin recommended was that the king should keep Alfonso under strict control and not allow him to leave the palace; he should be under continual surveillance in case he started trying to put a rival party together in order to reclaim the throne.[10]

When the king arrived at the cathedral on that Christmas Day, the first thing that Father Martin pointed out to him was that Alfonso had not ridden in the procession. The king searched the congregation and failed to spot Alfonso; that worried him. However, his participation in the mass required him to pay close attention to the priests, and that soon distracted him from Alfonso's absence. Even so, once in a while he kept sneaking glances to see if Alfonso was there.

---

10 According to some sources, Witiza had three sons.

Chapter 8

The Interrogation

Once the mass was over, the king and his entourage left. He looked around for Alfonso again but did not find him. Mounting his horse, he told Father Martin to accompany him. They spent the ride back to the palace discussing the reasons for Alfsonso's absence. When the procession was getting close to the palace, Father Martin spotted Alfonso galloping as fast as he could past the palace. He already knew about Alfonso's relationship with Florinda and realized that that explained his absence. However, he merely alerted the king to the fact that Alfonso had just arrived.

The king returned to the palace and dismounted by the main gate. Climbing the wide marble steps to the palace courtyard, he made his way through a colonnade to a hall where corridors branched off to different parts of the palace. The main one led to the audience chamber, and that is where the king went, accompanied by his priest, by way of a private corridor. Courtiers, including delegations that had come to congratulate the king on the major feast day, now started making their way in by the public entrance. The king sat on an elevated silver throne with legs carved like those of a lion. He was wearing his official robes, with a gold-embossed silk cloak over his shoulders. On his head he wore a gold crown encrusted with precious jewels, and in his hand he held a golden scepter tipped with a bejeweled cross. Roderic was about forty years old, portly and with a distinct paunch. He was powerfully built, and his expression was one of defiance. He had large, bulging eyes and thick eyebrows; his long mustache made his beard seem even longer, not to mention his hair.

Above the throne where Roderic was seated was a portrait of the crucified Messiah; on the walls of the chamber hung a number of other religious paintings. Father Martin seated himself beside the king, and his retinue arranged themselves in front of him. People now came forward to offer him their congratulations, Alfonso among them. He entered, greeted the king, and offered his congratulations as did everyone else. He then sat down among the attendees. When everyone stood up to leave, Alfonso tried to do the same, but Roderic signaled to him to stay. That made Alfonso very uneasy, but he managed to keep himself in check until the chamber was empty and the only people still left were the king and Father Martin. He responded to the king's signal and stood in front of him.

"So, Alfonso," the king asked, "what kept you from accompanying my procession today?"

Alfonso was shocked. He had not expected the king to be so bothered about the fact that he had not been there. Even so, he stayed as calm as he could.

"I had some private business to attend to," he replied. "It prevented me from fulfilling my obligation to pray along with his Majesty the King."

"It's odd," the king continued, "that this business of yours happened to occur on Christmas Day, and at the very hour of my procession to the cathedral."

With that he looked over at one of the paintings that showed the Virgin Mary carrying her baby child. He started playing with the edge of his beard.

"Yes," Alfonso replied, "it's a strange coincidence. But it happened, and I had no choice. I am very sorry about that..."

All the while, Father Martin had occupied himself reciting some prayers very quietly in front of the painting of the Virgin Mary so no one could hear him. When he had finished, he came back, adjusted his cape and beretta, and took his seat beside the king. He had heard their conversation. When Alfonso realized that Father Martin was involved, he began to worry because he was well aware how much he and the priest loathed each other.

The king was not willing to accept Alfonso's apology, but he thought it best to postpone delivering any kind of verdict until he had

had the time to discuss things with the priest. Just as he was about to dismiss him, he heard the priest addressing Alfonso.

"It seems," Father Martin said, clearing his throat, "that your business was either inside the palace or very close to it." With that, he started wiping his mouth with a handkerchief.

That made Alfonso furious, but he was worried that, if he responded, he would be revealing yet more information.

The king got the strong impression that there was more to what the priest had said than was apparent, but he could not fathom what it was. He was eager to learn more when he and Father Martin were left on their own, so he did not bother to wait to hear what Alfonso had to say. He gave him a derisory and dismissive wave and told him to go.

"You can go, my boy," he said, "but make sure you don't do this again!"

Hearing that, Alfonso felt relieved that he had managed to avoid trouble, and that made him feel better; a huge burden had been lifted from his shoulders. Walking toward the door, he exited the hall, hardly aware of the space in front of him, such was his panic. But no sooner had he left the hall than he recovered his senses. He became newly aware of his current status and of quite how much he had lost. In his father's day, people had fallen over each other to greet him and show him respect; everyone would stop for him. But now, those days were long gone. Among all the people thronging in the palace courtyard, only his friends noticed him, and even they were wary of showing him any affection for fear of annoying the king.

As Alfonso left the courtyard behind him, feelings of envy began to flood over him. Florinda's words were still ringing in his ears. He remembered how he had promised her to recover his kingdom, and that made him even angrier with the king. Mounting his horse, he rode immediately to his residence, his mind racing with ideas and misgivings. He decided that he would stop at nothing to exact vengeance for his father's sake and to make Florinda happy.

Chapter 9

The Visit

Once Alfonso had departed, Roderic let it be known that he wished to relax. Entering his private quarters, he had his servants come, remove his official uniform, and dress him in his normal clothes. He did not say a word to any of them because he was so preoccupied with what Father Martin had told him about Alfonso and the palace. Once he had changed his clothes, he invited Father Martin to come and have lunch with him. When the priest arrived, the king did not discuss the topic at lunch because the queen was sitting with them. He preferred not to discuss such matters with her around because she was inclined to be very jealous. Once they had all finished lunch, the king spoke to his priest.

"Father," he said, "please say grace for us now that lunch is over. After that I'd like you to accompany me to my room."

That kind of request did not sound at all strange to the queen; her husband frequently spent time alone with Father Martin so he could get his opinion about something or other, discuss important issues, or hear the king's confession.

"What did you have to say about our dear colleague today?" the king asked Father Martin as soon as they were alone.

"If you're referring to Alfonso," the priest replied in a shocked tone, "I think you treated him far too leniently. How did he come to be absent from today's procession for heaven knows what reasons?"

The priest made it all sound urgent so it would have a greater effect on the king. If Roderic had not been so used to his mode of speech and the way he always muttered, he would not have understood a thing...

"But I heard you talking about the excuse he offered," the king went on. "I didn't understand what you meant."

The priest now realized that the king was angling to learn some more about Alfonso and Florinda. He was pretending not to know and trying to convince Father Martin that his question was entirely innocent.

"I didn't say anything," the priest replied, going along with the pretense. "All I said was that he arrived late at the palace."

"Which palace?" the king asked.

"Which palace?" the priest replied. "Your Majesty's palace, of course. You don't realize his connection with the royal palace?"

"No," the king replied, taking the pretense still further, "I don't know of his connection to this palace now that his family has been dethroned and I'm the monarch."

"I'm not talking about his connection with the throne," the priest said. "I'm talking about his relationship with Florinda, the daughter of Count Julian. A few days ago Your Majesty ordered that she be transferred to the small palace."

When the king heard her name mentioned, he was shocked. Love and jealousy made his heart leap. However, his pride prevented him from showing his true feelings, and he managed to convey the impression that the entire matter was of no interest to him.

"Are they related, then," he asked, "or what is the relationship?"

"As Your Majesty is well aware," the priest replied, "Count Julian, the governor of Sabta, is Florinda's father. He and Witiza are related, on the female side, I believe. But what I mean is that Alfonso and Florinda are linked in a very special way..."

"And what is that?"

"I thought Your Majesty knew about it," replied the priest with a laugh. "Their engagement was well known before Your Majesty became king of Spain!"

Roderic found the news of the engagement hard to take because he himself was also deeply in love with Florinda. He had not known that they were engaged. Even so, he was not too worried that she might avoid his clutches; after all, he had complete authority over not only her but Alfonso as well. He made up his mind to woo her with money and power; if that failed, then he would force her to leave Alfonso and live with him.

Not wanting to let the priest know how he really felt, he pretended to be satisfied with his response. With that he stood up, a cue for the priest to leave. Father Martin rose to his feet and departed.

Between the king's chambers and those of Florinda, there was a hallway leading to the other palace. It was the only way of walking from the royal palace to the small palace where Florinda resided, and the complex had been built that way for this particular purpose. The king made up his mind to reveal his love to Florinda, in the hope that she would abandon Alfonso. But he was not prepared to bring her to his chambers, for fear that the queen would find out. Locking the door to his private chambers that led to his own palace, he opened the door that led to Florinda's palace...

Chapter 10

A Knock on the Door

When Alfonso had left the garden, Florinda had returned to the palace with her great aunt. Her intense love for him now completely preoccupied her thoughts. She started rehashing every word that they had spoken to each other and regretted the way she had pushed him so hard to get his kingdom back. She felt like being on her own so she could think over what she had said and maybe come up with some ideas to lessen her worries. She went into her private chamber, which overlooked the gardens on the river side. A large almond tree blocked her view of the river. The branches had grown out and thickened to such an extent that, when Florinda sat at the window and looked out, she could only catch a few glimpses of the river through the branches, even in winter when the tree was almost leafless. Florinda sat down by the window and stared through the branches at the river and the country beyond. She noticed that the boat had now moved off, and that reminded her that her very own beloved had been in it. She allowed her thoughts to wander off...

Meanwhile, the old woman left Florinda to contemplate her worries. She went over to an icon by Florinda's bed, which showed a picture of the crucified Messiah. Kneeling in front of it, she kissed the image and started beating her breast in penitence. She asked the Messiah to protect Alfonso, to grant him success, and to bring to pass his marriage to Florinda. Once she had finished praying, she kissed the icon again and left the room, closing the door behind her. She instructed the servants not to go to the room so as not to disturb Florinda, nor to let anyone go upstairs in the palace. They should all stay downstairs. If Florinda needed anything, she would send them a message with the old woman.

Florinda spent so much time by the window wrapped in her own thoughts and worries that she lost track of time; she felt exhausted and wanted to take a nap. She lay on her bed and was soon sound asleep. In her dreams Alfonso appeared to her, his face radiant with light as he approached her; she wanted to kiss him, but could not. That upset her, and she woke up with a jolt. Just as she was wiping her eyes to make sure that it had only been a dream, she heard footsteps. When she looked up, she saw the old woman coming in with a frightened expression on her face.

Florinda sat up. "What's the matter, Auntie?" she asked in surprise. "What has happened?"

"Everything's fine," the old woman replied. "Don't worry."

With that she fell silent, and that made Florinda even more worried. "What's happened?" she exclaimed. "Has something bad happened to Alfonso?"

"Good heavens, no!" the old woman replied. "But the king wants to see you."

When Florinda heard those words, she was really flustered and forgot all about her worries for Alfonso. This invitation from the king did not augur at all well.

"Where is he?" she asked. "What does he want with me?"

"I don't know, my lady," the old woman replied. "I was in my room tidying up, and noticed the king in person slinking his way in here like a thief. I was astonished to see him behaving that way. He asked me where you were and told me to ask you to come to the north room in this palace. You are to come immediately, exactly as you are. I've come to carry out his instructions."

Florinda leapt out of bed, fully aware that the danger she was now facing was just as bad as she had feared. Even so, she put her reliance on God and plucked up her courage. Going over to the icon, she kissed it and prayed to God to give her courage and protect her from the talons of evil. She also asked her great aunt to pray for her. Wrapping herself in the cloak she was wearing, she went on her way, all the while pleading with God from the bottom of her heart to save her from this particular trial.

A Knock on the Door

In circumstances such as these, the only resort for mortals is a plea to the higher, unseen powers...

As Florinda made her way to the north room, it felt as though she were walking to the gallows. Small wonder then that her knees were shaking and her entire body turned to jelly. She wished that the room could be miles and miles away. Even so, she took comfort from the fact that she was placing her reliance on God. As she approached the room, she heard footsteps. There was the king, emerging from the room to greet her with a smile on his face. He seemed to imagine that a simple smile would be enough to make her bend to his will, that, as soon as he made clear to her how happy he was to have her company, she would make every effort to please him.

Chapter 11

Chastity

Florinda entered the room with a confident stride, her heart a zone of conflicting emotions between pride and modesty, her expression a blend of anger and fear. The king walked ahead of her, sat down on a couch, and invited her to sit beside him.

"Your Majesty," she said, modesty and shyness written all over her face, "it's not fitting for me to be seated in your presence."

"Come and sit down, Florinda," the king replied with a laugh. "I didn't invite you here to subject you to all the bother of formalities. I wanted to see you when you were feeling happy and relaxed. Come and sit."

"Forgive me, Your Majesty," she went on, "but…"

The king did not give her a chance to continue but seized her by the hand and made her sit next to him. When his hand came into contact with hers, she felt as though she had been touched by the devil. Moving away, she withdrew her hand, but stayed sitting there, trying to make sure that their garments did not come into contact. Roderic was conscious of the way she had withdrawn her hand; when he had touched her, his reaction had been exactly the opposite of hers. He did not like the fact that she was resisting him but decided that she was pretending to be shy.

"I don't blame you for looking so shocked, Florinda," he told her with a smile. "After all, you're feeling overawed by being in the presence of the king of Spain. It's the first time you've been in that position. But you should understand—you queen of beauty—that I've only come to see you in order to offer you a life of real happiness. I don't want you to address me as the monarch, but rather as an ordinary man who loves and adores you and is eager to make you the happiest woman in the whole world."

When Florinda heard those words, her worst fears were confirmed. However, she decided the best way to rebutt his advances was to remain cordial.

"Heaven forbid, Your Majesty," she said, standing up, "that someone such as myself should be anything but a humble servant in the presence of the king of Spain, whose authority symbolizes the people as a whole, and…"

Once again the king interrupted her. "What's to stop you being my beloved?" he asked. "Not only that, but my lady, queen of both my heart and kingdom?"

As he spoke to her, his emotions got the better of him; his eyes reddened and his lips were quivering. He kept trying to keep his words and gestures as gentle as he could, but his words and demeanor were still gruff and crude.

"No, no, Sire," said Florinda, "I could not possibly be anything like that. Your Majesty seems to be overlooking all the things he's achieved during his life. I'm completely unsuited to such lofty status."

He got the impression that she did not believe how much he was in love with her and was afraid that he was just trying to trick her.

"It seems that you don't believe me," he said, standing up as well. "You're right to be shocked by my apparent willingness to overlook my status, but I have to tell you, Florinda, that you have won my heart and soul and are mistress of my every emotion. So take pity on me and accept my offer."

As he spoke, he bowed like some pathetic petitioner and stretched out his hands, shaking with passion.

Florinda paid no attention to these phony gestures and remained calm and collected.

"Accept what?" she asked quietly.

"To be my life partner," the king replied, assuming that her question implied that she was about to accept. "To live a life of happiness and ease and to be my ultimate authority!"

Florinda gave him a contemptuous look. "What about the queen?" she asked.

That question struck the king like a lightning bolt. He had not expected Florinda to act so proudly because he had no idea of the value of chastity and personal freedom. He had simply assumed that, if he gave Florinda a single smile, she would fall at his feet and surrender herself to him. What he had not realized was that chastity to her was much more valuable than the treasuries of kings, loftier than the thrones they sit on, and more sublime than the levels achieved as part of their civilizations. More than that, chastity is the sharp sword that a young woman can use against a king to demonstrate that she is thus more powerful and prestigious than he. Florinda's posture in facing Roderic was that of one monarch confronting another. The modest behavior she had used at first was aimed at extricating herself from this situation in as cordial a fashion as possible. But, now that she had discovered that he was crossing the line, she had responded to him by using a word, "queen," that shook him to the core; a word that reminded him that he was tied to the queen by a sacred bond that did not permit any form of intimacy with other women.

Roderic was annoyed that she had chosen to humiliate him by raising the subject of his wife. Even so, he decided to ignore her intended message and maintain his pleasant demeanor.

"I'm surprised that you can be so ignorant and deluded," he said. "Here I am, offering you happiness and honor and paving the way for you, and all you do is set up barriers. Don't you realize, Florinda, that what I'm offering you now is something that any young woman in this kingdom or anywhere else would make any kind of vow to achieve? Be sensible, and think about it; you're turning down the kind of bliss that very few of the elite manage to achieve in their lifetime, prestige of a kind that mothers of young girls would do anything to acquire. Don't you realize that, if you accept my offer, you will gain a level of honor that none of your family can ever aspire to? If you continue to be so stubborn, you'll be hurting your own father. If you accept the offer I'm making, I'm prepared to make your father one of my closest confidants at court."

When Florinda heard him say that, her temper got the better of her. At the same time she was aware that she still had the upper hand.

What she had to say was not the kind of thing that should be said to kings.

"So Roderic," she said, pointing to herself, "you're claiming that you can offer me happiness and prestige, but what you're actually offering is misery and contempt. When you use such terms—even just hints, you insult me and belittle me. Merely by thinking that I would accept, you make me the lowliest of creatures. Give up the idea and leave me alone. You are a prestigious monarch, with power and authority over people and great wealth as well. All I possess is just this one jewel. Do you propose to take it away from me? Do you presume that, simply by wanting it, you can have it?"

She was so worked up that she had turned pale.

"No, no!" she went on, hands shaking and lips quivering. "No one can take this jewel away from me. It's worth more than all the treasuries in the entire world. It's my weapon, my compass, and my shield, indeed my path to eternal bliss."

The king was so put out by her angry words that his beard kept bouncing on his chest. Even so, his innate sense of justice and truth forced him to keep his temper in check. He did not dare insult her, but he was still nourishing some hope of persuading her to accept him. He decided to keep the conversation going by introducing some levity into the serious discussion.

"So," he asked, "does that boy deserve you more than I do?"

That question made her even more determined to stick to her principles, since she realized at once that he was trying to disparage Alfonso.

"Whatever the case may be," she said, "he is my lot in life. We are engaged according to God's own law."

This brazen response shocked him even more. He told himself that he should now give her the cold shoulder and treat her unkindly. However, he decided to postpone that until he had had a chance to use the last arrows in his quiver of tricks.

"Well, Florinda," he said, "it seems to me that your young age is having an effect on your reasoning. If that weren't the case, you would certainly not be preferring a young boy with no importance or prestige to the king of Spain. So I'm prepared to forgive your impetuous behavior and give you some more time to think about things; you can return to your senses and not turn down the kind of boon that I'm offering you. Don't waste this golden opportunity for the kind of futile fancies and vacuous expressions you keep clinging to. That is all the advice I have to offer you, so think about things carefully."

When Florinda saw that her censure of his behavior was not working, she collected her scattered thoughts and decided to use his own reasoning as a way of convincing him.

"What Your Majesty is saying," she told him in a logical, calm tone, "is that I'm clinging to futile fancies and vacuous expressions. What would you have to say if Her Majesty the queen decided to have an extramarital relationship with a young man and asked him to live with her and be her life partner?"

The king now realized how valid her argument actually was, quite apart from the implied insult that her remarks contained. He was furious and almost decided to strike her in order to make her change her mind. He was on the point of issuing orders that she be arrested and tortured until she gave up her relationship with Alfonso, assuming that the only reason why she kept refusing his offer was because she was in love with Alfonso and hoped he would one day be powerful and rich. The king still believed that, once Florinda could be convinced that Alfonso was weak and powerless, she would leave him and decide that the king of Spain was the best alternative.

Roderic had all these illusions because he did not understand the meaning of pure love, nor did he appreciate the importance of genuine chastity. He had no conception of the fact that, when two hearts are pledged to each other, that very pledge is the source of all happiness. Wealth and status have no part to play. Roderic also imagined that, if he managed to humiliate Alfonso in Florinda's eyes, he could make her give him up.

"Don't you realize, Florinda," he told her, "that Alfonso is one of my retainers? He's completely under my authority, and I can do with him what I wish. You don't seem to be aware of that fact. Maybe you think things are still the way they were before the monarchy slipped from his grasp..."

Chapter 12

Fervent Prayer

When the king made this veiled threat against Alfonso, that only served to increase Florinda's determination and her intense love for him. When true love encounters adversity, it only grows stronger; adversity serves to heighten its intensity. She was still annoyed that this tyrant ruler should see fit to talk about the subject, but at the same time she was scared that, if she responded angrily to his overture, he would take out his anger on Alfonso and harm him. She decided instead to try to charm him, hoping thereby to calm his anger until such time as God would provide a way out of the situation.

"If it's true," she told the king, "that people should only fall in love with those who have wealth and status, how is it that Your Majesty has fallen in love with a lowly maiden like me, to such an extent that he's eager to make her mistress of the entire kingdom? If the principle dictates that we should ignore the poor and never fall in love with them, then what you should really be doing is to throw me out of your court because I cannot possibly rival the power and prestige that you possess. I beg you, Sire, to do just that. It will be more suited to your lofty status and will better preserve your honor."

As she was speaking, her cheeks reddened due to the intensity of the emotion she was feeling and the anxiety that was overwhelming her. Her knees kept shaking so badly that she could scarcely stand upright, but she pulled herself together and occupied herself in toying with her hair. She stood there, waiting to hear the king's response.

The king realized, of course, that she was not to be tempted and indeed that her argument could not be countered. He decided instead to play a trick on her and abandon any idea of resort to physical violence till his trick had had a chance to work. Realizing how very fond of Alfonso she was, it occurred to him that, if he exiled Alfonso, he would be able to change her mind and win her over. With that decided, he pretended that he had some urgent business to attend to.

"I still think you're allowing fanciful ideas to get the better of you," he said. "I've just remembered something that requires that I go back to the royal palace. That's very much to your benefit, because it gives you more time to think about things and come to your senses. If you fail to do so, you'll only have yourself to blame."

Having delivered those words in a threatening tone, he went out of the chamber and left Florinda on her own.

For her part, Florinda was happy to have this time so that she could come up with some means of escape. Once Roderic had left, she made her way back to her own room. By the time she got there, all her worries and anxieties had returned in force, and she was feeling very uneasy. The old woman met her at the door and asked her what had happened. Florinda did not say anything but kept walking until she reached the icon of Jesus. Kneeling in front of it, she started beating her breast, stifling tears as she did so. Now the stolid demeanor she had managed to maintain in Roderic's presence gave way to grief and misery. Her only mode of release was to burst into tears. As the hot tears coursed down her face, she prayed to the Messiah with heartfelt pleas from a soul that was overflowing with love and piety...

When the old woman saw her on her knees, she knelt down beside her and prayed along with her. Every time Florinda uttered a phrase, the old woman added her own "Amen." The gist of her pleas was, "Savior, save me from this trial and change this king's heart so that he may return to your will and sense the foulness of the deed he is proposing to commit. Guide me, Lord, along a path that will rescue me from this trap. Keep your servant, Alfonso, safe; guard him and stay with him. Dear Savior, bring us both together so that we may live a pious life with one another, one that will be pleasing to God. Pour your sympathy on this poor young woman, this wretched maiden who has no other haven but you. You are the resort of the wretched and helpless. Dear Lord, do not allow this evil deed to happen on the festival on your birth."

Every time she mouthed a phrase, she beat her breast and her great aunt intoned, "Amen." Both of them were shedding copious tears as they did so.

When they had finished their prayers, they both stood up. Florinda now felt more relaxed. Having shared her burdens with God, she felt as though the dangers had passed. Only someone with a firm faith can have such feelings; show such a person all the problems in the world, and he will show steadfast endurance, using prayer to lessen their effects. Tears also can remove feelings of stress; when anyone feels that he is under great pressure, crying will often alleviate those feelings. Such emotions are encountered more often in women than men.

Once Florinda's uneasy feelings were calmed, she sat down and started thinking about a way out of her dilemma. As she pondered her fate, the old woman sat cross-legged and watched her.

Chapter 13

Ya'qub

Let us now leave Florinda to her thoughts and go back to Alfonso to see what happened after his return to his own residence, which was not far from the royal palace. When he reached the door, he dismounted and handed his horse over to one of his servants. He was about to go inside but had the feeling that something was holding him back. After pausing for a moment, he went in and headed for his own chamber. He noticed his personal servant waiting by the door to receive his orders.

This servant was a short, middle-aged man with bulging eyes and an eagle-shaped nose. His chin jutted out and his short beard was divided into two cone-shaped segments that pointed outward. The tips were already tinged with white, whereas the hair close to his chin was still dark, or rather chestnut-colored. His name was Ya'qub. He never bothered to trim his hair, as was clear from the state of his beard; looking at it, one might think it had been sheared off an ewe, all tangled and matted. In summary, then, his face was funny to look at, with his bent nose, bulging eyes, and scruffy beard. Beyond all that, he was always on the go. He was good-natured and always wore a smile. He had been brought up in Witiza's house before he became king, and, once he assumed the monarchy, he had kept Ya'qub with him, trusting him implicitly and sharing many of his personal opinions with his faithful servant. Other personnel in the palace were jealous of Ya'qub because of his intimacy with the king, particularly since he was not a Goth himself. They had no idea of his origins or how it was that he had managed to reach such a lofty position. The whole thing left them all amazed...

Witiza had loved his servant and confided in him. Once he realized that his end was near, the king entrusted his own children to his care, and vice versa—in the latter case, Alfonso especially. He told his son to trust Ya'qub completely. In fact, Alfonso had already learned to respect and trust Ya'qub while his father was still alive, and the servant was utterly devoted to him. At first glance, when people noticed how jolly and boisterous Ya'qub could be, they may not have realized that he was actually someone with serious opinions and concerns. In fact, he was the most prudent and serious of men when the occasion demanded it.

When Alfonso got to his room, Ya'qub greeted him with a laugh, but Alfonso went straight inside without saying anything, which was very unusual for him, since he would always crack a joke or something. Ya'qub immediately realized that something really serious was going on, so he did not say anything for fear of interrupting Alfonso's train of thought or adding to his worries.

The first thing Alfonso did when he entered his room was to take off his cap and sword and hang them on the wall. Sitting on a wooden chair by the window, he stared out at the meadows of Toledo in the distance. It was still a bright, clear day, and he allowed his gaze to wander over this lovely space and linger in silence.

"Ya'qub!" he exclaimed, turning around abruptly and finding Ya'qub right in front of him. "Has my uncle come here while I've been out?" he asked.

"No, sir," Ya'qub replied, "he hasn't. Didn't you find him in the cathedral?"

As Alfonso recalled the mass, it occurred to him that his uncle must have been in the congregation because he was the metropolitan bishop, but then he remembered that, because there was such a level of estrangement between his family and the king's, his uncle had gone to pray in another church.

"Do you think he went to church?" he asked Alfonso. "Why didn't you go to church to pray?"

"I was busy with household matters," Ya'qub replied. "I said my prayers here. Isn't that enough?"

"Oh, forgive me!" Alfonso said, as though he had just remembered something. "I forgot my solemn promise to my father not to question you about praying. But what do you think about my uncle, the bishop? I need him."

"Just say the word," Ya'qub replied, "and I'll go and fetch him at once, even if he's in the Roman church!"

He smiled as he made that comment, because he was well aware of the antipathy Alfonso's family felt toward the Roman church.

"Oh," Alfonso replied, appreciating the joke, "I don't think he's that far away. Go and get him!"

Ya'qub went out to the servants' quarters and ordered one of them to go and look for the bishop at the church, another at his house, and a third in another likely place. He came back and was obviously concerned about Alfonso's state of mind. Even so, he was unwilling to find out what was wrong. When he reached Alfonso's room, he told him what he had done then stood to one side, toying with his beard and waiting for further instructions.

By now Alfonso was so deep in thought that he did not even notice. Many concerns were crowding together inside his head, but chief among them was the king and the way he had treated him with such disdain and contempt. Whereas before he had been the object of the adoring gazes of the nobility, now he was lower than the lowest. He tried to think how he could wrest the monarchy back from Roderic's hands, but at every turn he found that he was unable to come up with a solution. He had neither money nor men, no means to put up any resistance. At this point he remembered Florinda and the vow he had made to her to get the monarchy back. How could he possibly go back on his promise, weak and defeated? The entire prospect suddenly overwhelmed him, and failure loomed before his eyes. He came to regret ever making such a vow to his beloved Florinda. He began to despise himself and fell into deep despair. In spite of his valiant efforts, he could not help crying. When there seems to be no way out of a difficult situation, tears can often lighten the blow.

Ya'qub was still standing by the door; hearing Alfonso let out a big sigh, he realized from his movements that he was actually in tears.

Ya'qub was aware that Alfonso would only be doing that if he thought he was alone, so he sneaked out—without Alfonso even realizing—and sat on his chair by the outside door. Now he was really worried about Alfonso and decided to ask the bishop about him once he had arrived since Alfonso's uncle clearly had a big influence on him.

Chapter 14

Bishop Oppas

A short while later, one of the messengers came back and informed Ya'qub that the bishop was on his way. The servant took that as a pretext for going in and talking to Alfonso. Once inside, he discovered that Alfonso had stopped crying and his mood had improved somewhat. When he heard that his uncle was coming, he could not help breaking into a smile because he trusted his uncle implicitly; he was a man of firm resolve and powerful intellect, quite apart from his fondness for his nephew Alfonso.

The bishop's name was Oppas[11] and, like Alfonso, he regarded Roderic as an interloper. He had done his utmost to prevent Roderic from acceding to the throne, but he had failed, largely because the party of Roman bishops had ganged up on him and prevailed, and also because he was the only Gothic bishop. All the rest of them were Romans who adhered to the Roman king, and that is how they had managed to win. Since Roderic had become king, Bishop Oppas had avoided involvement in public affairs unless it was absolutely necessary. On this particular day, for example, he had conducted the Christmas mass in his own house and then gone out to sit in the garden. He could not stand the thought of watching Roderic in procession to the cathedral rather than his own nephew. So, when the messenger arrived asking him to go and see Alfonso, he put on his beretta and cloak and came hurrying over.

Bishop Oppas was an impressive figure, lively, tall, and lanky. His shoulders and forehead were both broad, and his jaw and cheekbones jutted out. While his skin was tawny-colored, he had black hair aplenty, most notably his beard, which extended from his chin all the way to his

---

11 'Abbas in Arabic. *Translator's Note.*

waist. People with traits like these normally have a strong will coupled with considerable bodily strength, a strong sense of what is right, and an awe-inspiring presence. They figure prominently in a number of different domains: war, commerce, politics, or anything to which they choose to turn their minds.[12] For the most part, they are distinguished from people with other traits and are superior to them. In spite of all that, Oppas always walked at a slow pace. He was often deep in thought and was a man of few words. When he spoke, however, his voice was loud and clearly audible, and what he had to say was always to the point and pertinent.

It was not long before Alfonso heard his uncle's footsteps, which were easily recognizable because of their slow, steady pounding on the floor. He got up to greet his uncle. When the bishop reached the door, Alfonso went over and kissed his hand; in return he received a blessing. Ya'qub did the same, and the bishop gave him a blessing, too, accompanied by a smile, something that he rarely bestowed on anyone.

The bishop entered Alfonso's room, and the nephew quickly shut the door so they could be alone. The bishop took off his beretta and let his hair loose; it was very long but still had no grey tinges even though he was almost fifty. Oppas stared at Alfonso and immediately noticed that, while he was making an effort to smile, there were still traces of tears in his eyes and he was looking unhappy.

"What's the matter, my boy?" he asked, much affected by what he saw. "Why are you looking so downcast?"

Alfonso could hardly manage to keep his face calm and not burst into tears again, but he gritted his teeth and took a bit of comfort from his uncle's presence.

"I don't think you're unaware of what is bothering me," he told his uncle. "You have the same problem…"

"I understand what you're saying, my son," Oppas said, "but in your case that's old history now. Something else must have happened to make you so unhappy all over again."

"How right you are, Uncle!" Alfonso replied. "Here's what has happened. This morning I presented myself before this ravening beast of a king like some servant groveling in front of his master. I felt so

---

12 The modern science of physiognomy.

insignificant that I almost died of shame. If the audience had gone on much longer, I cannot say what might have happened. When I left the palace, the royal retinue completely ignored me, whereas in earlier times they would have been fighting each other to kiss my hand."

"Why were you placed in such a position?" Oppas asked. "Roderic has rarely been interested in talking to you before."

"I was late for the royal procession this morning," Alfonso replied. "I only realized it when I was on my way back to the palace."

"Couldn't you have avoided being late, so you would not be subjected to such abuse and censure? What was it that made you so late?"

Alfonso had no problem telling his uncle what the reason was because he was completely in the know about Alfonso's relationship with Florinda; in fact, it was the bishop who had paid the pledge money for their engagement.

"The reason is that this morning I went to see Florinda," Alfonso replied. "I had not seen her for ages. You realize that, ever since the disaster happened to my father and me, I've been cut off from the palace and its environs. I was worried that Florinda might have changed her mind, so I paid her a visit to make sure she still loved me. We talked for so long that I completely forgot about the procession. I only realized what the time was when they were on their way back from the cathedral. I rushed to join them, but I didn't realize that the king would be watching my movements so closely. When I went in to see him, he told me to stay behind until all the other people who had come to offer their congratulations had left. Then he proceeded to upbraid me for my conduct; it wasn't all that fierce, but it still struck me like a thunderbolt."

As he was speaking, tears began to swell in his eyes. Oppas was used to ignoring such signs—symptoms of human frailty that they are—so he made no comment. He waited for Alfonso to finish what he had to say. For his part, Alfonso noticed that his uncle was still listening, so he continued.

"What made me even more upset is that that dreadful priest is still trying to trap me. He drew Roderic's attention to my relationship with Florinda, and I could read evil intentions in those sunken eyes of his, not to mention in his sinister remarks."

"My dear Alfonso," Oppas said, "I can see that you're very upset, indeed, but there's no point in that. You should not pay any attention to the odd phrase or random gesture that you hear or see; they are but dust in the air, with no truth to them. So relax, be strong, and use your intelligence."

Chapter 15

Composure

Alfonso was surprised by what his uncle had to say; it made him feel weak and puny. Even so, he managed to keep his feelings under control.

"But how can we pay no attention to what people are saying?" he said, his voice tinged with genuine anger. "How am I supposed to endure such utter contempt? My dear uncle, are you content for us to be treated like slaves by this interloper?

"No, I'm not," his uncle replied calmly.

"So how are we supposed to accept such treatment?" Alfonso went on. "'Mere dust in the air,' you call it, but I can't stand it. If I'm to be treated this way, I'd rather be dead than alive..."

"I didn't say that such contempt is like dust in the air," his uncle replied. "What I do believe is that speaking in anger and without due thought is just like dust in the air. There's no point to it!"

This well-meaning rebuke made Alfonso feel duly ashamed, but his emotions were still very much in command.

"So, Uncle," he went on, "are you blaming me for being angry when they've killed my father and stolen my kingdom? And not only that, they've restricted my movements as though I'm one of their slaves. What am I supposed to do?"

"What I want you to do," the bishop continued in the same calm voice, "is to consider the situation logically. All anger does is to remove all common sense and encourage wrong decisions. You may be assuming—wrongly—that my calm demeanor and my patience means that I'm somehow less disgusted with these interlopers, but the truth of the matter is that I'm thinking a lot and saying little. When you've calmed down and listen to what I have to say, you'll come to realize that I've spent the last two years working on the very issue that has only occurred to you today. The only reason you're so worked up now is that you've met your fiancée today and she's blamed you for being so weak. But I'll never give way to anger, nor do I intend to take offense at stupid talk. Instead, I look at things realistically. I've expected you to behave this way ever since you lost your kingdom, not to mention the insults you've been suffering and the reprimands you've been getting."

Alfonso was very impressed by what his uncle had to say and fully appreciated the serious resolve that lay behind his sage advice. Realizing the harassment that his uncle had also been enduring without complaint over the past two years, he again felt humbled. He felt the need to correct the impression of his own lack of resolve.

"You're absolutely right, Uncle," he said enthusiastically. "I've let things slide. I had no idea that you were so involved in things. So please give me some advice. Tell me what I need to do in order to get back what this interloper has stolen from me."

While Alfonso was talking, the bishop was looking somewhat distracted and even gloomy. Staring out of the window, he seemed to become even more contemplative and serious. To look at him, one would think he was staring off into the void, as though in his imagination he could see a cluster of images that invoked a blend of fear, anger, joy, and energy.

Reflections of these differing emotions were clearly visible in the bishop's sparkling eyes. Had Alfonso known anything about physiognomy, he would have been able to read the contents of his uncle's thinking and thus avoid the need to find out more details. However, he possessed no such skills. So, once he had finished speaking, he waited patiently to hear what his uncle would have to say. But the bishop was still deep in thought, toying with his hair as he did so. It was as though he had not heard a single thing his nephew had said. The entire scene left him somewhat awestruck, and he did not dare to interrupt his uncle's thoughts. He did not say a word but simply waited.

For a while they both remained silent, but then Oppas spoke.

"Are you really aware, Alfonso," he asked, "of the major project in which you're involved? Do you fully appreciate the thing to which you aspire?"

"Of course I do," Alfonso replied. "How could I not? The thing I seek is my right, and no one can challenge me on that."

"So you do understand," said Oppas, "but have you come up with a plan to restore yourself as king?"

"I'll tell you what I think," Alfonso went on, "but it's your opinion I want."

"Tell me," Oppas said.

Chapter 16

Philosophy of History

"I'm sure you're well aware, dear Uncle," Alfonso said, "that the power that made it possible for Roderic to ascend to the highest office was the Roman church and especially its bishops. The Goths, who are our people and our family, do not want him. They're a large community of people. If they and their followers could unite, they would be able to form a large army that could defeat Roderic's forces. Then it would not be hard to recover the throne. He could either step down, or else be killed."

Oppas gave a wry smile to show how aware he was of the young man's naivete; he had had so little experience.

"My boy," he said, "You're right that the Goths support us. But do you really think that they would actually fight for us in a war? As far as I'm concerned, their grumbles about this king will never venture beyond mere words. You can't blame them for that; they're thinking about themselves and their property. The majority of them don't mind having Roderic and his Roman cronies in control; they all belong to the same religious grouping. They're all adherents to the Roman Catholic church; the Roman bishops have managed to win over their hearts and minds in the same way as they did their government before. They've actually forgotten to which nation they belong."

The bishop spoke quietly and deliberately. For the most part he remained calm and collected, but when he got to the end, his expression grew more excited. He stopped talking for a moment. Alfonso stared at him, waiting for him to finish.

"God forgive Reccared!" Oppas went on, fiddling with his beard. "He's the one who brought us to this sorry pass."

Alfonso did not understand why Oppas was blaming Reccared this way. Reccared had been one of the Gothic kings of Spain who had ruled the country for a long period in the sixth century AD. He was a man of war and politics.

"What did Reccared do," Alfonso asked his uncle, "to deserve such reproach? What I've learned is that he preserved the Spanish kingdom and expelled the Franks."[13]

"You're quite right, my boy," his uncle said. "He did indeed save us from the Franks. But unfortunately he exposed us all to an even greater danger."

"What was that?"

"Don't you know?" Oppas asked. "Reccared was the one who lost us our identity and broke our community apart."

Alfonso still did not understand what Oppas was talking about. "No, Uncle, I still don't know. What did he do?"

"My dear Alfonso," his uncle went on, "Reccared was the one who made Roman Catholicism the official government religion of Spain."

"Yes," Alfonso commented. "Wasn't that a good thing to do?"

"Now all of us are its adherents," Oppas replied. "We've been brought up to love and respect it. There's nothing wrong with that. But I'm looking at it from a political angle, our identity as a community. When the Goths came to this country several centuries ago, it was governed by the Romans. The Goths seized it from them by force and became its rulers. I'm sure you realize that the faith of our ancestors who came to Spain wasn't the Catholicism of the Roman church, but Arianism, a faith community that traces its origins back to the famous Arius of Alexandria. Before the Goths left their own domains and came to the Roman kingdoms, Arianism was the predominant faith.[14] So we conquered this country and spent almost two centuries as adherents to the Arianist faith system, even though the people of Spain have been Catholics.

---

13 Romey, part 2.

14 Gibbon, *Decline and Fall of the Roman Empire.*

"You should know that our kings of old made no effort to proselytize, nor did they see any particular connection between religion and politics. However, the Romans made a point of seizing every possible opportunity to use religion in order to regain control of the country. Bit by bit, they started poking their noses into the country's affairs and using a variety of methods to evangelize their brand of religion among the common people. A century or so ago, Reccared became king, and the Romans managed to influence his mind to such an extent that he discarded his own faith and adopted Catholicism, making it the official state religion. Now Roman influence was everywhere. The synod of bishops that gathers in this Toledo monastery can now control things just as they wish. They may even be getting orders from Rome itself. Roman Catholicism is still the official religion of this country, and there is only a tiny vestige of Arianism. I have no doubt whatsoever that the people who converted to Catholicism early on only did so because they were going along with Reccared's ideas, not because they were in any way convinced. Arianism, after all, is much closer to the logic of the human mind than any other Christian sect."

At this point Oppas became aware that he had probably gone into too much detail for his nephew; the somewhat glazed look on his face seemed to confirm as much. Ever since Alfonso had been a boy, he had heard people saying bad things about Arianism; in fact, he had often heard his own uncle make negative comments. Oppas realized what was going through his nephew's mind and decided to take a different tack.

"You're aware, Alfonso, aren't you," he said, "that I've not tried to make you show any favoritism to the Arian belief over any others? It's not a question of preferring one sect over another. I'm talking to you now about politics, not religion. I'm trying to show you how mistaken Reccared was—God forgive him!—when he joined the Catholic faith and thus lost his sense of Gothic identity. After all, dear boy, religion is the strongest and most inclusive of community bonds. In our day, Goths, Vandals, Romans, Greeks, Saxons, Arabs, and others as well, all existed alongside each other. But when they joined one particular sect, they lost their sense of group identity over time and became a single religious community."

"There is, to be sure, another unifying factor like religious affiliation; I'm referring to language. It, too, is inclusive, but as a rule it's linked to religious belief. Didn't you notice that, once we joined the Catholic faith, Latin became the predominant language in most of our churches and communal gatherings because it is the official language of Catholicism? Our own Gothic language began to decline and disappear. If we had adhered to the Arian belief, kept our own language, spread it among the common people of Spain, and brought them back from Roman Catholicism to the Arian belief system, their language would have been ours and their beliefs ours, and they would have been our supporters. However, we simply ignored the fact, and what actually happened was the exact opposite. Once the Romans had robbed us of our beliefs and language, they used the fact that Roman bishops had acquired so much influence in political matters to try to wrest the monarchy from our hands. That is why there is no other religious community in the whole of Europe that has as much influence in government affairs as does the Toledo church community of the government in Spain."[15]

"The first Gothic king to realize the danger was your own father, Alfonso—may God watch over his grave! He made every effort to keep Roman influence out of government affairs, to such an extent that I can almost hear him now expressing his own desire to abandon the Catholic faith and the power that its church managed to wield. The majority of the Spanish bishops had been brought up in the Catholic faith and were devoted to both it and its archbishop. They all refused to accept your father's expressed desire. Indeed, it did not take long for them to achieve their goals, of which I will spare you the details at this point since it hurts me just as much as it does you. They put Roderic on the throne, he being firmly in the Roman camp even though he claims to be Goth by birth. By so doing, they managed to ruin everything that your father had managed to do."

---

15 Kizu, *History of European Civilization.*

Chapter 17

Oppas's Views

Alfonso listened closely to what Oppas had to say. He was impressed by the philosophy and wisdom that lay behind it all, something that had never occurred to him up to this point. When Oppas mentioned the loss of the monarchy, Alfonso could not restrain himself.

"So how did they manage to put Roderic on the throne," he asked "when Witiza's children were still alive?"

"They got round it," the bishop replied, "by stating that the monarchy is elective, not hereditary.[16] If it had been hereditary, you, of course, would have been the most suitable candidate, but since it was elective, you were robbed of the opportunity. They were supposed to choose you because you were the king's son, and in fact they have done that several times before. But their choice of this Roderic to be king was the clearest possible sign of their larger national goals stemming from a complete lack of any sense of Gothic identity. But for that, we would not have come to this sorry pass..."

Oppas paused for a moment as though emerging from some kind of trance. "I realize that I've wandered off the main topic," he went on. "The point I've been making is that the people whom you consider to be Goths and who you hope will support you in your attempts to defeat this man Roderic have completely lost their sense of identity through both religion and language. They're more likely to support Roderic than us; they're not to be relied on or trusted."

Once Alfonso had listened to the conclusion of Oppas's statement, he lost all hope. He had been expecting to use his own people to bolster his

---

16 Romey, *History of Spain*, part 2,

cause. Once he realized that all was lost, his resolve collapsed. He just sat there, staring at the floor. "I'm out of ideas," his posture seemed to be saying.

Oppas noticed that his nephew looked dispirited and tried to cheer him up.

"Have you given up hope?" he asked.

"Why shouldn't I?" Alfonso replied. "I have neither men nor money. Not only did they rob me of the throne, but they left me empty-handed as well. Do you know what they did with my father's money?"

"They had every right to take the money," Oppas replied. "King Recceswinth, who ruled about sixty years ago, passed a law requiring that the king's money and property be returned to the state treasury.[17] There's no point in laying all the blame for what has happened on our enemies; the real question is how do we achieve our goals. If you're out of ideas, then tell me so I can come up with some thoughts, in the hope that they'll set us on the right track..."

Alfonso was amazed at his uncle's modesty. But he was so tongue-tied that his hands and eyes had to act as substitutes in urging his uncle to proceed; he was obviously more intelligent and experienced. Oppas adjusted his chair in preparation for what was going to be a lengthy statement. Even though he was certain that the two of them were alone, he still looked around as though searching for eavesdroppers.

"You should realize, my boy," he told Alfonso, "that whenever you plan anything, you have to think of the consequences before you start. Otherwise things can turn out very badly. You realize, don't you, that the Spanish people fall into a number of different groups? One, the nobility. They have all the property and high offices, some as provincial or city governors, others as estate owners, and still others as well. Two, the clergy. Three, civil servants, employed by the court and the government. Four, tradesmen, mostly middle-class and city dwellers. Five, servants and slaves, the rest of the population—and the largest group, peasants, house-servants, and most of the soldiers in the army."

"If we wish to regain the monarchy, we will have to get the support of some of these groups. So let's see which of them are most sympathetic to us..."

---

17 Romey

"The nobles are of either Roman or Gothic origin. The Romans are opposed to us, of course. I've just explained to you the situation with the Goths. By adhering to the Roman faith, they have lost their influence and power. So the nobility will be of no help. The same is true of the court officials. As for the clergy, well, as you already know full well, they are in fact the basic cause of the change that has occurred. When it comes to tradesmen, the fact that they've been living in cities for so long means that they've lost the kind of fortitude that is necessary for this kind of revolution, in addition to the fact that each one of them is tied to his particular profession and scared of losing what little money he has. You need to realize that the majority of European countries are made up of cities and countryside. City dwellers pay hardly any attention to what goes on outside their walls.[18] Every city is only worried about itself, so we can't expect to rely on the people of a single city because Roderic has whole armies and aides and will also ask his provincial governors to support him. All our efforts will be in vain..."

"So we need to take a look at the other class, the populace— servants and slaves. They're the largest segment, and the other groups can't do without them. In spite of that, the rulers still manage to tyrannize them. As you are aware, the majority of those who are now slaves were reduced to that status as the result of wars. They're all strong, not least because they're used to hard work and have suffered a lot from long hours working in the fields. The nobles' estates, their houses, and all their wealth are within the grasp of these slaves. Even so, the slaves are persecuted and regularly suffer humiliation at the hands of their masters—quite apart from the ignominy of slavery itself. I'm sure you also realize that, when it comes to innate abilities, these indentured workers are not less gifted than their masters, but they have become so inured to bowing and scraping before them that they're more compliant than the masters' own shadows. Everything a slave has belongs to his master. The slave cannot do anything without his master's permission, not even get married. Everything a slave acquires, whether by thrift, agreement, barter, or war—even his own children—all belong to his master. The slave, his property, and his children can all be sold without any redress."

---

18 Montesquieu

"In spite of all that, some masters do grant their slaves freedom as reward for good work that they may have done for them. Such freedom, however, is rarely that much different from slavery itself. Even though the slave may have been manumitted, he is still at his master's beck and call. If he gets a job, half of his pay goes to the master. If he decides to move elsewhere, he has to give back all the weapons and furnishings that he may have with him in his house. Such a manumitted slave only becomes considered as a free person in the fourth generation of his descendants.[19]"

"To summarize then, I'm not going to go into any more detail because you already know enough about such slaves. However, you've probably not given much thought to the humiliation and wrongs that they suffer. In fact, it may never have even occurred to you that their temperament is very similar to ours. That's the way you've looked on them while you've been growing up."

---

19 Romey

Chapter 18

The Method

At this point Oppas stopped and coughed. He looked at his nephew to see what effect his ideas were having and noted that he was giving them his fullest attention. With that, he continued.

"The principal point I want to make to you, Alfonso, is that it's precisely these oppressed slaves who represent the people's strongest segment; they're more numerous and have not only greater bodily strength but also a greater endurance of hardships. If we make use of them in this plan of ours, they'll be able to turn the monarchy on its heels. We may not even need them to pretend to be our allies and helpers; the simple fact that they will be a united force will be enough to scare the king, his governors, and the nobles as well. In that way, we'll be able to achieve our goal without war or bloodshed. But what will bring them together? How can we make them into a party that will come to our support?"

Alfonso was still listening closely to what his uncle was saying, realizing that every single word was right on the mark. But, when Oppas stopped after posing that particular question, Alfonso was a bit flustered. He had not expected to be asked such a question and had no response.

"You should realize, my boy," the bishop went on, "that the method we need to use to unite these oppressed slaves under our own banner is the most virtuous and noble of all; indeed it is a virtue that will cause our name to be remembered throughout the ages and make all previous kings of this realm jealous of our good fortune in making such a decision. Beyond that, it will earn us a justifiable reward from God Almighty... Do you know what I'm talking about?"

Alfonso did not bother responding because he could tell that his uncle was about to provide the answer himself.

"The best way of getting all these people together, my boy," Oppas went on, "is for us to offer them their freedom. Every one of them who joins our group will have the right to procure his own freedom after a certain amount of time. If he acquires that freedom, he'll immediately become just like all other free people. No one will be able to take a portion of his labor or profits. However, all that will be based on the fact that you will become king. Once you are enthroned as monarch, you'll make manumission much easier and use it as a way of getting these wretched people on your side."

Alfonso was absolutely dumbfounded by what he had heard. He now realized how far apart the two of them were in their perception and willpower. He even started thinking that everything was now so well settled that he could actually visualize the reins of power and was on the point of grabbing them back. In fact, Alfonso was not stupid by any means, but it was only in comparison with his uncle that his intelligence and thinking seemed less effective. Alfonso could not help himself shedding a couple of tears, so happy did he feel. He leaned over to kiss his uncle's hand, but it was swiftly withdrawn. Oppas was not feeling either happy or annoyed, but he managed to fake a laugh, put his hand on his nephew's shoulder and squeezed it hard. Alfonso felt the force of his hand and waited to hear what his uncle would say next.

"I see you're convinced by what I've suggested," he said. "But you haven't given any thought to the obstacles that stand in our path."

Alfonso looked shocked. He began to realize that his hopes would not be fulfilled. What could be the obstacles, he wondered, that would prevent the implementation of this plan? But he had no chance to answer because his uncle started talking again.

"I'm sure you're well aware," he said, "that this project of ours will need financing so that we can pay the soldiers, hire mercenaries, build fortresses, and subvert our enemies."

Chapter 19

A New Secret

As soon as Alfonso heard those words, he became distressed all over again. He had no money of his own, nor did the rest of his family. He started wondering how on earth he could have been so taken in by his uncle's initial ideas and imagined that he was about to achieve his primary goal when he knew full well that money was going to be a major problem. A little while before, he had been on the point of complaining to his uncle that he had been left virtually penniless after his father's death, but he had decided not to do so when he convinced himself that Oppas's plan was one that would work. His confidence in his uncle was something that had been developing ever since he was a boy. Ever since he had learned to crawl, he had always watched as his uncle came to visit his father wearing his clerical garments. Everyone used to revere him and treat his opinions with the greatest respect. As a result, Alfonso had grown up to respect his uncle's opinions and go along with them; whenever Oppas said something, Alfonso assumed that it was correct without giving it much thought. The same thing was happening on this occasion as well. No sooner had Oppas mentioned the question of funding than Alfonso realized that their discussion was essentially useless. He remained silent, his expression such a picture of frustration that there was no need to respond to his uncle's observation.

When Oppas noticed that his young nephew was listening so carefully and beginning to give up hope, he smiled again.

"So, Alfonso," he asked, "are you giving up already? Your mood changes so quickly, from hope to despair. Don't despair, my boy. I'm not going to allow your blind trust in your uncle to go to waste. I haven't been spending these last two years asleep in bed. It's true, I've been discussing things with you from all sides, but in fact I'm going to suggest a plan to you that I've worked out in great detail. Every aspect has been carefully organized. If that weren't the case, I certainly would not have even discussed the subject with you."

With that, the bishop stood up. Alfonso stood up as well, although he had no idea what his uncle's gesture meant. He was thoroughly confused and eager to hear more about his uncle's plans to get hold of some money, but he did not dare ask him for specifics. He remained silent in anticipation of what his uncle would say next.

Oppas picked up his beretta and put it on his head; Alfonso assumed he was going to leave. But then he heard his uncle yell for Ya'qub.

In a trice, Ya'qub rushed in, his nose and beard leading the way. He stood in front of the bishop, his face wreathed in smiles as befits someone who felt at ease in his presence. Once Ya'qub had come in, Oppas sat down again and signaled to Alfonso to do the same.

"You sit, too, Ya'qub," Oppas told him.

Ya'qub looked shocked. "My lord," he said, "Heaven forbid that I should sit in your presence and that of my master." He pointed to Alfonso. "Please allow me to remain standing."

Oppas laughed, something that he rarely did except with Ya'qub. Stretching out his hand, he grabbed hold of one side of Ya'qub's beard and pulled it gently downward until Ya'qub was seated on a rug on the floor. He made a big show of pulling his hand away and wiping his fingernails with a handkerchief.

"How often do you wash your beard, Ya'qub," he asked. "Isn't it about time?"

When Ya'qub heard the bishop say that, his mood changed all of a sudden; out went the saucy side, and in its place there appeared a serious mien.

"Your Worship knows better than I," he replied. "But it'll be soon, I hope…"

Alfonso could not work out what all this meant, especially when he noticed how quickly Ya'qub's mood had changed. Even so, he waited to see what would happen.

"I hope so, too," the bishop said. "But getting it washed costs a lot of money. Can you afford it?"

"Oh yes, sir," Ya'qub replied. "As you well know, I don't stint on either money, children, or breath itself when it comes to washing it."

For Alfonso, the entire conversation was only getting more and more peculiar and obscure. He could not understand why the bishop had called his servant into the room, nor could he work out why such a serious topic was being treated so frivolously. He was not aware that his uncle had this jovial side to him, particularly when it involved his servant, Ya'qub. He assumed they were simply joking, so he said nothing on the assumption that they would soon get back to the primary topic of discussion.

"I'm already aware of that, Ya'qub," Oppas went on, "but now it's time for me to see that you get your beard washed. Are you quite sure about the money, however much it is?"

"Oh yes, sir," Ya'qub said, "as you yourself already know."

"Yes, I do know," Oppas went on, "but has there been any change or adjustment?"

"Oh no, sir," Ya'qub replied. "It's still the way it's been."

At this point Oppas spent a long time in deep thought, almost as though he were trying to solve a serious problem and thinking through something that had only just occurred to him. He stood up, and so did Alfonso and Ya'qub.

"I shall want to see you at my house tonight," he told Ya'qub.

The servant acknowledged the command with eyes, hands, and lips. With that, he left the room and closed the door behind him.

Chapter 20

Florinda's Letter

Once Ya'qub had left, Alfonso expected to hear his uncle say something to calm his worries. When he noticed the bishop sitting down again, he did so, too, waiting to hear what his uncle would have to say.

"Don't worry, Alfonso," he said. "I have the money in hand when it is needed. We'll need another conversation for me to explain all the details to you and put the final touches on the plan that we'll need to follow in this very dangerous situation."

"But what I don't understand," said Alfonso, "is what all this has to do with my servant Ya'qub and his beard."

"God willing," his uncle replied, "you'll learn all about it later this evening. Will you come back with me and have dinner at my house? No, I've a better idea. You stay here, and I'll go home on my own; then I can work out the plan we'll need to adopt."

With that, he got up and moved toward the door, walking slowly as he usually did. Alfonso followed behind him to say farewell. But just as they reached the door, they heard a knock. Ya'qub came back in carrying a small flat purse of purple silk that looked just like a book. It was tied with a string of blue silk. No sooner did Alfonso set eyes on it than his heart started pounding. He realized it was from Florinda; she often used it to send him letters. He hurried over, took it from his servant, and asked Ya'qub who had delivered it.

"A servant from the royal palace," was the answer.

Even before he heard the answer, Alfonso had started opening it. Once it was open, he brought out a square piece of wood with both faces coated in wax; a metal pen had been used to write on it, that being the way correspondence was conducted at the time, several generations before the invention of paper writing.[20] Alfonso took it over to the window, completely forgetting that he was supposed to be saying farewell to his uncle. He started reading it, but as soon as he had reached the end, his hands started shaking and his entire expression changed. Oppas realized that there had to be something momentous in the letter, so he let Alfonso read it undisturbed. But he soon noticed that Alfonso turned the tablet over and started reading it all over again, tilting it toward the light coming in from the window and scrutinizing its every word. It was almost as though Alfonso could not believe what he was reading. His face reddened, and he looked furious. Looking at his nephew, Oppas decided to close the door again so he could be alone with him. At this point, Alfonso looked up and saw his uncle coming quietly toward him. The very sight of his uncle calmed him. He did his very best to control his emotions so as to replicate his uncle's calm demeanor, but it was too much for him. Going over to his uncle, he handed him the letter.

"What a disaster!" he said. "We seem to be going from one catastrophe to another, and all because of this debauched interloper, Roderic."

Oppas held out his hand, took the letter calmly, and examined it closely. It was written in Latin with a few Gothic phrases included[21] and had been carved into the wax with a wooden stylus.

Here is what he read:

My beloved Alfonso,

The one thing that I most feared as a result of my being transferred to the royal palace has almost just happened. If you don't hurry up and rescue me, I will fall into the lion's clutches. You say you love Florinda, so hasten to rescue her before it is too late. Failing that, she has only a few hours of life left to her, since it will come to an end before she leaves

---

20 *Encyclopedia Britannica*, "Paleography."

21 Romey, Part 2.

this palace. If I am not to be rescued, then I entrust you to our God and assure you that I will be departing as a martyr to chastity and purity. Remember me to my dear family. We will meet again in heaven along with the saints above.

Your wretched Florinda.

When Oppas read it, he was as much affected by it as Alfonso, but he was better able to deal with emergencies such as this. He realized that he was primarily responsible for the predicament in which Florinda now found herself because he had arranged her engagement to Alfonso. However, Alfonso could not restrain himself.

"Forgive me, Uncle," he said. "My patience is at an end, and I've forgotten all about the throne. You're the one who blessed our engagement, so you have to ensure that the marriage takes place, in addition to the fact that we are related to each other. But apart from all that, I really want to hear what you think we should do."

Oppas gave Alfonso a calm look and stroked his beard.

"Calm down, Alfonso," he told his nephew. "God willing, I'm going to get Florinda out of the royal palace safe and sound."

For a moment he raised his eyebrows while he thought about things, but then he frowned.

"I'm absolutely amazed at the way this man is behaving," he said, "ignoring the problems his people are facing in order to indulge in a passion that will please neither God nor His servants. I see it as a clear sign of the imminent demise of his monarchy. God will never lend His support to a king who goes against His clear injunctions."

Alfonso was still deeply concerned, his heart in flames over his concern for Florinda. While his uncle thought things through, he read through Florinda's letter again. His eyes fell on the phrase, "I will be departing as a martyr to chastity and purity," and could not help wondering what lay behind such statements that made him feel insanely jealous.

Just then, his uncle called out to his servant. "Ya'qub!"

Ya'qub came in, cap in hand. "At your service, sir," he said.

"Can you think of two servants in this household," Oppas asked, "who could be completely trusted if we asked them to perform a special task, even if it was against the petty tyrant who happens to be the ruler of Toledo at this point?"

"Me, sir," Ya'qub relied immediately.

"No, Ya'qub," Oppas went on. "We'll be using you for something else. What we need are two or three young men whom you trust implicitly and whose energy and courage you can count on. The task we'll be asking them to undertake requires courage, initiative, and total reliability."

Ya'qub looked down, deep in thought, and started twisting his beard between his thumb and first finger. Eventually it was so twisted that it looked like the end of a piece of rope. After several moments of thought, he suddenly let go and his beard returned to its normal shape. As he looked straight at Oppas, his expression suggested that he had thought of something.

"Normally I don't trust such people," he said, "even though most of them have grown up in this household and shared in its benefits. Humans are too weak to be willing to sacrifice themselves in the cause of loyalty and trust. Even so, there are two men I know who are suitable for this task."

"Who are they?"

"Their names are Ajilla and Chantilla," Ya'qub replied.

"Why have you selected those two in particular," Oppas asked, "when neither of them has grown up in the king's household?"

"I've chosen them," Ya'qub responded, "because I believe they can perform the task, and they still aspire to higher things. You realize, sir, that they were originally slaves. Your brother freed them before he died. When he realized how competent and astute they both were, he added them to his own retinue. After they were manumitted, I came to realize that both of them have higher aspirations. When people eat a dish they haven't tried before and like it, they develop a taste for it and want more, whereas people who are used to eating fine food rarely ask for more. These two young men grew up as slaves, but now they've had a taste of freedom. It's a long story, but the late king noticed how they longed for better things, and so he gave them their freedom and made them part of his retinue. Now they want to advance. If the task you have planned for them will give them the right opportunity, they'll do their utmost to make it happen. Otherwise they'll refuse to consider it. But they won't let you down..."

"I can see," Oppas commented, "that you're an astute ethicist! Bring them both to my house after sunset."

With that, he turned to address Alfonso. Ya'qub realized that he was supposed to leave, and he departed. Alfonso, meanwhile, had started worrying again.

"How are we going to reply to this letter?" he asked as his uncle approached.

"Tell her to get ready to leave at two in the morning," Oppas said. "Say you'll be waiting for her in a boat by the palace."

Alfonso took a piece of thick fabric, the kind they used to write on,[22] and with shaking hand wrote the following:

To Florinda, queen of my heart,

Greetings, my beloved! I shall be waiting for you at two in the morning tomorrow night. Be ready to leave with whatever you can carry with you. Look out of the window on the river side. When you see a triangular light, you'll know that I'm there waiting for you. Take courage and don't be afraid!

Your beloved Alfonso, who would ransom his very heart for you.

He folded up the letter, sewed it together, put it in the purple purse, and sealed it. He then handed it to Ya'qub to give to the messenger who had brought it, with instructions that he was to keep it safe so no one else would read it. Ya'qub took the letter and went out.

---

22 *Encyclopedia Britannica.*

Chapter 21

Another Letter

It was already almost sunset by the time Alfonso prepared to accompany his uncle to his house so they could discuss what they were going to do. Alfonso had been really surprised to learn about what Ya'qub had already been doing, but he was still perplexed as to the precise details of what he had heard. By now the weather had changed; it had turned cloudy and very cold. Alfonso put on a heavy fur cloak, while his uncle wrapped himself in his clerical garments, which rarely left him feeling cold. But, just as the two of them were preparing to leave, each one deep in his own thoughts, the door suddenly opened and Ya'qub came in carrying a purple leather cylinder. Alfonso immediately realized that it was a letter from Roderic; his letters to governors and commanders were always written on leather, wrapped up, and then put into purple calf's leather cylinders. When Alfonso noticed the cylinder, he went over to take it from Ya'qub. His uncle stood in his way and took it instead.

"Who brought this?" the bishop asked Ya'qub.

"A troop of the king's horsemen," Ya'qub replied. "Their commander asked me if Alfonso was here. I was hoping to delay him while I obtained the appropriate answer, but he wanted to know at once. I was ordered to convey this letter to him as quickly as possible wherever he might be. So I told him you were here. He gave me the letter and said he would be waiting…"

Oppas stared at the seal on the letter and saw that it was indeed the king's own. He broke it and took out the letter. It consisted of a piece of parchment that was used by the government to issue orders. The letter was folded over, so Oppas opened it up and read its contents, with

Alfonso standing beside him. It consisted of an official command from Roderic to Alfonso. Here is what it said:

From Roderic, king of the Goths,

To the fearless champion, our dear friend, Alfonso,

Dear Friend, we have learned that slaves and vassals in the dukedom of…have stirred up a revolt aimed at opposing the government there. Upon receipt of this letter, you are hereby enjoined to hasten to our military headquarters in Toledo. A battalion of soldiers is waiting for your arrival to lead them to that city in order to quell the rebellion. Haste is of the essence here. It is a sign of the urgency of the situation that this letter of ours is being dispatched on Christmas Day when no one is supposed to work. If you are now on your feet, do not sit down. If you are walking somewhere, do not stop until you have executed our command. Farewell.

Written in the royal palace of Toledo on the twenty-fifth of December 710.

No sooner had Alfonso heard the conclusion of the letter than the entire world closed in around him. "I won't go there," he yelled angrily. "I refuse…"

Oppas gave him a derisory look. "How can you not go?" he asked. "Is that even possible? Don't you realize that this letter is full of compliments to you? If you refuse, you'll be causing yourself all kinds of trouble."

"What kind of trouble?"

"If you refuse to go," Oppas pointed out, "you'll be accused of disobedience to the king, and he'll have you arrested. Do you have any men at hand to help you resist the monarchy at the moment? What you'll be doing is to bring down all kinds of trouble not only on yourself but on all the rest of us as well. The clergy collegium will make use of your disobedience to do just that. The only sensible thing to do is to calm down and go along with their scheme until such time as God wills something else to happen..."

In fact, Alfonso was well aware that such was the case, but it was his anger about the way Florinda had been treated and the fact that he now had to leave Toledo before he could rescue her that made him stop thinking logically.

"So what's to be done?" he asked more calmly, once he had taken in what his uncle had said. "How can I get to see Florinda?"

"Leave all that to me," the bishop replied. "I'll make sure to rescue her tonight and hide her somewhere. I'll write to you wherever you happen to be. We'll have to see what the fates decide to bring us. But don't be alarmed. Instead, think ahead to the time when this particular journey of yours is complete and we can move ahead with our plans. Trust in God. As the Muslim Koran puts it: 'You may hate something which turns out to be the best for you.'"

Alfonso looked over at Ya'qub. "Tell the letter-bearer that I'll be on my way shortly."

"As I told you earlier, sir," Ya'qub replied, "it's a whole troop of horsemen. They've been told not to come back without you..."

Oppas interrupted Ya'qub. "Go now, my boy!" he told Alfonso. "On your way, and I'll take care of everything while you're away. But I'd advise you to take Ya'qub with you and rely on him. He can advise you on matters that are of concern to you..."

"I hear and obey," Ya'qub replied immediately and rushed away to put on the appropriate clothing. Alfonso did the same. Both of them went out, with Alfonso doing his best to remain calm as he placed the entire burden of his worries on his uncle.

Chapter 22

Back at the Palace

Let's leave Alfonso now, as he prepares to travel, and go back to Roderic's palace. We left Florinda in her room pondering her situation after finishing her prayers, during the course of which she had placed all her burdens on God. When Roderic had left, he was already harboring evil thoughts toward her. The first thing he did was to look for Father Martin, who was reciting some prayers of his own. The priest had been aware that the king had gone to Florinda's palace quarters and realized that, once he came back, he would be bent on finding a way to get rid of Alfonso or banish him somehow. When he encountered the king on his way back to the palace, he immediately sensed from his eyes and general expression that the king was in a rage. Anyone who set eyes on him might have been surprised that he had not murdered the girl, particularly since, whenever he was sufficiently angry, he was quite capable of killing hundreds of people without batting an eyelid.

However, love can always quell anger and exert itself over both heart and mind; it can tame lions and imprison tyrants, since its primary mode of action involves affection and sympathy. If you encounter a man who is still uncouth and gruff in his manner, you can be sure that love has yet to take up residence in his heart. To be sure, in this case Roderic's love had its sinister aspects, but that did not prevent it from gaining control of his heart. The reason is that love has but a single cause, but it can manifest itself in a variety of ways depending on a person's temperament and circumstances. When Florinda rebuffed Roderic and resisted his advances, he may well have felt inclined to kill her but refrained from responding to his baser instincts because he was still hoping to win her favor and get her to change her mind. Signs of this involuntary forbearance were clearly visible in his expression, so much so that when Father Martin set eyes on him, he assumed that he was furious. With that in mind, the priest greeted the king with a laugh. The king's response was to pull himself together, greet the priest, and try—albeit in vain—to hide his real feelings. He decided that the best thing he could do was to engage the priest in conversation.

"It seems that that youth, Alfonso, has some particular interests inside the palace," he said, trying to make light of the situation.

"It would seem," the priest replied with a stutter, "that Your Majesty did not understand my reference to precisely that subject this morning."

"Oh, I understood," the king replied, "but I..." With that, he fell silent.

The priest realized that there was more to the king's words than was immediately obvious, so he too remained silent. Tapping his jutting lip with his finger, he stared at the king, assuming that he would finish what he wanted to say. The king could see no harm in sharing his secret with Father Martin, since the priest served as the depository for all his secrets except for his passionate love for Florinda. He had kept that secret because he was ashamed of what people might say and scared in case his wife found out. He was well aware, too, of the power that priests have over women. If Father Martin disapproved of his behavior, the queen might find out about it and stand in his way. Even so, he was eager to let the priest know about decisions he had made.

"I think it would be a good idea to banish that young man from this city of ours," he told the priest. "That will take him away from the palace and his family..."

The priest nodded in agreement, seeing that as a preferable way of responding rather than saying anything.

"If you banish him," the priest went on, "we may be able to do two things at once: get rid of him and make use of his services. But, as the saying has it, the snake is not dead if the head is still alive."

Roderic was well aware, of course, that he was referring to Oppas. He was just as eager to exile him as well. "Actually," the king went on, "keeping the snake's head close by is a better idea, especially if the tail is far away."

Once again Father Martin nodded in agreement but said nothing.

The king got up at once and composed the letter. As we have already seen, it was sent to Alfonso. The king waited until he was sure that his orders had been carried out, meaning that Alfonso had actually arrived at the barracks and was preparing to leave.

By now the sun had disappeared below the horizon, and it was getting dark. It seemed that the arrival of darkness only served to amplify the king's blind passions and evil intentions; he could no longer wait till the following day. He ate dinner with his wife and drank a great deal of wine in order to hide the devilish flames that were raging inside him.

When he left the table, his stomach was sated and the wine was swirling inside his head. He went immediately to his room, while the priest remained at the table with his wife. Once Roderic was inside his room, he locked the door behind him and opened the other door leading to the passageway to Florinda's room.

Florinda had been giving a lot of thought to the letter that she had written to Alfonso and given to the old woman to deliver. She, in turn, had sent it by way of a servant whom she trusted implicitly. So now Florinda was waiting for an answer. For an hour she could think of nothing else; in fact, it felt more like a month or even a year. Sometimes she looked over at the door and at other times at the window overlooking the river; occasionally she summoned her great aunt and asked her why it was taking so long. The old woman kept trying to calm her down. Eventually the messenger came back, and Florinda was overjoyed. The very first thing she did was to kiss the icon and give thanks for the way her prayers had been answered. She started packing light clothing and jewelry, and the old woman helped her till the sun went down. Florinda now left everything else, went over to the window, and sat there, her eyes focused on the river as she waited for the triangular light to appear. She realized that the rendezvous was still some time away, but it made no difference; there was a sense of panic that made her think it would be soon.

The weather had turned cold and clouds were gathering. The sky turned dark, the winds picked up, and there was thunder and lightning.

Not long afterward, it started raining. Even so, she kept on staring out at the river, her knees shaking with hope and joyful anticipation. Every time there was a flash of lightning, she assumed it was her beloved's lamp shining. Occasionally the clouds would break up and a few stars would be reflected in the river. Florinda kept assuming that they were a triangular light. In fact, some twenty stars may have been visible, but she assumed that the effect was caused by the way the river waters were refracting the light. In fact, tree branches in the gardens were blocking her view of the river, especially the big ones directly outside her window.

Chapter 23

Another Trial

Comforting herself with the thought that she was about to be rescued, Florinda concentrated all her thoughts and emotions on the window looking out over the river. All of a sudden she became aware that Roderic's footsteps were approaching through the passageway. Her strength gave out, and her heart started pounded so hard that she almost fainted. In an instant she realized the peril she was still in, something she had not been taking into account. She sat on the rug and started beseeching God to come to her aid and save her. The only person around was her great aunt.

"Isn't that the king approaching?" she asked.

Before she even had time to finish her sentence, the old woman left the room then came back.

"The king wishes to see you in the other room," the old woman told her.

"Woe is me!" Florinda wailed. "What a disaster. O, my God!" She slapped her own face and started to cry.

The old woman came over and tried to calm her down, although this time she had no idea of anything to say that might console her. Even so, the only effective thing she could think of was to resort to the greatest of all consolations, religion.

"Put your trust in God," she told Florinda. "He saved you last time, and He will do the same now. For God, that does not present a problem…"

Florinda was a person of deep religious faith, so she begged God to come to her aid this time as well.

"I beg you, Auntie," she said, turning to the old woman, "pray for me and ask God to save me from this dreadful trial."

"I shall stay here," the old woman replied, "kneeling in front of this icon until you return. If I went with you, it would do you no good. Against such an enemy, only God will be of any help."

That was somewhat reassuring for Florinda. She went out of the room, like a sheep ready for slaughter, and proceeded, step after reluctant step, till she reached the other room. Roderic was sitting on the other side and did not bother to stand up. This time, he looked angry, something that had not been the case when they last met. His eyes looked red, and his expression was askew from the effects of all the wine he had drunk. His breathing was labored and heavy, sounding almost like a snore. At first Florinda assumed that his facial expression was that way because the room was very dark, but as she drew closer, her heart started pounding again. Seeking refuge in God, she pulled herself together and moved forward till she was standing just a few paces away from him, head lowered. She had combed and braided her hair and changed her clothes, ready to leave the palace as arranged. When Roderic looked at her, his passions intensified, the more so since the wine only served to amplify his baser instincts. He was still sitting down, legs stretched out in front of him and arms spread wide to either side.

"So, Florinda," he asked her, "has your heart told you anything new?"

She did not reply but merely looked down at the ground.

He asked her the same question again, leaning on his knees as though he were about to stand up.

"Answer me, Florinda," he said. "You're clearly aware by now of the happiness that I'm offering you. That's especially so now that you realize that I've freed you from the clutches of that boy who was tempting you with his declarations of love. He doesn't love you or deserve to command the passion of your heart."

When Florinda heard him say that, she was afraid that the king had arranged for Alfonso to be harmed in some way. Looking up, she stared straight at him to see if her worries were justified. However, she quickly lowered them again when she noticed in his expression signs that made her quiver to her very bones. What she saw could only be described as evil personified. By looking down again, she hoped to hear the truth about what the king had done. The king jumped up and moved toward her.

"Why won't you give me an answer?" he asked, twirling his beard between his fingers then letting go. "Are you ashamed of being in an intimate situation with the king? God has already forgiven you for your past behavior." As he said that, he was about to place his hand on her shoulder as an affectionate gesture.

As soon as Florinda realized what he was trying to do, she moved back and lifted her arm to protect herself; it was as though he were a ravenous wolf about to devour her.

Roderic moved back, too, looking perplexed. "What's the matter with you?" he asked. "Why are you running away, as though you're scared of getting hurt? All I want to do is to come close and make you happy."

Florinda was still deeply worried about Alfonso and wanted to find out if she was right in her suspicions. By now it was raining heavily, and the pattering of rain was mingled with the sound of gutters, lightning strikes, and thunderclaps. Florinda, however, was in such a panic that she was completely unaware of all the noise. She knew full well that she had to talk to the king and eventually realized that the noise the storm was making was so loud and her tone of voice so soft that the king could not hear anything she was saying.

"I have already explained to Your Majesty," she said in a loud, quivering voice, "that this situation has nothing to do with me. God has determined that my destiny lies with someone else…"

"It seems," the king replied, "that you didn't understand what I just said. The young man whom you say is your destiny has now left. There's no way…"

When Florinda heard him say that, she assumed that the king had killed Alfonso. She let out a loud scream, shaking all over as though someone had just poured boiling water all over her body.

"What are you saying?" she yelled. "What have you done to Alfonso? What have you done? Have you killed him?"

Chapter 24

Asking for Help

When Roderic saw the way Florinda reacted, he was afraid that the shock might kill her, whereas all he wanted was to keep her alive, if only for just one hour.

"What's all this screaming about, Florinda?" he asked. "Have I killed Alfonso, you ask? No, I haven't, but he's completely in my hands and his life is entirely at my discretion. If I so wish, I can have him killed with a single command any time I want. You seem to be forgetting who it is that's talking to you now, and who is the other person whom you're calling your destiny. Yes, indeed, I have not killed Alfonso; instead I've made do with simply exiling him. But, if you continue to be so stubborn, I will kill him; and, if you persist in your stupid ways, I'll kill him first and then you. I've noticed how impertinent you still are being with me; I obviously have not been able to convince you or win your sympathy. So, hear me well: this very hour marks the divide between your continuing stubborn resistance and my own wishes."

Having shouted those words at her, he turned toward the door and closed it behind him. But then he came back in.

"So choose which door you wish to use," he told her, "and then leave."

He threw himself down on a couch, groaning like some lowing ox. His eyes were now even redder, and his nostrils were flared in anger.

Florinda now realized what his evil intentions really were; she was clearly in imminent danger. She looked all around her, as though to search for someone she had lost track of or to ask a friend to help her;

she had no idea what she was trying to do. She was about to answer, but Roderic anticipated her response.

"So who are you looking for?" he asked. "There are only two of us here; no one else. No one on earth can stand between me and what I want. So give up and submit; it'll be better for you and bring you greater happiness."

When Florinda heard the words "only two of us here," she remembered some of the words from the Holy Bible that she had read and heard: whoever trusts in God will never falter, and God is to be found in every place. We've already seen that Florinda was a very devout person. For that reason, she suddenly felt more confident, as though she were surrounded by a host of angels who were there to protect her. Plucking up her courage, she now looked straight at Roderic, who was staring at her ravenously.

"You claim that we're alone," she told him, "and that nothing stands in your way. You seem to have forgotten that God is everywhere; He will not permit anyone's authority to outweigh His own. So I heard you threaten me with death. So, go ahead and do it! Kill me! My life means nothing to me. But the one thing I beg you is not to harm Alfonso. Oh dear, my beloved Alfonso!"

No sooner had she mouthed that name than she burst into tears and let them flow unchecked.

When Roderic heard her crying like this, he became yet more furious, especially when he heard her still talking about Alfonso. However, he had come to realize how pointed her reference to God had been and how determined she was, not to mention her love for Alfonso and her plea that he be allowed to live. With all that in mind, he decided to offer her a deal.

"If Alfonso's life means so much to you," he told her, "I'm quite willing to let him live; in fact, I'll even promote him and make him one of the happiest people in Toledo. All you have to do is to stop being so stubborn with me."

"The thing that you want me to give away for your sake," she replied with a derisive smile, "is the most valuable thing I possess in this life; in fact, it's even more valuable than my own life, even more priceless than Alfonso himself. Without that costly jewel, that diadem without peer, I would not merit even a single glance from Alfonso, or any other man, for that matter. I would be worth nothing. If that were not true, do you really think I would dare to address the king himself in such a direct fashion?"

The king realized that she was trying to prolong their conversation. He had no arguments to counter hers. In any case, he was in no mood to be persuaded because his animal instincts had completely overwhelmed his mind and will. As he was flirting with her and trying to convince her, he might well have been persuaded that he was actually embarking upon an action that would be reprehensible and that her protests were fully justified, but he had lost control of his own passions.

In such situations human beings find themselves at the great divide between virtue and vice; everyone has similar passions when it comes to the desires of the flesh, but they also recognize the dividing line that separates virtue from vice. But in situations such as this one, they prefer to see the force of will prevail over evil passions and behave in accordance with the dictates of their conscience. Those who are closest to a life of virtue are those with the strongest wills. People who live a pure, chaste life are not distinguished from their peers by their ability to differentiate between good and evil, nor do they necessarily possess a superior understanding of the dimensions of virtue and vice. What distinguishes them is their ability to control their emotions in particular circumstances and for short periods of time that may not exceed a few minutes. If they manage to keep themselves under control, they can preserve their own honor throughout their lives and live in peace and happiness. The best evidence for this is that people who are unable to control their emotions surrender to their desires and soon come to regret their actions—but too late.

Chapter 25

Desperation

Roderic may have had a powerful build, but he was still weak-willed. No sooner had he heard Florinda's rebuke than he realized how wrong his behavior had been. In spite of that, he ignored his better instincts and plunged blindly on, pursuing his sinful intentions, regardless.

"So, Florinda," he yelled, leaping to his feet in fury, "I see you're determined to put up a useless defense. I've lost patience with all your pretty words. Don't you realize the danger you're in? Well, if you're not willing to go along with my plan willingly, then it'll have to be by force."

So saying, he moved toward her and seized her arms with quivering hands. Florinda shivered all over and felt as though she were being clasped in an iron grip.

"A curse on you, you blackguard!" she yelled. "A pox on you, you pimp! Have you no fear of the Day of Judgment? Do you not fear God? May God blacken the face of a monarch who is supposed to treat the oppressed fairly, when in fact he's the greatest oppressor of them all! God curse a man who claims to have been enthroned to keep rebels at bay, when he himself is unable to control his own passions!"

Looking up to heaven and raising her hands, she prayed. "O beloved Savior," she cried, "I seek your aid. With you I seek refuge from this perfidious tyrant!"

As she was saying this, Roderic kept trying to grab her other hand, and she was desperately trying to escape his clutches. He brought his mouth close to her face, and she could smell the stench of wine. She was about to say something, but just then there was a flash of lightning, followed a few seconds later by a huge clap of thunder that came close to the palace. The entire building was shaken to its very foundations. The lightning bolt came in through the windows like some fiery lance. The entire thing gave Roderic an enormous jolt and for a moment distracted his attention. He began to be scared because for the first time he realized that fate was threatening him. This often happens with people who are brought up within a tradition of faith. They come to believe that the fates are observing their every move and gesture; nature never does anything without considering as part of the process both the good and evil aspects—rewards for good deeds, punishment for bad ones. Such people may regard one particular action as a reward at certain times and as a punishment at others, according to the dictates of their conscience. Conscience itself is rarely deceived, unless, that is, it has been dulled by continuous indulgence in sinful acts and the dominance of passions in one's personality.

This is exactly what happened to Roderic when he heard the thunderclap and watched the lightning. For the first time, he was really scared; he turned pale, and his heart started pounding. He might well have been inclined to regret his actions so far and to forget about his evil intentions, but unfortunately this particular sensation lasted for no longer than the lightning flash.

Florinda, meanwhile, had taken advantage of the situation and withdrawn her hand, regarding the lightning as a response to her plea for help, an answer to her prayers.

"Don't you realize," she now said, turning to look at him, "that there exist in the world powers to grant the weak victory over the strong? Is this force now capable of raining down on you and your palace thunderbolts to dispatch you to an early grave?"

Roderic was totally dumbfounded by the way the fates had come out to support Florinda's cause but told himself that now was the time for revenge. His evil desires were now intensified. Moving toward her, he grabbed her shoulder with one hand and stretched his other hand to grasp hers, kicking her as he did so. She struggled to escape his clutches and managed to break free because he had not managed to fully clasp her to him. Once she had managed to free herself, he became even more furious and attacked her like a raging bull, totally oblivious to what might happen to her.

Now that Florinda knew that his blind fury was at such a pitch that he was about to assault her, she realized she was in real danger. She decided that she would kill herself before he could achieve his evil goal. Falling to her knees, she looked up to the heavens as though begging for help, since she believed that divine intervention would still be able to help her. When she saw that Roderic was almost upon her, she rushed away, placed both her hands around her neck, and tried to throttle herself.

"Come, sweet death!" she screamed. "Death is better than ignominy! O beloved Savior, I surrender my soul to you!"

So saying, she grabbed her dagger. All the blood drained out of her face, and her eyes bulged. Roderic immediately pulled her hands away from her neck and held them tight. Her strength gave out, and she collapsed to the floor. There she lay on her back, motionless.

Chapter 26

Spray her with Water

When Roderic saw what had happened to Florinda, for just a moment he felt some twinges of humanity and decided to be gentle with her. Kneeling down beside her, he took her hand and sat her up, hoping that she would come round from her fainting spell. But her eyes remained closed, and her limbs were completely limp. His heart was pounding as he did this, and his conscience started pricking him badly. He assumed she was either dead or almost so. Leaving her on the floor, he rushed to the door in search of some water he could use to sprinkle on her face. Opening the door, he headed for Florinda's quarters. There the old woman greeted him as she was coming out of the room. She had been surprised to hear the door opening because, at that very moment, she was still kneeling before the icon, praying desperately for Florinda's safety in this dangerous situation. In fact, she was praying so fervently that she was oblivious to everything going on around her; she had closed the windows overlooking the river, so she did not hear the thunder, nor did she pay any attention to the lightning and wind—like someone who is half asleep and hears background noise. But, once she heard the door opening, she came to herself, as though waking up after a dream or something, and rushed over to the door, where the king met her, shock and panic written all over his face.

"Bring me a cup of water," he told her. "Hurry!"

With those instructions he hurried back to the other room, and the old woman followed him, bringing a cup of water. She was so worried about Florinda that her knees were shaking. Roderic went in first.

"Pour some water on her face," he told her.

No sooner had the old woman set eyes on Florinda than she yelled, "Florinda! What happened to you?"

When the old woman sprinkled her face with water, Florinda came round and sat up at once, staring all round her.

"Oh, woe is me!" she screamed when she set eyes on Roderic. "I am still alive, and this evil creature is still standing in front of me. I thought I'd escaped his clutches in death!"

Roderic ignored her and spoke to the old woman, "Have you seen what Florinda has done to herself? She is impetuous and stubborn. I offer her happiness, and she refuses..."

All the old woman could do by way of reply was to burst into tears; she could not think of any way for Florinda to escape. With that in mind, she decided that the best plan was for her to flatter the king.

"Your Majesty," she said, still crying, "I beg you to treat this poor girl kindly and let her be. There are hundreds of other girls like her in the palace who are at your beck and call."

That made the king angry; he had been expecting her to help him. He gave her a kick.

"Get out of here, you foul old woman," he yelled. "You're as bad as she is!"

As Florinda's great aunt left the room, she remembered the rendezvous with Alfonso and wondered whether he might have some men with him who would be able to climb up and rescue Florinda from this evil man's clutches, by force if necessary. She rushed back to Florinda's quarters and opened the window a bit. The wind blew in her face, and she got soaked by the rain. Looking toward the river, she could not see any kind of light, triangular or otherwise. Closing the window again, she went back to her prayers.

Roderic, meanwhile, closed the door again and went back to Florinda, who was still sitting on the carpet. By now she had rested a bit and recovered her strength; the color was gradually coming back to her cheeks. With all that, she was still looking downcast. Roderic went over to her, with his hand clasped to his belt. When he took it away again, he was holding in one hand a dagger with a blade that glistened as though dipped in poison, in the other something that looked like a ring.

"My patience is at an end, Florinda," he told her, stretching out his hand. "For the last time, I'm offering you happiness. Either you take it, with this ring as a token of my intentions, or else I shall plunge this dagger into your breast. Answer me now!"

Getting to her feet, she turned her breast toward him. "Go on then," she said, "plunge it in. Stab me with your dagger and rescue me from this foul life. At least then I shall be able to face my God innocent and pure... Go on, Roderic, do your killing!"

"Think carefully," he told her. "Don't for a second imagine that I'm just threatening you. I'll do it! If you come to your senses and fulfill my desires, you can take this ring as a token of my love for you. Then you'll be the happiest girl in all Toledo!"

"And don't you imagine that I'm joking either!" she replied. "I'm not scared of dying for the sake of purity and chastity. For me, death is infinitely preferable. Perhaps it is you who needs to return to your senses and repent before it is too late. Whatever happens, you'll live to regret this. If you perform this dastardly deed and then regret it later, that will do you no good. If you decide to go ahead and kill me, you'll live to regret killing an innocent young maid whose only crime was to insist that you behave as God has enjoined you to do."

With that, she turned away and looked up to the heavens. "O my beloved Savior, my Lord and my God," she said, "will You not reveal to this man how foul and evil is the deed he plans to do? Please remove from his eyes the crust of ignorance that is covering them..."

Roderic guffawed. "Maybe you're expecting some more thunder and lightning," he interrupted, "to answer your prayers like last time. But in this age when miracles don't happen..."

Chapter 27

Unexpected Footsteps

Roderic had the dagger raised in his right hand as though to plunge it into Florinda's breast, but, without being able to finish what he was saying, he suddenly stopped. He could hear the sound of footsteps approaching along the corridor. As he listened intently, he could hear the sound as the footsteps drew rapidly closer. His heart started pounding, and he shivered all over. Once again the religious sensitivity that had been part of his upbringing took over, and he told himself that God seemed to have answered Florinda's prayers yet again, sending some of His angels down to rescue her. He was convinced that no human beings could possibly have gained entry to the palace at this time of night; even if they did, they would never dare to come up to this room, when the doors were all locked and clear orders had been issued not to disturb the king.

For a moment or two, both Roderic and Florinda were transfixed, standing there with their eyes glued to the door and waiting to see what would happen. Florinda stayed where she was, quivering with embarrassment, while Roderic put the dagger back in his belt. He could still hear the footsteps as he went over to the door. Before he got there, he heard a loud knock that reverberated around the palace and sent a shiver through Roderic's bones. He hurriedly opened the door. Imagine his shock and surprise when he discovered Bishop Oppas coming in, someone whom he well knew to be august, determined, and self-possessed. The bishop's clothing was dripping wet.

When Florinda saw him, she imagined that it was an angel dressed in Oppas's clothing. She stayed standing where she was, holding her breath; the shock of it all had left her mouth dry.

Roderic was unable to suppress his shock that the bishop should behave in such a bold manner.

"What brings you here at this hour?" he asked the bishop. "How were you able to get into the palace without permission?"

Oppas ignored the implications of his remarks. "What brings me here," he replied, as though addressing a silly boy, "is a matter of importance to the kingdom that I need to present to you. As far as my admission to the palace, the king is well aware that bishops such as myself have no need to ask permission in order to speak to the monarch. After all, they speak to God without asking permission."

Roderic now realized that he was confronting the authority of the clergy, and most especially the bishops who had placed him on the throne. Even so, Oppas was not one of them, as we have already explained. So, while Roderic was angry at the way Oppas had intervened, he also knew that he had committed a grievous sin. Even if the sinner happens to be a king, he still feels weak and disconcerted, particularly when faced with a revered figure such as Oppas. For that reason, Roderic decided to cover up his sin by devious means; he would divert Oppas's attention and come back to Florinda later.

"Wait for me in the public rooms," he said. "I'll come in a while."

"If the matter I've come about could wait," Oppas replied, "I would not have come here through the pouring rain to speak with you."

As he said that, he pointed at Florinda, although he pretended to be addressing the king. "If you look out of the window overlooking the river," he said, "you'll see that what I've just told you is true. You can see that it's not just raining; it's snowing. If the matter were not really serious, I would certainly not have disturbed the king. I will only leave this room in your company."

Florinda was attending to what Oppas was saying with eyes and ears poised. When she heard him talk about the window, she immediately realized that he was referring to the rendezvous to rescue her. That made her very happy.

Roderic now looked at Florinda. "Go back to your chambers," he told her, "till I return."

With that he rushed out of the room. Oppas followed but at his usual pace, totally unbothered by the king's haste. When Roderic reached the end of the corridor, he turned around and noticed that he had left the door open. Once Oppas had left the room, the king went back and locked the door behind him to stop anyone from coming and snatching Florinda from his clutches. Oppas paid no attention to these moves on the king's part. Eventually they reached the public rooms where council sessions were normally held. Roderic sat down and invited Oppas to do likewise.

"The thing I wish to discuss with you," Oppas told the king, "is not one that can be discussed in this place."

Roderic was astonished. "Where then?" he asked.

"In a private place," the bishop replied.

Roderic stood up, clearly annoyed by this stubborn insistence on Oppas's part. They went to a private room where the light was very dim. The king sat down again, and Roderic sat facing him.

"So, Metropolitan," the king said impatiently, "what is it?"

"I've come to see you," the bishop replied, "on a matter that God has enjoined me to tell you."

That made Roderic sit up and pay attention.

"God has granted you authority," Oppas began in his usual calm manner, "and through that authority you are to rule over people, right the wrongs done against them, and punish all those who oppress them. Do not use that authority as a means of annoying God."

The criticism implicit in Oppas's statement astonished Roderic. The way he knitted his eyebrows indicated that he would treat such brazen behavior with utter contempt.

"Is that all you have come here to talk about?" he asked.

Oppas was well aware that the king was furious; he was trying to show his contempt and parry the criticism. Obviously the bishop could not tolerate such a posture.

"Do you believe perhaps," he asked the king, "that what I'm saying is somehow fanciful or completely unimportant?"

"I don't believe," the king replied, anger written all over his face, "that you have any business whatsoever objecting to whatever I do inside my palace. If there's something connected with the way I rule the people, with public safety, or with the country's politics that concerns you, then tell me."

Oppas smiled in contempt. "Your Majesty," he said, "don't you realize that you're responsible for everything that goes on either inside or outside your residence? From that point of view, vagabonds have more freedom than kings. You've been entrusted with the interests of your people, their souls, their wealth, and their honor. God has given you that authority so that you will both preserve and defend those values. So what do you do? You use it as a way of robbing people of them, and then start engaging in such practices yourself. So, when a wise counselor comes to warn you, what do you do? You berate him and treat him with contempt. This is not appropriate behavior for kings who are members of the faith."

Roderic was utterly astonished at the insolence of the bishop. Oppas's calm, staid posture only made him more angry.

"So," the king asked, "was your late brother any more in tune with these values than I am?"

Chapter 28

Stammerings

Oppas realized that Roderic was simply trying to put him down by referring to the fact that his brother had lost the kingdom. He could not tolerate such an insult, so he raised his voice while still maintaining his calm demeanor.

"Let's not bother talking about the dead," he said. "They have their own reckoner to deal with. We're talking about the living here. In any case, I don't believe that Witiza would have even contemplated indulging in the kind of evil you're perpetrating here."

Roderic leapt to his feet in anger. "Forget about it," he yelled. "It's none of your business. I know best what I need to do for my people..."

That said, he turned his back as a way of indicating that he desired the conversation to come to a close. Nevertheless, Oppas remained seated.

"If you really knew what your duty was," he went on, "then you certainly would not be harassing a pure young girl, given that you're married. But, instead of repenting of such a foul deed, I see you're trying to defend it."

That said, he stood up. "You should know, Roderic," he said to finish his statement, "that your indulgence in these kinds of activities and your contempt for the clear meaning of God's words and instructions is one of the very first signs that this dynasty is heading for downfall."

No sooner had Roderic heard Oppas's prediction concerning the dynasty's downfall than he turned toward him again.

"So you threaten me with the dynasty's downfall, do you?" he yelled. "You'd never be able to bring that off, even if you filled the entire world with conspiracies and invoked all the powers of heaven and earth together!"

"If we did indeed have any desire to take over the monarchy," Oppas said, "the powers of heaven could certainly wrest it from your grasp."

Oppas had not even finished his sentence before the door to the room opened, and in rushed Father Martin, stammering his way across the floor as though he were trying to say something but could not get the words out because he was so worked up. Finally he managed to put the words together, albeit in a jumbled fashion.

"Y...y...you, you're threatening His Majesty the king? The dynasty is heading to a fall? Wh...wh...what impudence! Ou...ou... outrageous!"

Before the priest had managed to get everything out, his beard was covered in spittle, which came flying out of his mouth. Once he had managed to get to an end, he started wiping his beard off and pacing around the room, head lowered and still mumbling.

Oppas was well aware that the priest had launched a phony accusation against him so as to shift the blame, so he maintained a contemptuous silence.

Roderic, meanwhile, was delighted and relieved by the priest's intervention and put on a display of both anger and victory.

"No matter," he said. "We've heard quite enough about good and evil for one day."

With that, he left the room, trailed by Father Martin.

Oppas stood up, utterly unconcerned by what he had witnessed in this room. His only concern had been to rescue Florinda from the king's clutches.

The reason Oppas had come to the palace and entered the private quarters was that, when the appointed time for the rendezvous had come, Ajilla and Chantilla had arrived at Oppas's house. He had instructed them to get a boat ready for the river. Once they were in it, the storm had started, the wind had started blowing hard, and the river had become very choppy. None of that had bothered them; in fact, they regarded it as being propitious because it would be easier to cover their tracks. When they reached the palace walls, the king and Florinda were in the room, and the old woman was praying. The window was locked, so the two men, accompanied by Oppas, climbed up, not bothered by the pouring rain and the raging storm, till they were right under Florinda's room close to the leafless tree. None of the guards or retainers even noticed them. Oppas signaled to Chantilla to climb up the tree and knock on the window. He did so, reached a branch right in front of the window, and tapped lightly on the panes with the tip of his sword. It made a fairly loud noise, but no one inside heard it because the old woman had gone to get some water to splash on Florinda's face. Chantilla shinnied down the tree and told Oppas that no one had responded to his knock.

Oppas stood there for a moment, thinking. "If Florinda was able to do what she wanted," he told himself, "nothing on earth would have kept her from looking out of that window. She has to be in trouble, and that can only mean Roderic."

He realized that she had to be in great danger. If he did not do something quickly, the king might well kill her. He told the two men to tie up the boat alongside the palace and wait where they were; when they heard the window open, they should climb up the tree and carry Florinda and anyone with her down to the ground.

Once he had given those instructions, he headed for the palace's public gate. Questioning the palace guards about the king's whereabouts, he learned that the king was in the palace. No one stood in his way as he entered the palace grounds; it was very common for bishops to enter in order to discuss confidential matters, particularly where Toledo itself was concerned because its clergy were far more involved in political matters than was the case in other European monarchies. That was even more so in Roderic's case because he had only managed to become king with their help.

True enough, Oppas had not been among the bishops who had put Roderic on the throne, but the guards on duty at the palace gate were not the kind of people to make distinctions between one bishop from another; all they had to do was look at the ecclesiastical garb. As it was, Oppas's august demeanor was quite sufficient for him to earn respect and for his commands to be obeyed, particularly at this moment when his urgent concerns gave him an even greater air of dignity and seriousness of purpose.

As he made his way through one door and gate after another, no one stood in his way, until he eventually arrived at the door to the king's apartments. He knew the place well because, of course, the same rooms had belonged to his brother, Witiza, not too long before.

"The king is in his chambers" the guard told him, "and no one else has come in."

Oppas paid no attention. The king had left the doors unlocked, so Oppas went in without anyone noticing. He saw immediately that the door leading to Florinda's rooms was open, so he went through. There were no servants to be seen. His stride was that of someone who had nothing to fear from kings. He started looking around him and noticed a light in one of the rooms; he could hear an argument going on inside. Knocking on the door, he went in. He decided to knock in case he found Roderic and Florinda in a compromising situation, the very thought of which made his entire body quiver in fury. He found it impossible to control his anger. Decent, God-fearing people hate the idea of spying on other people and surprising them in their most intimate quarters, even if the purpose is to benefit one of them...

Once he had entered, however, it took only a single look at Florinda for him to realize that at least she was safe and sound. All he had to do was to get Roderic away from her so she could go back to her room and escape. That's why he asked to speak to Roderic on his own. He had two reasons: firstly, to set Florinda free so she could escape; and secondly, to reprimand him severely for committing such an outrageous act. He did not care whether or not this angered Roderic; he had done what he had to do, and Roderic's anger would have to be dealt with. The way he had left the room so precipitously made that clear enough. From now on he would obviously be out for revenge, especially once he came back to Florinda's apartments and only found the old woman there.

Chapter 29

Revenge

Roderic had been fuming with rage when he left the room. Father Martin trailed behind him, still muttering and utterly amazed at the way he had witnessed Oppas addressing the king in such a blunt and inappropriate fashion. He assumed that the king would not leave him that night until they had come up with a plan to bring about Oppas's downfall. But he watched as the king left him and went back to his chambers. The priest now sat on a chair in one of the palace corridors so that, when the king did come back, he would be bound to pass by. But, when the king did not return immediately, Father Martin returned to his own room.

Roderic had gone back to Florinda's quarters, of course, his heart aflame with anger and malice. His mood was not in any way improved when he could find no one in that palace. Instead, Florinda's room looked a mess because everything that was precious and light enough to be carried off had been removed.

As he made his way back to his own chambers, he could hardly contain his fury. In spite of the lateness of the hour, he sent for the palace superintendent. Without even giving him time to say a word, the king asked the man who had left the palace that night. When he asked the servants the same question, they all replied that they resided on the first floor of the palace and were not allowed to venture upstairs on any account. They were, however, quite sure that the palace gates had not been opened that night, nor had they been able to see anyone coming out of another exit because the night was so dark. The rain and stormy weather had made it impossible for them to check on what was going on outside. He then asked the guards, and they too responded that the stormy weather had prevented them from paying attention to anything else. Eventually he checked on other modes of escape and discovered the window overlooking the river. There they found on the tips of the tree branches some tufts of fur that had been torn off Florinda's cape.

Once that became clear, Roderic realized that Oppas had helped Florinda escape. That sent him into a towering rage. He was now hell-bent on bringing Oppas down. As he returned to his quarters, he was feeling utterly exhausted; the sense of failure had an even greater effect on him. It felt as though he were recovering from a bad hangover. He needed to be left alone and lay down on his bed. However, his mind was still churning, so he could not fall asleep; his anger at Oppas would give him no peace. His only resort was to summon Father Martin, the confidant of all his secrets. Getting out of bed, he found a guard standing by his door and ordered him to fetch Father Martin immediately, even if he were asleep in bed.

The guard went to Father Martin's room and knocked on the door. The priest had taken off his clothes and put on a nightshirt. He was sitting on the bed, beginning his nighttime prayers. The guard waited outside till he had finished praying, then went in and informed him that the king had demanded his presence. The news delighted him because he was sure that the reason was to plot Oppas's downfall. Getting up at once, still in his nightclothes, he put on a roomy fur cape but left off his beretta. His hair was mostly white and looked like a pile of cotton on top of his head. When he reached Roderic's quarters, he found him similarly informal in his appearance, since he too had just rolled out of bed. His hair was a mess as well, tangled up with his beard and mustache. He looked angry and frustrated. The priest's entrance made him feel much better, and he rose to welcome him. Kissing his hand, he invited him to sit down beside him. The priest did so.

"I hope," he said, "that Your Majesty has called me here on some suitably enjoyable matter."

"I think you know full well why I've invited you here," Roderic replied. "You saw and heard what happened with Oppas tonight."

Martin decided to flatter the king. "His impudence was truly astonishing," he said, "only surpassed by Your Majesty's patience."

"It's the kind of impudence I haven't expected from such people," the king went on. "After all, we've trained them to be humble and submissive and wrested power and authority from their hands. Is Oppas not scared of my anger?"

"I suspect," Father Martin said, "that Your Majesty did not pay full attention to what he had to say. Oppas is famous for saying little and thinking a lot. Whenever he says something, you have to think about it carefully because he'll never say anything at random. Didn't you hear him say to you, 'If we had our eyes set on the monarchy, the powers of heaven would be able to wrest it from you'? It's a peculiarly bold statement, one that shows the extent to which he is scheming and planning conspiracies. I can only assume that what he's plotting is to convene secret assemblies and cooperate with our foes to seize the monarchy back. But he's bound to fail..."

When Roderic heard this explanation, he was relieved because the priest had come up with a pretext for charging Oppas with a crime. Now he could be arrested, along with everyone else in his house. Perhaps Florinda would be there as well. He was convinced that that was where she had fled, since she had no other relatives.

"So, Reverend Priest," he asked, "what do you think about this traitor?"

"I think he should be arrested immediately," the priest replied, "before he has the chance to hatch any more conspiracies. As he left your palace, he uttered threats against you. Don't be lenient in this case; at such a moment as this, prudence would be a sign of weakness."

Roderic was in no need of further encouragement since that was what he himself devoutly desired to do. But he decided to do even more than Father Martin was suggesting. He would have the whole of Oppas's household arrested and imprisoned in the hope of getting them to reveal some fresh conspiracies.

"Call the head of the royal guards," he said.

Martin left the room and ordered some of the guards to summon their commander. He then went back into the king's room.

Chapter 30

Oppas in his Palace

As soon as the king had left, Oppas had got up and rushed back to his residence to meet Florinda and the two servants. He was anxious to work out a way of getting her out of Toledo. When he reached his house, he asked the servants if anyone had asked after him. They told him that no one had. He had assumed that they would get there before he did, unless, that is, something had gone wrong or they had encountered an obstacle of some kind. He contented himself with waiting for them to arrive, but after a while he decided to go out and look for them on the road they were expected to take. Just then, however, he heard commotion outside, the sound of horses' hooves. He told himself that Florinda and the servants were arriving on horseback and went over to a balcony to take a look. It was still very dark, but he was able to make out a group of horsemen approaching the palace and encircling it at a distance without talking to any member of his household. It was so dark that he could not make out any faces, but his intuition led him to believe that they had to be Roderic's men; their arrival was thus a matter for alarm. Even so, he retained his calm demeanor, thanks to his self-confidence and a firm conviction that his cause was just. He decided to persevere, duly bolstered by his clear resolve and the sheer force of his arguments. However, he was really worried about Florinda and her companions. If they came to the house now, they would inevitably fall into the trap.

After a few moments' thought, he came to realize that he needed to take the initiative; that was better than simply pacing around his room. Putting on his cape, he went out the door and called the nearest guard. The man came over, dismounted, and greeted the bishop with great respect.

"What are you doing here?" Oppas asked.

"We've been told to stay here till morning," came the reply.

"On whose orders?" Oppas asked.

The man did not reply but turned away and summoned the commanding officer. He came over, dismounted, greeted Oppas, and was about to kiss his hand, but Oppas withdrew it sharply.

"Who ordered you to stand guard here?" he asked. "What is the purpose in all this?"

"One of the king's deputies," the officer replied. "Why have you disturbed yourself and come out on a night like this? Go back to sleep!"

"Officer," the bishop replied in his usual calm manner, "either explain to me why you are standing guard here, or else go back the way you came."

"We have been ordered," the officer said in a lowered voice out of respect for Oppas, "to arrest you as soon as you leave this house."

That made Oppas furious, but he remained calm. "Ordered to arrest me?" he said. "Who gave such an order?"

"Forgive me, my lord," the officer replied, "I'm only obeying orders. I can only do what I'm commanded to do. The orders come from our commanding officer acting on behalf of the king. How can we not obey such an order?"

"No, you're right," replied Oppas. "I would always encourage you to obey orders."

Oppas was thinking fast, well aware of the fact that Florinda might arrive at any moment.

"I will leave with you now," he told the officer. "There's no need to wait till morning."

"There's no need to panic like this, my lord," the officer said. "Even if you stayed in your house for a month, we'd still wait for you."

"No, I'm coming now," the bishop replied. "Let's go..."

The officer signaled to his men, and they regrouped. A horse was brought for Oppas, and they formed an escort around him. No one said a word since they were afraid to speak in his presence.

On the way, he started wondering what could be the reason for his arrest, but he remained calm and steadfast. He was still preoccupied, of course, with Florinda and kept worrying in case they might run into her on the way. Fortunately they arrived at the palace without seeing anyone else.

When they reached the palace, Oppas was about to dismount, but the officer indicated that they were ordered to accompany him to a guardhouse near the palace, where he would have to stay till morning.

"That's why I suggested, your eminence," the officer told him, "that it would be better to stay at home till morning. I wanted to make sure you were at your ease."

Oppas realized, of course, that he had done the right thing by leaving the way clear for Florinda, even though it might cause him some slight discomfort wherever he was to meet the king and see what it was he wanted. So he went into a room close by the palace, and a guard was posted by the door.

Oppas spent the rest of the night pacing around the room, wondering what the king had in mind in "inviting" him to the palace in this fashion. Many ideas occurred to him, not to mention a number of charges that he might be deciding to level against him. But the fact that Florinda had managed to escape made him very happy. For his own part, he had nothing to fear in defense of the cause of truth and liberty. Free men are never flustered by any situation, nor are they bothered by doubts. Even their enemies respect them, but the cunning tricks of conspirators and the despotism of tyrants may still place such people in danger.

Chapter 31

The Message

With the arrival of dawn and daylight, things began to assume an urgency for Oppas; he was anxious to know why he had been summoned in this peculiar fashion. But a significant part of the day went by without anyone requesting his presence, and that made him even more anxious. He summoned the guard commander who was in charge of arrangements, and the man duly appeared.

"When is this period of confinement supposed to end?" Oppas asked him.

"I don't know, my lord," came the answer. "Maybe it'll all turn out for the best. If I knew the answer, I would certainly let you know."

"I need to return to my house," Oppas said. "If there is no urgency about this meeting, then they should let me go. When the king needs anything, I can come back."

The officer's look convinced Oppas that he was keeping back something that he would much prefer not to reveal.

"What information do you have?" he asked the officer.

"If you return to your house," he replied, "you'll find no one there."

Oppas was stunned. "How can that be?" he asked.

"Everyone in the house, servants and slaves, they've all been arrested," the officer replied. "They're in prison, and the doors of your house are locked."

When Oppas heard that, he was sure that the king was planning to do away with him. But he still managed to retain his composure. The thing that continued to worry him was Florinda. It occurred to him that the only reason for arresting his household was because they had seen Florinda. But at this point he was not bothered about details.

"That won't do them any good," he said calmly, looking straight at the officer. And with that he went back inside and the officer returned to his post.

This officer was one of the people who was well aware of the excellent qualities of Oppas and his entire family, but, like most people connected with government authority, he had no choice but to follow its policy. Even if he thought otherwise and might actually say so, he had to enforce that policy—not what he himself believed. This is a typical situation with dynasties in eras of decline and collapse. Even in such periods, there can be intelligent men who fully realize the shortcomings in the operation of the government and criticize its actions outside the framework of their official positions. They will even claim that, if they were to be put in positions of authority, they would be able to introduce reform measures. However, if one of them were to actually achieve such a status, he would soon go along with the general scheme of things, albeit against his better judgment, just as his predecessors had done. Should he try to resist such normal trends, he would be exposing himself to great danger. Very rarely does someone adhere to his former resolve when placed in such an executive position; individuals find it very hard to go against the general pattern of things. Dynasties only reach such a stage of decline when their problems last several generations. If the human body gets sick when a person is old, there's no hope of going back to days of youth. However, if a reformer in high office does come along, he may be able to achieve genuine change, but then he, too, will go his own way...

Many people in Toledo at this time were quite able to witness the decline in progress, but they had no recourse against powerful administrative positions. All that junior officials like this particular officer could do was to grit their teeth and endure...

So Oppas went back inside and sat down. He was so lost in thought that most of the day went by. When he noticed a servant bringing him in some food, he realized that he was going to be in the room for a long time. That made him even more worried. He refused to eat anything and sent the food back. He summoned the officer again.

"I cannot eat this food," Oppas said, "until I know why I am being treated this way. Can you ask someone?"

"The best plan, my lord," the man replied, "would be for you to write a letter that I can take to the king's councilroom. Then I can bring you the reply."

Oppas took a wax tablet out of his pocket and start writing on it with a stylus.

Your soldiers have brought me to this place, when I have committed no wrong. The king is well aware that it is entirely inappropriate to treat a member of the clergy in this fashion. Clergy are under the control of the church. I have no idea why I am being imprisoned, except for the fact that it is just one more sign of the rot eating away at the life of this regime.

The officer took the letter and went to the palace. He soon came back.

"Father Martin is on his way to talk to you," the officer said.

Oppas was, needless to say, not delighted to hear this piece of information, but in spite of that, he was still hoping to hear why he had been imprisoned. He realized that he would only be coming because the king had told him to do so. As Oppas was sitting in his chair, Father Martin came rushing in, muttering to himself as though he were saying some prayers. He stopped in front of Oppas and greeted him. He was about to kiss the hand of his clerical senior, but Oppas could not be bothered with such formalities. Father Martin sat down on a chair facing Oppas, smiling gleefully. Nothing makes a man happier that having the upper hand over his enemy.

Father Martin coughed several times and wiped his face and beard as he prepared to say something. But his stammer made that impossible until such time as God might release his tongue.

"H...H...His Majesty has sent me," he stuttered, "to inform you that he is well aware of the privileges of the clergy. They may only be imprisoned or tried as a result of actions by ecclesiastical courts. The order to have you imprisoned is only for a short time until the council of bishops can be assembled and investigate your actions…"

When Oppas heard what Father Martin had to say, he was as astonished as ever. He did not understand what was being implied because such ecclesiastical meetings only occur once or twice a year.[23] The only reason for summoning extraordinary sessions is to consider important matters such as the selection of the king or investigation of a serious danger that threatens the kingdom or other matters of similar import. In order to summon such a meeting, letters have to be sent to all the bishops and primates in the provinces, a process that takes several days. Oppas stared at the ground, deep in thought, but said nothing.

Father Martin was staring straight at Bishop Oppas to see how he would react. He expected him to get angry because his plan was to treat him with contempt. But when Oppas did not react in that way, Father Martin felt that the insult was thrown back on to him. Once he realized that Oppas was not going to flare up or change his usual demeanor—no temper, no protests, no questions—he assumed that Oppas was not fully aware of the danger he was in, evidenced by being summoned to such a session.

"You're aware, your eminence," he said to Oppas, "that it normally takes some time to convene all the bishops. However, since they have all come to congratulate the king on the occasion of Christmas, it won't take too long to convene this one. So don't worry about it."

Oppas still remained calm and said nothing. He had already worked out those details for himself.

When Father Martin noticed that Oppas still refused to be provoked but remained his normal calm self, his anger got the better of him and he decided to make a reference to the charge that was to be leveled against him.

"August Metropolitan," he said, "I was shocked to hear the way you insulted the king yesterday evening. Is it appropriate for someone such as you to threaten the king with deposition? If I hadn't been there and heard it for myself, I would never have believed it possible. Not only that, but you said much the same thing in the letter you've just written to him."

---

23 Romey, *History of Spain*, pt. 1.

Chapter 32

Disaster is Worse in Anticipation than Actuality

Oppas was now fully aware that they intended to charge him with sedition against the king, something that he found utterly outrageous. Even so, he felt quite relaxed about the whole thing because he knew what had actually happened. People are always much more alarmed when they have to wait for information than when they have actually heard it. That accounts for the old maxim: "Disaster is always worse in anticipation than in actuality." Once Oppas realized the situation, he saw no point in discussing things any further with Father Martin, quite apart from the fact that the priest would be relishing the opportunity to confront him. Oppas stood up calmly.

"So let's wait for the council to be convened," he said. "It seems as though Roderic still wants me to remain convinced of the imminence of his dynasty's downfall. The way he's treating me at the moment makes that quite clear."

With that, he went away without even giving Father Martin the opportunity to respond.

Father Martin stood up as well. "You dare to say such a thing?" he said, showing a certain degree of sympathy. "Amazing! How can your conscience even permit you to conspire against the king's person, authority, and very life? You realize full well that it was the church that installed him as monarch by unanimous vote of the bishops…"

Oppas realized that Father Martin was trying to trick him into saying something he did not want to so it could be added to the list of his crimes and help the priest get his revenge. Oppas turned his back and looked out of the window at the garden outside.

Seeing that, the priest let out a guffaw and hurried over to the door. Summoning the guard, he told him that the king's orders were that he watch the prisoner carefully because he was facing serious charges. "Make sure he doesn't get away," Father Martin said as he left.

The officer indicated that he understood. As Father Martin went on his way, he would have thought he had emerged triumphant, had it not been for the calm and resolute manner that Oppas had shown during the encounter. Father Martin would have much preferred for the bishop to lose his temper so he could reprimand his superior and have the satisfaction of revenge.

Oppas started thinking again, still worrying about what had happened to Florinda. He recalled that Alfonso was supposed to have left the city the day before at the head of a troop of soldiers. Wanting to find out where he would be heading, he went back to the door and summoned the officer.

"Can you confirm," he asked the officer when he stood before him, "that Prince Alfonso has left Toledo?"

"I know that a troop of soldiers left Toledo yesterday," the officer replied, "but I don't know whether or not the prince was with them."

Oppas assumed that Alfonso had indeed left with the troop, but he was still concerned about Florinda since he had no idea what had happened to her. He was afraid she might have been taken prisoner along with everyone else in his household. It was entirely his fault that they had all been put in prison. He dearly wanted to find out what had happened to her, and it occurred to him to ask the officer about that as well. But he held back because, even though the officer seemed well disposed and even friendly toward him, he could not be sure. Few, indeed, are people whose outward demeanor conforms with their inner one, and even fewer are those who follow the dictates of their conscience. Oppas was scared that, if he talked about Florinda and seemed in any way concerned about what had happened to her, the officer would tell someone else and it would be used as yet another charge against him. So, while he thought that the officer still respected him, he was inclined to assume the worst and to believe that everyone was a potential spy.

Oppas spent several days in prison waiting for the bishop's council to be convened, but he was unable to find out anything about Florinda's fate or even hear a single word about her. He assumed that she had been captured and taken back to the king's palace. The very thought of what might have happened to her there made him shiver all over, and he totally forgot about the danger that he himself was facing.

Chapter 33

The Procession

There came the day in Toledo when the church bells were rung and the streets decorated, particularly the main road leading from the royal palace to the cathedral. Slaves were kept busy sweeping and cleaning the streets while guards stood in two ranks by the palace and the great church; they were all holding staves and wearing their dress uniforms, which were reserved for major occasions. People wondered what this was all about. They crowded into the streets, looked out of windows, and watched from rooftops, expecting to see a wonderful and important spectacle. It was a clear day, and the sun was shining on Toledo's buildings as well as on the river and gardens.

At noontime,[24] a loud noise was heard. When people looked, they could see that a platoon of royal cavalry in their military uniforms had left Roderic's palace and were telling people to clear the way for the royal procession. About twenty meters behind them came a procession of deacons in brilliant white robes with gold embroidery; some of them were carrying crosses mounted on wooden poles, while others carried candles. Occasionally one could see their flames in the sunlight, but most of them had been blown out by Toledo's winter wind. Even though it was a sunny day, there were gusty winds because the city was situated in a mountainous region. Still others were carrying olive branches and thuribles from which clouds of incense smoked. They were all chanting in Latin. Behind the candle-bearers came Roderic, wearing his crown and surrounded by priests in all their regalia, followed by bishops, deacons, and other members of the clergy. Bringing up the rear was another platoon of cavalry.

24 Romey, part II.

When people saw this procession, they realized that the bishops were gathering for a council of some kind, but they were curious as to why they were meeting at this particular moment. It was not the time when they usually held their convocation. People were confused. The council only ever held extraordinary sessions if there was a matter of real importance to discuss, so that made them start speculating about the real reasons for this convocation.

In Spain at this time, there were three types of convocation: the major, the regional, and the diocesan. The first type was convened in Toledo at the king's command to consider matters of significance to the kingdom, such as the selection of the monarch, consenting to laws and the like, including issues like today's, namely the charge directed against Bishop Oppas. The regional convocations would meet upon order from the bishops and happened once a year. The diocesan gatherings were attended by abbots of monasteries, priests, deacons, and other such people.

So when the people of Toledo saw how involved everyone was in this particular convocation, they started worrying that the issue had to involve war, deposition, or some major appointment.

The procession wended its way through the city till it reached the cathedral. The cavalry moved to either side, and the deacons with their crosses and thuribles also divided into two groups. Each group entered the church through a side door. The king, bishops, and priests all dismounted and entered through the central door.

The cathedral servants had been up since dawn, cleaning and putting out chairs and benches in the configurations needed for such a convocation. Candles had been lit and doors opened. They stood there, waiting for the procession to arrive and stopping anyone who had no business with the convocation from entering the church. The people who were entitled to enter were the bishops of Toledo and the regions adjoining it, the metropolitan bishops, the abbots of monasteries, canons and priests, certain members of the king's retinue, and the king himself.

As the procession entered the cathedral, everyone took his appropriate seat. The chairs had been arranged in rows. The bishops sat in the front according to their age, then behind them the adjutant bishops, also seated by age. Behind them were the priests, with deacons standing beside them. Right in the middle of the nave was a single chair for the recorder. An ornate throne had been placed in the middle for the king himself, alongside which were a number of other chairs reserved for members of the king's personal retinue. Father Martin, being a priest, was supposed to sit with the other priests—perhaps at the front because of his great age—but he preferred to sit beside the king, for reasons that will not be lost on the reader.

Chapter 34

Opening the Convocation

When everyone was in place, the doors of the cathedral were closed, and silence reigned over the entire church. It stayed that way for a while, but then the senior canon of the cathedral spoke from a chair alongside the altar: "Oremus," meaning "let us pray." His voice echoed around the church, and no sooner had he intoned the word than the entire congregation fell to its knees; everyone started saying his own prayers in muted tones. Then the senior bishop interrupted the private devotions with a prayer that he intoned loudly so everyone could hear. When he came to the end, everyone said, "Amen." The senior canon now said "Surgite fratres," meaning "Rise up again, brothers," whereupon everyone sat in his chair. Once the prayers were concluded, the recorder of the convocation opened the session by reciting the creed ("We believe in one God," etc.) as required in the Constantinian rite and closed his recitation with an acknowledgment of the four ecumenical councils.[25]

A canon in a gleaming white robe now stood up. In front of him, right alongside the place where the recorder was seated, was a lectern with a large book. He opened the book at the place he had selected. The bishops and everyone else inside the church were waiting to see what the canon would read out so that they could learn why this council had been convened. The book contained the law of the kingdom, and it was customary for the canon to read out sections of the law as a preamble to the proceedings. Those particular sections would be related to the purpose for which they had been assembled. Thus, when the canon read out sections about selecting the monarch, people trying to subvert the intentions of the majority, attempts to depose the monarch, and things

25 Romey, part II.

of this nature, everyone immediately realized the exact purpose of the convocation.

When the canon had finished reading the particular sections involved, the recorder turned toward the congregation.

"You may be surprised that I should read out such materials to you today," he said, "when everything in the kingdom seems to be peaceful. However, priestly brothers, I have to inform you that we have gathered here today to consider a charge that has been leveled against one of our own number; regrettably, that person is indeed a bishop. You may be surprised that he is not present at this convocation, even though he lives in Toledo. You all certainly know him very well."

When the recorder finished what he was saying, there was a burst of conversation among the bishops. They were all talking about Oppas and not a bit surprised that he was being accused of wanting to overthrow Roderic; they were all fully aware of his connection to the former king and his desire to see the monarchy restored to his brother's children.

"We will be bringing him in," the recorder went on, "so that he may stand before you as a defendant. He will either exonerate himself or else face the penalties."

Once the recorder had finished, one of the bishops sitting in the front row spoke. "We need to know," he said, "who is making the accusation and on what grounds. We have now learned that the defendant is our brother, the Metropolitan Oppas, but we have no idea who is making the accusation..."

"You will be told," the recorder replied, "once the defendant is present."

The entire congregation now fell silent, awaiting the arrival of Oppas, at which point they would hear what the charge was to be. When the canons moved over to a room that led to a secret door, all the bishops looked over in that direction. It was not long before they saw Oppas coming in at his usual pace, back straight, and as imposing and dignified as ever. His expression showed not the slightest sign of anxiety or tension. Once he reached the center of the nave, he looked around at all the bishops, then at the king, but he ignored Father Martin as though he were not even there.

Chapter 35

The Trial Opens

Oppas stood there, looking more like a judge than a defendant. It was as though he were looking at a group of weaklings; neither their number nor their purported authority concerned him, especially where the king was concerned. Oppas regarded him as a spoiled child, and his impression had only worsened after he had seen the way he behaved with Florinda. People are always assessed on the basis of their qualities, not the position they occupy, although it is true enough that in general people tend to respect high positions, wealth, and influence. However, deep down they still prefer to judge people on the basis of their character and fine qualities. The only reason for doing otherwise is when they are afraid of being badly treated or are out for gain. Even so, there are always people who are ready to pander to influential people, thus betraying themselves and exposing themselves to even greater risk. If there are large numbers of such flatterers at the court of a weak ruler, he himself will be duped and will surrender willingly to his own baser instincts. He will base his actions on their advice—and flatterers are never good counselors—with the result that things will go from bad to worse and the entire country will fall into wrack and ruin. God preserve us all!

Oppas was one of those people who only acknowledge the truth; the only thing that could cause him concern was when people abandoned the principle of freedom. He had no particular aspirations when it came to the lower world inhabited by humans. High office and such ephemeral goals were of no interest to him. However, ever since he had abandoned the life of the secular world and joined the ranks of the clergy, he felt he had become the servant of higher values that were firmly implanted in his mind; indeed, it amazed him that people did not recognize this. He saw himself clearly as a prisoner of what was right, a servant of truth and freedom of thought. For him there could be no sycophancy or political maneuvering. Thus, it was no surprise to see him standing before this convocation and showing no fear of any of them; as far as he was concerned, truth was greater and demanded more respect than any of them.

With Oppas standing there, the recorder stood up and turned to him.

"I hereby inform you, Metropolitan Bishop, that we have brought you here because a charge has been leveled against you. Every one of us here hopes that it will prove to be unfounded and that you will be acquitted. You stand accused of a plot to overthrow His Majesty, the king. You are well aware, of course, that such a charge does not involve the king alone, but is a matter of grave concern to this convocation, in that it was this convocation of bishops that selected him as monarch and installed him on the throne."

While the recorder was speaking, Father Martin was staring straight at him, his neck fully extended. When he heard the recorder read out the charge, he closed his eyelids and nodded his head as a sign of approbation, his thought being that, by so doing, he would be able to persuade the bishops and other clergy to be yet more severe in their verdict on Oppas.

Oppas, on the other hand, seemed to be entirely oblivious to other people. Once the recorder had finished reading the charge, the entire assembly fell silent. Everyone craned his neck to hear what Oppas would have to say.

"I have heard what you have to say concerning the charge," Oppas replied in a calm voice. "However, I cannot respond to it without knowing who is making the charge..."

The recorder looked over at the king and bowed.

"His Majesty the King in person," he said.

"What are his proofs of this charge?" Oppas asked.

Father Martin was doing his very best to maintain the same level of composure as Oppas, so he remained seated and gave the bishops a look of derision and contempt. With open mouth and raised eyebrows, he seemed to be saying to them, "Just look at this idiot. He's asking the king to provide witnesses."

All the recorder could do at this point was to look at Roderic as though expecting him to respond to Oppas's question. The king gestured to Father Martin to respond on his behalf. The priest lost the composure he was trying to maintain and returned to his normal demeanor. When the bishops saw that he was about to start talking, they all leaned forward to listen carefully because they were worried that, with his usual stammer, they would not be able to understand what he was saying. They would have to base their reaction to the charge on what Father Martin had to say.

"How can you ask for evidence," he told Oppas, "when every normal faculty can provide sufficient proof? Ever since the late king was alive, you have been trying to get rid of the authority of the Catholic church and return to Arianism. The appointment of this king was a severe blow to all of you. You tried every trick in the book to oppose him, but his support comes from God and the church. What is most amazing is that you are actually demanding proof of the king's veracity!"

By this time everyone was tired of hearing his stammering voice. Oppas turned to the assembled clerics and smiled.

"No," he retorted, "what is even more amazing is that anyone is trying to find proof for a charge directed at a metropolitan bishop who holds a position of high prestige among the people. The best you can say about this charge is that it is contrived. Yes, I mean contrived, even though it is the king who is making it. But then truth stands above both monarchs and bishops. Beyond that, I have no idea what the components of this charge actually are. How can anyone claim that I have conspired to dethrone the king? With whom? Where? How? If there's a conspiracy, there has to be a group of people. So who are my accomplices supposed to be? It's all utterly absurd. I'm not saying that in order to avoid the penalty involved. Such things are of no concern to me."

Chapter 36

Declaration

Listening to what Oppas was saying, the king could not contain himself.

"I'm astonished at such blatent impudence!" he said, eyes bulging and eyebrows knotted. "How can you say such a thing when I heard you with my own ears threatening me with the imminent collapse of this government? You went on to say that it would be no concern of yours if I were to lose the throne. Do you deny saying such things? Father Martin also heard you. Can there be any clearer evidence than that?"

As the bishops sat there listening, they were inclined to believe what the king was saying, and for a number of reasons. Most of them actually hated Oppas because he was always so frank and liberal in his views and so utterly devoted to the truth. Then each person's instincts could tell him that the charge was probably true because the population of Toledo was well aware of the hatred that the entire family of the late king Witiza felt toward Roderic. Everything that might be advanced by way of evidence, particularly where the bishops were concerned, suggested that the charge was genuine. Once they had heard the king's evidence and that of Father Martin, they were all inclined to pronounce Oppas guilty, added to which was the fact that they could convict him without even holding an actual trial. On the other hand, it was clearly an obligation of this convocation to follow proper procedures. Thus, once the king had finished speaking, they all turned toward Oppas in order to hear what he would have to say.

They all noticed that he remained completely calm and in full control of himself. However, before he could even reply, one of the bishops interrupted.

"What surprises me," the bishop said, "is that certain Visigoths still bitterly resent the appointment of His Majesty as monarch. The process of his appointment was completely in accordance with the laws of this country and the church. Anyone who chooses to claim that the sons of Witiza and other descendants in his family have any right to the monarchy is in error. The monarchy in Spain at this point in time is by election. Everyone knows that, including you. No one sits on the Spanish throne unless he has been selected by this holy convocation. Do you deny that His Majesty was elected in such a fashion?"

When Oppas heard this statement, he realized that they were trying to lead him into a trap. In spite of that, he decided to pursue the matter to its conclusion.

"That particular issue, Your Grace," he replied, "has no relevance to the current charge. Even so, I will respond. Yes, indeed, this monarchy in Spain is of all its peers the one that is most beholden to the church. As you have noted, it is its bishops that select the monarch. I do not deny that the king was seated on the throne by the elective process of his convocation. His particular election was legal, although I do not believe that this convocation followed all the necessary legislative channels in transferring the scepter of power from the previous ruler. But I do not intend to explore that issue here. But, sirs, I will not hide from you all my view that the church in this land has extended its authority in a way that transcends its legitimate limits. I say that as a member of the church, but I suspect that none of you would be willing to support it, even if you were to believe it to be true. Each one of you is too worried about his own personal interests."

As soon as Father Martin heard Oppas make these objections to the role of the convocation in selecting the monarch, he made sure that the recorder wrote it down as a matter to be brought up against him later on. The recorder duly did so.

The bishop who had raised the issue now replied to Oppas's statement. "It would appear," he said, "that you are denying the benefits afforded by the church in this country. Are you not aware of the fact that it is the Catholic church that has managed to preserve proper order and civilization on this continent? When your German ancestors, with their different tribes, most of which were pagans, came to Spain, they conquered the Roman kingdom and spread around its cities—nomadic tribes with no learning and no culture. It was the church that brought them into its bosom, taught them proper manners, and turned their rule into communities and kingdoms. It was the church that preserved learning and wisdom and trained them how to conduct politics, administration, and social works. But for the church, Europe would still be in total chaos, with no learning and no order."

Oppas was on the point of answering, but the recorder rang a bell to indicate silence. No one spoke. When they looked around, they noticed that the king was about to speak, so they all pricked up their ears to listen.

The king sat there on his throne, his chest thrust out and his hair flowing down beneath his crown to his shoulders.

"We have no need," he said, "to discuss issues here that have no relevance to the topic at hand. What we have heard him say here in total contempt of the operation of this convocation in selecting the monarch is surely enough. He has suggested that you have not used canonical means in selecting the king. When someone can make such an accusation in a judicial setting, is it any surprise that he should be charged with conspiracy?"

Oppas looked at the king. "Your Majesty," he replied, "there is no connection whatsoever between my approval or disapproval of the means of election and the alleged conspiracy that you claim I have organized in order to depose you. It is true that I have my doubts concerning the canonical methods adopted in the election process, but I have never constructed a conspiracy on that basis. Since I am standing here in this position, you have to be assuming at the very least that I have indeed done something of the kind."

Father Martin objected, "How is His Majesty supposed not to believe it when he heard it from your own lips, as did I? It's unbelievable!"

He now turned and looked at the king. "This argument has gone on for a while," he said, "but the charge is clear enough."

Chapter 37

Prejudice

The king turned and looked at the bishops.

"You've heard what this man has said," he told them. "Either King Roderic's assumption of the throne in Toledo is illegitimate, or else Oppas has no right to wear ecclesiastical garments."

By now anger had got the better of him, to such an extent that he had come down from his throne and started pacing around without even realizing it. Once he became aware of what he was doing, he went back to the throne and sat down angrily.

Oppas now realized that Roderic was suggesting that his punishment should involve his being stripped of his priestly functions.

"Do not for a second imagine," he told the king, "that this threat of yours in any way diminishes my determination to tell the truth. It is not my garments that make me a bishop, nor your crown that makes you a king. Deeds are assessed on the basis of the intentions that lie behind them. Whatever kind of punishment you have in mind for me, it in no way diminishes my own beliefs. However, Roderic, what it does do is to intensify your own sin in the face of God Almighty because He—exalted be His Name!—knows full well the real reason why you want to take revenge on me and have brought me in front of this convocation. You are well aware, and so is this reverend priest beside you, of the reason for your desire for revenge by bringing me to this place. I have no fear of a situation in which I see myself as being the one to tell the truth, even if it means that I will not be treated fairly. God is my buttress in that belief, and He knows full well what lies in people's hearts…"

Once the king heard Oppas referring to the matter of Florinda, he started to worry that the convocation might try to probe into the matter further; that would involve making the whole thing public and mentioning her name.

"A curse on you!" he yelled, leaping out of his seat in a fury. "Is that the way you address the king of Spain?"

"If you persist in listening to this man's statements," he said, looking at the assembled bishops, "I shall relinquish the throne. Either that, or else he must be defrocked immediately."

So saying, he busied himself adjusting his gold-encrusted belt.

"It is no great matter, Your Majesty," Oppas replied, still maintaining his composure, "if I am to be defrocked as you suggest. But that still will not absolve you of the foul crime that you were intending to commit. That was the real reason for the reprimand that I issued to you, but the truth was obviously too much for you to tolerate. So now you've decided to take your revenge on me. But the real avenger is God Himself…"

"Esteemed Metropolitan," the chief bishop interrupted, "in the name of the church I ask you to say no more."

Oppas could only respond to his request by speaking no further.

For a while the entire convocation was silent, everyone was staring at the floor. Some bishops may have been whispering to each other, but nothing was audible. All the while, Father Martin was casting his eye over the assembly to see what kind of expressions were on the bishops' faces. When his eyes locked with one of the bishops, he gave a disapproving gesture with both eyebrows and lips, pointing towards Oppas, as though to say, "Do you see what a rogue this man really is? How dare he behave this way on such a holy occasion?"

Oppas still stood where he was, looking like a stolid and open-hearted man and gazing expressionless at the assembled bishops. His composure and solemn expression nevertheless conveyed the clear impression that the consequences of this trial were of no concern to him; the fakery and ill intentions involved were already abundantly clear. At the same time, he recalled the conversation that he had had with Alfonso before the young prince had departed, especially the part concerning the status of the monarch, all of which made him realize that that particular aspect of the charge against him was true. As he recalled that conversation, he could think of nothing he had said that prevented him from declaring his rejection of Roderic's right to the throne. While he was engaged in these thoughts, he happened to look at a large painting hanging on one of the cathedral walls: it showed Jesus standing before Pontius Pilate. Oppas recalled that Jesus had accepted crucifixion in his defense of the truth. All of which made Oppas yet more convinced of the rightness of his path.

Roderic had now returned to his seat. When he noticed how quiet the convocation had become, he started to worry that they might insist on investigating the matter that Oppas had mentioned. The king looked over at the chief bishop.

"We've heard enough by now," he told the bishop in as calm a tone as he could muster, as though he had the authority to direct the agenda of the convocation as he saw fit. "If you all decide that this matter needs further investigation in spite of all the clear evidence that you have already heard, then I shall bring this session to a close. We will postpone the inquiry to some future session."

Now Father Martin rose to his feet. "Your Majesty," he told the king, "please do not conclude from the silence you are witnessing that the bishops in any way doubt the veracity of your statement or that they have the slightest hesitation in corroborating the charges against our brother cleric, the metropolitan bishop. Your Majesty has given clear evidence, and the bishop has not denied it. Indeed, the outlandish remarks he has made here which clearly show his annoyance at the current church structure and those responsible for it only make his attitude that much plainer for all to see. It's as though he had actually declared that this convocation has betrayed the country by electing Your Majesty as monarch."

In making these remarks, the priest was spitting out the words as though scattering straw in a completely random fashion so that it stuck to people's clothes and faces. People kept closing their eyes so it wouldn't hit them and cause them an injury!

Oppas had been listening to what Father Martin had been saying and realized the effect it would have.

"You have all heard what Father Martin has just said," he responded, addressing his remarks to the chief bishop, "but I'm not sure you all understood. Maybe you all expect me to deny the charge so as to avoid any penalty. That's not the case. I do indeed have doubts about the legitimacy of this king's election, as I have already indicated. Had I had the choice, I would certainly have chosen someone else. However, the reason why I have been brought here has absolutely nothing to do with that matter. This Roderic, whom you call king, has convened this assembly in order to try me. He has leveled this accusation against me because I counseled him against commiting a grave crime at the eleventh hour. Were it not for my fear of besmirching this holy place, I would reveal the nature of the crime so that everything would be made public. Were I to do that and were you all to treat me justly, you would immediately chastise this criminal with your own hands..."

With that, the entire convocation erupted. The king was enraged but also feared that yet more details might emerge about his conduct. He put on a big show, looking very upset and astonished. He had no idea of what to say, but once again it was Father Martin who came to his rescue.

"It is His Majesty's opinion," he told the recorder, "that our brother, the metropolitan, has gone too far and is now resorting to sheer nonsense. He is so scared of what might happen to him that he's gone crazy. His statements no longer make sense. For that reason, the king hereby orders that this session come to an end at once. The trial is to be postponed to some future session. Once this order has been promulgated, no one may utter a further word at this session except to repeat the closing prayer."

Father Martin's statement was like a refreshing shower for Roderic. The recorder had no choice but to accede to the command; the king, and no one else, had the right to both open and close the session. After making his statement, Oppas was no longer concerned and showed no reaction to the announcement. The chief bishop rose to his feet and recited the closing prayer.

The convocation over, everyone went back to their houses, except for Oppas, who was taken under guard to another guardhouse with instructions that he was to be closely watched.

Chapter 38

Alfonso and Ya'qub

Let us now leave Oppas to his problems and return to Alfonso to see what happened to him after he followed the king's orders and went away. He left his house accompanied by Ya'qub. They both went to the army barracks, a big building in a Toledo suburb. They were escorted by the cavalry troop who had been sent by the king to bring them to the barracks.

When Alfonso entered the building, he was greeted with great respect by the soldiers. Dismounting from his horse, he walked in with Ya'qub leading the way, but no other servants. The soldiers were surprised at the way he had neglected his beard and clothing. When they reached the commander's office, a servant was standing there waiting for Alfonso with a letter in his hand. Even without opening it, Alfonso could tell that it came from the king. His heart started pounding because he could well remember how the previous letter had so shaken him. Nevertheless, he did not ask for it until he had gone inside and sat down in the center of the room. This messenger asked Ya'qub for permission to enter, and the latter communicated the request to Alfonso.

"He doesn't need to come in," Alfonso replied. "Just give me the letter."

Ya'qub took the letter and brought it in to Alfonso.

"Don't get angry, my lord," he told Alfonso. "Maybe it contains orders for you to return to your house."

Alfonso took the letter without saying a word. Breaking the seal, he discovered that it was indeed from the king. Here is what it said:

From Roderic, king of the Goths, to the fearless commander, Alfonso: We previously instructed you to go to a certain dukedom, but we did not specify the city where you should reside. That city is Astigi in the Dukedom of Baetica. You and your men should billet yourselves in one of its fortresses there until such time as I write to inform you of your eventual destination. Along with this letter I have included another, which you should give to the Count of Baetica so that he may accord you the appropriate welcome and provide you with necessary funds when needed. Farewell.

Written in the Royal Palace of Toledo.

When Alfonso finished reading it, he ordered Ya'qub to get the other letter from the messenger. He took it, brought it into the office, and closed the door behind him. As he presented the letter to Alfonso, he was looking closely at his expression. When he noticed that Alfonso was looking withdrawn and dejected, he decided to lighten the atmosphere as best he could. He sneezed loudly enough to rattle the entire room. Alfonso came to and looked up at Ya'qub, who was laughing, nodding his head, and rubbing his chin with his fingernails. Alfonso was astonished and was on the point of upbraiding him, but then he recalled the enormous respect that his uncle, Oppas, had for Ya'qub and the way he relied on the servant's counsel. He recalled that there was always a reason for the way Ya'qub behaved.

"So, Ya'qub," he asked, "what's making you laugh? At least you can!" And with that he let out a sigh.

Ya'qub let out an even bigger sigh. "You should be laughing, too! Fate has given you such a good deal!"

"A curse on this fate!" Alfonso replied shaking his head. "Just leave me alone!"

With that, he stood up. "There's no point in sticking around here," he went on. "We're supposed to leave tonight. I have to summon the commanders and tell them to prepare to leave. Go and tell them to come here."

In the Gothic era, the Spanish army consisted of brigades, each one of which had a thousand soldiers; the commander was called brigade commander (Praepositus Ostis in Latin). Below him in rank were two other officers, each of them in command of five hundred men; they were called quingentenarus; each group of five hundred was then subdivided into hundreds, with a commander called centenarus, leader of one hundred men. Each one hundred was then subdivided again into tens, with a decanus in charge. The senior general would communicate his orders to the commanders of the five hundred, and they would be charged with organizing the troops.

Ya'qub left and came back a short while later to inform Alfonso that the two commanders were on their way. When they arrived, they were in travel uniform. As with the rest of the Goths, their hair reached down to their shoulders. They both looked healthy, and their dress suggested prosperity. They saluted Alfonso upon entering, having both known him since the time when his father was still alive; that made them respect him a lot. They had been delighted when they heard that he was to command this brigade since he was known to be both fair and even-tempered. Both of them were proud of their Gothic heritage and were only reconciled to have Roderic as king as a figurehead. Whenever they were left on their own, they would talk about the way that the Roman church had gained influence after Roderic had become the monarch. However, they never dared say such things in public, even to Alfonso himself because he was in the same position as they were.

When Alfonso saw them both, he remembered that he had seen them before, but he was amazed to see that they were already prepared for travel before he had even issued any orders to that effect.

"Why are you in travel uniform?" he asked them.

Chapter 39

Wamba

One of the two men, a tall man with vivid black eyes and hair, whose name was Wamba, replied, "We've already received orders to that effect from His Majesty the King," he said, "in order to accelerate our departure. At this point the soldiers are ready to move. They're simply awaiting your orders, sir."

When Alfonso heard Wamba mention his name, he felt more at ease.

"We'll leave the barracks at once," he said. "I would like you both to take charge of things during the course of the march until we reach our destination."

Wamba bowed to indicate that they would do so. Being more forward than his colleague, he then asked Alfonso, "Will you tell us, my lord, where exactly we are going?"

"We're going to Astigi," Alfonso replied, "a city on the river Sinyil[26] in the Dukedom of Baetica. Do you know how to get there?"

"I know it well. The route takes us to the southwest, to Merida on the river Anas.[27] We cross it and proceed southeast to Cordoba, then go southeast again down to Astigi on the river Sinyil. I know the city;

---

26 The Synyil or Genil River is the main tributary of the river Guadalquivir in Andalusia. Known to the Romans as the Singilis, its modern name derives from the Arab rendering of the Roman name. *Translator's Note.*

27 The ancient name for a river in southern Spain located on the Portuguese–Spanish border presently known as the Guadiana or Odiana river. *Translator's Note.*

I've prayed in its church, resided in its castle, and traversed its bridge. Its monasteries and markets are all well known to me."

"Bless you!" Alfonso replied. "I've already given you instructions regarding preparations for this expedition during our journey, but now I want to tell you something else that concerns me greatly. During the journey I don't want any soldiers assaulting peasants, nor do I want them to steal money or food. They're not to treat anyone roughly. If any soldier does such a thing, I'll punish him either with a whipping or death. If the offender is someone of rank, I'll strip him of it and his possessions and humiliate him. This expedition is to proceed on its way calmly and in good order."

Wamba eyes gleamed as he listened to his commander issuing this order. "And may God bless you too, sir!" he said. "Your late father trained us to behave in such a just and kind manner..."

When Alfonso heard that, he bit his lip and stared at the ground, as though to suggest that this was no time to bring up such matters.

"I want you to pass this command on to the priests who are in our company," Alfonso went on. "Make sure they share the instructions with the soldiers. You're already aware that what our soldiers do best is wage war as infantry. So don't wear them out with forced marches and don't make them carry heavy loads. The shields, lances, and spears they normally carry will be quite sufficient."

When Alfonso had finished speaking, Wamba simply acknowledged the instructions again.

"Aren't you going to bring some retainers and aides with you, sir," he asked, "to be your personal servants?"

Alfonso was planning to make it clear that he never felt any need for retainers, but just then, he happened to look over at Ya'qub. His servant made a gesture to the effect that he should not say anything like that, and he took note.

"I don't need anyone," was all he said. "I have my own personal servant here. He can arrange anything I need. If I find I need something else, I'll ask for it."

The two commanders went outside with Alfonso, clearly delighted by what they had heard.

"I noticed you gesturing to me in there," Alfonso said when he and Ya'qub were left on their own.

"We're among enemies here," Ya'qub replied, "and I was afraid you'd say something you might live to regret. I'd suggest keeping what has transpired between you and Bishop Oppas a secret till we see what's going to happen. Allow me now to finish what I began to say earlier. You should realize, sir, that by God's good graces you are very fortunate. The situation we were discussing, one that would inevitably involve spending lots of money and recruiting men, is now in your hands quite by chance..."

"What do you mean?" Alfonso asked.

"I'm speaking about the plan you were developing with the metropolitan bishop to force this enemy king out of office. The plan is now completely ready. Here is an entire brigade of soldiers under your command. So now you need to gain their trust and affection with money...money..."

As he said that last word, he broke into a smirk, as though relishing the very taste of the idea.

"Where are we supposed to get money from, Ya'qub?" Alfonso asked. "It's all very well to talk about it, but far more difficult to actually get hold of any."

Ya'qub placed his hand on his chest, bowed his head, and closed his eyes.

"I have the money," he said, "and I can get hold of it."

Chapter 40

Wine

Alfonso recalled that Oppas had made a similar undertaking that very morning. He was eager to find out what lay behind it.

"You've just reminded me of that previous promise that was made," he told Ya'qub. "You must be aware that I'm really keen to know what it's all about."

Ya'qub's expression changed from a smile to something more serious and reserved.

"I'd ask you, sir," he said, "to postpone that request till later. I'll explain how we're going to get hold of the money after we get to Astigi. Everything comes in its own good time. So, be of good cheer, sir. I may be ugly and crafty, but you can rest assured that I also have good qualities. Now we have to get mounted, because I can hear drumbeats; that means we're about to depart."

"Get my horse," Alfonso instructed. "I'll mount it while you attend to the servants and whatever food and other supplies we may need. You'll serve as my spokesman in everything. Don't let any of the servants come near me. If any of them needs something, they should go through you."

Ya'qub left and came back with one of the troop's finest horses, with a very costly saddle on it. Alfonso was dressed in his general's uniform, which was only enhanced by his youthful good looks. Just before sunset he gave the order to leave, and the troop set off. On its way out of Toledo, it passed through suburbs and eventually came to a high spot overlooking the city. Alfonso looked back at the city, which was also sited on an elevation. He could see the cathedral clearly and then turned to look at Roderic's palace on the banks of the Tagus River. When his gazed alighted on Florinda's palace, his heart started pounding, and he was overcome with emotion. Recalling their meeting earlier in the day and everything that had happened since, he looked up at the sky with its looming clouds, an apt reflection of the longing that he felt within him. At this particular moment, nature, it seemed, was sharing his mood.

It's common for human beings to relate natural phenomena to their own feelings and to use them to justify their beliefs and imaginings. For humans, nature tends to be seen as something targeted solely at them, intentionally causing things that are either good or evil. If it happens to rain while someone is on a journey, he immediately regards it as being intended to impede his progress. If someone else begs for rain to help his crops grow, he treats nature as being at his disposal. With all this in mind, it is no wonder that, when Alfonso looked up at the sky, he pictured it as glowering and frowning at him because he was leaving his beloved behind. Lovers will often entertain such fancies as long as it conforms with their feelings, even though all this is completely contrary to the laws of nature.

No sooner had the sun set than darkness fell. Rain started to pour down, and the winds picked up. They could travel no further. Alfonso ordered a halt, and tents were erected. That included one for him, which they put up as quickly as possible. Ya'qub came over, and Alfonso invited him inside. It was a bitterly cold night, and Alfonso was suffering just as many agonies of loneliness and passion as was Florinda.

In fact, Alfonso had been completely distracted because he was under the impression that he would soon be seeing her; that very evening he was going to rescue her, the plan that he had entrusted to his uncle Oppas. When the appointed time drew near, Alfonso had imagined Florinda escaping from Roderic's palace with Ajilla and Chantilla; they would have gone by boat to Oppas's house. He had imagined that she would be safe there until someone brought her to him wherever he happened to be. Just then, he realized that Oppas had no idea where they were actually going, and that made him realize why the king had altered his orders. He looked over at Ya'qub, who was ensconced in a corner of the tent. He had wrapped himself up in a heavy cloak and huddled up because of the extreme cold. The wind kept blowing, and thunder was rumbling as well.

"Do you know why the king changed his orders?" he asked in a loud voice, not caring about whether the noise would be drowned out by the thunder.

"I think I know," Ya'qub replied with a nod, his beard quivering with the cold. "I know others things, too; if it weren't so cold, I would tell you."

"What do you know?" Alfonso asked. "Tell me. If you're feeling cold, then get a cup of wine. That'll warm you up."

So saying, he pointed to a saddlebag in the tent. "Pour me a cup, too."

Ya'qub was still shivering with cold, but he managed to pluck up the energy to stand up, went over and pulled out the wineskin, poured the wine into a silver goblet, and handed it to Alfonso, who took a drink. He took another cup, poured some for himself, and took a drink. He then filled up both cups again. He was soon feeling warmer, and the sound of the thunder faded away. Taking the cup in his hand, he stood in front of Alfonso.

"I drink this wine in celebration of the secret that is between us," he said, looking around him as though he were worried that someone might hear him. "Let's hope that our plan will succeed. Let's drink as well to the high hopes that our Master Alfonso has, even though he imagines that Ya'qub isn't aware of them. But the secret has to be revealed, because he will have to make use of Ya'qub if he is to attain his goals."

He said all that with a smile, then drank some more wine. Alfonso was staring at him all the while, amazed that Ya'qub should mention another secret, which had to be his love for Florinda. He decided to make sure that his hunch was correct.

"What hopes are you referring to, Ya'qub?" he asked.

Ya'qub laughed. "The wine's been fooling with my head," he said, "so forgive me if I've forgotten protocol and spoken the truth. Those high hopes lie in Roderic's palace. She is the reason why this tyrant king has decided to send you on this mission. But vengeance will be had, there's no doubt about it, and you'll return to Toledo a clear victor."

He was laughing as he spoke those words, wiping the wine off his beard as he did so. Drops of it had spilled while he was downing his last cup. He now walked over to Alfonso and lowered his head.

"Roderic imagines that he's achieved his goal by sending us to Astigi," he said, "but in fact he's served our purpose very well. We needed to go to that particular city in order to carry out the project that we have in mind."

Alfonso was duly amazed, but he became impatient with all these cryptic statements and lost his temper.

"Ya'qub," he said, "I'm fed up with all these allusions and mysterious statements you keep making. Why don't you tell me straight out what you have in mind?"

Once again Ya'qub's expression assumed a serious mien. "I told you, sir," he replied, "that, God willing, things would be happening soon. Please don't insist that I reveal anything, since that would be dangerous. Please be patient with me, and I'll reveal everything very soon. You should realize that it's Roderic who's accelerated the need to reveal the secret by sending us to Astigi."

Alfonso now regretted that he had been so impetuous. He had a very high regard for Ya'qub because he realized how discreet he was. He decided that he needed to cheer him up again.

"So what do you think about this campaign that Roderic has sent us to complete?" he asked.

"I think it's simply one of those uprisings in certain cities," Ya'qub replied, "the kind of thing that tends to happen every year when people are oppressed. Now that we see things the same way, sir, I'll not hide from you the fact that the people of this city are feeling particularly aggrieved by the treatment they're receiving from their rulers. They used to complain bitterly about the Romans as well. So, when the Goths arrived, they thought that they would be relieved of the hellfire the Romans had brought. But instead they discovered that now they were living with not one, but two, hellfires; now they were slaves, with no freedom, no status, no lands, and no property. Once they realized how weak the current government actually is, they became more recalcitrant and rebellious.[28] What made the whole thing that much easier for them was the mistake the recent Gothic kings made in dealing with the Jewish community. They forced the Jews to reject their own faith and convert to Christianity, and that made the Jewish community support the Goths' rebellion…"

Alfonso interrupted him at this point, "But the Jewish community in Spain has essentially died out by now. As you are well aware, there are none left…"

"I'm aware of that, sir," Ya'qub replied, "and I'm also aware that the Gothic kings before your late father treated the Jews very badly; they had the choice of either being killed, converting to Christianity, or going into exile. Some left, and the rest converted. The Jewish faith has disappeared, but it's not been obliterated. Even if it had been, there are still Jews to be found in Spain."

"We seem to have gone off the topic," he said, wrapping himself up in his cloak again. "But, with regard to the charge that we've been given, the long and short of it is that I can guarantee that we'll be able to bring it to an end without drawing a single sword or throwing a spear. So calm down and be patient until we reach Astigi. At that point, all will be revealed to you."

He went back to his original spot in the corner. "Now it's time to get some sleep," he said. "Aren't you ready for that, sir?"

"Before we go to sleep," Alfonso responded, "pour us another cup of wine and drink it as a conclusion to our conversation."

Ya'qub poured some more wine. They both drank it then lay down to sleep. Alfonso, meanwhile, prepared himself to become privy to a lot of secrets once they reached Astigi.

---

28 Dozy, part I.

Chapter 41

Peasants

Even though there was thunder and lightning and the winds were howling, they both slept soundly that night because the journey had been exhausting. Ya'qub woke up early and left the tent to prepare the things Alfonso would need. The sun had not even risen when they were ready to move out. Everyone packed up their tents and mounted their horses in good order, but Alfonso and Ya'qub rode by themselves, not saying a word. For his part, Alfonso kept looking back at Toledo, which was still visible. Before long they were crossing the bridge over the river Tagus, and that was Alfonso's last glimpse of the city as it rapidly disappeared behind the surrounding hills.

The troop made its way to the southwest, carrying all its equipment. It was a clear day; the sun was shining on all the orchards, fields, valleys, and hills they passed by. Alfonso was surprised and delighted to see the fertile terrain, with its varieties of trees and crops. But what really amazed him was that there was no one to be seen. He had only expected to see slaves, peasants, and farmers, because the nobles and landed gentry used to treat such people like slaves. The nobles themselves would reside in cities, and few indeed were those who actually lived in the countryside. At that time Europe consisted of cities and countryside; the former were where the rulers and nobles lived, while the latter consisted of farmland where peasants lived and worked on the land. Those peasants, the land itself, and any animals and cattle on the land were all the property of the nobles.[29]

---

29 Guizot, *History of European Civilization.*

Alfonso had rarely left the city environment and had never bothered to think about these peasant people. But now that he had had the conversation with Oppas about proper kingship and they had decided to manumit all such slaves and rely on them to liberate the kingdom, he realized that he needed to study carefully the rural situation and the circumstances of the people who lived there. As they made their way across the countryside, it was obvious that people could not be bothered about cultivating the land and reaping its fruits; they hardly ever saw anyone. When this scenario was repeated time and time, Alfonso turned to Ya'qub, who was riding behind him. When Ya'qub saw Alfonso looking back, he spurred his horse till he was alongside and gave him a questioning look.

"I expected to find the fields teeming with people," he said in a low voice. "We've gone quite a long way by now, and I haven't seen a single soul."

"Oh, there are lots of people around," Ya'qub replied. "But, whenever they spot a troop of soldiers passing by, they usually hide. That way they can avoid whatever hard labor or other exactions they normally suffer in such cases. It would never even occur to them that a troop of soldiers like this one could pass through their territory without harassing them in one way or another. The only reason these soldiers are not behaving that way is because you, sir, have issued orders to that effect."

Alfonso was much affected by what Ya'qub told him and came to realize the grave mistake that tyrannical governments make by mistreating their citizenry. The end result is a loss for both the country and its people.

Alfonso's troops spent several days traveling, during the course of which they traversed fertile plains, mountains with several gold and silver mines, and valleys with flowing streams that irrigated fields and orchards. Land in Spain is exceedingly fertile and productive; all it requires is someone who will let it flourish and treat it justly. And then there are the big cities. The first one they passed through was Merida, where they crossed the river Anas, then they continued to Cordoba, crossed its river as well, and made their way to Astigi.

Chapter 42

Astigi

At this time, Astigi was a populous city on the left bank of the river Sinyil. The Romans had constructed a wall around it with guard-towers. To get into the city, anyone approaching from Cordoba had to cross the bridge over the river. The troop arrived there at noontime, and Alfonso dispatched a messenger with Roderic's letter to meet the governor of the city. The messenger soon returned accompanied by an escort of city soldiers. Their commander was carrying instructions that Alfonso's forces were to be given the big fortress overlooking the river from the right bank, with the river between them and the city on the other bank. It was a large fortress built specifically to billet soldiers.

Alfonso's troop took up residence, and Alfonso himself went into one of the rooms, the nicest and biggest of them all, with a window overlooking the river and the city and, beyond them, orchards and fields. When Alfonso climbed upstairs to his room, he found Ya'qub already there and all necessary arrangements in place so that he could relax and get some rest. He ordered some food from one of the servants. He brought it in, put it down on a table in the room, and invited Alfonso to eat and drink.

Ever since Alfonso had reached the room, he had been sitting by the window, lost in his own thoughts. He was thinking about his beloved Florinda, about his uncle Oppas, and about the fact that he had come to this city against his will. The only possible explanation for his banishment from Toledo was that Roderic wanted to put a distance between him and his beloved Florinda. When he thought some more about the king's real intentions towards Florinda, his entire body shivered and he felt as though someone were pouring boiling water over his head.

But then he also remembered the measures that had been put in place to rescue Florinda from the palace, and that calmed him down somewhat.

While he was lost in thought, he heard footsteps approaching the room. Turning round, he saw that Ya'qub was standing facing him, his arms crossed over his chest as though in prayer. When Alfonso set eyes on Ya'qub, the faithful servant came rushing over to his master with a smile on his face.

"Isn't it time for you to eat something, sir?" he asked.

By now Alfonso had relaxed a bit, so he could not resist the smile on Ya'qub's face. Standing up, he hurried over to the table without saying a word. Ya'qub walked behind him. Alfonso sat down, but Ya'qub remained standing like any other servant. Alfonso gestured to him to sit down, but he refused and offered his excuses.

"After all the things you've told me about your lofty intentions and your determination to see the truth prevail," Alfonso told him, "it's no longer appropriate to treat you as a servant."

"Forgive me, sir," Ya'qub replied, "but as yet you know nothing about me. Everything you've heard is just words. If, after seeing me in action, you still want me to sit and eat with you, then I'll indeed do so."

Alfonso now remembered Ya'qub's promise to reveal the big secret to him once they reached Astigi, but he was unwilling to remind him about it because he didn't want Ya'qub's response to be yet more procrastination. He decided to wait patiently until Ya'qub decided to tell him in his own good time.

"You can decide for yourself what you want to do," Alfonso said. "But I gather from some of the things you've already said that you're aware of what's been happening with Florinda."

Ya'qub nodded to indicate that, indeed, he was aware.

"So," Alfonso went on,"what do you think about her situation and ours? She doesn't know where we are, and my uncle doesn't know either. Shouldn't we send them some information so that they can join us, as long as we're stuck here, far removed from that tyrant in Toledo?"

"Don't presume that we're that far away," was Ya'qub's response. "Don't you realize that most of the troops with us here are serving as spies, watching your every move? They'll be trying to curry favor with the king by causing your downfall. When dynasties grow old and things start falling apart, the number of spies multiplies, as do the means of betrayal. All noble motives have become corrupt, and now brother spies on brother, son on father. They are only spurred to greater efforts by the fact that the king dabbles in frivolities and is distracted from political matters by the sycophants and miscreants who surround him. Don't rely on or trust anyone unless you can be sure that their loyalty suits your purpose and your interests are one and the same. That even applies to me..."

So saying, he pointed to his own chest. Alfonso was amazed by what he had just heard, having had no real experience in dealing with people and no realization of the ways in which human beings can become so morally corrupt. He remained silent and continued eating his food till he had finished. Ya'qub remained standing at a distance.

Alfonso now stood up.

"Get some rest, sir," Ya'qub suggested. "Permit me to go into the city and come back before sunset. Tomorrow we can go there and check on its markets and open spaces."

Alfonso was suddenly aware that tomorrow was actually Sunday. "We'll go to Mass as well," he said.

"Very good, sir," Ya'qub replied. "We can deal with that tomorrow. May I leave now, sir?"

"Yes, you may," Alfonso said. "But before you do, go and find the troop commander so I can talk to him about the soldiers."

"Very good, sir," Ya'qub replied and left.

Alfonso now returned to his seat by the window, still wearing his traveling clothes. He started thinking again about Florinda, Oppas, and Roderic, but then he remembered what Ya'qub had said. He felt happier at the thought that the secret would soon be revealed. He heard footsteps approaching and turned to greet Wamba, the commander. The soldier saluted Alfonso with a big smile as a way of showing his great respect and admiration for Alfonso. Alfonso returned the salute and asked how the soldiers were faring.

"Everything is fine and in good order," Wamba replied, "and they all devoutly wish that their fearless leader may be victorious."

"Have you heard anything about the circumstances of the people living here?" Alfonso asked.

"Only that things are quiet," the commander replied. "There are no signs of unrest. Perhaps they decided to quiet down once they heard you were on the way."

"In any case," Alfonso went on, "I trust that you will keep a close eye on things and find out whatever information you can. I have complete confidence in you."

Wamba realized from Alfonso's statement and his gestures that his commander had said what he wanted to say. Saluting him once again, he left the room. Once Alfonso was left on his own again, he changed his clothes. He then decided to spend the rest of the day in the room so he could relax a bit after the exhausting journey.

Chapter 43

Sunday

Ya'qub still had not come back by the time the sun went down. Alfonso wondered what was keeping him. He sat by the window looking toward the bridge, which anyone coming out of the city toward the fortress would have to cross. It was not too long before he spotted Ya'qub crossing the bridge with a bag under his arm. Alfonso assumed it was something that Ya'qub had picked up in the city. He decided to be patient until his servant reached the fortress and came up to see him. Once again Ya'qub took his time, and, when he eventually climbed the stairs and entered Alfonso's room, his hands were empty.

"What did you bring back from the city?" Alfonso asked.

"Nothing," Ya'qub replied. "We're going there together tomorrow."

"I saw you with something under your arm."

"Oh, it was nothing!" Ya'qub replied with a laugh.

That made Alfonso even more eager to find out what the package had contained.

"Is there a reason why I shouldn't know?" he asked.

"Wait till morning, sir," his servant told him. "Then you'll find out."

When Alfonso got up the next morning, he was eager to find out what was inside the bag. He was hardly out of bed before Ya'qub was with him, bringing his clothes for the day. Alfonso washed, combed his hair, and put on the clothes in preparation for his visit to the city. He waited patiently with regard to the bag's contents until Ya'qub decided to tell him of his own accord. Once Alfonso was ready and all they had to do was leave, Ya'qub came back in with the bag and locked the door behind him. Alfonso stood up, waiting to see what was inside it. Ya'qub opened it up and took out something made of black material that looked like a priest's cassock. There were two garments, both of them long enough to cover the entire leg. Ya'qub took one of them and handed it to Alfonso.

"Put on this jallaba, sir," he said. Alfonso did so, putting it over his shoulders and wrapping himself in it so that it covered the rest of his clothing. Ya'qub did the same with the other garment. He then reached behind his neck to the collar and pulled up a hood that hung down the back and put it over his head till it completely covered both head and face. There were three slits in the face cover, two for the eyes and one for the mouth. Once Ya'qub had finished, he looked just like a black ghost. He came over to Alfonso, pulled up his hood, and arranged it so that he looked exactly like him. While Ya'qub was busy doing this, Alfonso remained quiet so he could see how this operation would end up. When Ya'qub had finished, he told Alfonso that these garments were what he had brought from Astigi. For the time being, he should take it off. It would be needed later.

All this left Alfonso perplexed. "When are we going to need it?" he asked.

"Soon enough, God willing," Ya'qub replied. "Don't be in too much of a hurry."

So saying, he helped Alfonso out of the black garment, wrapped each one of them separately, and put one of them under his breastplate till it was completely concealed. He gave the other one to Alfonso and told him to do the same. Alfonso had no idea of what was going on, but he did so nevertheless.

"Now let's go to the church," Ya'qub said.

As Alfonso and Ya'qub were leaving the fortress, they ran into Wamba. He stood up to greet them both.

"I'm on my way to church," Alfonso told him. "Look after things here."

Wamba nodded and saluted to show that he fully understood.

Alfonso now proceeded into the city, with Ya'qub following behind. They took no other servants or retainers with them. As they crossed the bridge and entered the city, they said nothing to each other because Ya'qub was fully accustomed to dealing with royalty and not speaking unless spoken to. Alfonso was lost in his own world and completely oblivious of everything around him. His mind was totally preoccupied with thoughts of Florinda, Roderic, what Ya'qub had told him, and this mysterious black garb he was carrying. It was only when they reached the markets and encountered lots of people making their way to the church that he finally came to himself. It was not long before the road brought them to the big square in the middle of the city where people used to meet. Alfonso had no idea how to get to the church, but merely followed Ya'qub's instructions. Once they had crossed the square, they found themselves facing a huge gateway with people scrambling to get either in or out.

"This is the gateway to the main street in the city," Ya'qub said after stopping for a moment, "and there's the church."

He pointed to another big gateway nearby. They both went over to it and walked through along with everyone else. The people had no idea who Alfonso was, but his long hair and clothing told them that he was some kind of noble and figure of authority.

They remained silent as they performed the prayer liturgy. Once it was over and people started to leave, they went outside. However, Alfonso had no idea where to go until Ya'qub started walking in a particular direction. Alfonso followed behind as he made his way out of the city by another gate. Once again Alfonso was perplexed, and he could not help asking Ya'qub where they were going.

"To that hill over there," Ya'qub replied, and pointed to a hill close by with no buildings on it. They soon reached it and climbed to the top, but Alfonso still had no idea what they were doing.

"Look down at Astigi," Ya'qub said. "Take a look at its wall. Do you see a high tower on it?"

Alfonso responded in the affirmative because the tower was very close to the city itself.

"If you come up here at night," Ya'qub went on, "you can't mistake that tower because it is so high and there's no other tower like it. Remember that. Now follow me..."

So saying, he started down the other side of the hill. They found themselves facing an isolated cave.

"Do you see this cave?" Ya'qub asked Alfonso who was standing by his side.

"Yes, I do," Alfonso replied.

"Now let's go back to the city," Ya'qub said. "We'll spend the rest of the day there, then come back up here."

Chapter 44

The Lesson and the Vault

Alfonso had been expecting to hear about the secret, so now he was even more perplexed by the whole thing.

"Where are we going to spend the day?" he asked Ya'qub. "I'm finding it long already…"

"I'll be making it very short," Ya'qub replied.

With that, he set off, Alfonso trailing behind him till they had reentered the city. Alfonso kept looking up at the tower and thinking about it. They traversed several market squares and eventually entered a narrow alley leading to a small gateway.

"Wait for me here, sir," Ya'qub said, "till I get back."

He went into a house, then came out and gestured to Alfonso to come in with him. From all the household utensils Alfonso spotted, he could tell that people were living there, but even so he did not see anyone else. Followed by Alfonso, Ya'qub went into one of the rooms. By now Alfonso had run out of patience and was beginning to get annoyed.

Ya'qub closed the door, sat Alfonso down on the carpet, and knelt beside him.

"Now, sir," he said, "I'm going to teach you some strange phrases. You need to memorize them."

"Why?" Alfonso asked.

"The phrases and gestures I'm going to teach you now," Ya'qub replied, "are the key to revealing the secret and getting the project started."

"Very well then," Alfonso said, "go ahead."

"Say 'Shalom 'alay-khem'," Ya'qub told him.

Alfonso repeated it, although his tongue stumbled over the consonants kha' and 'ayn. Ya'qub kept on repeating it over and over again until Alfonso had it memorized.

"Now say 'Ohil maw'id."

Alfonso duly repeated it for him until he had learned that phrase as well.

Now Ya'qub stood up and grabbed Alfonso's hand. "Stand up, sir," he said.

Ya'qub now took several steps in Alfonso's direction, walking in a manner that was not normal for most people. "Walk the way I just did," he asked Alfonso.

Alfonso did so and repeated the steps till he had them mastered. He then also learned some hand and finger gestures and others as well, acting like a parrot as he learned the various phrases and gestures, none of which he understood.

The rest of the day was spent this way. Once the sun went down, they both went outside, although Alfonso was more and more perplexed by what was happening. By now he had completely forgotten his concerns over Florinda and Oppas. The two of them kept walking until they exited through one of the city gates. It was a clear night and extremely cold. Ignoring how cold they were feeling, they climbed the hill again and looked over at the tower. Searching all around it, they found no one, because at nighttime people made sure to go back to their homes inside the walls. Ya'qub went down to the cave, followed by Alfonso, and they both stopped by the entrance. Inside was pitch black. Ya'qub grabbed Alfonso's hand and took a few steps inside. All the while, Alfonso was hanging on for dear life and treading carefully as though he were walking on spikes. Ya'qub stopped.

"Now take out your garment," he told Alfonso.

Once he had taken it out, Ya'qub helped him put it on. When they had put the garments on, it was a case of black on black, clothing and darkness. They now took a few more steps, with Ya'qub leading the way, but then he stopped suddenly. Alfonso was aware how suddenly he had stopped and was afraid that something bad had happened. He noticed that Ya'qub was bending down to the ground. He heard a scratching sound as though someone were digging in the soil with his fingernails. Ya'qub let go of Alfonso's hand, leaving him standing there like a totem pole; it was so dark that he had no idea where he was supposed to go.

Ya'qub had let go of Alfonso's hand so that he could use his own to lift up a heavy stone. A few minutes passed, with Alfonso standing stock-still. Just then he heard the sound of the stone being lifted and felt a cool breeze emerging from the opening.

"Follow me, sir," Ya'qub told him. "Move slowly."

Alfonso followed Ya'qub down seven steps, leading to a vault tall enough for a man to stand up in. They moved on, with Ya'qub leading and Alfonso behind him. To Alfonso it seemed as though they were walking in a circle, but actually they were walking straight down a gentle slope. It was getting darker and darker. After a while, Ya'qub stopped again.

"Wait here, sir," he said. "Don't move till I get back."

With that, he left Alfonso and moved off, although his footsteps were inaudible. Alfonso was left feeling strangely alone; the minutes that Ya'qub was away seemed like hours. Eventually he grew tired of waiting and told himself that he should try to follow Ya'qub's tracks. But then he remembered Ya'qub's injunction to stay where he was. He stopped for a moment, but Alfonso, like all people, was eager to find out secrets even though they might place him in danger. However, he had forgotten the direction in which they had been moving, so he stretched out his hand. He found nothing to touch, so he told himself he must be in some open space. While he was still working out what to do, he saw a faint light approaching from a distance, and eventually made out the shape of the person carrying it, who was wearing a black garment just like the one he was wearing. He assumed that it was Ya'qub and called out his name, but the other person did not respond. He concluded that his silence must be a form of concealment. Just then, he noticed another figure behind the first one, also wearing the same black garment. This second person uncovered his face, and that turned out to be Ya'qub. Alfonso now realized that he had almost reached their destination.

However, he hardly had time to think before Ya'qub rushed over and seized his hand. Alfonso looked at his face in the dim light and noticed that his beard was more scruffy and dirty than before; because of all the tension, his expression was now that much more anxious. Alfonso was afraid that something bad was going to happen to them in this place, but he allowed Ya'qub to take charge of the situation. Ya'qub held his hand and pulled him along as they followed the man with the light. Ya'qub warned him to watch where he was walking. When Alfonso looked down at the floor, he noticed that there were several ditches into which people might fall in broad daylight, let alone in the dark. Now Alfonso realized why Ya'qub had gone to get some light. He walked slowly and carefully for several minutes, then the light was put out, and there was complete darkness yet again.

"No!" Alfonso shouted without even thinking.

Ya'qub squeezed his hand, as though to tell him to keep quiet.

"We've arrived," he said.

Chapter 45

The Session

Alfonso was fed up with the hood he had pulled down over his face, so he raised it. He took a deep breath then lowered it again. Suddenly Ya'qub came to a stop and whispered in his ear that, once the door was open, Alfonso should do exactly what he did. Whatever he saw, he should not be scared. Ya'qub now knocked seven times on the door in a particular way, then waited a moment before knocking three more times in a different way. The door opened on to a small vestibule, which was faintly illuminated. On each side of the doorway stood a man wearing clothing identical to what they were wearing. Each one was holding a drawn sword; the two weapons formed a kind of arch over the doorway. Alfonso started at the sight and moved back, but then he heard Ya'qub say, "Shalom 'alay-khem!"

Alfonso said the same thing, and with that they both entered the vestibule while the two sword-carriers remained in place like idols. Ya'qub now walked across the vestibule in that particular way he had demonstrated to Alfonso earlier in the day. Alfonso did the same, although he was so confused that he stumbled. Eventually they reached another closed door; for this one the special knock was five times. As the door was opened, the light went out. For a moment Alfonso panicked, but then he remembered what Ya'qub had told him and steeled himself. He heard himself addressed in a language he did not understand, but heard Ya'qub respond.

"Ohil maw'id," he said, and Alfonso repeated the same phrase.

As they made their way through the darkness, Alfonso felt they were going up some stairs. Another door opened, and Alfonso could feel warm air coming out, mingled with the smell of human breath. Feeling warmer now, he forgot all about the cold he had felt in the vault. Passing through the doorway, they emerged into a large hall with a kind of table in the middle on which was a lighted lamp. Beside it was a large scroll. All around the walls were seats on which shrouded figures wearing the same clothing as theirs were arrayed, all of them with their faces covered. In front of each one were a drawn sword and dagger that gleamed in light. The whole thing unnerved Alfonso. He felt he was in a critical situation; never in his entire life had he imagined he would be witnessing anything remotely like this or running such a risk.

Looking around, he watched Ya'qub proceed using the same walk he had taught him. So he followed in his footsteps and walked twice around the table and lamp. He kissed the scroll with its thick leather covering. They then made their way to two empty seats at the other side of the hall and sat in them, with two drawn swords in front of them.

All Alfonso could see were black shrouded figures; they all looked identical. He felt that he was in danger and regretted ever coming to this place, but then he remembered once more the extent to which he had complete trust in Ya'qub. That helped him relax a little. For a while no one spoke, but then one of them left his seat, moved over to the table, picked up the scroll, and opened it in the lamplight. Alfonso could make out that there was writing on it that he did not understand. When the man started to read, everyone stood up, Alfonso included, till he had finished the recitation. The man kissed the scroll and returned to his seat. Everyone else sat down as well, still saying nothing.

The same man then started a long statement in that same language, to which some of those present responded. Then Ya'qub spoke in Gothic.

"The presider hereby allows the convening of a special session to be attended by himself and whoever wishes in order to discuss a crucially important matter…"

The first man now stood up with a small sword in his hand and made a particular gesture, at which everyone stood. Three other men now came and stood in front of him. Ya'qub and Alfonso moved forward and joined them. The presider now moved toward a door behind him, opened it, and went inside. He was followed by the rest of those present. They made their way along a dark corridor till they reached another door. The presider opened it and entered a dark room. Standing by the door, he gave instructions, and another man came over with a lighted candle secured in a bronze holder. The presider took it from him, and the other man turned round and closed the door behind him. The presider went inside the room, carrying the candle, and put it on a stone shelf high up in a corner of the room.

Chapter 46

The Secret is Revealed

When Alfonso looked around him to see where he was, he found himself in a small room with black walls and a black ceiling. On the floor was a box that looked like a large coffin with a small scroll on top. All around this box was a carpet on which they all sat, with the box in the middle. Alfonso found the entire scene scary; after everything he had witnessed that night, his heart was pounding. By now the sight of so many shrouded figures was wearing on him; he could not see their faces or make out who they were.

Once they were all seated, Ya'qub spoke, again in Gothic. "Does the presider think that the sustenance is ready?" he asked.

"You're the one who should know the answer to that," the presider replied. "After all, you lit the fire."

"I hope it's ready," Ya'qub went on, "but it needs a lot of flesh. Sustenance with no flesh is inedible…"

"There's plenty of flesh," the presider responded. "This box has enough in it to feed the entire world, and that doesn't even include what's in the kitchen and can be brought in when needed…"

Alfonso had no idea what all this symbolic talk was about and could not stop himself from making a request.

"We're on our own here," he said, "and there are just a few of us. I'd appreciate it if you would talk openly."

The presider let out a sigh but said nothing. Ya'qub now got to his knees and turned to Alfonso.

"To be frank then, the materials that you need to complete your project are contained in dozens of boxes like these. The collection has been made over years but has only been spent in times of dire need."

That said, he gestured to the presider, who took a key out of his pocket and opened the box. Once the cover was removed, there was immediately a glimmer of brilliant yellow. Alfonso saw that it all consisted of pure gold coins. The presider now closed the lid again and put the key back in his pocket.

Alfonso was astonished by the sight of so much gold and realized that he was in the presence of really influential people. He was eager to find out more about them.

"I notice that you go to enormous lengths to preserve your secrecy. However, we're gathered here to discuss something of great importance. So who are you?"

"Don't try to find out anything more than you can see," the presider said. "You should realize that you already know things that the people you saw in the other room do not know. They have been part of our assembly for years, contributing money and spirit to our cause..."

"You should be content, sir," Ya'qub continued after the presider had finished, "to have seen what you've seen and to know that in Spain there are thousands of oppressed people such as these with large sums of money collected in boxes like this one here. Now they're ready and willing to devote themselves to your service along with their money."

Hearing the word "oppressed," Alfonso realized he was in the company of an anti-government secret society; from the peculiar phrases he had heard and learned for himself, he assumed they were Jews. He was aware that the Jewish community had dwindled drastically under the current government, either by being exiled, or killed, or forced to convert to Christianity.[30]

"So now I understand the secret," he told Ya'qub. "Now you should speak frankly to them since you are the one who knows the most about my goals and ambitions, not to mention those of my father before me..."

Ya'qub now turned to face the presider. "I now have to reveal another secret to you," he said. "You need to be aware, sir, that the person

---

30 Dozy, part I.

whom I have brought here tonight is our only protector in these regions. Once I tell you who he is, the fact that he now knows about us will be easily justified. He is none other than Alfonso, son of the late King Witiza. That is all you need to know."

No sooner had Ya'qub finished speaking than the presider posed the obvious question.

"Are his pledges exactly the same as those of his father?"

"Yes, indeed they are," Ya'qub replied. "He is the protector of the oppressed in this land. He's set himself to rid our land of this accursed tyrant who dares to call himself king. What he needs is money, and we have it. Now that I've made this frank statement about the situation, allow me to explain things to him."

Ya'qub now turned to face Alfonso.

"Your Majesty," he said, "and I use that term because we recognize no one else in that role but you, you should know that you are in the presence of a Jewish organization. Everyone you see here is Jewish, and they still practice the faith of their fathers and grandfathers. They represent thousands of their fellow Jews who are now scattered throughout the Spanish kingdom. They pretend to be Christians, attending Mass in churches, receiving Communion, and fulfilling all the other obligations of Christians, but it is all a pretense. They are still Jews, and they perform their own prayers in secret. This morning, there were hundreds of them in church, and we watched as they knelt in front of icons and made a show of reciting prayers. You may even have heard them praying for Roderic's success, when what they really want is to see him dead. For years the community has tolerated such oppression and swallowed its anger. All the while, they've been collecting money and keeping it hidden so that they can take advantage of the opportunity to remove this heavy burden from their shoulders. They had almost achieved that goal during the reign of your late father, but people with evil motives replaced him with this tyrant. He has no right to the position; you are the only legitimate heir. We all hope that you will be the one to rescue the country..."

When Alfonso heard what Ya'qub had to say, he understood all the secrets that he had wanted to know about ever since Oppas had first mentioned them. Now he was satisfied by what he had heard and seen for himself. He decided to wait for another occasion before asking for any more details. As he chewed over the various mysteries that were still unclear to him, he said nothing. He realized that the one thing he did not know was who these people actually were, particularly now that they knew who he was by name. Ya'qub actually anticipated his next question.

"That's all you need to know at this point, sir," he said.

"True enough," Alfonso replied. "All I want to know is, who are these wonderful people in whose presence I find myself, especially since they now know who I am?"

"They don't even know that themselves," Ya'qub told him. "The reason why they shroud themselves like this is that they're afraid someone may reveal their secret, even if it is one of their own number. Now that you have learned about these crucially important secrets, you'll still be able to leave this place as though you'd never entered it. You haven't seen anyone's face, so you can't accuse anyone of being involved. Some of these men may be soldiers, rabbis, businessmen, or farmers, and they're all considered Christians. The only one you need to know is me."

Alfonso was duly impressed by this level of precaution. He knew, of course, that Ya'qub was Jewish and remembered the way his personal servant had asked him to be lenient in his demands that he perform prayers and the like. His uncle Oppas had been a big help in that as well. Among the many thoughts that were swirling around inside his head was the question as to what Ya'qub's relationship with his late father had been like, but, as with other aspects of the situation, he decided not to pursue this for the time being.

These thoughts were interrupted by a noise over their heads. Alfonso was momentarily panicked and looked up at the ceiling.

"Don't be alarmed, sir," Ya'qub hurried to explain. "That noise comes from the city streets that are directly above us. People pass by day and night. The only people in Astigi who are aware that this structure exists beneath the city street are the members of this particular community."

Hearing that, Alfonso was even more amazed by the cunning and secrecy of everything he had witnessed that night.

"Any group," he told himself, "that can be so clever, committed, and patient fully deserves to achieve its goals."

Chapter 47

Another Knock on the Door

As these thoughts were going through Alfonso's mind, he heard another knocking in the distance, which seemed to be coming from the door at the end of the corridor. This time, however, the number and rhythm of the knocks were different from the ones Ya'qub had used. He noticed that the presider, Ya'qub, and all the other people who were sitting there with him were listening carefully to see what would happen next. He was afraid that their posture meant that there was cause for alarm; if only their faces had been uncovered, he would have been able to tell from their expressions. But then he heard another series of knocks in a different rhythm again, and that was barely finished before the assembly needed to listen no further and moved to action.

"A messenger has arrived with new information," the presider said. "Perhaps he's coming from our colleagues in Syria, Egypt, or Africa..."

Alfonso was amazed that the presider seemed able to recognize the new arrival simply from the knocking, but the statement he had just heard made it clear that this particular group had a broad network of connections in Syria, Egypt, and elsewhere.

"How could you tell who it was simply on the basis of a distant knocking?" he couldn't stop himself asking. "Does this group have members in other countries?"

"I was able to recognize who it was by using a set of rules established specifically for that purpose; everyone in the group knows what they are. With regard to the extent of our group, we do indeed have members in far-off lands, whom I've sent to search for ways to rid us of this enslavement."

He paused for a moment. "Some of our members," he went on, "have been prominent public figures and politicians, while others have worked as servants and suffered a life of misery and contempt. In fact, they've not actually been servants at all, but rather the group's most assiduous members in working for our cause. They've only donned servants' garments in order to bolster our endeavors."

While the presider was talking, Alfonso was gradually beginning to understand what was going on. Ya'qub, his faithful servant, was obviously a senior figure in this group and one of its most important members. Even so, he was still eager to find out about his relationship to his father and uncle, because some of the things that Oppas had said made it clear that they had both known about Ya'qub's secret. Once again, he decided to do that later.

As he waited with everyone else for the messenger to come in, there was complete silence for a while as they listened to the sound of movement in the big hall. Then there came a special knock on the door of this dark room. Ya'qub stood up and opened the door. A tall man wearing the same black garment came in, headed straight for the presider, and spoke some words in Hebrew, which Alfonso could not understand. The presider responded, and they spent a short time conversing, although Alfonso did not understand any of it. What amazed him was that the new arrival had headed straight for the presider even though there was no evidence he had a superior rank. His dress was no different than that of everyone else in the room; they were all wearing the same black garment. So, while the presider and the new arrival were talking, Alfonso asked Ya'qub what the secret was.

"If you look closely at the presider's garment," Ya'qub told him, "you'll notice a symbol on his shoulder that distinguishes him from everyone. You'd only notice it if you looked really carefully. In this group, every office-holder has a particular symbol: the scribe, the treasurer, and so on. But they're subtle, and you only notice them when you look carefully."

Alfonso now took a look at the presider's shoulder and spotted a black knot just by the collar. He then looked at the other members' shoulders, and noticed that Ya'qub's had a knot like the one on the presider's shoulder but of a different shape. He was about to ask Ya'qub what his symbol meant, but just then the presider spoke to the new arrival out loud.

"I'm delighted that you've joined us tonight," he said. "We wish to hear the news of your journey. We have among us someone who will be keen to hear what you have to say, and we too are anxious that he should hear. We are in the Eternity Room, and only the senior members are present. So where exactly are you coming from?"

The man had now sat down around the central box along with all the others.

"I'm coming from Sabta," he said, "and I have a lot to tell you. I can't go into detail now, but I can summarize the things that are of concern to both you and all of us. If I were to uncover my face, you would see good news written all over it. It seems to me that the era of our imprisonment and humiliation is very soon coming to an end."

When he made that statement, everyone sat up and stretched their necks to hear what the new arrival had to tell them.

"May God give you a good reward!" the presider told him. "Perhaps the end of our captivity will be like that of our forefathers in Babylon dozens of centuries ago."

Chapter 48

A Woeful Account

"As you well know, sir," the messenger said, addressing himself to the presider, "I've lived for many years in Sabta on the African coast in Morocco. That city and its environs are under the control of this tyrant in Toledo, even though it also has to be under the suzerainty of the Eastern Roman Empire because it's in Africa. However, the Byzantines essentially gave up control of Africa following the Arab conquests. The Arab armies managed to gain control of almost all the coastlands in Africa, apart from Sabta and its surrounding region, which they were unable to capture. Its governor sought protection in Spain, and thus, as you know, Sabta became part of its domain…"

"It would appear," the presider interrupted, "that the sons of Isma'il have done extremely well with their new faith…"

"Yes, indeed, sir," the messenger replied.

Alfonso had no idea what this question was all about, nor did he understand the meaning of "sons of Isma'il." He decided that it was not the right time to interrupt the conversation, so he said nothing.

"These cousins of ours have turned the entire world upside down," the messenger went on. "Their rule now stretches as far as Iraq, Syria, Africa, Persia, Khurasan, and to the edge of the known world."

Now Alfonso was even more perplexed. What did he mean by "these cousins of ours?" He turned to Ya'qub, who immediately realized what was bothering him before he was asked.

"The Arabs who have launched this new faith," he said, "are descendants of Isma'il, the son of Abraham," he told Alfonso, "and the Jews are descended from his brother, Isaac. In that way they are cousins."

Alfonso now listened carefully to the rest of the messenger's
report so that things would become clearer.

"My travels were both for commercial purposes," the messenger
went on, "and to work on behalf of our society. I went to both Egypt and
Syria and mingled with the populace there. I found several of our Jewish
brothers who had managed to rid themselves of the humiliating treatment
they had suffered by traveling to those lands. They're all in Africa, Egypt,
and Syria now, living in peace and tranquility, untroubled by anyone on
account of their religious beliefs. They pray as and when they wish and
can practice their jobs and professions in complete safety. That doesn't
apply only to Jews, but to everyone who lives in those regions, no matter
what community they belong to. Of course, the Jews were systematically
persecuted in those regions when they were under Roman governance
and suffered all kinds of agony, the same way that we in Spain did a few
centuries ago, before we were forced either to convert to Christianity or
go into exile or be killed. As you well know, we had the choice of either
fleeing or pretending to be Christians.[31] Our brothers in the Byzantine
regions were better off than we were, but even so they could not tolerate
the cruel treatment they received either. They often clashed with the
Christians and resisted the government in question. When the sons of
Isma'il emerged from the Arabian Peninsula to conquer those countries,
the Jews helped them, which turned out to be a good thing because they
were thereby released from the bonds and slavery of the Byzantines. They
could now protect their souls and their wealth and be taxed a lot less as
they lived a life of ease."

"How could that be?" the presider asked. "Were they not simply
transferring from one authority to another, one set of taxes to another?
Didn't the Arabs impose their swords or their influence on other people?
Didn't they impose their own set of taxes?"

"Yes, sir, they did," the messenger explained. "In conquering
those territories, the Arabs resorted to either the sword or peace treaties.
The lands then came under their control, but in fact they rarely involved
themselves in the affairs of the regions concerned. Indeed, they only rarely

31 *History of Islamic Civilization, part 1.*

lived in the cities or mingled with the populace, and then only at specific times and for temporary purposes.[32]"

"How can that be?" Alfonso now interrupted. "How can they govern a country without actually living there?"

"I don't blame you for being so surprised," the messenger responded. "Such behavior is totally unprecedented according to what we know of the history of that particular region, where rulers have traditionally poked their noses into every aspect of the people's lives, regarding them essentially as their slaves. But the Arabs are different. Once they conquered the country and imposed their poll tax and land tax, they moved on to the outlying regions. They built their own cities, and no one else can live in them: thus, Kairawan in Tunisia; Fustat in Egypt; and Al-Basra and Al-Kufa in Iraq. They left the people of those regions entirely untouched, the way they had been previously under the Byzantine and Roman empires. As a result, everyone is able to go about their own business, and all they have to worry about is paying the appropriate amount of land and poll tax each year. Compared with the levels that the Byzantines used to charge and force people like us to pay, the taxation rates are trivial. It is true that people were better off in the early days than they are now. That is because of the cruel treatment meted out by certain governors during the Umayyad caliphate. One of them in Iraq, named Al-Hajjaj ibn Yusuf, was particularly harsh in the way he treated people, imposing huge land taxes because he needed funding for the wars he was conducting. However, their chief ruler, known as the caliph, was residing in the city of Damascus and would often instruct his governors to treat people more gently. Whatever the case, the Jewish and Christian peoples have been much better off under Arab rule than that of others, especially if we go back to the period of the early caliphs who advocated justice, courtesy, and equality. Without those qualities in place, it would not have been so easy for them to embark upon a series of conquests that extended their domains to large swaths of the inhabited world in the East."

"And wouldn't it be wonderful," the presider said, "if they came to our land as well and took control? If they were less oppressive than the

---

32 Ibid.

Byzantines in the East, then they would have to be better than the Goth government here."

"No, sir," the much-traveled messenger objected. "We have no right to complain about the Goths as a group. Some of them treated us very well, especially Witiza the late king. He was determined to set us free and allow us to practice our own religion.[33] Unfortunately death got there first, or rather they killed him. What followed was Roderic, who's the worst of them all—may God blacken his very name!"

---

33 Romey, part II.

Chapter 49

Julian

The presider was well aware that Witiza's son was in their midst. He was somewhat surprised to hear this traveler extol the virtues of his father in this manner.

"You're right, of course," he said. "At any rate we would all be happy if these Arabs came to Spain. They probably wouldn't find it too difficult to conquer the country; there's hardly a communal group that doesn't complain bitterly about the current government..."

"The wish you've just expressed while sitting here is the same as the one expressed by our brothers over there, and I'm among them. We've often urged the Arabs to invade and told them how wonderful this country is. Whenever they've expressed doubts about it, we've told them that conquest would be relatively easy. Now it seems that they're on the point of starting an attack."

"Do you really mean that?" the presider asked enthusiastically.

"Yes, sir," the traveler replied. "That's why I've come. I wanted to surprise you, but we've gone off the topic a bit. I've explained that Sabta in the province of Mauretania is under Roman suzerainty. When the Arabs conquered Africa, Mauretania was detached from the Roman Empire, and its ruler went over to Spain so he could be under the protection of a Christian country. The capital city is Sabta on the Straits.[34] When I left Spain and went over to Africa, the governor there was a man named Julian. I pretended to be a Christian and focused on my trade,

---

34 Later to become known as the Straits of Gibraltar—a word coined from the Arabic *Jabal Tarek* or Tariq's mountain through which the Arab invasion of Spain was to take place. *Translators' Note.*

traveling to other lands and then returning to Sabta. All the time I was resentful of the savage and cruel treatment that our Jewish community was suffering under the Visigoths. I had the opportunity to take revenge for our community on Julian, and in a manner that I won't discuss here. Even so, I was one of his close advisers; he trusted me and confided in me. I, in turn, showed him a certain affection and used the opportunity to achieve my own goals, namely persuading the Arabs that invading Spain would be a good idea. However, I realized, of course, that the only way that might happen would be if they captured Sabta first, since it lies on the Straits[35], the shortest distance between Africa and this country.

"Most recently, the Arab governor in Africa has been Musa ibn Nusayr, who is both determined and courageous. He has sent his troops to capture Tangier. From that base he has set about besieging Sabta by land. Julian is holed up inside, sticking doggedly to Gothic overlords even though he is well aware that it will do him no good. However, he cannot relinquish his loyalty to Roderic for reasons of which you are all well aware..."

When Alfonso heard the name Julian, his heart did a leap; he knew, of course, that he was Florinda's father. He strained to listen in case something was said about her as well. When the traveler said that Julian could not relinquish his fealty to Roderic for known reasons, he realized that the principal cause was that Florinda was trapped at Roderic's court, a pawn, as it were, to make sure that Julian remained loyal. Alfonso remembered how things were with Florinda and that she had actually managed to escape Roderic's clutches. His entire body felt as though it were on fire, but he gritted his teeth and simply listened to the remainder of the conversation.

"Yes, indeed," the presider said, "we're all aware of what those reasons are. But then what?"

"While the siege was underway," the traveler went on, "I was in Julian's fortress and sat with him a lot. He was relying on me and keeping me close because I was wealthy and had a good trade. While the siege is still in process, he's going to need money or provisions. As you're all aware, I am as anxious as anyone to maintain this close contact. A few days ago I was at home when one of Julian's messengers arrived and asked me to go

---

35 The reference is to the Straits of Gibraltar. *See footnote above.*

to his residence immediately. Once I got to the fortress and approached his room, I spotted a young man emerging who seemed to have come from a distant land. He looked like a man of Toledo, and I suspect he was one of the king's men. The man walked past me without saying a word. I went in, something I usually did without asking permission. Julian was sitting by the window that overlooks the Mediterranean. He was clutching something in his hand and was deep in thought. When he heard footsteps approaching, he jumped up and tossed me the message in his hand. He was obviously furious. 'Just read this,' he told me, 'and see how utterly miserable I feel! The disaster that struck me when I was still young is apparently not enough, so now I have to suffer further torment, and all at the hands of a man for whom, as you well know, I'm going through the fires of hell so that he can keep his throne!' I bent down to pick up the thing he had thrown at me. It was a piece of cloth, from a shirt or gown probably. It had some red writing on it, as though written in blood. When I read it, my body shuddered in disbelief, but at the same time I was utterly delighted because I realized that this letter constituted a solution to the crisis that was affecting us all."

As Alfonso listened to what the traveler was saying, he was beside himself with worry. Everyone else was listening carefully to whatever the fresh news was going to be.

"So I read the letter," the traveler continued. Here's what it said:

My dear father,

You've handed your daughter over to a man who calls himself a king, when in fact he's a rabid beast who is utterly unconcerned about honor, chastity, or respect. But for divine protection, I would by now have become a victim of his vile lust. I'm writing to you on this piece of my own clothing, as I wander from place to place with nowhere to hide from the evil intentions of this feckless tyrant. I have no idea when I shall see you again. What is to be the recompense for someone who treats your daughter so badly? The bearer of this message—should he manage to reach you— can tell you in person about things that you may well find difficult to comprehend.

From the hand of Florinda.

Chapter 50

Incentive

You do not even have to ask how Alfonso reacted to all this. He was completely beside himself, and his heart was pounding. Had it not been for the mask covering his face, he would certainly have revealed himself. He was dumbfounded to hear the words "as I wander from place to place," because he had assumed all along that she was safely under the protection of his uncle, Oppas. It was all too much for him, but he managed to keep his emotions under control as he listened to the rest of what was being said. Ya'qub was just as shocked as Alfonso, because he was aware, of course, of his master's relationship with Florinda.

"When I finished reading the letter," the messenger said, concluding his report, "I made it clear how angry I was. I then asked Julian how long such a monarch should stay in power, when he showed not the slightest concern for honor, chastity, or respect for others. I went on to inquire as to whether it was worth his while to expose himself to danger and endure all kinds of hardship in order to protect such a king's throne, particularly when he behaved in such a way toward his daughter. Julian had already been deeply depressed because of a disaster that had struck him and his family, and now I was able to play on his emotions."

"'I must have revenge on this traitor,' he eventually said, 'and surrender this region to the Arabs. They are far more inclined to do what's right. Nor will that be sufficient. I'm going to encourage them to conquer Spain so they can kill Roderic and quench my thirst for vengeance.' I was delighted to hear him state such an intention; it was the goal toward which I'd been striving for ages. I started giving him even more encouragement. 'If you so wish,' I told him, 'I can serve as an intermediary to the Arabs and arrange for you to surrender the town to your and their advantage. In that way, it won't appear to be a matter of either weakness or cowardice.'"

"He was clearly pleased by the idea, and with that I left. I proceeded to tell Musa ibn Nusayr, the Arab commander. He, too, was pleased and gave Julian a friendly reception. Julian proposed that he cross the Straits to the other shore and conquer Spain; he offered to join them and give them information about the deficiencies in the Visigothic defences.[36] Musa was delighted by the idea. No sooner had I heard this news than I was anxious to share it with you. What do you think?"

When the traveler finished his report, everyone was astonished, not least Alfonso, who found himself torn between two worries: firstly, his love for Florinda, about whom he had become increasingly worried when he heard that she was not in fact under his uncle's protection; secondly, his feelings of despair about the monarchy since, if the Arabs were to invade Spain, that would put an end to the Gothic monarchy altogether. Ya'qub could tell what was going through Alfonso's mind and worried that his mood might have a negative impact on his desire to fight Roderic. But then he remembered how much Alfonso loved Florinda and how he loathed Roderic for that very same reason. He realized that at this point there was no way of calming Alfonso down, particularly after he had heard what Florinda had written to her father. Even so, Ya'qub wanted to make sure that Alfonso remained wedded to his purpose.

"This news that our colleague has brought us," Ya'qub said, addressing himself to the presider, "is clearly momentous. The Arabs are bound to conquer Spain, especially if Julian is with them to show them the way. Needless to say, we will be helping them, too, since it serves our larger purpose. But none of that alters our primary goal, namely the restoration of the monarchy to His Majesty here." Saying so, he pointed at Alfonso and continued, "We've heard that the Arabs prefer to leave the countries they conquer with considerable autonomy. Once they learn that our king is one of their supporters, they will no doubt hand over

---

36 History tells us that Julian had actually heard about his daughter some six or so years earlier. He surrendered to the Arabs and suggested to Musa ibn Nusayr that he invade Spain. Musa in turn informed the caliph Al-Walid so that everyone should be in agreement about the invasion in the year 92 AH (710AD).

executive authority to us. They'll be happy to receive the land and poll taxes and only maintain general control from afar."

As Alfonso listened to what Ya'qub was saying, two things were still bothering him, but it was Florinda's situation that concerned him the most. He was eager to leave now and go looking for her. However, before departing, he was anxious to confirm the one matter for which he had come.

""My colleague Ya'qub believes," he said, "that my sole purpose in taking revenge on Roderic is out of a desire for power. However, my real quest is to rid this country of his tyranny and grant religious freedom to the Jews who have been forced to convert to Christianity. I want that criminal thug to realize that tyrants always pay for their misdeeds. If we manage to achieve that, I am not concerned with who assumes the throne."

"I can assure Your Majesty," Ya'qub replied, "that, once the Arabs have conquered Spain, they will do as you have suggested. With the conquest completed, I don't think they'll want to dispense with Your Majesty's legitimate authority. They've already placed a Berber man named Tariq in charge of Tangier even though the Berber tribes have not completely submitted to them as yet. The Arabs do such things because they are actually few in number when compared with the sheer size of the region that they've conquered. That's why they need to make use of non-Arabs to administer the territories. So who better to help them run the affairs of Spain than its own king? At any rate, we'll be sparing no effort to convince them that this is the best plan."

The presider got to his feet, and so did everyone else. "If you need to leave," he said, "then by all means do so. However, we hope that you'll feel assured of our genuine loyalty to you. The Jews throughout this country will be willing to devote their wealth and themselves to foster your interests. You have our pledge before God to that effect."

"I've told of you my intention to cooperate with you," Alfonso replied by way of thanks. "God alone can assure eventual success."

Ya'qub headed for the door and signaled to Alfonso to follow him. They went out into the big room again and passed from one door to another till they ended up in the corridor and thence to the cave.

Once they reached the open space, they realized that dawn was breaking. It now occurred to Alfonso that they had spent the entire night underground. He was feeling really cold. Once they had taken off the black robes, they both left the cave and headed back to the city. The gate was already open, so they entered the city and cut across it toward the bridge. Alfonso's mind was so preoccupied with images of the things he had witnessed that night that he did not say a word. Now that he had found out that Ya'qub was a senior official in the Jewish community, he did not know how to deal with him, but he was still eager to learn the rest of the secrets. Now that they had emerged from the subterranean corridors, his head was aching: after spending the entire night underground, he could feel the cold wind blowing on him. He could not think straight. The image of Florinda kept imprinting itself on everything else, and he could not get the contents of her letter out of his mind.

They reached the fortress. Alfonso was still not saying anything, while Ya'qub was keeping a close eye on his gestures and noting his glum appearance. He had some idea of what was going on in Alfonso's mind but decided not to ask him any questions, apart from what he wanted to eat and such mundane things. They both went up to Alfonso's room. Ya'qub got everything ready for Alfonso and prepared his bed. With that, Alfonso went to sleep, and so did Ya'qub.

So now let us leave the two of them asleep on the outskirts of Astigi, and take the reader to the land of the Berber peoples in North Africa—with cities like Barqa, Tripoli, Tunis, Algiers, and Marrakesh. We will investigate the situation of the Arabs in the region up to the conquest of Spain.

Chapter 51

After the Islamic Conquests

The Umayyad caliph, 'Abd al-Malik ibn Marwan, had died in 85 AH (704 AD), to be succeeded by his son, Al-Walid ibn 'Abd al-Malik. The father, 'Abd al-Malik, had been caliph for twenty years. For the majority of that time he had been at war with his rivals. He was often worried that the caliphate might fall from his grasp. However, he was astute and cunning, and Al-Hajjaj ibn Yusuf, the craftiest and meanest of his governors, made sure that he stayed in power. When 'Abd al-Malik died, his son, Al-Walid, who had managed to escape from his rivals, was eager to expand the Islamic dominions. He therefore dispatched Qutyaba ibn Muslim to the east to conquer Transoxania, and he managed to cross Turkish territory till he reached the borders with China. The new caliph also sent his brother, Maslama ibn 'Abd al-Malik, to the north to raid Byzantine territory, where he conquered Amoreum, Heracliopolis, Qamuniya, and other towns. He sent Musa ibn Nusayr off to Africa and made him governor, with orders to complete the conquest of the region.

In fact, the province of Ifriqiya (Tunisia) had been conquered in the early days of Islam and annexed to Egypt. However, it had been largely ignored because it was far away and difficult to reach. The original inhabitants of the region were the Berber tribes, who had their own particular languages and customs. There were many such tribes, and their territory was rich in animals and pasturage. The Umayyads had largely ignored Ifriqiya during 'Abd al-Malik's caliphate: they were so busy squabbling amongst themselves that the Berber tribes seized the opportunity to rid themselves of Muslim suzerainty. They had rebelled and refused to acknowledge the authority of the Muslims. 'Abd al-Malik had sent Hassan ibn al-Nu'man to the region. After attacking the tribes, he had managed to bring them back under control and inculcate the Islamic religion among them. But the Berber were tough, and it was not long before they were making trouble again. When Al-Walid became caliph, he was informed that the Berber tribes were split, so he decided to make use of the opportunity to bolster his authority in Ifriqiya and complete the conquest of the region. That is why he had dispatched Musa ibn Nusayr to complete the task, he being an Arab of Lakhmid origins who was not only a fearless commander but a devout Muslim as well. Musa settled in the fortress city of Kairawan, and from there he pursued the fleeing Berbers all the way to the Sous region in Morocco. Once the Berbers realized they were not going to win, they came to Musa and surrendered. They swore an oath of fealty to the Muslims, and Musa appointed some of his commanders to organize their affairs and teach them the Koran and Islamic obligations.

Among his followers was a Berber man named Tariq ibn Ziyad. A courageous soldier, he had converted to Islam and was a stalwart supporter and defender of the faith. As Musa's conquests of Ifriqiya expanded further and further, he appointed his loyal lieutenant Tariq governor of Tangier and supervisor of its affairs as his representative, leaving him with a cavalry of nineteen thousand, themselves stalwart converts to Islam. Musa then returned to Ifriqiya itself. In the entire region, only the city of Sabta was still not under Muslim control. It jutted out slightly into the Medterranean and overlooked the Straits.[37] The governor of Sabta was Julian, who has been mentioned above. Historians tell us that he remained loyal to Roderic[38] until the latter mistreated Julian's daughter, whereupon Julian decided to take revenge and encouraged the Arabs to invade Spain. European historians are inclined to discount this version and suggest instead that his support for the Arabs was based on the fact that he was a relative of Witiza. The reason he wanted to exact revenge was that he had been robbed of the monarchy.

The Berbers in the Western part of Africa were idol-worshippers, except for a minority who had had some contact with the Romans on the shores of the Mediterranean and had converted to Christianity, but they were few in number. Every tribe had its own set of idols and rituals;

---

37 The reference is to the Straits of Gibraltar. *See previous footnote.*

38 Also known as Ladhric.

shamans used to direct their affairs and interpret the law for the people. They would also be responsible for solving any problems that came up, just as the shamans used to do in pre-Islamic Arabia. The Berber shamans were known as marabouts. People would come to see them for advice in times of war and peace, bringing gifts in the form of animals, crops, or black or white slaves.

Roman and Gothic merchants used to dominate the Berber tribes, kidnapping infants and young boys and transporting them far away to barter away. They did the same thing with white boys from Spain as well. The majority of them were prisoners of war, and the sale of such prisoners was common during this era. The Berbers from the Maghrib were also famous horsemen.

Chapter 52

Tariq ibn Ziyad

Among the Berber tribes was one called Al-Sadaf, and it was from that one that Tariq ibn Ziyad hailed; for that reason he was often called Al-Sadafi. He grew up in the mountains and lived the nomadic life of the Bedouin, worshipping pagan idols like his tribe and companions. He was both sturdy in build and extremely brave. From a very early age his companions recognized him for his strength and horsemanship.

One of his childhood friends had a light complexion, unlike the rest of the tribe; his facial features were different as well. Most Berbers have thick lips, broad faces, and short noses. Their hair is normally black, and their skin color is a deep brown. By contrast, this young man was light-skinned with blond hair and blue eyes. However, since he had grown up with the Bedouin and taken part in raids on horseback, his skin color was somewhat bronzed, and his bodily frame had grown bulky. By now, he had thick neck and arm muscles, a broad chest, calloused hands, and a whole mop of hair. They all called him Badr[39] or "moon-face" because of his light skin color compared with everyone else in the tribe. Everyone liked him for his good humor and his bravery. The general belief was that courage went with brown skin color, while light-skinned people were puny and cowardly.

While Tariq was growing up, this young servant was working in his father's house. He realized that Badr was not his own brother because the tribal chief had offered him to Ziyad and told him to take care of the boy and supervise his education and upbringing; he could already see good things in him. So the two boys became friends and loved each other.

---

39 The literal translation of Badr is "full moon."

Tariq was only happy when Badr was with him, while Badr admired Tariq and loved him just as much. In fact, Badr regarded Tariq as his brother; they would only ever say anything in a spirit of brotherhood, and the two of them were well known for that in the Sadaf tribe.

When Musa ibn Nusayr arrived in Ifriqiya and became its governor, Tariq ibn Ziyad was one of the retainers he took with him on the journey. Noticing how courageous and devout he was, he promoted him to be commander of the Tangier garrison, as we mentioned. In fact, Badr was always in Tariq's company, but Musa had not paid attention to him because he was still so young. Even so, Badr managed to show tremendous courage in the various battles that were fought; he was not afraid of death, especially because he was in the company of his "brother" Tariq.

When Julian suggested to Tariq that he should invade Spain and that he, Julian, would assist him, Musa sent word back to the caliph, Al-Walid, in Damascus, asking for permission to move ahead. The caliph sent back a message that he could, but that he should use only prisoners and not risk Muslims on such a dangerous stretch of water.[40][41] Musa realized that he could do no better than make Tariq commander of the invasion force. What Tariq actually decided was to make use of non-Arab Muslim forces. Seven thousand troops were equipped, both client peoples[42] and Berbers, and a few Arabs as well. Making Tariq their commander, Musa gave instructions for them to cross the Straits and invade Spain.

Crossing the water in boats provided by Julian, they passed by an outcrop on the far shore, which since that time has been called Tariq's Mountain.[43] Tariq had no trouble capturing it. At that point he learned that Roderic was preparing a large army to meet him on the battlefield. Tariq now sent back a message to Musa, who provided him with five

---

40 Ibn al-Athir, Part IV, where it is noted that this occurred in the year 91 AH (709 AD). Musa dispatched Tarif, who invaded an island that adopted his name. Then he sent over Tariq.

41 *History of Islamic Civilization*, Part II.

42 "Client peoples" is a translation of the term in Arabic (*mawali*) used to designate non-Arab muslims. *Translator's Note.*

43 *Jabal Tariq* in Arabic or Gibraltar. *See previous footnote.*

thousand more troops. Thus, the entire army consisted of twelve thousand men, among whom was Julian, the governor of Sabta. He pointed out to them the various weak spots in Roderic's forces and provided them with intelligence. He also went around telling people in Spain that the Arabs were not coming to conquer and occupy the country, but only to get enough plunder for themselves and then leave. He persuaded the Spaniards to make it easy for them to defeat Roderic so they could finally be rid of him and restore the monarchy to their original royal family. Meanwhile, Tariq continued his march till he reached the Valley of Lakka near Cadiz. There, as the history books tell us, he met Roderic's army.[44] The Valley of Lakka[45] is in southern Spain, between Astigi and Gibraltar, and the river's estuary opens on to the Gulf of Cadiz.

The two armies clashed on the banks of this river at the beginning of the year 711 AD. The Gothic army was eventually defeated, and the Muslim conquest of Spain was now able to continue, with Tariq ibn Ziyad the Berber leader still in command, as we shall see...

---

44 Al-Maqqari, *Nafh al-Tib*, Part I.

45 Guadalete in Spanish. The Guadalete River runs through this valley located in the Spanish province of Cádiz. The Spanish name came from the Arabic phrase meaning "River of Forgetfulness." *Translator's Note.*

Chapter 53

Roderic and Oppas

As we have just seen, the Muslims were fully prepared and equipped to undertake the invasion and bring victory to their ally. As we have also noted earlier, Roderic continued to indulge in all kinds of luxurious and frivolous pursuits. When we last came across him, he was absolutely furious with Oppas because Florinda had managed to escape his clutches after being in imminent danger of falling victim to his lust. He had tried to get Oppas convicted in the bishops' assembly, but, when he realized that there was a danger of his own behavior being exposed, he had hurriedly brought the assembly to an end on the pretext of postponing any investigation of Oppas's charge till a later date (as noted earlier in our story). In fact, he had no intention of returning to that particular item, but he was simply using it as a way of keeping Oppas in prison while he searched for Florinda.

When the assembly of bishops had come to an end, Roderic had returned to the palace with Father Martin at his side, duly extolling the way they had been able to defeat Oppas and cut him down to size. In fact, Roderic knew full well that Oppas had bested him at the assembly, but even so, he allowed himself to be taken in by Father Martin's fawning account. He came to the conclusion that his own observations were wrong and that in fact he had scored a clear victory. It was as though he had somehow managed to forget the thunderbolts that Oppas had unleashed upon him during the assembly. If he had not brought the proceedings to a rapid close, with the assembled bishops being inclined to exonerate his behavior merely in order to keep their own positions, his very throne might have come crashing down.

However, we all know that human beings are narcissist by nature, and that makes it very easy for many of them to be convinced that they are superior to other people in intellect, opinion, and power. That conviction is only strengthened whenever intellect and perspicacity are weak. Our narcissism automatically leads us to believe that we are actually the most resolute and right-minded of people; not only that, but it conveys the illusion that our every quality is better than those of others. As a result, we all believe that our children are better than anyone else's and our wives are superior to all other women. If the person concerned happens to be a writer, he is convinced that his writings are as eloquent as can be or his poetry is the most exquisite verse imaginable. Mankind is bewitched by his own ideas. However, the more astute and critical a man happens to be, the more his judgments will be trustworthy. We still have to admit that unfortunately we all rarely indulge in critical self-assessments; that is even more the case when we surround ourselves with those who are willing to flatter us and extol everything we do simply in order to make us feel content. It is kings and other people in lofty positions who are the most prone to these dangers. Courtiers will try to outdo each other in offering encomia and phony flattery, all with the goal of gaining profit or influence. That was clearly the case with Father Martin and Roderic.

Roderic returned to his palace, convinced that Oppas had done him a grievous wrong and deserved to be further punished. He decided to keep the metropolitan bishop in prison while he worked out a way to discover where Florinda was and then take his full revenge on him. He decided not to have him killed immediately in case he had useful information about Florinda. His first decision was to enhance the surveillance activities in Toledo's suburbs and on all the roads leading out of the city. Large rewards were offered to anyone who was able to arrest her and whoever might be traveling with her.

As Oppas went back to his prison, he felt quite serene, since he was convinced of the correctness of the path he was pursuing and the sheer nobility of his cause. That was especially so, now that he had had the opportunity to reveal to the entire assembly the precise nature of Roderic's behavior, if only by allusion. Even so, he had no hopes of the assembly actually turning against Roderic. What concerned him was that the truth and submission to the inner conscience should eventually prevail—that being typical of those men of religion who choose to avoid the temptations of this lower world. Whenever such people are sincere in their faith, no one can possibly match them when it comes to ensuring that truth is triumphant. The reason is that they reject fame and fortune and show contempt for the fripperies of this world. The essential goal of their existence is to shun all such things. Oppas was such a person. The reason he was working so hard to restore his nephew to the throne was based solely on his desire to see the truth prevail.

Oppas spent several weeks in his temporary prison, and the thought of spending years there did not bother him. However, he was worried about Florinda; he had no idea where she was or where Ajilla and Chantilla had taken her. Even so, he assumed that Roderic had not been able to catch them, a belief that was bolstered by the confidence he had in the two young men's bravery and loyalty to him. But he was anxious to find out where she was and how she was faring. He was thinking about Alfonso as well and the mission that Roderic had sent him to complete. Oppas realized that Roderic had only done that in order to damage Alfonso's chances because he was well aware that he would try to rescue Florinda and restore the throne to himself. But in spite of all this, Oppas was so firm in his belief that the truth would prevail that he was not actually worried about those who held the opposite convictions. Truth was bound to emerge victorious, and sinners would inevitably be confounded. He could foresee Roderic foundering on the basis of his own evil actions, something that he had told the king himself to his face.

An intelligent person will make decisions as to how to lead his life on this earth, in the process duly acknowledging the pitfalls involved. For that reason he will inevitably view any relapse into evil as a kind of madness. That is because truth always wins and is the only thing that endures…

Chapter 54

Jerez and its Vines

Jerez is a city in the province of Cadiz in southern Spain; it lies between the city of Cadiz and Seville. It is some seventeen miles from Cadiz and is situated on the banks of a small river, the Guadalete, which has its source in the mountains of Cadiz province to the north and flows towards the southwest, leaving the city of Jerez to its right as it continues its way toward the Atlantic in a bay close to Cadiz. Jerez itself lies in a plain between two mountains that overlook it to east and west. A number of crops and plants are grown on the land between the city and the river, including vines. The city is actually renowned for its vines, and especially the wine known by the city's name, sherry, which is well known throughout Europe and is expensive. They age it themselves and offer it at mealtimes. Most of the sherry exported worldwide comes from winepresses on the outskirts of this city.

Sherry vines occupy a large portion of the land down to the river and also on the flats and slopes on the other bank. Vintners' homes are scattered among the vines, along with other strangely shaped buildings that are actually big rooms standing on rows of thin columns with high ceilings and copious windows along the walls to let in the air. This is where the vintners age the wines.

Close to where the Jerez valley branches off from the Guadalete is a plain that the historian, al-Maqqari, calls the Jerez Test.[46] It was there that the armies of Tariq the Berber commander and Roderic the Goth met, and it was to be a decisive blow in the Arab campaign to conquer Spain. The Arab invaders made the most of the booty and products that they

---

46 Dozy, part I.

managed to acquire. Beyond that, the chaotic state of affairs in Europe and the weakness of its forces led the Arabs to contemplate invading the continent as a whole. Had they actually continued their invasion to the north, they would not have encountered any opposition; no one would have stood in their path. However, they delayed their advance, and the opportunity was lost.

In the summer of 710 AD, in other words, a few months after the events in Toledo that we have already described, the vines in the Jerez region and its environs were fully ripe. Some farmers were already busy picking them, others were making props to support the weight of grape bunches that the trellises were supporting, others were getting the winepresses ready, and still others were transferring wines stored the previous year to other locations to make space for this year's crop.

The people doing these tasks were often from families who traced their origins to this region, but others were former prisoners of war who were now slaves. Some of this latter group had been members of the gentry in other lands,[47] but they had long since become inured to the humiliation involved. In any case, such servitude was not as hard as it might seem for such people at this particular time because everyone was suffering the same kind of treatment. Even so, the peasants were continually complaining about their lot. They were particularly critical of the king in Toledo; for reasons that we have already examined in some detail, the public was deeply dissatisfied with Roderic as monarch.

On the other hand, these people had heard that the Arabs had crossed the Straits and invaded their country, but they were not especially bothered by that fact nor did they worry themselves about it. Among their number was an old man who had spent most of his life traveling around Spain and neighboring regions in Africa; in fact, he had even gone as far as Egypt and Syria. He had observed the way things were in the East following the arrival of Islam. Whenever the Arabs were mentioned in his presence, he would always reply, "Only the Arabs can save us from this dreadful king of ours." So, when they told him that the Arabs had in fact crossed the Straits, his response was, "We'll soon be free!"

---

47 Dozy, part I.

Chapter 55

Maria

In the final days of July in this particular year (92 AH or 710 AD), this sheikh, whom we have just mentioned, was sitting in his cottage with his children and grandchildren all around him. The women were busy preparing the meal and making yogurt and cheese, while the children fed the animals or made baskets to carry the grapes when they were picked. Their only conversation was about the quantity of grapes and wine that would be harvested that year, although, truth to tell, there was not really any point to such discussion because none of it belonged to them. Peasants and their ilk were not allowed to acquire land or own buildings. That right was the privilege of the nobility, most of whom were either Romans or Goths. Peasants were only entitled to a meager share of the product. Even so, humans are always inclined to investigate the unknown, and that may explain why the sheikh and his children spent most of the day estimating the crop yield for the year, to such an extent that an argument broke out between two of them that distracted them from everything else going on around them. They were all seated in the shade of a large trellis whose branches created a kind of tent shaped like a bower. Underneath it, they had channeled a small canal where animals could take a drink and people could collect water. The people on this particular farm liked to shade themselves at this spot, among them the sheikh, his children, grandchildren, and married women.

This is the way they all were disposed as evening fell. Everyone who had spent the day repairing and propping up trellises, cleaning the storehouses, making baskets, and bringing in dry sticks for firewood had come back. One man might be carrying a basket on his head, while another might have a bag on his shoulder, a jug under his arm, a purse in his pocket, a loaf of bread in his hand, or something to chew in his mouth. Behind him would come a whole group of boys, one leading a lamb, another pulling a donkey. Yet another boy might be carrying a cluster of grapes that were not fully ripe yet and thus were not acidic enough. His father may well have tried to stop him doing that, but he had managed to hide it in his pocket and take a few surreptitious nibbles. By his side, his brother was threatening to tell his father if he did not give him a few grapes to eat, so the boy rushed over and hid himself in his mother's skirt—that very place would be able to protect him from all the disasters and catastrophes that fate might decide to hurl at him—as though it were the flag of Chosroes Anurshirwan, the mighty Persian king himself!

This life of natural simplicity, whereby mankind is nourished by the fruits of his own cultivation and the milk of his pasturage, is one in which his only ambition is to gather enough to feed and clothe his family for the rest of the year. Intentions are honest, and hearts are pure; loyalty and honesty prevail. If someone says that he is longing to see you, he really means it. It is not something that a person says habitually just in order to deceive or flatter someone else. True happiness—if indeed such a concept has validity—can only be found in these lowly homesteads and meadows where leaves grow again on the trees and people's hearts come to bloom along with them. Mankind's needs are few and his demands are simple, so there is no spite, or hatred, or greed, or slander, or hypocrisy. If humans have few demands in their lives and are not concerned with acquiring things, emotions like hate, envy, and other evil intentions rarely enter their hearts. It is only weak people who acquire such feelings when they have high expectations that they are unable to achieve through their own efforts. It is for that very reason that civilization is plagued by so many base motivations.

The peasant with his simple style of living is thus happy to live a life of security and justice, but he is nevertheless the most miserable of God's creatures because tyranny inevitably ruins his happiness by robbing him of the very source of that happiness, namely the products of his land. How could it be otherwise when he is not the owner of the land that he works, as was the case with the peasantry in Spain during the Middle Ages? So this sheikh cannot really be blamed for desiring a different form of government, even if it were to involve someone foreign.

The sunset's golden rays always delight the heart. People in cities spend a good deal of time hoping to see them, but they rarely have the chance. Peasants, on the other hand, can watch the sunset every evening, but unfortunately they are all otherwise preoccupied, preparing a meal or gathering under someone's roof or beneath some trees. As the sun set on this particular day, the members of this family—dozens of them, babies, young children, adolescent boys and girls—gathered together, the youngest of all being the happiest.

The person who was most concerned at this point was the sheikh himself, because he could never relax completely till he had made sure that all his children and grandchildren were safe and sound under this bower. That was especially so since, on direct orders from Roderic, the governor of the region had dragooned some peasants to serve as reinforcements to fight the invading Arabs from across the Straits.

The sheikh assumed that all his family was present, but, when he looked closely, he realized that one of his daughters had not arrived. She was kind and gentle and was his favorite daughter. Even so, he waited for a while in the hope that she would arrive. However, when she did not come, he asked his wife, "Where's Maria?"

"Hasn't she come back yet?" she replied.

"No," he said. "Where did you leave her?"

"I left her at the big storehouse on the hill," she replied. "She was washing some vessels and moving some full vats from one side to the other. Her brother, Butrus, was with her."

With that, she looked around her. "Butrus!" she called.

Butrus duly rushed over.

"Where did you leave your sister?" she asked him.

"I left her in the big storehouse," he replied. "Hasn't she come back yet?"

"No," his mother replied.

No sooner had the mother said that than Butrus dashed off in the direction of the hill.

"I'll be back soon," he said.

What made him move so fast was his realization that he should not have come back without her.

The moon had been waning for some time, and by now it was dark. The track between the vines was muddy and full of ruts. Even so, people who dealt with vines could easily walk along such paths with their eyes shut without tripping over branches or rocks. As the sheikh and his family waited for Butrus to come back, they were all on tenterhooks, trying to estimate how long it would take him to get there and where he might be at that point. But by the time they assumed he would be back, he still had not returned. They all waited impatiently, but Butrus was away for a very long time. Eventually the two parents could stand it no longer. The old sheikh leapt up like a young man and took a shortcut to the place where Butrus had gone, a route that his son did not know. Going by way of the river, the distance between the bower and that particular storehouse was over a hundred meters. The storehouse itself overlooked the river and most of the vineyards in that region.

Chapter 56

Guadalete

The sheikh reached the storehouse, panting for breath. He climbed the stairs to get to the door, but it was locked. There was no one there. He banged on the door several times, but there was no response. When he looked closely at the door, he noticed that, as usual, it was locked from the outside. He assumed that Maria must have left and locked the door behind her. As he stood at the top of the stairs to catch his breath and looked around him, he could see the city of Jerez on one bank of the river and the vineyards on the other. It was very dark, but he could still make out a whole series of lights on this side of the river; their number and the way they were scattered around suggested that there was a big group of people involved. The only people he knew around these parts were peasants and farm workers, and they would never have fires burning like this. It all made him very worried; for a moment he forgot about his missing daughter. As he stood there watching the fires, he could see the glow reflected in the river, like tiny lights glowing beneath the surface with their beams refracted in the waves. But for that, he would not have realized that the fires themselves were coming from the riverbank.

All of a sudden he came to himself and remembered his missing daughter. It occurred to him that she might have returned home by now or else her brother had come across her on his way back. But soon afterward he heard the sound of people running fast between the grapevines. When he listened carefully, he could make out his wife's voice, along with several of his children. He realized that they were trying to find out what had happened to Maria, so he called out to them. The first voice he heard was that of his wife, wondering where Maria was. When the sheikh heard her asking, his whole body shuddered and he began to panic.

"Where's Butrus?" he asked. "Has he come back yet?"

By now the old lady had reached the bottom of the stairs and bent over to extract a thorn that had stuck in the sole of her foot while she was running.

"Yes, Butrus has come back," she replied, "but he didn't find her."

The sheikh came down the stairs and joined his wife and a number of his children.

"It seems," he told them, "that Maria must have lost her way coming back home from here. Let's split up and take different routes back to our house. If anyone finds her, he should give a yell so the rest of us will stop looking for her. The code will be to say 'O, St. Peter!' If I don't get back any time soon, don't get alarmed."

His wife wanted to know why he had said that, but he did not wish to hang around and hear what she had to say. Leaping from one outcrop to the next among the vineyards, he made his way down to the river, stumbling once in a while over some animal fodder or rocks. It was still pitch dark, so he made sure to keep an eye on the river in order not to lose his sense of direction. Whenever the river disappeared behind some high trellises or hills, he worried that he might lose track and have to walk a lot further.

Fortunately for him, the river rarely disappeared from view. Once he was close, he could make out the lights on the bank. He heard lots of noise, too, which he recognized as camel sounds; he had heard them before during his travels abroad, but there was nothing like this in Spain itself. No sooner had he heard the din and caught the scent of Arabs than he realized that he was quite close to them and then recalled the things he had heard about their arrival in Spain. While realizing that he was now right alongside their camp, he was still perplexed at the apparent ease with which they had managed to reach this spot.

Before long, he reached a hill that served as a vantage point from which he could survey the scene laid out in front of him. He was looking down on a broad plain stretching as far as the river. On the far bank were tents with fires burning in between them, while on the near bank he could make out a fire burning. Close to it was a huge tent, although it was so dark that he could not make out the color. He paused for a moment, thinking about his daughter Maria, and considered searching for her somewhere else, but then he decided to go down to that tent and check on the people inside before returning home. His lengthy travels in Africa and Syria had taught him that the Arabs were honest folk who always dealt kindly with the peoples of the territories that they conquered. He had even learned a few Arabic phrases, even though the language itself was strange and far removed from his own. The years had taught him both courage and forbearance.

As he made his way down the hill, he was more and more curious about this tent. While most of the tents were clustered on the other bank, this one was set apart. It occurred to him that the force must have reached the river that night and started to cross it, but then it had grown dark before they had been able to complete the operation. So they had postponed things till tomorrow.

The sheikh kept walking till he was close to the tent. As he listened, his heart took a leap. He could hear his daughter's voice inside, sobbing as she spoke. Utterly fearless and overcome by emotion, he could not stop himself surging toward the tent out of fear for his beloved daughter. As he approached the fires, he came to the tent's entrance and was challenged by a sentry with sword and lance fully drawn. The man was on the point of arresting him.

"Who are you?" he asked.

The sheikh understood what he meant and gave a terse response to the effect that he wanted to enter the tent.

The man made him wait outside while he entered the tent and asked permission for him to enter. He soon returned and indicated to the sheikh that he could go inside. As he entered, his beard was all aquiver. But, in spite of his old age and grey hair, he was still fit and alert, that being a common feature of villagers and peasants.

Chapter 57

Badr and Julian

Once the sheikh was inside the tent, he looked all around in search of his daughter. He spotted her sitting on the ground in a corner. The light was very dim inside the tent, but even so, she saw her father, jumped to her feet, and rushed over to him.

"Father, Father!" she cried.

The sheikh hugged her, while for her part she was so shocked and delighted that she started to cry. As he looked further into the tent, he saw a man with a big head wearing a turban and cloak; he realized that he must be a Berber. By his side was another man wearing Gothic clothing, and he did not have to look at him for long before recognizing him as Julian, the governor of Sabta. That did not surprise him because he had already heard that Julian had reached an agreement with the Muslims to fight against the Goths. He had assumed at first that it was simply a nasty rumor, but, now that he had seen Julian in the tent, he realized it was true. The Arabs were bound to win.

As the sheikh hugged his daughter and tried to calm her fears, all sorts of thoughts were running through his mind.

"Is this girl your daughter perhaps?" he heard the governor of Sabta ask him.

"Yes, my lord, she is," he replied.

"You have nothing to worry about," Julian told him, "she is quite safe. Do not imagine that your arrival has changed our plans regarding her. The commander had every intention of returning her to you safe and sound. She is only crying because she's scared. She assumed that these

Arabs were going to treat her the same way your overlord Roderic treats women. That's why, God willing, he's about to lose his sway."

He scowled as he made that last comment, but no one present realized why he did so.

"The reason why she was brought here," he went on, "is that one of our commander's men went out to do something this afternoon, spotted the girl walking on the road, and brought her here, assuming that she was a female prisoner. When the commander got to hear about this, he proceeded to upbraid the man. They were still arguing fiercely when you arrived and entered the tent."

No sooner had Julian finished what he was saying than a young man in Arab dress and a turban on his head leapt to his feet. But his facial features showed clearly that he was neither Arab nor Berber; he was clearly in the prime of youth and full of energy and vitality.

"So," he said angrily, addressing Julian, "I see you've deprived me of my booty, simply in order to placate your own community."

"Don't be so impetuous, Badr," Tariq told him with a smile. "You'll get booty enough in good time. This is just the beginning. Tomorrow we'll confront the Toledo army. Any prisoners and booty you capture then will be entirely yours. But for the moment, we're not at war with anyone. We can't treat this girl as a prisoner. This is her father, and he's an old man. You've seen for yourself how much he loves her. It's not right for us to ruin their lives without due cause. Islam demands both fair treatment and justice. Prisoners of war belong to their master; that's fair enough. Someone who is as courageous and bold as you will certainly be able to get the best booty and the most beautiful slave girls."

"Return to your home safe and sound," Tariq said, turning to the old man. "Our only purpose in invading this land is to deal kindly with its people. Charity and fairness are both enjoined on us by our faith. You and the entire people of Spain can rest assured that anyone who does not make war against us will be under our protection and need have no fears whatsoever. But those who take up arms against us will find themselves being dealt with by the sword."

"Boy!" he yelled, whereupon a Berber servant entered.

"Accompany the sheikh and his daughter back to their home," he said.

The sheikh was on the point of kissing Tariq's hand, but he withdrew it. Wishing him well, he told him to leave. As the old sheikh departed, he had the best possible impression of Tariq.

"That's how rulers are supposed to govern the people," he told himself, "not by using force and compulsion."

Meanwhile, Badr remained silent out of respect for Tariq, but he resented Julian's behavior because he believed that it was his intervention that had robbed him of his spoils. Even so, he kept his emotions in check and left the tent so as to keep his feelings to himself.

Chapter 58

Escape

A while ago, we left Florinda, her aunt, and the two men, Ajilla and Chantilla, making their way around the Toledo outskirts. As we saw earlier, the reason was that Ajilla and Chantilla had been waiting for Florinda at the bottom of the palace wall on a cold and thundery night. Once Oppas had surprised Roderic by appearing late at night at the palace, it was easier for Florinda to get away. She had rushed over to the window carrying as much clothing as she could and a small icon of the Virgin Mary. Florinda placed tremendous faith in the Virgin's kindness to women, so she covered the icon in her gown and wrapped herself up in a big cloak. Her aged great aunt helped her get ready. Once they had done everything they could, the old woman looked out the window and shouted. The two men were ready, shinnied up the tree, and eased Florinda safely down to the ground. The old lady followed, bringing all the necessities with her. As they left the gardens, the winds were blowing a gale, and it was thundering. Until they reached the boat, they were so scared that they forgot about everything else. Florinda was expecting to find Alfonso waiting for her, because that is what he had written to tell her. When she saw that the boat was empty, she became even more scared and started to panic. She was too shy to ask the men about it, but she spoke to her aunt. The old woman looked at the two men.

"Where is Prince Alfonso?" she asked them.

"He hasn't come with us, madam," replied Chantilla.

"Where is he, then?" she asked.

Chantilla was afraid to say anything to make Florinda even more worried. He already knew that they were in love with each other;

in fact, the two men were well aware of the reasons for Oppas giving them this particular task, even though the bishop probably imagined that they were simply dumb machines only fully capable of carrying out his mission. Alfonso still imagined that no one else knew about his relationship with Florinda, but then that is the way it always is with people in love. A young man will fall in love with a girl and she with him, and they will consort with each other, assuming that people are not aware of the fact, even though there will probably be some people who know every syllable and sentence that has ever passed between the two of them. The people who are most knowledgeable on the subject are always the household servants. They will give the impression that they are actually preparing meals or setting the table, but the truth is that their ears are always pricked to listen to secret conversations between guests and dinner companions. They pride themselves on their ability to pass on such information and even embellish it in accordance with their feelings with regard to the person making a particular statement. If they like that person, they will turn his negatives into positives—and the best quality where servants are concerned is generosity—otherwise it is the opposite, and any good qualities become faults. Ajilla and Chantilla were both servants of this kind, but, as noted above, they were also former prisoners. They were both aware of the love affair between Alfonso and Florinda; in addition, they knew from gossip that Roderic was also in love with her. When Oppas had told them to undertake this task, they already knew the secret and were determined to do their utmost, all out of love and respect for Alfonso and because they loathed Roderic and his courtiers. They had observed Alfonso following the king's orders by leaving the city at the head of a column of horsemen and realized that he had been sent away on a mission.

Chantilla saw how flustered Florinda was as she asked about Alfonso. He was afraid that any answer he might give would alarm her even more. He had not prepared himself for such a situation. Instead, he concentrated on rowing the boat along with his brother to take advantage of the river's current. The wind was blowing so hard that the lamp had gone out. But in spite of all his concerns, he realized that he had to tell her something.

"As far as we know," he told Florinda, "Alfonso is at the metropolitan's house. He was the one who told us to bring you there."

That calmed her down somewhat, but she was still worried. In spite of the intense love Alfonso had for her, she had not expected him to tell anyone else about the plan to rescue her. Her feelings at this point were thus a mixture of reproach and doubt. Even so, she decided to keep her feelings to herself until she could actually see her beloved Alfonso and confront him face to face. In any case, blaming someone involves friction between people's hearts and affections, something that only serves to intensify their feelings of love and attraction...

They kept following the river in the hope of reaching the bank near Oppas's house, since they were supposed to rendezvous with him and bring Florinda with them. The river was churning, and the wind was still blowing hard, so it was very difficult to make any headway, quite apart from the fact that it was dark. Every time Florinda felt scared, she sought refuge in God, taking out the icon and kissing it. Once she had done that, she felt calmer and more relaxed. That is one of the benefits of a strong faith, and there is no better means of consolation known to mankind.

Almost half the night had passed before they were able to reach dry land. Once they had clambered ashore, they discussed what to do next.

"I think you should wait here," said Ajilla, who was more astute and daring than his brother. "I'll go to the metropolitan's house and bring back someone to carry all these things."

Everyone agreed with his plan, and so he hurried off until he reached a point close to the bishop's house. He immediately noticed that it was surrounded by the king's troops. Astounded, he withdrew, trying to imagine why so many soldiers were there. Before long, he spotted some of them talking to Oppas and hid in an alcove so he could pick up bits of the conversation. He gathered that the soldiers had come to arrest Oppas, but that did not worry him because he had complete faith in the bishop's abilities and authority. People will always have great confidence in their priests, teachers, and parents. Every pupil believes that his own teacher is the cleverest of all, his priest is the most devout, and his father is capable of doing anything, even if there is no evidence to justify such a belief. But in Oppas's case, we have already noted his dignity, nobility, and sheer intelligence. With that in mind, Ajilla had no fears about the bishop, but he was now very worried about Florinda because he realized that Oppas was only being arrested because Florinda had managed to escape.

Once the troops had left with Oppas, he edged his way toward the palace in the hope of talking to some of the servants. As he made his way toward the entrance, he assumed that it would be easy to get in now that the troops had left. But to his astonishment there were yet more troops surrounding the palace again; they were forcing everyone inside to leave, smashing their way into the house and treating the servants very harshly.

As Ajilla watched the scene, he was soon aware of the danger he himself was in and the enormous peril that Florinda would face if the king were to find out where she was. As he rushed away, his only concern now was with Florinda, especially when he realized how important she was to both Alfonso and Oppas. He made up his mind that he would do whatever he and his brother possibly could to rescue her and protect her, to the very last breath of their lives.

Chapter 59

The Letter

Meanwhile, Florinda was sitting on the ground, with her arms wrapped around a purse in her lap. It was still very cold and windy, and she kept looking around her. Everything that had happened to her that day and night had made her feel incredibly tired, not least her worries about having the entire scandal exposed. She started feeling drowsy, the more so since, now that she had managed to escape the clutches of the lecherous king, she felt able to relax a bit. Leaning her head on her hands, she closed her eyes and fell asleep. When her aunt noticed that she had fallen asleep, she too felt able to relax a bit, but Chantilla remained fully alert. He was worried because his brother was taking so long, wondering what on earth could have happened to him. He started blaming him for leaving them in this spot where they were so exposed to the wind and cold, and convinced himself that, if he had been the one to undertake the mission, he would have been able to finish it sooner than this and solve any problems that might have arisen. Even so, it was not long before he saw his brother coming back. He was amazed to see him alone.

"Come on," Ajilla told him, "we need to get out of these Toledo suburbs as soon as possible. Starting tomorrow morning, the king's bound to be sending out scouts to look for us."

Florinda woke up with a start. "Woe is me!" she cried. "Where are we going? Help me, O my Savior! Where's Alfonso?"

"There was no one in the house, my lady," Ajilla told her.

"Not even Oppas?" she said. "Did you see Alfonso there?"

"Alfonso wasn't there, my lady," he replied.

"So where is he, then?" she asked in a panic. "Oh my God, where's Alfonso? How do you know he wasn't there?"

"Because I watched Oppas being led away under guard to the royal palace," Ajilla replied. "I saw another troop of guards going into Oppas's house and bringing all the servants out. None of them even mentioned Alfonso. Maybe he's still in his own house."

"No," Chantilla interrupted, "our master, Alfonso, had not returned to his own palace before we left."

"Where was he, then?" she asked.

"He'd left on a mission," he replied, "under orders from the king himself."

Florinda now remembered what the king had told her about Alfonso being banished. At the time she had assumed he was simply threatening her, but now she realized that it was true. But she still did not know if he had been actually banished or put in prison.

"Are you sure he's left the city?" she asked. "Do you know where he's gone?"

"I'm certain he left his palace under royal escort, but I've no idea where he was going. We must assume that he's been sent on a mission to certain cities in the realm…"

Ajilla interrupted his brother again. "I think," he said, "he was dispatched as head of an expedition to certain cities to quell a rebellion or else to check on some recalcitrant provinces. It's happening a lot these days. But, God willing, all's well! Once we've settled somewhere and can feel safe from spies, we can start making inquiries to find out exactly where he is. We've done everything we can to make both you and him as secure as possible. We're both devoted to him and will always work assiduously in his interests. But now we must leave here at once. Fleeing tyranny is always a good thing to do. So let's leave discussion of our next moves till later. We'll go back to the boat and follow the river until we're out of the city. It's raining and thundering so hard that people there, especially the guards, have other things to worry about. Once we're safe and sound somewhere else, we can start planning what to do next."

So saying, he went over to Florinda to help her stand up. She was still very worried, of course, but even so she managed to get up on her own and headed straight for the boat. Her aunt followed her with the bag of clothes. That left just one box, and the two men helped each other carry it to the boat.

By now the storm had abated somewhat, and the river's current helped them get out of the city limits. They reached a place where they could not see a single soul; the only sound to be heard was frogs croaking. By now most of the night was over, so they took refuge in a cove behind a hill, which provided shelter from the winds.

"Now we're safe, my lady," Ajilla told Florinda. "If you feel like sleeping until it's morning, that's fine, and your aunt as well. We'll keep watch in turns till the sun comes up. Then we can check which way we need to go next."

So Florinda slept for the rest of the night, albeit fitfully, since her worries kept piling up on her. She could not stop thinking about her beloved Alfonso and what might have happened to him, also about the fact that Roderic was solely responsible for ruining their lives. She remembered her father as well, and how fond she had been of him ever since she was a child. How angry he would be when he heard what had happened to her, and what a sense of failure and disappointment he would have when he had to grit his teeth in the face of Roderic's dreadful behavior and avoid confronting him with it. She told herself that she should write to her father and complain about the way Roderic had dealt with her and urge him to take revenge on her behalf. So, when she woke up, she took a piece of cloth and wrote on it the letter that has already been mentioned. She called to Ajilla. When he came over, she handed him the letter, the tears she had shed while writing it still visible in her eyes.

"You and your brother have been so noble and brave on my behalf," she said. "You've promised me to look for Alfonso. Now I'd like to request that you send this letter to my father. Do you know who he is?"

"Yes, my lady," Ajilla replied. "He's Count Julian, the governor of Sabta."

"That's right. Can you take this letter to him?"

He nodded his head to indicate that he would do so willingly.

"However," he went on, "before we do anything else, I think we need to find somewhere safe for you to stay. I must know where I am to go when I return with an answer."

Florinda looked over to her aunt.

"What do you think, Auntie?" she asked. "Where can we go so we're safe and secure?"

The old woman stared at the ground but said nothing for a while. Florinda asked her a second time. With a broad smile on her face, the old woman lifted her head.

"I think I've come up with an answer," she said. "In these circumstances it'll be the best thing for us."

"What's that?" Florinda asked.

"You all know," she said, "that this country has a lot of monasteries where monks go from all over the world in order to worship God Almighty. They're usually situated in desolate spaces or on mountains; lay people rarely go there. The monks are cut off from the entire world. If we stayed in such a monastery, we'd be safe until the whole situation becomes somewhat easier to deal with."

Chapter 60

The Mountain Monastery

Ajilla now stepped forward, as though he had just remembered something important.

"Your aunt's idea has just reminded me about monasteries for unmarried women," he said. "That would obviously be best for my lady because she would be among women in the same position as herself."

"You're right, Ajilla," Florinda's aunt interrupted. "I'm aware of the existence of such monasteries, but I haven't finished what I was saying yet. They would be fine for Florinda and me, but we still need to keep one of you with us. Where would you stay, since you can't stay in the monastery?"

She paused for a moment, but her expression made it clear that she had more to say.

"In Spain," she went on, "there are some monasteries for both monks and nuns, although they never mix. The reason for their existence is that some widows decide after the death of their husbands to retreat from the world into a life of prayer and devotion. So they stay in special monasteries; there may be unmarried nuns with them as well. But others will take their asceticism and renunciation of the world to such lengths that they never leave the monasteries where they are residing. There are many such institutions in Spain, as I'm sure you already know. I happen to know of one of these institutions quite close to Toledo, with one wing for monks and another for nuns. Each group occupies a part of the monastery building, but there's no contact with the other one and only rarely with the outside world, either. The only place where the monks and nuns meet is during prayer times in church. One of the rules, I've discovered, is

233

that the nuns cannot speak to anyone, including the abbot or his deputy, unless there are other nuns present.[48] Such precise requirements are intended to avoid any kind of untoward conduct. If Florinda agrees to the idea, I think we should make our way to that monastery. She and I can stay in the nuns' quarters, and you can stay with the monks. We can stay there as guests till we find out what's going to happen..."

"God bless you, Auntie!" Florinda said, turning in her direction. "That's clearly the right thing to do. Let's go to the monastery. Is it far?"

"It's about a day or so's journey from here," her aunt replied. "The road's not paved, so there'll be no one spying on us on the way."

"Do you know the way yourself?" Florinda asked.

"I think I do," she replied. "I passed by it a few years back. Let's get going with God's blessings!"

"But first, my dear Auntie," Florinda said, "I think Ajilla should take the letter to my father. If he comes back with news for us, he can bring it to this monastery."

"That's fine," her aunt replied. "Do what you wish."

Florinda now looked at Ajilla. "Go with our Lord's blessing," she told him. "When you come back, head for the mountain monastery we've been talking about. If you can find out anything about Prince Alfonso, you're too intelligent for me to need to tell you what to do."

Ajilla beamed to be receiving such praise. He gave them all a bow, said farewell, and rode off. The rest of them got out of the boat, each carrying some of the baggage. They then made their way through the hills and mountains, with the old woman in front as though heading for a house she went to every day.

They walked for several hours without meeting a single soul. Most of the hills were bare, apart from a few scattered trees in valleys that were obviously untended. The previous night's rainfall had flooded some of them, and there were streams to cross. Once the sun came up, the day was clear and warm. The path was muddy, and they were soon tired, especially Florinda, who was not used to such hardships, not to mention her continuing worries about her beloved Alfonso.

---

48 Ruhi, part II.

They walked for most of the day. At nighttime, Chantilla cooked some food, made all necessary preparations, and kept watch. They spent most of the next day walking as well, and their conversation was restricted to things they had already discussed. As the sun was setting, they finally reached a mountain slope from which they could look down on a huge building more like a fortress than a monastery.

"There it is!" exclaimed the old woman as soon as she saw it. "We've arrived, but we still need to climb up to it."

"Then let's start climbing," Florinda replied, gathering her skirts and heading swiftly upward. She was obviously eager to get there, take some rest, and send Chantilla back to Toledo to find out what had happened to Alfonso. They now all made their way toward the monastery building, which was situated on a flat outcrop on the mountainside. It was an ancient building with a peculiar shape, surrounded by an enormous stone wall; the entire structure may well have been the size of three or four kasbahs. The basic shape was a square, with each side about five hundred feet in length. The wall was extremely high and had no windows, except for a few vertical slits at the very top. There was just one door on the side. Compared with the height of the wall, it was minute; to the observer, it looked like a dot on a page. Above the door, there was a lofty tower at the top of the wall, looking just like a fortress, obviously a place for the watchman to keep a lookout.[49]

Florinda, her aunt, and Chantilla stood there gazing admiringly at this imposing structure. They were all panting with sheer exhaustion.

"May I knock on the door, my lady, and ask permission to enter?" Chantilla asked, after they had had time to recover their breath a little.

"Go ahead," she replied.

Chantilla went over to the door. It was steel plated. The thickness of the metal was obvious from the nail heads that protruded from its surface; it was only a bit taller than the height of an average man. He looked to the side to see if there was some kind of ring to pull but found nothing. Just then he noticed a rope dangling from the top of the door. He grabbed it and pulled hard. When he heard a bell ring inside, he knew he had done the right thing. After a moment's pause, a head poked out of

---

49 *Encyclopedia Britannica.*

the window in the tower at the top; all they could see was a mop of white hair, a protruding nose, a pair of eyes with prominent eyebrows, and a heavily wrinkled forehead. The old man looked down at them without saying a word. Chantilla knew how exhausted Florinda was, so he did not wait to see if the man would say anything.

"Will you give shelter to some strangers," he asked, "if only for a little while?"

Chantilla had not even finished what he was saying before the head disappeared without responding. Soon they could hear the jangling of keys on the other side of the door, which led them to believe that their long trek would soon be at an end. The jangling went on for a while; then they heard a creaking noise, so they went up to the door on the assumption that it was about to open. However, it stayed shut, and they had to wait longer. The jangling and creaking were repeated, but still nothing opened. They were getting tired of waiting like this and worried that something untoward might be about to happen. That applied especially to Florinda, who was standing there with her eyes riveted on the door.

The old lady was sitting on a rock, her eyelids dropping with exhaustion after the long trek. She was almost falling asleep, but just then she was roused by an even louder creak and noticed that the door was slowly opening, almost as though the person doing it were carrying an enormous weight. Florinda stayed where she was, but Chantilla moved toward the door. He was greeted by the old man, who was wearing the simple habit of monks, a single cloak-like garment that covered his body as far as the knees, below which his legs and feet were bare. The monk had obviously spent many years walking over rocks and tree trunks, so the soles of his feet were as leathery as sandals. The old man came outside, leaning on a knotted cane that he clutched in his bony fingers. His knuckles were swollen, sticking out from his hands so that he could no longer stretch them—almost as though they had been designed for this very cane and had frozen in place while he was holding it.

The monk's habit had short sleeves, so they could see his rough-skinned elbows, which, along with his feet, might have led them to think that he had spent his entire life crawling on his soles and elbows.

Chapter 61

Waiting

The old monk stood there by the door, staring at them. They all hurried over. Chantilla, who was ahead of the others, took off his cap and leaned over to kiss the man's hand. Florinda and her aunt did the same.

"So what's brought you here?" the monk asked in his gruff, rustic tone.

"We've come to seek the blessing of the abbot," Chantilla told him. "Is there any problem with that?"

"Certainly not," the monk replied. "The monastery is in two parts, one for monks, the other for nuns. Which of the two do you want?"

"As you see fit," Chantilla said.

"In any case," the monk went on, "the decision rests with the abbot."

He now went inside and signaled to them to follow him. Doing so, they found a door leading to a short corridor with two other steel-plated doors. Eventually another corridor led out into a large courtyard covered by a blue dome. They had barely crossed this space before they heard the door closing behind them. Looking around them, they could see the enormously high walls of the monastery. They were in a yard paved with solid stone, or it may actually have been part of the mountain itself. Florinda felt as though she were in some kind of fearsome prison.

The monk took them a few paces to the left, where they reached another door built into the wall. He opened it, and they went inside. There was a room adjoining a number of others.

"This is our guesthouse," the monk said as he showed them the room. "Stay here while I go to see the abbot and tell him about your arrival. Whatever he says will be done."

That said, he turned to leave, but just then they heard a bell ringing. As the monk listened to the number of chimes, he threw down his cane, crossed himself and bowed in respect. They all did the same, although none of them knew why they were doing so.

"I can't go to see the abbot now," he told them as he turned around to talk to them. "It's time for Mass. Everyone will be going to the church, and I must go, too. Once the Mass is over, we'll see what happens…"

When Florinda heard the word Mass mentioned, she was delighted. She remembered her fervent prayers of a few days ago and the way God had rescued her. She went over to the monk.

"Sir," she asked in her sweet voice, "Is it permitted for us to attend the celebration of the Mass?"

"Our Savior never forbids anyone," the monk replied. "The church is never closed to any soul."

They all followed the monk across the courtyard till they reached the center, where there was a huge door. Before they even reached it, they could smell the scent of incense and knew that it was the entrance to the church. They entered behind the monk and immediately noticed the altar in the center. The nave was divided into two: one side for monks, the other for nuns. The monk showed them to a place where they could stand and listen to the Mass. Of the group, Florinda was the most fervent in her devotions; how she beat her breast, how she begged God and Christ Jesus to save her beloved fiancé Alfonso from danger and bring him back to her safe and sound!

Once the Mass was over, the congregation went its own way, the nuns through one door and the monks through another. The monk took Florinda and her companions back to the guesthouse. As they were leaving the church, he noticed that Florinda took some money out of her pocket and put it underneath the icon in front of which she had been offering prayers. He noticed the gleaming gold coins and surmised that these guests of theirs must be wealthy; they might endow the monastery treasury with a lot of money. Leaning on his cane, he hurried back to the abbot's quarters and told him about these strangers who had just arrived.

"From their appearance and accent," he said, "they seem to be from Toledo. That's confirmed by the amount of money they've given us. Shall I allow them to come and see you?"

"No," the abbot replied, "I'll come to their quarters to see them."

So saying, he stood up and put on his modest cloak. It was somewhat finer than the one the monk was wearing, and longer, with a rope around the waist; he also put on wooden clogs and a black beretta on his head. The abbot was middle-aged, portly in appearance, handsome and well built, with a keen eye. He used to read a lot and spoke well. It was, in fact, these qualities that had led him to assume the role of abbot when he was still relatively young, with dozens of monks under his control, many of whom were just as old as the old monk himself. In the clergy, promotion is normally based on merit; nepotism or favoritism of any kind play no part in the process. Everyone is equally cloistered and sequestered, and heritage and profession are irrelevant. All monks must do their part when it comes to activities and share equally in the duties and chores. If a monk is elevated to the abbot's position or something similar when he is still young, that means that he has been deemed superior to his colleagues in the fulfillment of that function. As a result, the person chosen often becomes the object of jealousy or even hatred. But, in the case of this particular abbot, it was the opposite. His kindness, modesty, and generosity of spirit were natural gifts of his, and his decision in this case to go to the guest quarters in order to greet them was a typical example of his humility and thoughtfulness.

Florinda had returned from the Mass and was seated in one of the guest rooms. Her mind was preoccupied worrying about Alfonso, and she was lost in her own thoughts. The old lady was seated by her side without saying a word; she was so exhausted that she had dozed off. Chantilla was standing by the door, waiting for the monk to return. The sun was about to set; in the mountains, that was an awesome spectacle, especially when there were so few people around.

Chapter 62

A Conversation with the Abbot

Before long, the abbot himself arrived, carrying a piece of parchment that he had been perusing when the monk had spoken to him earlier. When Chantilla saw him, he stood up out of respect, thinking that he had either seen him before or someone very like him. But on this particular occasion, he did not have much time to reflect on the thought. When the abbot arrived at the guesthouse door, Chantilla indicated to Florinda that the abbot had arrived. Going over to the abbot, he took his hand and kissed it, but the abbot looked extremely uncomfortable about such phony gestures. As he neared the door, Florinda emerged to greet him, and she too kissed his hand, as did her aunt. As the abbot greeted the young girl, he did not meet her eyes, as was the custom with monks. However, when she sat down in front of him, he remembered that he had seen her before.

"Is this lady your mother?" he asked.

"No, Reverend Sir," Florinda replied, "she's my aunt."

As she replied in this way, she asked God to keep the number of questions few. She was scared in case he asked for her own name and origins. Had he done so, she would have felt bound to reply truthfully, since she abhorred lies. She much preferred that the questions be addressed to Chantilla since he was much more adept when it came to wriggling out of telling the truth. But then, she remembered that people always put their trust in men of religion; they are quite willing to confess to things and admit all the terrible things they have done, even if they are particularly bad. That realization made her change her mind; she decided that, if the occasion demanded, she would confess everything to the abbot.

All these thoughts went through her mind in a flash, so, when the abbot posed the next question, she was fully prepared to answer.

"Where have you come from?" he asked.

"If you would allow it, Reverend Sir," she said, turning in his direction, "I would like to suggest something that will, I trust, not cause offense..."

"Not at all," the abbot replied. "Go ahead."

"If you need to ask questions about us," she went on, "I trust that it can be in the form of a confession, since our story involves a secret that cannot be revealed to a single soul. That would be the only way..."

The abbot nodded his agreement.

"The only reason I've been asking about you," he went on, "is that I want to make sure that we can be of service to you in some way. You are entirely free to choose whether to answer or not. At all events, you are our honored guests."

"We are very grateful to you," said Florinda, impressed by the abbot's kindness. "But for that, we would not feel safe telling you our secrets. But revealing such things to a person such as yourself is a form of release and mercy. May we close the door?"

Chantilla had heard some of what Florinda had been saying and moved away from the door. The abbot, meanwhile, went over and was about to close it when he gestured to Florinda's aunt, as if to say: "Should she be allowed to hear your confession?"

Florinda realized what he meant. "This aunt of mine," she told the abbot, "is the repository of all my secrets. There's no harm in her staying."

The abbot closed the door, and the room grew dark. He went back, opened the door, and clapped his hands. A monk soon arrived with an oil lamp, placed it in a niche on the wall, then left. The abbot now closed the door again and sat down to listen to what Florinda wished to tell him. No sooner had she started talking than he was eager to hear the entire story.

"We come from Toledo," she said. "We had to get away to avoid being killed. Fleeing the city was our only means of escape."

"Why did not you seek the aid of the king?" the abbot asked. "He's supposed to be responsible for the care of oppressed people."

Florinda did not know what to say. The abbot immediately realized that she was troubled and was eager to hear what had actually happened.

"The king appears to be one of the people you fear," he commented.

This time the aunt took over.

"What's the point in keeping things hidden?" she said. "Yes, indeed, we're afraid of the king himself."

Florinda was shocked that she was being so frank, but she took comfort from the fact that this was in the form of a confession, which could never be revealed to anyone else. The abbot duly noted how shocked she was.

"Who is the man who came with you both?" he asked.

"He's one of our family retainers," Florinda replied.

"Isn't he one of Prince Alfonso's men?" the abbot asked with a smile.

When Florinda heard Alfonso's name mentioned, the color rose in her face till she almost choked. Unable to respond, she turned to her aunt as though to beg her to find a way out.

"Yes, Reverend Sir," the aunt replied, "he is indeed one of the aides of Prince Alfonso, son of King Witiza, the former king of Spain. Do you know him?"

The abbot's smile now turned to a frown, but he realized that he had to respond.

"Yes, I know Witiza, and his sons and entire family. Who in the clergy does not also know his brother, the Metropolitan Oppas? Who has not benefited from his wise counsels, his sterling example, his prudence, and his learning? Time rarely gives us such a man, but..."

Once Florinda heard the way the Abbot praised Oppas, her mind was put at ease. The abbot obviously supported the cause of the former king, so she could reveal her secret without fear. Even so, she noticed that he seemed reluctant to tell her what was on his mind for reasons that she would have been afraid to probe if it were not for the institution of confession. For that reason she made up her mind to find out what he really thought, confident that it would remain a secret.

"Don't you know where Oppas is now?" she asked.

"No," the abbot replied. "Where is he?"

"For two days he's been in prison."

"Who put him in prison?" the abbot asked in astonishment.

"King Roderic," she replied. "He sent a squadron of cavalry to his house and dragged him out of bed."

The abbot leapt to his feet, clearly furious.

"They dragged him off to prison," he said. "Someone as eminent as Oppas can be put in prison? May God forever disclaim sheer ignorance! How can they even dare to touch his hand without kissing it? How can they even address him without using words of the utmost respect and reverence?"

Florinda could now be sure that the abbot was a supporter of Oppas. She now felt safe in asking the abbot for help and advice about Alfonso. However, she felt bashful and looked down at the floor.

Her aunt continued the conversation in her stead.

"Alfonso..." she asked. "Do you know him?"

"Of course," the abbot replied, "I've known him from childhood. We'd often meet in Toledo on feast days in the days of his late father."

The old lady now stood up and gave the abbot a piercing look.

"The time for concealment is over," she said. "I can tell you that the young girl you see in front of you is Alfonso's fiancée. The king tried to wrench her away from him by force and has sent him off on a mission to some distant part of Spain. Once she realized what the king's intentions were, she fled from the palace. Since then, we've learned that Roderic arrested Oppas because he helped rescue her from the king's clutches. That is the way things are..."

Chapter 63

A New Task

The abbot now took a closer look at Florinda. "This is the daughter of Julian, the governor of Sabta, Alfonso's fiancée, isn't it?" he asked. "I was the primary witness at the ceremony of her betrothal to Alfonso, which her family had been discussing ever since they were children. The betrothal took place, and Oppas was the main agent for the match. So how can Roderic even dare to sever the bond?"

Once the old lady had heard what the abbot had to say, she remembered that she had seen him frequenting the Toledo palace during Witiza's reign, but wearing different vestments.

"Aren't you Father Sergius?" she asked.

"Indeed I am," the abbot replied. "I was a priest representing this monastery at the Toledo court. But when I saw the way the conspiracies were piling up against the late king and was unable to help him in any way, I decided to live in this monastery. Eventually I became its abbot. If Oppas had taken my advice, we could have both lived here safe and sound."

The abbot now looked at Florinda.

"Rest assured, young lady," he said, "that your secret is safely buried in a deep well here. Let me tell you that I am here to help both you and Oppas, come what may. God forgive him! How many times did I tell him to leave Toledo and come to the monastery where we would be able to worship God and distance ourselves from the world's intrigues and the cravings of men? We have enough provisions and wealth here to last us a lifetime. In spite of my suggestions, he refused to stay here. It's my belief that he decided to remain in Toledo to protect his brother's children, most of all Alfonso."

He lowered his head. "So," he said sadly, "Oppas is in prison…"

"We've been told they took him away to prison," Florinda said, "but we don't actually know whether they put him in prison or killed him. After we settle in this monastery, we plan to send this young man back to Toledo to try to find out what has really happened. He could bring us back the actual facts."

"No, no," the abbot interrupted. "That's no good. They'll recognize him and realize that he's one of the retainers of Prince Alfonso or Metropolitan Oppas. They may well arrest him, or even put him in prison or kill him. Leave it all to me. I can see it's my duty to investigate this entire matter. Try to relax till we get some news." So saying, he stood up.

"Try to get some rest now," he said. "You've traveled a long way. The monastery is at your disposal; we're all supporters of the late King Witiza. We'll stand firm with his son and all those who choose to put their faith in him. Would you prefer to stay in the nuns' quarters and your servant Chantilla in the monks', or would you rather stay here in the guesthouse where you will be the only occupants?"

Florinda stood up as well, feeling as though a heavy load had been lifted from her shoulders. She gave thanks to God because He had again answered her prayers as she clung to the hope that she would soon be free. Bending down, she kissed Sergius's hand, then asked her aunt's advice about where to stay.

"I think we should stay here," her aunt replied, "far removed from other people, with Chantilla close by. We can wait here to see what happens next."

"So it shall be," said the abbot.

When he left, night had fallen. Monks came in with lamps, which they placed around the hall to provide both light and warmth. Chantilla had been talking to the monks outside, but, even though they plied him with many questions, they had not learned anything useful. When the abbot emerged from the guesthouse, the hubbub died down, and the monks set about preparing the meal. The abbot, meanwhile, sent for the superintendent and told him to prepare food and other necessities for the guests.

A New Task

As the abbot made his way back to his own room, he was furious at the news he had heard about Oppas. The bishop was someone for whom he had the greatest respect; he loved and revered him—such was the bishop's intelligence, probity, and prestige that everyone shared those feelings. The abbot started thinking about ways to help him escape, but then he recalled that no one was sure of his current location. He decided that he would have to undertake the investigation himself. Sergius had been far removed from all these events because he had not visited Toledo for some time. He had not even attended the High Mass on Christmas Day or gone to congratulate the king because of some personal business that had kept him away. Maybe he would not have done that, had it not been for his natural inclination to distance himself from Roderic because of his feelings of loyalty to Witiza. The abbot had actually been present at the council where the decision had been taken to replace him with Roderic. He had not supported that decision, but it had been a majority vote, and he had been afraid to voice his opinion for fear of annoying the new king. He could not bear to see something so contrary to his beliefs actually happening, so he had stayed away from Toledo as much as possible. This past Christmas, he had found a pretext for not going, and so he had not been aware of the things that befell Oppas. Had he been there, he would have witnessed the trial in the cathedral and heard his arguments, even though his being there would not have helped Oppas in any way because the king's party was still in the majority.

So Sergius decided that he had to go to Toledo himself and apologize to the king for his absence on Christmas Day. He was still afraid that the king might accuse him of something or doubt the real reason for his coming to Toledo. The very first factor in his thinking was Father Martin, because he was all too aware of the kind of priest he was. For that reason, the abbot decided to postpone his visit until New Year's Day. He could then congratulate the king on both festivals, and Roderic would have no cause to question his decision to come to Toledo. Even so, he could not stand the thought of waiting so long to get some news of Oppas, so he decided to send a monk to question the king's retinue on the matter without seeing Oppas or hearing what he had to say. Sergius spent a restless night as he turned these thoughts over in his mind.

Chapter 64

The Abbot's Room

Next morning, the abbot sent for Florinda. After the exhausting journey and all the anxieties she had suffered through, she had slept well; that was particularly the case now that she was reassured that Abbot Sergius shared her views and was willing to help her. The sound of chiming bells woke her up. She got up, fully intending to go to Mass. However, while she was getting ready, she heard footsteps outside her door, not those of Chantilla. Hearing a knock, she stood up. Her aunt went over and opened it. Standing there was a monk whom she did not recognize, so she asked him what he wanted.

"The reverend abbot invites you to visit him," he replied.

They proceeded on their way, with the monk walking in front of them.

"My days of suffering are not over yet," Florinda mused to herself. "The abbot seems to have changed his mind about helping me..."

The monk preceded them across the square till they reached a spot behind the church and climbed some stairs to a room. Knocking on the door, the monk went inside without asking permission to enter. He came out again and invited Florinda and her aunt to enter. They found themselves in a room that was simply furnished but well arranged. The walls were covered with portraits of saints of various shapes and sizes, among them portraits of Roman provenance representing the major events in the Gospel accounts: Christ's birth in Bethlehem, His baptism in the River Jordan, and His crucifixion and ascent into heaven. As Florinda looked around the room, her heart was overjoyed by the sight of all the pictures, and her own sense of devotion intensified the feeling.

All the trials she had gone through had only increased her attachment to religion; coming into this room, she had felt the same way as she did on entering a church.

The abbot stood up and invited her to take a seat. Before doing so, she made sure to kiss an icon of the crucified Christ close by where she had been standing. With that, she sat down.

"There are no longer any secrets between us," the abbot began. "We all know how the others feel, so we can talk freely. I've promised you, Florinda, to try to find out what has happened to Oppas. I was planning to do that myself, but then it occurred to me that, if I went to Toledo today after staying away from the Christmas celebration, it would look suspicious and might interfere with our plans. I've decided to postpone my trip until New Year's Day, which is coming soon. What do you think?"

Florinda was relieved. The delay was obviously a way of solving the problems involved, and her emotions showed clearly in her expression. The abbot was fully aware of how worried she was.

"Even so," he went on, "I'm going to send one of our monks today to see what he can find out from Roderic's courtiers. If he can get any information, it'll help us plan for my own visit."

Florinda now felt more relaxed and was happy to learn that the monk would be going to Toledo. Actually, she really wanted to make clear to the abbot that she was more anxious for news of Alfonso than of Oppas, and to know how Roderic had reacted to her escape—was he sparing no effort to track her down? But her innate shyness prevented her from asking such questions directly.

"If the monk you're going to send is clever and can find out enough reliable information, that would be much better than Your Reverence going to Toledo for the same purpose."

"So let's discuss what we want him to find out," said the abbot.

"I won't hide from you, Reverend Abbot," Florinda's aunt said, "that the most important thing is to find out what's happened to Oppas. But we'd also like to know about Roderic's reactions because we managed to escape from his palace against his will. We'd also like to find out where he dispatched Prince Alfonso."

"I fully understand these requests," the abbot said. "I'll pass them on to the monk. We can expect him to return with firm information."

Florinda now stood up and kissed the abbot's hand, as did the old lady. They were anxious to let Sergius get on with the task, so they asked his permission to leave. He gave them his blessing, and they departed.

The abbot now clapped his hands, and the monk who served him appeared. He asked the monk to summon a particular monk, whom he named. The second monk now arrived. He was someone in whom the abbot had implicit faith, having often shared with him his opinions of Roderic. The abbot told the monk the information that he wished him to obtain and urged him to hurry back to the monastery as soon as possible.

Chapter 65

The Current Situation

The monk set off on a donkey with a saddlebag, as though he were simply going to Toledo to get some provisions and goods that the monastery needed. The monastery usually sent someone to the city for that purpose two or three times a year, but it normally happened in the summer because, like everyone else who lived in the mountains, they preferred not to have to travel in wintertime. Even so, there was nothing to prevent them going to the city in winter from time to time.

The monk spent five days in Toledo and then came back. Florinda grew tired of waiting; to her those days seemed like an eternity. She habitually went with her aunt to the monastery roof to look out over the hills and valleys in the hope of seeing the abbot's messenger coming back. It so happened that the weather was very clear at this particular time, so from their viewing spot on the roof they could look out over the mountains. There was little greenery, and some of the peaks and crags were even covered with snow. Every morning the valleys were shrouded in mist; one could almost imagine that it was a sea being buffeted by waves and the mountains that jutted out were islands surrounded by water. Just before noon, when the temperature was warmer, the mist would rise and the islands would turn into mountains again. Florinda kept telling herself that the messenger was actually quite close but the mist was keeping him hidden from view.

By now she was quite friendly with the old man who was the monastery doorkeeper because his room, or garret, was on the way up to the roof. From time to time, he used to come out, sit with her, and recount for her all the amazing things that had happened to him during his long life. Florinda was always delighted to hear what he had to say;

even though he was so old, he did not bore her with long-winded stories—the kind of thing younger listeners do not want to hear.

During the afternoon of the fifth day, Florinda spotted from the roof a rider between two ridges; upon closer inspection, it was indeed the monk on his way back to the monastery. Her heart skipped a beat.

"Here he is!" she cried to her aunt. "Let's go to the abbot's room to hear what he has to tell us."

Her aunt agreed, and they both made their way to the abbot's quarters. They found him sitting by the door perusing a scroll in Latin. When he noticed Florinda and her aunt approaching, he stood up and greeted them both. He could tell from Florinda's expression that she was excited about something.

"Good news, I trust, young lady?" he said. "What's happened?"

"I've seen your messenger coming back," she replied. "Call him in so we can hear what he has learned."

"Is he really back?" the abbot asked. "I've been even more anxious for him to get back than you. I've only been reading these texts in order to keep myself busy."

Standing up, he told his servant to summon the messenger quickly. The monk rushed out and returned almost immediately, followed by the messenger still in his riding clothes. Once in the room, the messenger greeted everyone, crossed himself, and sat down.

"So tell us now what you learnt," the abbot told him. "Begin with Oppas."

"The metropolitan bishop is indeed imprisoned in a room on his own," the monk replied.

"For what reason?" the abbot asked.

"They have accused him of plotting to overthrow the king," the monk replied, "and charged him in an ecclesiastical assembly."

"How could that be," the abbot interrupted, "when I heard nothing about any such assembly?"

"They did it quickly," the monk replied. "The king convened all the bishops who were in Toledo for the Christmas celebrations."

"And what was the result of this process?"

"I don't know," the monk replied. "But I did hear that the dignified and steadfast way the bishop conducted himself during the proceedings was enough to confound his enemies."

Florinda was listening closely to what the monk was saying and was, of course, anxious to hear some news about Alfonso.

"Do you think the accusation was genuine?" the abbot asked the monk.

"Shall I tell you what I heard?" he replied.

"Yes."

"The retainers in the royal palace told me there was a secret reason behind the bishop's trial," the monk went on. "Only a few people know about it..."

"And what's that?"

"Prince Alfonso is engaged to a young girl in the royal palace," the monk replied. "Roderic considers himself a rival and wants her for himself. Oppas chose to chide him for his behavior. That made Roderic angry, and so he decided to get his revenge..."

"So what's happened to Alfonso and his fiancée?"

"Roderic sent Alfonso off on a military mission to some remote spot so he could have the field to himself in Toledo. That's why Oppas decided to interfere. I heard that the girl managed to escape. People find that amazing because the palace was so heavily guarded. The king is said to be furious with her and intends to take revenge once he gets hold of her again."

"How can he do that?" the old lady asked. "Where is she now?"

It seems to us unlikely that this monk was not aware that the girl in the room was in fact the fiancée in question, but he pretended not to know—in accordance with the abbot's wishes.

"People told me," he went on, "that the king had all the roads blocked, set up watches, and sent spies all over the place. Hardly a day goes by now without one or more girls they happen to come across in some place or other being brought to the palace. But as soon as Roderic sets eyes on them, he has to let them go because they are not the girl in question."

When Florinda heard this bit of news, for the first time she felt really worried. However, she still thanked her God for letting her find refuge in this monastery where she was under the care and protection of this beloved abbot. She decided to stay put until Ajilla came back with news from her father. But she was anxious to hear where Alfonso actually was, so she signaled to her aunt to ask.

"Have you any idea," the old lady asked the monk, "where Prince Alfonso actually went?"

"I couldn't get any precise information," he replied, "but I did hear that the king sent him with a troop of soldiers to Astigi. I can't be completely certain because I didn't make detailed inquiries about him."

The abbot gestured to Florinda to make do with that response until such time as he himself could go to Toledo and make inquiries, so she said no more. The abbot stood up and said a short prayer. With that, Florinda left, her mind still reeling with all the news about Oppas's imprisonment and Roderic's intensive search for her. She now saw that she had no choice but to remain in this monastery till she could discover what fate had in store for her. Needless to say, she devoutly hoped to learn more details once the abbot had returned from his own mission to Toledo.

However, nature decided to impose its own restrictions. The weather changed, and rain and snow poured down, blocking off the mountain paths and impeding all traffic. For several days, the abbot could not leave, even though he was impatient to be on his way. We can only imagine how Florinda was feeling—the more so since over a month had passed by now, and yet Ajilla had still not returned from his mission to her father, all of which made her even more anxious and alarmed. She became very depressed, imagining that the entire world had closed in on her. She had lost her fiancée and was far away from her father; she had been a prisoner then had become a fugitive until fate had drawn her to this monastery. She felt like an incarcerated criminal. No sooner had she felt a modicum of joy at the abbot's decision to go to Toledo himself than nature had blocked his path and prevented him from leaving, piling up huge snowdrifts between the monastery and Toledo. Even so, whenever worries such as these began to pile up and she felt really depressed, she resorted to prayer. That alleviated her distress and restored her sense of hope. When she finished praying and the sky was clear, she would go up on to the roof with her aunt and look out at the distant trails in the hope of spotting a figure heading for the monastery, bringing news that would release her from these hardships. But all she could see was mountainous piles of snow extending all the way to the monastery door. If the monks had not spent much of the morning clearing it away, the path would have been completely invisible.

The abbot did his best to visit her often in order to calm her fears, promise eventual success, and discuss with her various means of rescue from her plight. The basis of his comments lay in Oppas's intelligence, learning, and persuasive abilities. Florinda herself admired Oppas just as much. As she had grown up, she had always heard Oppas described in words of praise and admiration, to such an extent that she imagined that he could do anything; no one could ever harm him or get the better of him in a discussion.

Sergius, meanwhile, was thinking how he might be able to get Oppas out of prison. Then he'd be able to come to the monastery and stay there in peace and quiet. However, when he heard that the king was keeping the closest possible watch on the bishop and guarding him night and day, the abbot realized that he could not come up with any specific plan.

Chapter 66

Snow and the Messenger

One morning in late February, Florinda woke up to the sound of roaring winds and pounding rain, most of which was actually hail and ice. For two solid hours, there was a gale, with thunder and lightning. Then, all of a sudden the rain stopped and the wind died down. That is quite normal in countries in the temperate zone; in a single day the weather can be clear and then change to rain and high winds before reverting to clear skies again. Once the rain stopped, Florinda took a look out of her room and saw that the entire courtyard was filled with snow, right up to her door. The sun was shining on the snow, and the reflected rays gleamed brightly, only to dissolve in some of the drifts. The glow contained all the colors of the rainbow.

Florinda stood there, enjoying the beautiful scene. Soon she noticed all the monks emerging from their quarters with picks and shovels; they started clearing the snow and heaving it outside. The entire scene delighted Florinda, and she began to feel more at ease than she had for months. Once rain has stopped and the weather has become clear again, human beings will always have such feelings, particularly when the rain is preceded by dense fog or looming clouds. However, when the sky is clear, it is always that much colder than when there is cloud cover. For that very reason, Florinda did not stay by the door for very long gazing out at the scene. Going back inside, she put on her fur-lined cloak, wrapped herself up in it, and came out again. She spotted the old monk, the gatekeeper, coming toward her. He had put his cane aside and was using the shovel he was carrying to move the snow with all the vigor of a young man—and his feet and arms were still bare. All he had done to keep himself warm was to put a headscarf around his temples and ears.

When Florinda noticed what he was wearing, she was amazed at the way human beings can learn to adjust themselves to circumstances. She stood there, watching the old man and the other monks as they shoveled away, with Chantilla working along with them. Before long the entire courtyard had been cleared, and some of them were working on the roof as well. Once they had finished, Florinda and her aunt, Barbara, came outside to enjoy the clear air and bright sunshine. They both went up to the roof and looked out over the mountain ranges. They were only there for a short while before Florinda started shivering with cold; her cloak and other garments were of no use. Just then, the sky began to cloud over again. It was clearly about to rain. Florinda was about to go back downstairs, but she noticed that the old monk was standing by the door of his room and gesturing to her to come over. She turned round and went over to the door, followed by her aunt. When they entered the monk's room, they found a stove like a brazier; as soon as they went in, Florinda started to feel warmer and had a strange sensation of pleasure.

"Sit down, young lady," the old monk said. "It's very cold today."

So Florinda sat down with her aunt by her side. They were both close to the window, while the monk sat directly in front of the stove. To keep them entertained, he started telling them stories of his youth and middle age, and Florinda's aunt kept on supplying extra details even though she was younger than he was.

All the while, Florinda was looking out of the window at the area around the monastery. Almost the only thing she could see was snow. The monk and her aunt were deep in conversation, assuming that Florinda was listening to what they were saying. At one point Florinda's aunt asked her a question and waited for a response, but soon realized that her ward was intent on watching something outside the window; that much was clear from her expression. When the aunt looked outside for herself, she noticed a horse heading toward the monastery, carrying a rider. She thought she recognized the person, but just then Florinda yelled out, "Ajilla, Ajilla!" When the monk heard her say that, he looked at the person who was approaching the monastery but did not recognize him.

"Who is that, young lady?" he asked.

"It's the messenger we sent on a mission," she replied. "He's just come back. Please hurry and open the door so he doesn't suffer too much from the cold."

"At once!" he replied, whereupon he grabbed his cane and went down to the door. Florinda and her aunt stayed where they were, watching what would happen. It was indeed Ajilla on horseback. Once he drew close to the monastery, the horse came to a stop. Ajilla looked up at the monastery and let out a loud laugh. When Florinda saw that, she felt relieved and happy.

"Ajilla!" she called out to him, but he did not answer, as though she had not made a sound.

For her part, she assumed that the roar of the wind had prevented him from hearing what she had said. Just then she saw the old monk come out of the monastery door, take out his cane and start beating Ajilla very hard; but he did not even budge. The monk kept on pounding him, and then called to other monks to come out and help him. Two others came out with thick clubs. While one of them grabbed the horse's reins, the other one started pounding Ajilla wherever he could—but still Ajilla did not react. Florinda stood there watching the entire scene in utter amazement, not least because they all seemed to be hitting Ajilla for no particular reason. She started yelling at the monks to stop. She asked them why they were hitting him so mercilessly, but they paid no attention. That angered her, so she decided to go to the abbot's rooms to complain about the monks' behavior. Once she reached the courtyard, with her aunt trailing behind her, she sent her aunt to see the abbot while she went outside to talk to the monks directly. She called for Chantilla but received no reply. Hurrying over to the monastery door, she went outside. There she saw Chantilla pounding his brother just as hard as the monks. They had taken him off the horse; one of them had grabbed his feet while another clasped his arms. The two others were still pounding his feet and shoulders. The whole thing shocked her.

"What on earth are you doing, Chantilla?" she asked.

He did not reply or even pay any attention to her.

A short while later, she saw them pick Ajilla up and carry him into the monastery. Florinda stood to one side and watched. Ajilla was still not moving, almost as though the pounding he had received had killed him. She felt so angry and sorry that she almost burst into tears, but the shock she was feeling overpowered everything else. Once they were inside, she followed them up to the doorkeeper's room but kept her mouth shut in case they might start hitting her as well. She kept looking left and right in the hope of seeing the abbot arriving; then she could ask him to help or find out what was going on. Just then the abbot did arrive from another direction, closely followed by Florinda's aunt, who signaled to her niece to calm down.

Florinda rushed over to the abbot and asked him what was going on.

"Don't worry," he said. "They're doing that to keep him alive."

"How can they be doing that," she asked, "when they've almost pounded him to death?"

The abbot laughed. "You obviously haven't heard of hypothermia," he said.

"What is that, Reverend Sir?"

"Death from intense cold," he replied. "Your messenger was clearly almost dead, so they have been pounding him like that to get his circulation moving and warm him up again so he won't die…"

"He wasn't saying he felt cold," she said. "In fact, I saw him laughing."

The abbot laughed. "When you're that cold," he said, "laughing is one of the symptoms of hypothermia."

With that, he went into the monk's room. "Give him some wine," he told them, "and put him close to the stove."

The old monk hurried over to a pitcher in a corner of the room, poured a glass of wine, and moved close to Ajilla. Florinda came over, too, and took a look at his face. By now he had opened his eyes, but he was still very weak, indeed. Florinda now realized that what the abbot had said was correct, and she thanked God for the effective methods that had been used to save him.

Chapter 67

Reliable News

They spent a good hour warming Ajilla up and giving him stimulants. Eventually he came round and returned to his normal self. Florinda asked them if she could take him back to the guest quarters, and the abbot gave his permission. They both went down, followed by Chantilla and her aunt. Once they were settled inside the room, she asked Ajilla why he had been away for so long. He told her that on the way back he had suffered all kinds of hardship, revisiting not only the dreadful weather but also Roderic's spies. Eventually he had been forced to sleep in daytime and only travel at night for fear that Julian's letter that he was carrying might fall into the wrong hands. That was how he had come to almost freeze to death from the cold.

She then asked him about her father. He gave her an account of his arrival at her father's residence and how furious he had been when he read her letter.

"I've decided to avenge myself on Roderic," he had said, "and it will be of a kind unprecedented in Spanish history."

The very thought of Florinda's father's steadfast intent made her eyes sparkle. Now she felt once again that she really belonged to someone after feeling neglected and uncared for all this time. She was eager to hear more about his plans for revenge.

"What does that mean?" she asked Ajilla.

"He has decided to dethrone Roderic," he replied.

"That's a great idea," she responded, "but..."

"Do you imagine that Count Julian would embark upon such a plan," he interrupted, "if he wasn't sure of himself?"

He then told her about his pact with the Arab forces to cross over to Spain with them and assist them in the conquest.

Florinda could not believe what he had just told her; she thought he was just saying that to comfort her.

"Are you telling me the truth?" she asked.

Putting a hand in his pocket, he brought out a sealed tube and gave it to her. She tore open the seal and found a piece of Coptic cloth inside. Opening it, she found a letter to her from her father and in his own handwriting. Her heart leapt up as she remembered how fond he was of her, and her eyes teared up. It was only when she had calmed down a bit and dried her eyes that she could read what it had to say. Here is what it said:

From Count Julian to his beloved daughter, Florinda:

My dear daughter, when I read your letter, tears flooded my eyes as my innermost thoughts overwhelmed me. I was furious to learn what that savage beast, Roderic, had done to defame the faith, virtue, and reputation of Julian himself. For the first two crimes, God can take His revenge, but, as for the third, which directly infringes my own honor, I intend to get my own revenge. So here is the good news: I am going to attack him and invade Spain with an Arab army. God will certainly grant them victory over his traitor, since we already know how the Spaniards and Goths detest him. The offense that you detailed in your letter to me is already enough to arouse the wrath of heaven and earth against this usurper. I will not go into any more detail here, because the conveyor of this letter will be able to explain any complexities to you. I have only penned these few lines in order to confirm what he has to tell you and to let you know that our deliverance is at hand. You will soon see Roderic the traitor dead or a prisoner in chains. So stay where you can be safe and wait until I can come to you. If you need to get in touch with me, I will be with the Arab commander, wherever he may be. Farewell! (written in Sabta)

When Florinda finished reading it, she stood up and went to see the abbot, who had returned to his own rooms. She went on her own, not really aware of anything going on around her because she was so overwhelmed by this sudden news. Her heart was dancing for joy at the thought of revenge, that being, as we all know, one of mankind's most satisfying pleasures.

As she approached the abbot's room, he was somewhat disturbed by the shocked expression on her face, albeit mingled with a certain delight. He stood up, so she went in and greeted him.

"I've come to see you on a crucially important matter," she said. "It's the definitive end for Roderic..."

That gave him a shock. "What's it about?" he asked.

"The young man who arrived this morning half-dead from the cold," she told him, "is the messenger that I sent to my father in Sabta. I gave him a short letter in which I complained about the way that Roderic had treated me. Today he has come back with this letter from my father."

With that, she handed the abbot the letter. He took it and proceeded to read it, hardly believing that he was actually wide awake. He then read it a second and a third time, while Florinda just stood there, anxious to hear his reactions. When he had finished, he looked up at her.

"What your father is planning to do will change the very face of this peninsula," the abbot said. "It'll certainly put an end to this particular dynasty. Roderic will discover what happens to those who infringe the sanctity of religion. We all seek refuge from God's wrath!"

He paused for a moment. "Did your messenger provide any details?" he asked.

"Yes, he told me a few things," she replied, "but I could not wait to tell you the news. If you allow me, we can send for Ajilla, and he can tell us what he witnessed."

"I'd like to hear," the abbot said. Clapping his hands, he asked the monk to bring him the man who had arrived that morning and was staying in the guesthouse.

The monk went away and returned with Ajilla, who bowed to the abbot, kissed his hand, and took a seat.

The abbot now started questioning Ajilla about the things he had seen. Ajilla related to them his impressions of the Arabs' fortitude, resolution, and endurance in battle, how they prayed regularly and obeyed their commanders.

"Not only that," he went on, "but Count Julian is providing them with assistance and guiding them as they proceed. They are also getting help from the Jewish communities who are disguised as Christians. They're prepared to do whatever it takes to support any invader; they loathe this king and his government because they have suffered such humiliation and contempt at their hands."[50]

The abbot nodded his head as he listened to Ajilla's account.

"That tyrant's regime is surely at an end," he told himself, "and maybe the entire Visigothic dynasty as well."

"So, if I go to see Oppas now," he said, turning to look at Florinda, "I can tell him this news and what's in the letter. I suspect that the people at court haven't heard it as yet. We can figure out a way to free him from prison and bring him to stay in this monastery. Your father often dealt with the Arabs, so we'll be quite safe if they conquer the country. But, if they're defeated, Roderic will have nothing against us because we did not oppose his campaign…"

When Florinda heard the abbot's idea of bringing Oppas to the monastery, she was even more delighted. Just a few days later, the snows melted and the roads were cleared. Abbot Sergius mounted his mule and took off for Toledo, accompanied by his servant.

---

50 Dozy, part I.

Chapter 68

General Kumis

By now Roderic had received a letter from the Governor of Baetica informing him of the Arab invasion. He told Father Martin about it before notifying any political figures. The priest reacted to the news by saying that all the Arabs wanted was to conduct a quick raid for plunder; they were not interested in undertaking a full-scale invasion. Once they had grabbed enough booty, they would go back the way they had come. They would never dare, the priest claimed, to launch an attack on the Gothic kingdom. Truth be told, the Arabs did conduct frequent raids into neighboring territories; they used to invade the country and then go back with whatever cattle and other booty they could lay their hands on.

Roderic was glad to hear the priest's opinion since it seemed eminently sensible. He decided not to tell his government officials about the letter he had received. But then other people arrived in Toledo with accounts of the Arabs and their horses and camels; they had already captured the Mountain[51] and were being escorted by Julian, Governor of Sabta, who was guiding them through the rough countryside and helping them in their forward march. These people also informed the general commander about what was happening.

The commanding general of Roderic's armed forces was a tough and ferocious individual named Count Kumis. He had a lot of influence and prestige with Roderic. This general had noticed that Roderic was interested in Florinda and advised the king to give it up, but the king had ignored his advice and now regarded him with a certain suspicion. When the count heard that the girl had escaped and Oppas was to be put

---

51 Jabal Tariq or Gibraltar. *Translator's Note.*

on trial, he had secretly advised Roderic not to proceed in case the king's behavior with Florinda would be exposed. The gist of his advice to the monarch was not to listen to Father Martin and the other members of the clergy. When the general heard that the Arabs had invaded Spain and that Count Julian was with them, he realized what he had told the king about Florinda confronted him with an even greater danger. All of this meant that the general now despised the king even more. Beyond that, he was astonished that the king had not even told him about the Arab invasion; he found it utterly implausible for the king not to have known about it.

For that reason, he decided to go to the king's palace one morning. The king was actually in council with his senior administrators, all of whom were also counts. In the Gothic governing council there were only ten senior posts: the supervisor of royal domains, known as the Count of the Country; head of the royal stables, known as the Count of the Stables; the royal secretary, known as the Count of Records; the chief judge, known as the Count of Benefices; the Army Commander; the Treasurer; and the Royal Chamberlain.[52] Among other holders of the rank of count were the chief steward and others who were in the king's service.

The council was attended by all these officials, and Father Martin was seated, as usual, beside the monarch. Count Kumis entered the council and delivered his greetings. His expression showed how furious he was. Once he was settled in his place, he asked the king if he had any news from Baetica.

"I don't know," the king replied. "Have you heard anything…?"

"I asked the king," he replied in a gruff tone, "if he had received any important news from that particular province."

The king was furious to hear such an impudent and bold-faced response.

"What is that response supposed to mean?" he asked.

"You heard what I said."

With that, the general changed his position and looked away, twiddling his hair, which hung down to his shoulders. He looked very

---

52 Romey, part II.

angry. The other counts kept looking at each other then at Roderic and Count Kumis, asking themselves what this confrontation was about.

Kumis realized that everyone had heard the disrespectful way he had addressed the king and was now staring hard at him in anticipation of what he would say next. He decided that things were getting out of hand. Army generals are always proud and impulsive. If they get really annoyed, they are never bothered by either crowns or scepters; all that matters is their own impulsive instincts. That was particularly the case in this era when the last word belonged to the person who controlled military power. Beyond all that, Count Kumis already despised the king because of what he had learned about his despicable behavior toward Florinda and Oppas. When the king had used such a tone of voice, he decided to respond in kind.

"I suspect," he said, "that His Majesty the King is not unaware of the import of my question, even though he pretends not to understand. What I mean by it is that something has happened in the kingdom that requires that we be informed, but he has kept it a secret from us. It is so significant that it places the entire kingdom in imminent danger."

The entire assembly was outraged and was eager to find out what exactly that news might be. At this crucial moment, Father Martin stood up in his usual fashion and took on the task of responding to Count Kumis in the king's place. He addressed his remarks to the count.

"I suppose that what you are referring to," he said deliberately and in a scoffing tone, "is that those pesky Arabs have landed on the shores of Baetica. They're just here on a quick raid for plunder; they'll soon be going back to their own country. If the news were of any importance, the king would have reported it to the bishops first of all."

Kumis despised Father Martin and paid no attention to what the priest had said. Instead, he addressed his remarks to the king.

"It is a grave error to treat this invasion so lightly," he said. "That's particularly the case when the king already knows full well that they are being guided on their march by Count Julian, the governor of Sabta." He said this in a particular tone of voice and continued, "As for informing the council of bishops about what is before us, well, the king may have his own opinions on that. But I think that, of all people, the army commander should certainly be informed well in advance of anyone else. After all, he is charged with the defense of the kingdom. Bishops are only supposed to fast and pray."

As he spoke, his contempt was clear in every single word. The entire matter was so delicate that no one else had any desire to get involved, but, even so, many of them realized that Kumis's reference to Julian, the governor of Sabta, was a less-than-subtle allusion. They all decided to say nothing.

Roderic was furious. He was well aware what Kumis was alluding to and appreciated that he himself was in a very risky position. He also realized that he needed his army commander much more than all the rest of his government officials. Even so, he was not willing to overlook the way Kumis was behaving.

"Count Kumis," he said, "you have absolutely no right to address me in that fashion! Quite the contrary, you should be behaving in a totally different manner so that we can understand each other."

"The king has provided us with no other way of achieving such mutual agreement," the commander responded. "He's allowed this priest here to be his mouthpiece, whereas everyone knows that he and other clerics like him are only useful in matters of worship. Instead, the king has made them his partners in running every aspect of the kingdom's affairs. If they had given him proper advice, the situation would not be so critical."

Obviously, any such brutally frank statement in that particular era, especially in Toledo, amounted to sheer heresy in view of everything we have learned about the power of the clergy at that time. If the army commander had not been so furious, he would surely not have expressed himself so forcefully on the subject, thus initiating discussion of a topic for which Roderic might well be criticized and indeed brought to account.

But the king now turned the entire discussion into a defense of the bishops, hoping thereby to distract attention from his own errors.

"Isn't it enough for you to be defying your own king?" he asked the commander. "Now you're challenging the bishops as well! That is well beyond the bounds of your position."

Father Martin was quivering with rage. Once he saw that the king was holding his own in the argument, he decided to speak.

"Are you not aware, Count," he asked, "that a mere word from the king or any one of the bishops is sufficient to deprive you of your position?"

The army commander had not been anticipating the kind of contempt that the king had already shown him, so what can we say about his reaction to this priest?

"With those very words," he said, clasping the sheath of his sword, "you have lost the sword of Kumis—and at a time when you are in the gravest need of it."

And with those words, he left in a fury.

It had been the king's intention to argue with the commander in his own defense but not to make him so angry. For that reason, Father Martin's words had made him even more angry than those of the commander himself. No one in the assembly dared mediate between the parties so as not to make things even worse than they already were. What they had feared might happen had, indeed, happened. The king now stood up, and everyone realized that he intended to bring the council to a close. Everyone left, except Father Martin. Once they had departed, the king turned to the priest.

"Is that the way you infuriate our senior general and army commander," he asked angrily, "when we need him so urgently?"

"Your Majesty," the priest replied, "are you blaming me for scolding him when he belittled not only you but all the bishops as well? Tolerating such behavior is out of the question."

"Kumis is our finest general," the king said, "and we have never needed him more than we do now. The enemy is at our gates, and our governors are showing them the weaknesses in our defenses. God forgive you this dreadful mistake! Is it not enough already that we've kept this information not only from him but also from the other members of the government? Now we've committed an even worse error!"

Father Martin was infuriated by the king's accusation. "It's almost as though you're accusing me of committing this error," he replied. "If the advice I offered was not good, then you shouldn't have accepted it!"

So saying, he walked to the middle of the hall with his left arm behind his back and his right one wiping the foam from his lips and beard.

The king regarded this, too, as an insult and was furious. "So," he said, "you're in the wrong and you lose us our army commander, and now you turn on us, belittle our words, and make it all our fault? Is that it?"

"You're right, Your Majesty," he continued sarcastically, nodding his head but not looking directly at the king. "It's all my fault, isn't it? I'm the one who's wrong. All the evils have come about because of my disgraceful behavior with the daughter of the governor of Sabta. If I hadn't done that, her father would not now be helping the Arabs invade my country."

With that, he did turn round and faced the king. He was in a towering rage, quivering all over, all of which made his stutter even worse than usual.

"Roderic," he shouted, "will you commit sin and then make me the culprit in my old age? Once the bishops have been insulted, is it not your job to defend them? After all, they are the ones who gave you the throne and have since helped you and supported you. Who was it who defended you just yesterday in the assembly in Toledo when they leveled a charge against an innocent man without the slightest pretext? Then you tell me that I'm responsible for the loss of this commander? You're the one who's lost him because of your poor judgment and the way you've been meddling in matters that are of no importance to you. It's that same poor judgment that has now lost you Father Martin as well, after he has served you so well by working for your best interests and defending you."

With that, the aged priest wrapped himself in his cloak and left the palace.

Once Father Martin had left, Roderic found himself alone as he contemplated the enormous peril that was enveloping him. Sitting on his chair, he put his head in his hands and thought back over the events of recent months. He thought about Florinda and her father and realized that Julian was only lending his support to the Arabs in order to take revenge on him. He became more and more annoyed and started to panic, especially since he had lost his army commander and deeply offended his priest-confidant, both of which augured ill...

Chapter 69

Sergius and Oppas

Abbot Sergius's arrival in Toledo happened to occur the day after this confrontation. He headed for the cathedral, as was the custom for all bishops upon their arrival in the city. There he met Father Martin, whom he had previously known in the royal palace. The two priests greeted each other and exchanged news about various things. The abbot bore in mind Father Martin's well-known proclivities, in that, in spite of his old age, the priest was a prickly personality who could be easily aroused, as should be clear from the way we have already described his temperament. Everything that had happened the day before involving Count Kumis and Father Martin was already well known to the abbot, so he assumed that the priest's hasty temper would now be leading him to bring about Roderic's downfall and condemn his monarch's views as though he were a diehard enemy. Such sudden changes of position only happen with people of a nervous or vicious disposition.

When Sergius had arrived in Toledo, he had obviously not expected to find an easy way to get to see Oppas or even rescue him. But once he ran into Father Martin in the cathedral, the whole thing seemed that much simpler. So he mentioned Oppas to the priest and told him that he had heard that the metropolitan was in prison. As soon as the abbot mentioned the name Oppas, Father Martin recalled the way they had disparaged him, put him in prison, and done him wrong by leveling a false charge against him. Bearing in mind that he was now furious with Roderic, he decided that by vindicating Oppas he could take revenge on the king and thus calm his own anger.

"Oppas is indeed in prison," he told Sergius, "on the basis of a trumped-up charge by Roderic. He was accused, but the charge was not

273

proven. The process was postponed, and he was put in prison until such time as the court case could be resumed. However, it seems as though the king has no intention of reopening the case."

"Do you think," Sergius asked, "that he would be acquitted if the case were to be reopened?"

"I've no doubt," Father Martin replied.

"So why doesn't anyone demand that?"

Father Martin smiled and nodded his head.

"But how can that happen," he asked, "when Oppas is locked away in a room and can't see anyone? Roderic's prevented anyone from having contact with him."

"Is there any way of getting to see him," Sergius asked, "without the king's authorization?"

"That's easy for me to arrange," Father Martin replied with a smile. "Do you think we should be encouraging our colleague to demand that the trial be reopened?"

In fact, he was not saying that because he wanted Oppas to come out on top, but rather because he assumed that Roderic would then be forced to make up to him, Father Martin. That was what the king usually did whenever he had managed to annoy his primary counselor. For that very reason, Father Martin was sure that, before the day was out, the king would be sending for him so he could be reconciled. But when morning dawned and still no one had come to fetch him, he had become even more furious. That explains why, when Sergius spoke to him about Oppas, he decided to urge him to get the trial reopened. He was convinced that Roderic would be dismayed by the prospect, particularly as he was already aware of how angry Count Julian and Count Kumis were with him. Roderic would have no choice but to do his utmost to please Father Martin so he would take charge of things again. That would not work to Oppas's advantage because, even if they agreed to reopen the case, they would have to reconvene the bishops from all over the kingdom; that would require weeks...

Sergius was delighted by what he had just heard.

"If you can get me in to see him," he told Father Martin, "I can let him know about the possible resumption of the trial."

Father Martin immediately stood up, grabbed a pen and inkwell, and wrote a note to the officer in charge of Oppas's guard. He was to allow Abbot Sergius to talk to the metropolitan. Sergius took the piece of paper, hardly believing what he had managed to achieve, and headed as fast as he could to the place where Oppas was being held.

Oppas, meanwhile, was still in his prison, totally cut off from the outside world. He had dealt with the situation with his usual aplomb, countering the difficulties involved by dint of sheer patience. He never felt lonely because the issues that were constantly on his mind were of the kind that can only be thought about in isolation; in fact, he was so convinced of his own innocence that he did not even regard himself as being in prison. On the other hand, he did feel a great deal of regret over the innate weakness of humanity. It was the reason behind so many problems that people had to face, particularly if those involved were monarchs and political leaders. In such cases, the mistakes made by one person could cause hundreds and thousands of innocent people to suffer. When he contemplated the reasons behind his own imprisonment, he felt sorry for Roderic and rulers like him because of the obvious delusions that governed their behavior and the crimes and misdemeanors that they proceeded to commit in a vain quest for temporary pleasure or some illusory fancy. As Oppas immersed himself in the world of philosophy, ruminations of this sort about the vagaries of human nature preoccupied his mind for whole hours and even days. He would definitely have reckoned himself to be living a life of ease while others were suffering hardships, were it not for the way that the problems that Florinda and Alfonso were facing kept impinging upon his consciousness. He was obviously unable to help them in any way or find a method of getting to them, so the only thing he could do was to entrust their fates to God.

On the day that Sergius came to visit him, his personal guard came in to his room.

"The abbot of the Mountain Monastery wishes to see you," he said.

As soon as Oppas heard the name, he recognized who it was. His heart leapt. After such a lengthy period in isolation, the whole thing was a shock. He told the guard to let the abbot in, amazed all the while that he had come to see him and even more that he had been allowed to speak to him.

Sergius had already heard about the long time Oppas had spent in prison, so he expected to see some changes in his general appearance. As he entered the room, he saw Oppas coming over to him in his clerical garments, since, apart from his beretta, he had not changed his manner of dress from the very first day of his imprisonment. His hair now reached his shoulders and continued down his back, but his time in prison had only amplified his dignified bearing. He walked over to greet the abbot.

When their eyes met, Sergius tried to kiss the metropolitan's hand, but Oppas stopped him. Instead, they hugged each other and shook hands. Sergius could not hold back his tears, while Oppas clasped the abbot by the shoulder because he was the taller of the two. They both sat opposite each other on a couch. Sergius was about to talk, but Oppas spoke first.

"Welcome, Sergius, my dear friend and colleague," he said. "Where are you coming from, and why are you here?"

"I've come straight from the Mountain Monastery," the abbot replied, "with no other mission than to see Metropolitan Oppas. I praise God that he is safe and well! May he bear the trials that he has gone through, since God always tests His loyal servants!"

"You're a person of sagacity and sound judgment," Oppas replied, "and yet you regard this room as a trial. Isn't everyone confined within the bounds of this earth of ours? Their lives are short, their powers limited, and their deeds often do not salve their consciences. For people who perform good deeds and are pious in their devotions, the only way out is through the eternal world, whereas evildoers suffer both in this world and the next. With that in mind, there is no need to feel sorry for a prisoner who is innocent and has a clear conscience; his imprisonment is actually short, though it may seem long. One should really weep for those to whom God has given power and authority over their fellow human beings. The goal is that they should rule people justly and support them in this life, whereas what they actually do is to tyrannize them and treat them badly, shedding the blood of thousands in the process. And it's all merely a quest for a bite to eat or a corpse to wallow in. They may not realize it, but they're actually doing themselves wrong."

As Oppas was speaking, there was not the slightest trace of anger, agitation, or psychological trauma on his part. Sergius was struck by the sheer wisdom and moral probity of what he had heard. Even so, he was eager to carry out the mission for which he had come.

"You are so right, my lord!" he said. "But God will often punish wrongdoers and reward the righteous while they are still in this lower world, all in order to serve as a warning to others. I have brought you some news that you will no doubt want to hear. Don't you wish to hear what has happened to Florinda after she managed to escape from Roderic's clutches?"

No sooner had Oppas heard that name than emotion got the better of him. He looked concerned, and all his philosophizing and contempt for worldly things were immediately forgotten. It does not matter how intellectual and ascetic a man may be, he will always become interested in life and people whenever love is involved. The ties that bind human society together would all dissolve if it were not for love. The same thing would happen to celestial bodies; if they ever lost their interaction with each other, they would all be scattered. Oppas loved Florinda for his nephew Alfonso's sake, and his feelings were only amplified by what he knew about her sufferings and the way he had managed to rescue her from Roderic's evil clutches. Human beings will always feel closer to young folk whenever they become aware of their weakness. So, when Oppas heard Florinda's name mentioned, he felt a strong jolt inside, although his expression gave little indication of the way he was feeling.

"Do you have some information about her?" he asked Sergius. "Where is she now?"

"She's at the Mountain Monastery," the abbot replied.

"How did she get there?" Oppas asked.

Sergius told him what he knew about her escape from Roderic's palace in Toledo and her arrival at the Mountain Monastery.

"She's safe and sound with us now," he told Oppas, "but she's very worried about you and Alfonso because she doesn't know where he is. In any case, she can't get to see him because Roderic has set up a whole system of spies and informers."

Oppas was relieved to hear about Florinda, but at the same time the news about the way he was hunting her down angered him intensely.

"How can that evil man still be pursuing and harassing that poor girl?" he asked.

"Before long," Sergius continued with a smile, "he's going to find himself in deep water, to the relief of everyone, not least the metropolitan bishop."

Oppas noticed a sparkle in Sergius's eyes, which suggested that he had something very important to communicate to him.

"And what might that be?" he asked with great interest.

Chapter 70

Chivalry and Knowledge of Duty

Sergius put his hand in his pocket and brought out Julian's letter to Florinda, still in its cylinder.

"When Florinda managed to get out of Toledo, as I've already recounted to you," he told the bishop, "she wrote a letter to her father, complaining about the awful time she had spent in Roderic's palace and the evil demands he had made of her. She dispatched Ajilla with the letter and received a firm response from her father about the current situation. Here it is."

He handed Oppas the cylinder. He took it, extracted the rolled up letter from inside, and unsealed it. He read it through, then read it again. Sergius was watching him closely to see what effect it would have on him but could discern no visible signs of emotion. That did not really surprise him; he was already aware that such traits were characteristic of self-assured and tolerant people. Even so, he did expect to hear Oppas make some comment or other.

"Did Ajilla give you any more information?" Oppas asked.

"Yes, he did," Sergius replied. "He watched as the Arab armies landed in Spain, with Julian showing them how to avoid difficult terrain."

"Does Roderic know about this?" Oppas asked.

"Yes, he does," Sergius responded. "He received the news several days ago but essentially ignored it, nor did he inform his council about it. That decision made matters worse, and now Roderic's in a real fix. He's bound to lose the monarchy."

"What caused this upheaval?" Oppas asked.

"Count Kumis, the army commander, found out about the Arab invasion from people who returned to Toledo from the south," Sergius told him. "He was thus able to confirm that Roderic had kept him in the dark, so he upbraided him in a council meeting that was attended by all the major figures in the government. His criticism turned into outright enmity, and Count Kumis left the meeting feeling furious with both Roderic and his priest-adviser, Father Martin. Once the meeting was over, Roderic turned on Father Martin and blamed him for the situation, whereupon they quarreled. Father Martin also stormed out and is now residing in the cathedral. That's where I met him and learned that he was out for revenge against Roderic; that explains why he helped me gain access to you by writing a note to the guard. Father Martin's opinion is that, if you demanded that your case be reopened, you'd certainly be found not guilty. At all events, God has now certainly brought the deceit of this tyrant down on his own head. King Roderic, who only a few days ago could have his own way in dealing with a person of Oppas's prestige, now finds himself deserted by not only his army commander but also his primary personal adviser. People are now treating him as a joke. Don't you see this as part of God's greater plan?"

As Sergius was speaking, he kept watching Oppas's expression. The bishop was staring at the floor, deep in thought, as he kept twisting his beard in his fingers. His knitted eyebrows and the concerned look in his eyes both showed how profound were his thoughts. When Sergius finished speaking, Oppas looked up at him, obviously still contemplating the situation. He stared at Sergius as though to assess what was in his heart. As for Sergius, he could no longer stand the fixed glare of those two eyes. It was as though some electric current were flowing from the activity of so many brain cells, and, every time the activity increased, the energy flow intensified. For several minutes, they both said nothing, but finally Oppas spoke.

"Is this the right time to take revenge on Roderic?" he asked.

"Will there ever be a better moment?" Sergius replied. "He's in a really tight spot: his enemies are threatening him, and his friends keep opposing him as well."

Oppas now stood up and started pacing back and forth across the room; he was still fiddling with his hair, which reached down to his shoulders. The fact that he was not speaking only amplified his august demeanor. Sergius kept watching him without saying a word. Suddenly Oppas stopped right in front of Sergius.

"My dear Sergius," he said, "do you think it's chivalrous for us to take advantage of our enemy's weakness and attack him when he's in such a tight spot? Does it make sense for us to lend our support to strangers against our own kin? Whatever else you may want to say about Roderic, he's one of us and we of him. We drink from the same stream, we read a single holy book, we talk the same language, and we pray the same prayers. We take Communion from a single cup and gather in the same church. How can we possibly take advantage of his hour of weakness and give assistance to people who are not part of us nor we of them? Their religion is not ours, nor is their country ours. Beyond all that, taking revenge on Roderic will bring ruin to the entire land of Spain; we'll be getting rid of a government that is familiar to us all and replacing it with a new one about which we know absolutely nothing. We have no idea what will happen to this country if the Arabs conquer it. Did our ancestors not shed their blood in the process of conquering this land and exploiting its resources? So how can we possibly hand it over for nothing? As far as our disavowal of Roderic's right to the throne is concerned, that's like a squabble between brother and brother or father and son. It's simply not right for us to seek the help of a people that is foreign to us in terms of race, religion, and country in resolving our internal disputes. On the matter of Roderic's attempts to discredit me personally, the pangs of his own conscience are quite enough, and that is easily left to God to deal with. No, my dear Sergius, you and I find ourselves in a situation in which we must put aside all rancor and challenge an invading enemy, all in the cause of saving our kingdom. We must overlook the evil deeds one person may have inflicted on another. I'll start with myself, by going to see Roderic and urging him to unite our efforts in the cause of our homeland."

So saying, he went over to a shelf where he had left his beretta, and put it on his head. His expression alive with emotion, he made ready to leave, but only then did it occur to him that he was actually in prison and would need the king's permission to leave the room.

As Sergius sat there listening to what Oppas was saying, he felt smaller and smaller. No sooner had Oppas finished what he was saying than Sergius convinced himself that he was the most despicable of men, while Oppas was made of some far more exalted clay. He went over and hugged Oppas and kissed his beard and cheeks.

"God bless you for being such a wonderful human being!" he said. "You're no mere human being but rather a marvelous angel. You've made me feel so inferior and lowered my own self-esteem. I'll follow you in whatever you decide to do and carry out your orders."

Meanwhile, Oppas had been adjusting his hair underneath his beretta and walking over to the door. As he came back into the room, he was somewhat shocked that he had not borne that in mind. He took a tablet, holding a candle to illuminate it, and wrote as follows:

From Oppas, Metropolitan Bishop, to Roderic, King of Spain,

I am writing from my prison, not out of any request for mercy or for fear of any dire consequences. I have now learned that the country is in peril. I wish to serve as a partner in its defense and to place myself in the ranks of its army. There is something that I wish to say to you, so command your guard to bring me to you.

Farewell.

He went outside, handed the letter to the guard, and ordered him to take it to the king. With that, he returned to his seat. The officer took the letter and left.

After Count Kumis had left, Roderic had no idea what he should do; he could not debase himself to the extent of initiating a reconciliation, and Kumis would certainly not be coming back of his own accord. If Father Martin had been there, he would have been able to help Roderic decide how to resolve the issue. Roderic spent most of the day in his own quarters, but then his personal servant came in with Oppas's letter. He could scarcely believe what he was reading, so he read it over several times. Once he had finished, he gave orders that Oppas should come and see him. With that, he left his personal quarters in order to await his arrival in the council chamber.

A short while later, Oppas entered with firm step and resolute demeanor. Roderic waited for a while without saying anything, to assess the bishop's mood.

"Don't be afraid, Your Majesty," Oppas began. "I am not here to upbraid or insult you. I have come because of a matter that concerns the interests of the country as a whole. I have heard that the Arabs have invaded our shores and are intent on conquering the country. Your army commander has managed to aggravate both himself and you and has abandoned you in your hour of greatest need. His weakness is of the same sort as that of Julian, governor of Sabta. They are both angry with a Gothic person and have decided to avenge themselves on the kingdom as a whole and on themselves as well since they belong to the same community. However, their bad judgment does not absolve the king himself from the mistake that he made, but we won't discuss that now."

This was said in a calm and moderate tone, Oppas's serious intent being obvious from his facial expression. Roderic was amazed to hear the bishop speak this way and had his own doubts about his sincerity, since qualities of this kind were so foreign to his own—in much the same way as a decent person will always dismiss the idea that anyone else might reward a good deed with mean behavior. He decided to find out what Oppas was really thinking.

"So what's your opinion, then?" he asked.

"It's good that you're confining yourself to the matter at hand," Oppas replied. "In my view, you should send for both Count Kumis and Father Martin. I shall undertake to upbraid them both for their behavior and encourage them to return to your service and thus save this country from the invading Arab forces."

Roderic immediately commanded one of the guards to go and fetch the two men at once. The man departed, and Roderic signaled to Oppas to be seated, hardly crediting that the bishop was actually conducting himself with such loyalty and fervor. Oppas's chivalrous and bold response had managed to utterly confuse the king, so he decided to say nothing more in case something inappropriate slipped out.

Oppas simply sat there, entirely unconcerned with the royal presence. The messenger soon came back with the news that the two men were on their way. Kumis arrived first, gave a respectful greeting, and sat down in response to a gesture from the king. He was surprised to see Oppas there. Then Father Martin came in and was equally astonished to see Oppas in the room. Turning to the king, Oppas asked for permission to speak. It was duly granted.

"Esteemed Count," he said, addressing himself to Kumis, "yesterday you left the king's council in a fury. How do you feel now?"

"The only reason I was so annoyed," the general replied, "was for the sake of our homeland. But no sooner did I get home and sit by myself than I realized that I had been too hasty. We're now in a situation that demands that we be united in order to defend the country against our enemies."

"You are a true warrior!" Oppas said before Kumis even had time to finish. "I was already well aware of your sterling qualities. I dearly hoped for such a response from you. Such people are always swift to see when they have taken a wrong turn."

He now turned to look at Father Martin, who was staring at the floor.

"I can only imagine," Oppas said, "that Father Martin feels the same way as well."

The priest continued to stare at the ground without saying a word.

"I have not the slightest doubt," Oppas said, turning to address the king, "that the Reverend Father fervently wishes to reach agreement and banish all rancor, all in accordance with the testament of Jesus Christ the Messiah. For that reason I suggest that we stop talking about such things and decide what we are going to do. Let the king summon a council meeting involving the men of state in order to consider the measures that need to be taken."

With that, Father Martin raised his head.

"How can the king undertake such a course of action," he asked, addressing the king, "without first proposing it to the council of bishops? His Majesty is well aware that the laws of the land demand that."

Chapter 71

The Decision to go to War

Those laws were not, of course, unknown to Oppas, but he was anxious to move ahead quickly because the council of bishops would take several weeks to convene. Even so, he was worried in case his refusal of the idea of bringing them together might lead Father Martin to ruin everything he had just put to right. With that in mind, he apologized for his insistence.

"I've no desire," he said, "to reach any decision without convening the bishops' council, but I was suggesting that the king's council be convened so as to decide what precisely should be presented to the bishops."

He had forgotten, of course, that the reason Father Martin wanted to reconvene the bishops' council was to complain about the fact that Oppas had managed to get out of prison. What annoyed Father Martin even more at this point was to watch Oppas playing the role of both adviser and homilist.

Roderic approved of the idea of summoning his council and sent for all the counts we mentioned earlier. They all duly arrived. However, before they actually met, Count Kumis insisted that they follow officially sanctioned procedures, which required that Father Martin withdraw because he was not a member of the king's council. With that, Father Martin left the chamber, barely managing to control his anger.

Once the council was assembled, Oppas stood up, raised his hand, gave his blessing, and intoned a fervent prayer in which he beseeched God Almighty to unite the hearts of all Goths in order to rise to the defense of their country. He then addressed the council.

"You are all well aware," he told them, "of the insulting way I have been treated by the king and the council of bishops, to the extent that I have just spent two full months in criminals' prison. The only people I've seen have been guards. They condemned me even though I had committed no crime, or at the very least that is what I personally believe. Even so, when I heard about the grave dangers that are now threatening our country, I asked for an audience with the king and offered my own services along with those of others in order to save it from ruin. Put more appropriately, each one of you needs to show a sincere and powerful desire to bring that about, most especially since you are its governing council and the organizers of its affairs. I will not counsel you about something which you know full well, but I merely wish to convince you all of the strength of my feelings on this matter even though I am a minor player in such matters."

Count Kumis was the one who responded, "Oppas's courage, dignity, and intelligence are all too well known to need mentioning," he said. "We should never expect to encounter such honorable emotions in any human being. So how can we possibly be aware of the important role that he has played and not commit ourselves totally to the king's service? That said, I don't think we should postpone things until the bishops can meet. There's no point in wasting time."

"On a matter like this," Oppas went on, "we have to get their opinion. As everyone knows, they played the major role in forming the current regime, composing its laws and regulations, and organizing its affairs."[53]

"No final decision about conscription and war can be made without consulting them," confirmed Roderic himself.

"There's no harm in asking their opinion," Kumis replied, "but time is short, and the moment is crucial."

Oppas was worried that Kumis might lose his temper again, and all his efforts would be in vain. He remembered that Father Martin had left the council chamber in a fury, which led him to worry about the priest. If he were not reconciled to the king, he might try to incite the bishops against the king. In that case, the kingdom would be divided

53 Guizot.

against itself, and the second disaster would be even worse than the first. He decided that the whole situation needed to be rectified.

"I think you've narrowed the time and defined the goal very clearly," he told Kumis. "As you pointed out, there's no reason not to consult the bishops; in fact, I'll go further and say that we have to respect them because they form the base of all these institutions, quite apart from the benefits that may accrue from their counsel. Beyond that, the need to present a unified front demands that we ask for their advice because any grievance that they might have would inevitably lead to schism. I'm sure you realize that such an eventuality would mean that the goal for which you propose to draw your sword and put your military talents to use could not be achieved. My dearest hope, therefore, is that you will come to terms with this peril that we face, as I'm sure you will. With that in mind, I suggest that we start here." Saying so, he gestured toward the door through which Father Martin had left the chamber. "If Father Martin can be convinced, then things will be that much easier."

He now turned to face Roderic.

"Would Your Majesty permit Father Martin to attend this council meeting?" he asked. "He could then take part in the deliberations."

By this time, Oppas had so overwhelmed everyone with his fervor and generosity of spirit that his words carried great weight, quite apart from the natural eloquence that he possessed. Roderic immediately gave instructions for Father Martin, who had been left on his own in one of the palace rooms, to be brought in. As he entered, Oppas stood up and smiled at him.

"Reverend Father," he said, "everyone in this room is aware of the fact that the bishops have control of affairs in the Gothic kingdom. However, young Count Kumis here is a soldier who likes to get things done quickly. His desire to protect our kingdom is such that he wants to move as swiftly as possible. When it comes to matters of war, he is clearly in the right, but I'm concerned about the need to consult the bishops on the matter. What worries me is that doing so will cause delay. Then we'll lose our opportunity, and everything will have been in vain. When the bishops meet and give us their opinion, I cannot believe that they won't counsel preparation for war as soon as possible. In fact, I think they might even blame us for delaying things until they have held their meeting. In my view—although it is for the king to issue the order—we should start preparing for war now, tell the various classes to start collecting troops and funds, and send a message to the bishops to convene, at which point we'll inform them of the decision of this council. Either that, or we can send them a summary of our decision in their own dioceses, because at this point in time we need them to be there. If the king permits, I shall be speaking on this topic, but the entire matter will be at the king's discretion. My reason for saying this is that the king should delegate the Reverend Father Martin as his deputy in informing the bishops of the decision of this council. If you think that I should be the one to undertake such a service, I hereby offer to do so. Or as you see fit…"

When Oppas finished talking, Father Martin could not come up with a response because he realized that the council's decision would be carried out, come what may. He was duly amazed to hear Oppas agreeing to make him the king's deputy in informing the bishops, because he would then be able to tell them all exactly what he was thinking. Even so, he did not like the idea of performing this charge, because he thought that Oppas was trying to keep him away from the king's council or else was trying to escape from his imprisonment for some other reason. Neither thought gave him any comfort. He saw no point in opposing the council's decision, so instead he decided to muddy the waters.

"I don't think," he said, "that the king will think ill of me if I demand that the bishops be convened. That is a perfectly legitimate request. As my brother the metropolitan bishop has observed, war is something that demands rapid action, and it is thus at the king's discretion as to how he communicates with the bishops. I personally would regard such an assignment as a great honor, but it would also require a good deal of time since I would have to travel from one diocese to another as delegated by the metropolitan bishop. It would be better for the king to delegate selected members of his retinue whom he would send out all together so that the news could reach all the bishops at the same time."

Oppas was not oblivious to the rancor and hatred that lay behind this particular show of apparent pliability, but he chose to overlook it in the broader cause of achieving the result he wanted. He therefore extolled Father Martin's suggestion and turned to speak to the king.

"With God's help," he said with a smile, "we have reached agreement. Now all the king has to do is to cooperate with his council in preparing for war. In that cause we are all his loyal and willing subjects."

Now that the king had seen the way in which Oppas's plan had worked out to his advantage, the king could do nothing else but show his respect and feel a little ashamed in his own eyes.

"God bless you, Oppas!" he said.

Oppas raised his hand to stop him for fear of further annoying Father Martin. He had no desire to hear any further praise heaped upon himself. Standing up, Oppas now asked for permission to leave and return to his prison.

"No, Oppas," the king replied, "stay here with us. You're a fine counselor. Leave prisons for people who belong there!"

"I thank you for that," Oppas said. "Even so, I would like to leave for a short while, then return."

The king gave his permission, and Oppas left, thanking God that his mission had succeeded. Sergius met him, and he told the abbot what had happened, all of which only served to increase the latter's admiration for the bishop's sterling qualities. They chatted about many things, and then Sergius left to return to the Mountain Monastery.

Florinda was waiting impatiently for his return. When Sergius got back and told her at the end of his report what Oppas had managed to do, she felt very awkward because it was exactly the opposite of what she had expected to hear, namely that the dynasty was about to fall thanks to her father's helping hand. She was scared to think about what might happen to her and her father if, in fact, the Arabs did not emerge as victors in the conflict. She did not know what to think, but she was unable to believe that Oppas could be in the wrong because all the laws of honor and chivalry supported his position. If it were not for the weakness of women and her own desire for revenge, Florinda would never have chosen to support something contrary to Oppas's wishes, but she strongly believed that her only path to happiness lay in Roderic's death, especially now that her father had declared himself to be the king's enemy. If Roderic were to win, the consequences for her and her father would be disastrous.

She asked the abbot about Alfonso and learned that he was in Astigi with a battalion of soldiers awaiting Roderic's further orders. She longed to go to Astigi, because she realized that, if Alfonso found out where she was staying, he would certainly come himself or else send someone to bring her to him. But she was afraid of Roderic's spies, so she asked the abbot for his advice.

"You should stay here with us," he told her, "until we can see what this forthcoming war will bring about..."

Chapter 72

The Journey

Florinda spent the rest of winter and all of the following spring at the monastery, getting whatever news she could by way of Ajilla, Chantilla, and the abbot. Because her father was with the Arabs, their victories were the only ones she heard about. After invading Spain, they had made their way across the province of Baetica. Meanwhile, Roderic was getting his forces ready and preparing to lead them south. In fact, she had heard that he had actually left Toledo accompanied by a number of his men. All Spain was in an uproar. As she knew full well, there were so many factions with different agendas that some people felt scared and regretful, while others gloated and were eager for revenge. When people in the monastery heard about all these goings-on, they felt cut off from it all—this because they were far from the field of battle. Florinda, meanwhile, was full of forebodings, being worried about both her father and her fiancé; she could not make up her mind whether to go to see just one of them or both, or indeed whether she should stay put in the monastery. The last choice seemed the most sensible, because she hoped that her father would do what he had said and send someone to bring her to him. When summertime arrived, the Mountain Monastery enjoyed fresh invigorating breezes and an abundance of pure water; the valleys were now covered in green.

One July day, Florinda woke up and was about to go out as usual for a walk in the surrounding orchards. Before she could do so, Ajilla arrived to ask her to go to the abbot's quarters. He had not invited her there for some time, so she was a bit worried. Hurrying over, she arrived at the abbot's room to find an old man there whose general appearance showed that he was neither Goth nor Roman. The clothes he was wearing reminded him of the kind of thing she had seen as a child when she was in Sabta with her father. When she moved closer, she could tell that he had been traveling. Not only his beard and mustache, but even his eyebrows and lashes, were caked with dust; in fact, he was dusty all over. She immediately assumed that this man was bringing fresh news, so she entered the room and extended her greetings. The abbot welcomed her.

"This man is a messenger from your father," he told her.

Her heart skipped a beat, and her cheeks suddenly reddened.

"What is your news?" she asked, turning toward the man.

"I'm a friend, admirer, and confidant of your father," the man replied. "I know about the letter you wrote to him and the radical change that it has brought about. Don't you recognize me, Florinda?"

Once Florinda had heard him speak and looked more carefully at his features, she recalled that she had seen this man several times when she was younger. He had often come to her father's residence in Sabta. The man decided to keep her in suspense no longer.

"Don't you recognize Sulayman the merchant?" he asked.

She realized at once who this man was. "Are you really Sulayman?" she asked him. "Of course I know you well. You used to visit our house often and bring presents and goods; you'd sell us crockery and clothing. Have you come from my father? Where is he now?"

"He's with the Arab army near Guadalete," he replied.

He gave her a look that asked whether he should reveal what he knew in the abbot's presence. In response, she signaled that he could indeed do so.

"The Arabs have penetrated far into Baetica," he said, "and they've only encountered minimal resistance. People in the country seem to regard them as liberators. They'll soon be in control of the entire country."

The abbot was shocked.

"What's happened to the Spanish army?" he asked.

"The Arabs have not faced Roderic as yet. We've heard that he's left Toledo with a huge army. But they'll be beaten. So spread the glad tidings!"

The abbot looked genuinely surprised.

"Do you really believe that?" he asked. "What's going to happen to us if what you say is true?"

"You'll certainly be better off than you are now," the man replied. "When the Arabs conquer a territory, they rarely impose measures on the inhabitants except poll tax and land tax. Monks and clergy are exempt from that requirement; they can stay in their monasteries safe and sound. That's exactly what has happened in lands they've conquered before, like Egypt and Syria.

The abbot stared silently at the floor.

"Why have you come here now?" Florinda asked.

"Your father, the count, charged me to come and pay you a visit. If you would like to go to him, I'm at your service."

That made Florinda very happy.

"But aren't you afraid something might happen on the way?" she asked.

"The people of Spain aren't going to hurt us," he said. "We're among them. The king won't be bothering us, either; he's too busy with himself and his army."

Florinda turned to the abbot, as though to ask him for his opinion.

"If you need to go," he said, "then this is obviously an opportunity that you shouldn't miss. We pray that you'll reach your father safe and sound."

Florinda now went back to her room and asked her aunt what she thought. The old lady advised that they should go. Next day, they made the necessary preparations and left the monastery, accompanied by Sulayman, as well as Ajilla and Chantilla. Florinda asked that they pass by Astigi on the way.

They traveled for several days, unimpeded by storms or rain. The terrain was covered with trees and grass, and the weather was beautiful. When they were close to Astigi, Florinda's heart started pounding at the very sight of the city. They were looking down on it from a high point, and she could see its cathedral. She considered the distant view of it as a blessing and started wondering to herself where Alfonso might be based. She decided to ask Sulayman.

"If Roderic sent a troop of soldiers to Astigi," she asked, "where would it be billeted?"

"I suppose you want to know where Prince Alfonso is?" he asked.

"Yes," she replied somewhat surprised. "How did you know that?"

"I've known that for several months," he replied. "When I came here, I heard that the prince and his soldiers had arrived. They were staying in that fortress by the bridge. Shall I go and look for him?"

Florinda gave him permission to go.

"Please do so, by God's mercy!" she told him. "Bring us news…"

He left them and was gone in an instant. Meanwhile, Florinda and her aunt dismounted and stayed there waiting for news. Florinda was looking forward to seeing Alfonso; every time she thought about it, her heart fluttered. She could still recall the last time she had seen him in the palace gardens in Toledo, wearing winter clothes, furs, and a wide belt. When he had heard the sound of the alarm, he had rushed away. That final image was imprinted in her mind. However, she did not have long to wait or worry, because Sulayman came hurrying back. When she saw him approaching, she looked up but felt too bashful to ask him for news before he even arrived. When he finally got there, he anticipated her question.

"There's no one in the fortress," he told her.

"Do you think they weren't billeted there?" she asked.

"I'm sure they were there," he replied. "I asked one of the fortress guards, and he told me that Roderic had sent a message to Prince Alfonso to meet him at Guadalete with his troops so they could engage the Arab army."

Florinda was shocked and looked down. She tried to keep her emotions under control while she was talking to this man, but she was really worried about Alfonso because he was going into battle, with him on one side and her father on the other. If one side were victorious, the other would have been defeated. And she loved them both dearly. Sulayman may well have realized what was going through her mind.

"If we hurry," he said, "I think we may be able to catch up with Prince Alfonso on the way. If not, we'll certainly find him at Guadalete. Once we get there, I can go and look for him and bring you whatever you need."

Florinda took comfort from this promise and gave instructions to proceed. They mounted and made their way forward till they reached Astigi and crossed the bridge. They kept moving south and passed by vineyards and orchards, although there were fewer and fewer workers in the fields as they drew close to Guadalete.

On the road next morning, they came across villagers who were hurrying along, as though to escape an enemy that was pursuing them. Florinda told herself that they must be close to the Arab army, or else the Arabs were already advancing. When she turned to look at Sulayman, he was already staring at the horizon as though he could see something peculiar. When she looked for herself, she could make out a cloud of dust and assumed that the Arabs were indeed coming.

"The Arabs seem to be very close," she told Sulayman, her heart thumping. "Isn't my father with them?"

"I don't think the people coming are Arabs," Sulayman replied. "They're moving north-south."

He stopped one of the villagers and asked him why they were running away.

"Don't you see the king's army coming?" the man replied. "They always wreak havoc on us poor folk. They take all our fruit and trample our crops. If they made do just with that, it wouldn't be so bad. But they attack people as well."

So saying, he sped off in case the person he was addressing happened to be a supporter of the king who would have him arrested.

When Florinda heard the man talking, she became very sad. She wanted to know if the king himself was with the army.

"Do you think the king is with the army?" she asked Sulayman.

"I think so," he replied.

Once she heard that, she realized she might be in imminent danger. Sulayman picked up on her anxieties.

"Don't worry, my lady," he told her. "You're quite safe. Let's go and hide till the army has passed."

So saying, he moved off, and everyone else followed him. They reached a desolate spot atop a hill far removed from the road.

"I think I should disguise myself as a man," Florinda said.

The men gave her and her aunt some of their clothes. When they put them on, anyone looking from a distance would assume that they were both men. They then hid where they were. Florinda was very eager to watch the army passing by, so she found a crevice through which she could observe the approaching cloud of dust. First came the banners, then the cavalry with colorful uniforms and shields. In the middle of the procession she could make out a whole cluster of other banners, carried by cavalrymen with jewel-encrusted uniforms. In their midst was a special carriage, gleaming like the sun; she realized that it had to be Roderic's. For a moment she panicked. No sooner had the procession come close to their hiding spot than her knees started to shake; she shivered all over and made the sign of the cross. Plucking up courage, she steadied herself and listened to the sound of beating drums, flapping banners, neighing horses, and the thunder of wheels. Provisions, treasure, and the clamor of shouting people all passed by, and then Roderic's procession came into view. He was seated on a kind of chair that looked like a hawdah, strung between two horses. Over his head was a brocade sunshade encrusted with pearls and jewels,[54] while in front a cross was embossed on one of the columns. Roderic was wearing a crown gleaming with precious stones and an embroidered pink sash. He looked just like a king sitting on his throne, hand on beard, as he surveyed the scene to left and right, taking in the huge number of men and amount of equipment he had with him. Father Martin was seated alongside, talking to him and making gestures, while Roderic kept staring at the flags all around his procession, satisfaction written all over his face.

There is no need to speculate about Florinda's feelings as she set eyes on Roderic. Sulayman was standing by her side and noticed how, when the procession passed by, her color turned grey.

---

54 Al-Maqqari, *Nafh al-Tib*, Part I.

"So, my lady," he asked her so as to distract her attention, "what do you think about the size of this army?"

"I don't know," she replied, "but it's clearly huge. Do you think the Arab army is bigger?"

"The Arabs have only a fifth of this number," Sulayman replied, "and that's not even counting the men who'll join Roderic's forces before they meet the Arabs. That's especially true of Prince Alfonso's troops. He'll be joining this army."

"So the Arabs are weak and in danger?" she said.

"If they were really weak," Sulayman replied, "they would not have been able to invade this country. Power doesn't reside in numbers but in fortitude. My lady, the Arabs have no more than twelve thousands troops in this country. Even so, no one has been able to stand in their way."

"But so far," Florinda said, "they haven't encountered an army this size."

"That's true," he replied, "but I've witnessed enough of their courage, unity, and endurance to know that there's nothing to fear. Even so, victory comes from God, and He will bestow it on whomever He wishes."

While they were talking, the remainder of the procession passed by, so they stayed in their hiding place for the rest of the day. Sulayman went off on his own to scout the place where the Arabs were camped. He came back and told Florinda that they were in the Guadalete valley close to the city of Jerez.

"Do you know where Alfonso's encampment is?" she asked.

"He's close by," he replied.

"So what's to be done?" she asked.

"If you want to go to see your father, the count," he said, "I can take you to him at once."

Florinda was of two minds. How could she go to the Arab camp without first going to Alfonso and finding some way of seeing him? For a while she said nothing. Once again, Sulayman realized why she was not saying anything.

"I gather that you'd like to look for Alfonso first. Is that right?"

"Yes," she replied.

"I happen to know the owner of a Jerez vineyard," Sulayman told her. "There's a building on a hill that overlooks the entire Jerez plain. You can stay there with your aunt and servants. I'll go to look for Alfonso and bring you news, or else I'll ask your father for advice…"

Chapter 73

Oppas's Letter

Florinda agreed with his plan and thanked him. They now proceeded till they were on the outskirts of Jerez. The area was surrounded by vineyards, among them the one owned by our friend, the sheikh, who was Butrus's father—he being the one whom Sulayman had had in mind when he mentioned it to Florinda. They climbed up and entered the vineyard, heading for the bower, but no one was there. Sulayman had never passed by this spot without seeing the sheikh, along with grandchildren and even great-grandchildren, ranging around the vineyard, either working or playing. "Something very unusual is going on here," he told himself. They carried on till they reached another bower at the edge of the vineyard, but before they got there, they heard a voice calling them, similar to the ones they would normally hear among the vines. Sulayman moved forward cautiously till they entered the bower itself, and there they spotted the sheikh and his entire household, all of them clearly in a state of panic. When they spotted Sulayman coming toward them, they were scared. Butrus got to his feet.

"What do you want?" he asked, but then he recognized who it was. "Welcome, welcome to Sulayman the merchant!"

When the sheikh heard that name, he too stood up and welcomed Sulayman. All the other members of the family were happy as well; they had all heard about him before, and some of them had seen him when he had come to Jerez to purchase wine in season. Now that they had recognized him, they were less scared. However clever and capable village folk are, they will always be convinced that city folk are their superiors. Once Sulayman saw how warm their welcome was, he dealt with them very delicately. Going over to the sheikh, he greeted him and asked him why they were all secluded in this bower in broad daylight, when the vines needed tending.

"You obviously don't know what we've been through," the sheikh replied.

"I suppose you mean the Arab invasion," Sulayman said.

"That's right," the sheikh replied. "We don't know what's going to happen to us once this war's over. Yesterday we watched the king's army setting up camp opposite the Arab army. The battle's going to start soon. We have babies here, so we can't simply run away even if we wanted to do so. And we can't abandon our fields either."

As he spoke, his voice almost choked, such was his love for his family and children.

"Don't worry, dear friend," Sulayman told him with a smile. "I'll pledge myself to defend you and your family from any harm. "I have some companions with me here whom I'll commit to spending the night in your company. Do you have room for them?"

"They're very welcome," the sheikh replied and pointed to the storehouse at the top of the hill.

"They can stay up there," he said.

Along with some of his children, he hurried over. When they reached Florinda and her party, they took the horses' reins and led them up to the storehouse. Some other children had got there first and swept it clean. Florinda climbed the steps, still dressed in man's clothes. Her aunt and their two servants followed, and then Sulayman. The sheikh's sons stayed at the bottom of the steps awaiting further orders from their father. Sulayman descended the steps, gave them some gold, and asked them to go and fetch some food. When he showed such generosity, the sons were all the more eager to serve him.

Once Florinda had climbed the stairs, she looked out of one of the windows. She could see the area below the vineyard. To the east was a wide plain as far as the eye could see; a river ran through it with trees and grass on its banks. On one side of the plain to the right, she could make out tents of a kind she did not recognize, with a huge red tent in the middle and a flag in front of it. There were smaller flags in front of the other tents as well.

Beyond those tents she could see others, with not only horses but also camels, something she had not seen for a long time. She deduced that this had to be the Arab camp, and she could almost feel her father's presence. By now Sulayman had finished dealing with the sheikh's sons and came back up.

"Isn't that the Arab camp?" she asked him.

"Yes, my lady," he replied. "The tent you see in the middle belongs to their commander, Tariq ibn Ziyad. My lord the count, your father, is in the same tent with him."

"What are those other tents further away?" she asked.

"They're for women and animal provisions," he replied. "When Arabs go to war, they take their women and children with them as well as their animals and place them behind their lines. Whenever their attacks fail and they're tempted to withdraw or flee, their families meet and give them encouragement. They can then return to the fray, invigorated and ready for battle."

Florinda then looked across the plain to the left. In that direction, she could see other tents, which she recognized as being those of the Spanish army. Among them would be both Roderic's and Alfonso's tents. She could easily tell which tent was Roderic's. It was enormous, with flags and banners flying over it and servants and retainers standing in front, although they could not be seen all that clearly because it was so far away. She could not tell which tent was Alfonso's, because the commanders' tents all looked alike, and there were many of them.

"Isn't that the king's tent?" she asked Sulayman, pointing in that direction.

"Yes, it is," he replied, "and I suspect you're anxious to know which one is Alfonso's. The only way to find out is by making inquiries. I've decided to go and check for myself because your father has always dealt kindly with me."

She thanked him for his offer.

"When are you going to leave?" she asked.

"As soon as possible," he replied, "after I've made sure you have all the food you need. You'll be safe here, with your aunt and the two young men, who are both energetic and reliable."

"When will you be back?" she asked.

"I don't know for sure," he replied. "I'll do my best to be quick."

After he had made sure everything was arranged, he said farewell and went back down the hill as the sun was almost setting.

Sulayman dealt with Spaniards a lot. He knew their language well in addition to Gothic. Whenever he spoke to people in either of those languages, they thought he belonged to that community. Beyond that, he knew Berber and Arabic as well. Our readers may already have deduced that he was actually the person who had come to the Jewish gathering in Astigi a few months ago when Alfonso was there, and he had told them about Julian's plans.

After leaving Florinda, he went back the way he had come and approached the Spanish encampment from the rear so no one would be suspicious, approaching as though from some local town or village. He was still staking out the territory without necessarily expecting to actually see Alfonso; he spent quite a while checking the area but did not come across any sign of him. After asking a few people in the know, he was directed to a spot directly behind Roderic's own encampment. He decided that the person he needed to find was Ya'qub, he being the fount of all secret information. The sun had already set by the time he reached the encampment. If anyone had challenged him, he would have claimed that he just happened to be passing by, but the soldiers were far too busy getting ready for battle to bother with him. When he got close to Alfonso's tent, he found some guards standing outside. He did not see Ya'qub, so he dodged behind the tent, pretended that he had swallowed badly, and made a special coughing signal that soon prompted a response from inside. That way, he learned that Ya'qub was there, and the latter in turn realized who was outside. He kept on walking, but fairly soon he heard another cough, which told him exactly where Ya'qub was. They met and exchanged the special modes of greeting by which they recognized each other.

"So I see you're still here," Sulayman said. "Haven't you been able to persuade him yet?"

"I would have managed it," Ya'qub replied, "if it hadn't been for Oppas's letter."

"Which Oppas do you mean?"

"The Metropolitan Bishop Oppas, Alfonso's uncle."

"But wasn't it through Alfonso that you were going to get rid of this dreadful regime?"

"That's right," Ya'qub replied. "I told you what we'd planned just a few months ago. You saw for yourself how we showed him the dinars in the chest at that meeting we had."

"Yes, Alfonso seemed to be on board with our plan. So what's happened since then?"

"When we left the meeting," Ya'qub replied, "he was totally convinced that our plan would work. I led him to believe that, when the Arabs conquered the country, they would let him keep his wealth and restore him to the throne. The achievement of his dearest wishes would come about as a result of Roderic being defeated. However, if Roderic were to win, then so much the worse for himself, his uncle, and his entire family. I told him that Roderic's downfall would depend on one crucial move, something that he alone, Alfonso, would need to take very seriously: on the first battle day, he and his troops would join themselves to the Arab forces. He was convinced by the argument, and we all agreed to the idea...."

"So then what happened?"

Ya'qub put his hand in his pocket and brought out a sealed tablet, the kind they used in those days, and handed it to Sulayman.

"We were all sure that everything was fine," he told Sulayman, "but then he received this letter from his uncle, Oppas."

Sulayman took the tablet and looked at it, but it was so dark that he could not read what it said.

"Don't bother reading it," Ya'qub told him. "I've read it so many times that I have it memorized. I'm furious with Oppas for writing it, even though I've always admired him enormously. I'll tell you what it says, so listen carefully.

From Metropolitan Bishop Oppas, to my beloved nephew, Alfonso: I have now heard about the grievous error that Count Julian has committed in launching an attack on King Roderic along with the Arab armies. In my opinion, he is only doing that to avenge himself because of his daughter. I suspect that, when the news reached you as well, you were delighted because it would salve the anger that you yourself were feeling. Now I'm afraid that that same anger may lead you to commit the same dreadful mistake as Count Julian, namely taking part in the deliberate loss of this kingdom and downfall of the dynasty. In a single day, everything that your ancestors have built up over generations will be destroyed, and the tables will be turned on us and everyone else as well. If you have even entertained such ideas, put them aside. They are the work of the devil incarnate. Instead, join with the king of the Goths to defend the Gothic kingdom of Spain. The entire matter of our rancorous dispute with Roderic can be discussed further once the Arab invasion has been repulsed. My dearest hope is that you will listen to my advice and not go along with the advice of other people. Farewell.

"That's the statement of a man of intelligence," was Sulayman's comment once he had heard the letter's contents. "Even so, if Alfonso follows that plan, then things will work out to our disadvantage as Jews. That will be especially true if Roderic comes out on top and learns about the ways in which we've been conspiring and intriguing against him and decides to interrogate prisoners about our secret associations. Even though the Arabs may be courageous and inured to hardship, I suspect that, as long as Alfonso decides to stick with the Goths, Roderic's side is going to come out on top. God help us all!"

"That's my thinking as well," Ya'qub replied, "but I've run out of ideas when it comes to persuading him otherwise. Sulayman, you know full well how many hours I spent during Witiza's reign saving the people of Spain from this kind of injustice. I myself gave up my position, got rid of my possessions, adopted Christianity, and turned myself into a household servant who would prepare the meals and serve at table. Just when relief seemed to be at hand, along comes Oppas to stand in our way. I had always assumed that he was our greatest supporter. Not merely that, but that he was the major motivator of our project to bring about change…"

"Where justice and truth are involved," Sulayman replied, "Oppas is correct and is to be commended. He does not wish the kingdom to be removed from the jurisdiction of his own nation, religion, and language community. He is unwilling to see it handed over to a people who are alien in terms of their religion, nation, and language. Our goal, however, is to rid our country of the Goths as a whole. As far as we are concerned, the Arabs will be better than they are. We have already observed the way they've treated Jews and Christians in Syria and Egypt. They have complete religious freedom, so everyone can practice the rituals of his faith as he sees fit, so long as he contributes a little bit of money that they call the poll tax. Not only that, but we Jews are closely related to the Arabs because, as you know, both groups come from a single ancestor, Abraham. They deal with us in a special way. With that in mind, we owe it to them in the current circumstances to support them in their conquest of this country. In so doing, we're serving our own best interests. The things that Oppas and others have to say are of no interest to us…"

"That's indeed what we would wish to see happen," Ya'qub replied. "The only way to bring it about is to convince Alfonso to switch sides. That will weaken Roderic's forces and cripple his resolve. You must be aware that the majority of soldiers fighting for Roderic here are doing so against their will; none of them like him. If they saw that their former king's son had gone over to the enemy, they'd all be either inclined to follow him or at least refuse to fight."

As he was speaking, he kept twiddling his beard, which was still caked with dust. Both of them remained silent for a while.

"In summary, then," Ya'qub went on, "if we can't persuade Alfonso to switch sides, all our plans, hopes, and money will have gone up in smoke. That'll be it!"

"True enough!" Sulayman replied. "If we could tempt them with money to make it happen, things would be a lot easier. But bribery won't work, neither with Alfonso nor Oppas. Even if we managed to bribe one of Alfonso's men, he himself still wouldn't change his mind. After all, you're one of his closest confidants, and yet you haven't managed to do it!" He grinned as he said that.

"This is no time for tomfoolery," Ya'qub responded. "The situation's both serious and dangerous. Time's running out…"

"When's Rodereic going to attack?" Sulayman asked.

"I heard tomorrow."

Sulayman was shocked. "Tomorrow?" he said. "Time's certainly running out, and we've lost our chance. Can't you hold things up for a day or two?"

"I don't think so," Ya'qub replied. "In any case, what's the point?"

"I'd try to implement a plan that I think might work."

"What's that?"

"I'll tell you in a while," Sulayman replied. "You can help me by getting the attack delayed for a day or two."

"I don't think I can manage that, Sulayman," Ya'qub said. "Roderic wants to attack the Arabs quickly before they can get reinforcements. That's what Oppas has advised him to do."

"Good grief!" Sulayman interrupted, "So who is this Oppas supposed to be? How has he managed to turn everything upside down?"

"If you've got a plan," Ya'qub told him, "then get on with it before it's too late."

"I'm leaving now," Sulayman replied. "I'll be back tomorrow morning with news of what I've got planned. If you can think of a way of delaying the battle, then do it! Farewell in God's name."

So saying, he made ready to return the way he had come. Ya'qub stood there watching him as he disappeared from view. It was early morning when he went back into Alfonso's tent.

Chapter 74

The Stratagem

It was pitch dark as Sulayman made his way to the Arab encampment and reached Julian's tent. No one stopped him because he knew the password. Julian had gone to his tent to get some sleep, but he had so many old and new worries to think about that he rarely managed to do so. When Sulayman arrived, Julian was sitting on his bed; he could not fall asleep, and that made him even more restless. As Sulayman watched him in the lamplight, he could see depression written all over his face, particularly after he had seen Roderic's army the day before. It looked huge and well equipped, while the Arab force was only a fifth as large. He was afraid that the Goths were going to win, in which case the consequences for himself, his daughter, and his entire family would be grim. Every time he thought about it, his entire body trembled.

Someone now told him that Sulayman was at the door of his tent, and he allowed him to come in. He greeted Sulayman and immediately asked him where Florinda was.

"She's well," he replied, "and will be coming either tomorrow morning or when the battle's over."

He proceeded to tell Julian where she was staying, and that put his mind at ease.

"So why have you come here now?" he asked Sulayman.

"On a matter of crucial importance, one that I think is already much on my lord's mind."

"The only thing on my mind at the moment is the size of Roderic's army," Julian replied. "It's very large, and it makes me afraid for the

Arabs. If they're defeated, they can go back without any problems. But it will be disastrous for me, my family, and everyone who's supported us."

"That's precisely why I've come," Sulayman told him. "But you should realize, my lord, that, even though the situation is very grave, it can still be resolved with relative ease."

He then told Julian about Alfonso and the conversation he had had with Ya'qub.

"I've come here now," he told Julian, "to ask you to write a letter to Alfonso in which you ask him to stop fighting. You'll need to give a guarantee that he won't lose any of his own wealth or his own and his family's lands. At the same time, encourage him to provoke Roderic. Give me the letter, and I'll take it to him. I know how to do it."

For a moment Julian stared at the floor.

"Come back tomorrow morning," he told Sulayman, "and I'll give it to you."

"Very well, my lord," he replied.

With that, he left to return to the vineyard. Florinda was on tenterhooks as she waited for him to come back, her mind full of emotions and premonitions that prevented her from sleeping. How could she possibly doze off when her beloved Alfonso was so close and she could not get to see him? In the words of the poet:

In the pain of love, the bitterest of circumstances I know

Is when the beloved is close by, yet there is no way to reach him.

She was still having such thoughts when the night was almost over. Every time there was a waft of breeze and the leaves rustled, she thought Sulayman was coming back. Her passionate love had convinced her that Sulayman would be bringing Alfonso with him. Just then she did indeed hear footsteps and the rustle of dry grass close by the wine store. She listened carefully, her heart pounding ever faster, and managed to make out the sound of footsteps coming ever closer. Hearing a whisper, she stood up, went over to the window, and looked out. There was Sulayman talking to Ajilla. He climbed the steps, and Florinda opened the door for him.

"So, Sulayman," she asked, "what's the news?"

"It's all good," he replied.

But his tone of voice suggested that there was something else, so Florinda got worried.

"You're holding something back," she said. "Tell me what it is."

The conversation woke her aunt up, so she sat up in her bed, rubbing her eyes.

"What's the news, Sulayman?" the old lady asked. "Did you see Prince Alfonso?"

"No, my lady, I didn't."

When Florinda heard that, she was very upset.

"So where is he then?" she asked.

"He's in the camp."

"How come you're back here without seeing him?"

"Seeing him would have done neither me nor you any good."

"How can that be?"

"Because at the moment, the only person he's listening to is his uncle, Oppas. The bishop has told him he has to devote himself heart and soul to Roderic's cause."

When she heard that, her face turned red, and she shuddered. For a moment she had nothing to say, but then she gave a smile as if to say that she could not believe what Sulayman was telling her. Above all, Alfonso would be bound to listen to her more than anyone else on earth.

"I think he'll listen to me," she said. "But how does all this concern us? What's the connection to the fact that you didn't meet Alfonso?"

"Something that's enormously important for your life, my own, and Count Julian's, as well," Sulayman replied, "not to mention for every Goth who still supports the family of King Witiza and all those who are not willing to live as chattels of Roderic."

"What does all that mean?" she asked.

Sulayman now explained it all as briefly as possible. "You should realize, my lady," he said, "that your own survival and that of your father and Prince Alfonso himself depend entirely on the Arabs winning a victory and Roderic being defeated. That all depends on Alfonso's decision. If he and his men leave Roderic's camp and join the Arab forces, Roderic is bound to be defeated, and the entire country will be rid of his evil tyranny. However, it seems that Alfonso is going to do what his uncle has asked of him. Oppas has asked him to fight for Roderic. If he obeys his uncle, so much the worse for all of us. God help us all!"

Florinda realized that Alfonso's position was enormously important, but she still thought that he would listen to what she had to say. She decided to write him a letter in which she would use every fervent expression she could muster to persuade him—encouragement, opprobrium, sympathy—touching every emotion in the book.

"I'll write him a letter," she told Sulayman. "Will you deliver it for me?"

"Yes, my lady," he replied, "I'll undertake the task."

"Come back in the morning," she told him, "and I'll give it to you. You can take it to him, and I can only hope and pray to God that it'll work."

Sulayman left, satisfied by the outcome of his conversation with Florinda. It was almost dawn when he lay out a rug on the floor of the sheikh's bower, hoping to get some rest. He closed his eyes and only woke up again when he heard the sound of beating drums and trumpet calls. Rousing himself, he looked at the two encampments. The Gothic camp was teeming with soldiers, arrayed in ranks and ready for battle, with flags and banners fluttering in front of them. In the middle were Roderic's troops, with his sunshade and throne duly protected by horsemen and other aides. Looking over at the Arab encampment, Sulayman could see movement there, too, as they all made ready to defend themselves. The whole scene horrified him. He felt that this was going to be a bad day; he told himself that they had wasted the opportunity. What made him feel so pessimistic was that there was an enormous gap in numbers between the two opposing sides, not to mention the equipment, cavalry, and provisions that the Spanish army had brought with them. Sulayman leapt up like a prowling lion and rushed down to the Arab encampment to take Julian's letter to Alfonso.

When he got there, he was panting from sheer exhaustion. He noticed that the Muslims, most of whom were Berbers, were drawn up for battle wearing white turbans to protect their heads from the sun. The tips of their swords and spears seemed to be emerging from their heads like some armor protection. Their number included spear- and lance-throwers and Arab archers. The cavalry were all wearing chainmail and helmets, so one could only make out the slits of their eyes. In front were special horsemen carrying banners with verses from the Koran on them.

No sooner had Sulayman reached the encampment than he started hearing cries of "God is great!" and "Praise be to God!" and others reciting the Fatiha of the Koran. As he looked at their faces, he could see no hint of what might happen in the battle, whether good or bad. For a while it made him forget that he had actually come to see Julian. But then he remembered his purpose in coming. He started looking along the ranks but failed to find Julian. When he asked someone standing there, he replied that Julian had gone off with Tariq to rally the troops so they would remain steadfast to the cause. No sooner had Sulayman heard that than he spotted some horsemen returning from one of the edges of the encampment, led by a cavalryman wearing a shield of Solomon and a huge turban. However, he was not wearing a helmet, so his features were clearly visible.

Looking more closely, he realized that this was none other than Tariq ibn Ziyad, the army commander. Sulayman had actually seen him before on more than one occasion, so he was already well aware of how imposing a figure he was, but he had never seen him looking the way he was at this crucial moment. On horseback he looked like a veritable mountain. He had pushed his turban back, so one could easily see his broad forehead, with its thick eyebrows, and his eyes reddened by so much effort. He had thick lips, and his beard was jet black with just a smattering of white. Sweat was pouring from his forehead onto his beard, but he could not be bothered to wipe it off. In fact, nothing seemed to be bothering him, and he did not look at any particular soldier. Reins in his left hand and sword in his right, he had pulled up his sleeve, so one could easily see his deep-brown arms. His stallion was no less impressive than he was. In fact, Tariq kept trying to get it to halt, but it would only do so for a moment before getting ready to charge off again. It, too, had sweat all over its chest and head, coursing down its head till it reached the muzzle. Its color was as black as the darkest night.

Sulayman was deeply impressed by this amazing Berber warrior. Alongside him he noticed another horseman, whose skin color and appearance were completely different, although he resembled the commander in his fearless posture and brave demeanor. He was younger than Tariq and seemed more lively. Sulayman stood to one side while Tariq and his retinue rode past, hoping to catch a glimpse of Julian and get a moment of his time so he could ask him for his letter. But at that very moment Tariq stopped, turned toward the serried ranks of his troops arrayed in front of him, and raised his right hand, which clasped his drawn sword. Everyone realized that he was about to speak and listened carefully to what he was about to say.

He began with praises to God, urging and encouraging the Muslims to fight in the cause of Islam.

"Ye people," he said, "where will you flee? The sea is at your backs and the enemy is in front of you. In God's name, all you have at your disposal is possession of the truth and endurance. I want you all to realize that in this peninsula you are worse off than orphans at the rogues' banquet. Now your enemy has come to confront you with his mighty army and weapons, while all you have to counter it all are your swords; the only food you can expect will be whatever you can extract from your enemies' hands. If this lack of food continues for a while and you cannot work out a solution, then everything will have been lost. The fear you have aroused in people's hearts will be converted into stalwart defense. Our best defense is to attack this tyrant. He has left his fortress city and come here to meet us, so we have a golden opportunity, provided that you will allow yourselves to risk death..."

"I'm not here to give you all advice about something that is of no concern to me. To the contrary, I'm urging you all to follow a path in which our own souls should be the very least of our concerns. I'll begin with my own self. You should all realize that, if you're willing to endure hardships now for the short term, your expectation in the long term will involve the very greatest luxury and ease. You've all heard about the lovely Greek maidens that this peninsula has managed to produce, all bedecked in pearls and coral, and the gorgeous gold-encrusted gowns worn by cloistered maidens in the palaces of crowned monarchs. From among the heroes of our people you selected Al-Walid ibn 'Abd al-

Malik as caliph of Islam. Your acceptance of the monarchs of this land as relatives and in-laws is a sign of his trust that you are prepared to fight and plunge into conflict against other warriors and horsemen. What he expects is that God will offer His reward to those who proclaim His word and spread His faith throughout this peninsula. So may its spoils be reserved for you alone and not for other believers. God Almighty will be the guarantor who will grant you victory, to be remembered in this world and the next."

"You should know that I will be the first to respond to this call. When the two armies meet, I intend to attack the tyrant Roderic in person and to kill him, God willing. Follow me into battle. If I should be killed at some point, I will already have dealt with that issue, and you will not find yourselves short of an intelligent commander upon whom you can rely. But, should I be killed before I reach the king, then pursue my goal to the end, attack him yourselves, and help bring about the conquest of this country by slaying its ruler. Once he is dead, they will give up."[55]

No sooner had he finished than shouts of "God be praised" rang out. By now they were all fired up, and Sulayman could tell from Tariq's words that the commander had managed to rouse their courageous spirits. Even so, he was worried about the shortage of time and set off to look for Julian. He spotted him in Tariq's group and hurried over. Julian noticed him and told him to approach, which he did.

"We thought you'd been held up," he told Sulayman, "so we sent the letter with someone else."

Sulayman was delighted to hear that the opportunity had not been lost and turned on his heels to go back to the vineyard and collect Florinda's letter. He needed to appeal to Alfonso's emotions and get him to change his mind. Reaching the vineyard, he found Florinda standing on the steps with the letter in her hand. To save valuable time, he took it without saying a word and rushed off; he was wearing clothing that made him look like one of Roderic's men.

By now the sun was high in the sky, shining on the Gothic encampment and reflecting off their uniforms, banners, and shields, especially those of Roderic's entourage. While the soldiers were

---

55 Al-Maqqari, *Nafh al-Tib,* Part I.

preoccupied with their preparations, Sulayman made his way around the back. He noticed that the Goth army was arranged in a phalanx pattern just like Roman armies, while at this time Arab armies preferred to use serried ranks.[56] Roderic's army had a left and right flank, each one led by a general. Alfonso was in command of the right, while the commander of the core was Roderic himself along with Count Kumis. Roderic was seated on his throne with an embossed canopy over his head to give him shade. He was surrounded by a veritable forest of banners and flags, while he was protected from the front by a troop of cavalry wearing embossed uniforms. He himself was wearing a coat encrusted with pearls, rubies, and emeralds; even his shoes were embossed with gold.[57]

Sulayman was struck by the huge difference between the simplicity of the Arab army and the utter extravagance of the Gothic one, quite apart from Roderic sitting on his throne as opposed to Tariq on his stallion. Just then, Sulayman noticed a tall man standing on a bench. He was wearing clerical garb and raising his hands to the heavens, holding in one of them a decorated cross. He lifted his voice in prayer, asking that God grant victory to the Gothic army. From his height and august demeanor, Sulayman could tell that this was Bishop Oppas. Almost in spite of himself, he stayed where he was till Oppas had finished, at which point the bishop did the round of the troops, urging them to be courageous and to remember the glories that their ancestors had wrought and the tremendous fortitude that they had displayed in shedding their blood in order to conquer this country.

Sulayman could delay no longer, so he hurried over to the army ranks. He searched anxiously for Ya'qub so he could hand him Florinda's letter but could not find him in the army ranks. He now tried looking in the tent. When he got there, he found a military-looking man by the door and recognized him as one of Julian's men. He realized that he had to be the one who had brought Julian's letter to Alfonso.

"Did you bring Julian's letter?" he asked the man so no one else could hear.

"Yes," the man replied. "Alfonso's inside reading it, and one of his servants is with him."

---

56 *History of Islamic Civilization.*

57 Al-Maqqari, *Nafh al-Tib,* Part I.

Chapter 75

Emotions Triumph

Ever since Oppas's letter had arrived, Alfonso had been trying to keep his emotions in check and assess the consequences of this conflict. He could envisage nothing good coming out of it, quite apart from the danger it obviously posed to both Florinda and her father. Every time he pictured the way Florinda had been so badly treated, his entire body shuddered. Ever since he had read the letter she had written to her father in that dark room, he had been trying to find her but had heard absolutely nothing. He could not keep up the search for fear of Roderic's finding out. Then he had heard that the Arabs had invaded and made their way through Baetica province and that Julian was their guide. At the time he had made up his mind to join them, if not to take revenge on Roderic, then certainly to honor Florinda's courage. But then Oppas's letter had arrived and had affected him deeply, almost as though he had been hypnotized. Some people, after all, possess a certain power that allows them to control the opinions of others whom they address, the kind of power that can only be described as enchantment. Oppas was just such a person, particularly where his nephew was concerned because he knew very well where his weaknesses lay.

Once Alfonso had finished reading Oppas's letter, he felt as though he were floundering in a bottomless sea. One part of him wanted to follow his uncle Oppas's instructions, but the other told him that they ran completely contrary to his own feelings; not only that, but it was also not in his own interest. When Roderic's order had arrived instructing him to join him at Jerez, it bolstered his sense that he needed to do what his uncle suggested, so he got himself ready to fight. The image of Florinda was constantly in his mind, and yet his emotions remained firmly tied to his uncle's authority. The whole thing made him depressed and nervous. He had completely forgotten how to smile. Totally giving up the idea of making up his own mind, he simply surrendered himself to fate.

When Roderic had arrived and set up camp the day before, he assigned to Alfonso the command of the right flank of the army[58] and told him to be ready to attack that very morning. Alfonso woke up at dawn, gave instructions to his commanders, and assigned each brigade to its allotted position. Alfonso went back into his tent to put on his armor. As Ya'qub accompanied him, his eyes peeled to watch for Sulayman or someone else with news. He started to panic in case the opportunity to avoid the battle would be lost. Just then, Ya'qub noticed someone whose demeanor suggested that he had some secret information to impart. This man knew Ya'qub and requested permission to meet Alfonso.

"Have you got a letter for him?" Ya'qub asked the man.

"I've a letter from Count Julian," the man replied.

So saying, he put his hand in his pocket, brought out a leather pouch, and handed it to Ya'qub. Going inside the tent, Ya'qub found that he was alone with Alfonso, who paid no attention to him. So Ya'qub went over and coughed in such a way that Alfonso realized he had something important to say. The prince had already taken off his coat and hat and was putting on his armor. He had begun with his breastplate and was about to put it on; bits of his hair hanging down over his shoulders kept sticking to the edges, and he had started pulling them off. When he heard Ya'qub coughing, he turned round and noticed that his servant had a sealed cylinder in his right hand, while his left was placed over his heart. Alfonso took the cylinder, broke the seal, and took out a letter. No sooner had he started reading and realized that it came from Julian than his heart leapt. His emotions were roused, and the blood rose in his face. He looked shocked, increasingly so as he kept reading it to the end. Ya'qub was still standing in front of him, with his hands crossed over his chest. Alfonso handed him the letter as though to ask his advice. Ya'qub took it and read the contents, which were as follows:

From Julian, Count of Sabta, to Prince Alfonso:

---

58 History tells us that he assumed the post along with his brothers.

My dear friend, I need not detail the disasters that have struck this peninsula ever since this tyrant king took over, not to mention the way he usurped the throne and threw out the royal family by killing your late father. The throne of Spain belongs to the descendants of Witiza, of whom you yourself are the most worthy. This tyrant has not been satisfied merely to infringe the laws, but has transcended that to commit outrages upon family honor. How can anyone obey such a person? Alfonso, the Arabs are a newly arrived system of rule. They govern their subjects justly and kindly. They are bound to defeat Roderic eventually because the citizens of Spain are all against him, even his closest relatives. Anyone who lends him support is actually supporting tyranny and deceit. You are well aware that I feel very close to you and am very fond of you because we are tied to each other by bonds of genuine affiliation. If you accept what I am saying and join the Arab army, I can guarantee that you will be allowed to keep all your late father's estates in Spain, some three thousand of them.[59] It is Roderic who has robbed you of them. If you do this, you and the entire royal family of Witiza will find yourselves restored to the prestige you enjoyed before this tyrant began his dreadful reign. I have written you this letter solely out of feelings of love and sympathy for your plight. Farewell.

As Ya'qub was reading the letter, Alfonso was staring at the floor, deep in thought. His hair was still spread over his shoulders and some strands still stuck to the armor. Once Ya'qub had finished reading, he looked at Alfonso.

"So what do you think, my lord?" he asked.

"What do I think?" Alfonso replied. "You know just as well as I do what my uncle the metropolitan bishop Oppas wrote to me. So do I now disobey his injunctions and go with Julian?"

"I can't advise you, my lord," Ya'qub said, rubbing his neck. "You must decide what is the right thing to do, and I'll follow you to the death. Even so, I am surprised by this advice from Oppas. After all, he of all people knows the way you and your family have suffered under this tyrant's regime. If I didn't believe in the sheer force of Oppas's intellect and his general good health, I would say he was suffering from delusions.

---

59 Al-Maqqari, *Nafh al-Tib,* Part I.

I can only imagine that he wrote you that letter and then came to regret it. In any case, you must make the decision."

"How can you claim he regretted it?" Alfonso asked. "He's still urging us to fight in Roderic's cause. The sound of his voice is still ringing in our ears, as he encouraged us all to unite our efforts and show courage on the field of battle. Oppas, my dear Ya'qub, is not one to indulge in trifles. If he didn't believe that this spirit of unity would work out for the best, he would never have asked me to join the effort..."

"My lord," Ya'qub replied, "your uncle the bishop is a sage and a philosopher. In hearing me say such a thing, you may perhaps think badly of me and wonder what my motives really are. But put such things aside. Take Count Julian's advice. He's Florinda's father, after all. He's only come to Spain with this unruly mob to defend..."

Alfonso stretched out his hand to block Ya'qub's mouth, albeit gently. "Enough, Ya'qub!" he said. "I'm going to stick with my uncle's views. After all, he has exactly the same information as we have. He's even more aware than you or I about the reasons for Julian's undertaking this mission. It's time I went out to take charge of the army."

He now resumed donning his armor. Meanwhile, Ya'qub stood there in despair, rubbing his nose as he watched his master. Just then Ya'qub heard a cough outside the tent. Realizing that this was good news, he went out and took another letter from Sulayman.

"This letter's from Florinda," Sulayman told him.

Ya'qub took it inside. Alfonso took it and unsealed it. He immediately recognized the handwriting as Florinda's. His heart started pounding even harder, and he looked utterly stunned. The way the letter quivered in his hand showed just how badly his fingers were trembling. He started shuddering, but then managed to control himself and look unconcerned. Needless to say, Ya'qub observed all his reactions but pretended not to notice. Alfonso started to read the letter, as follows:

I'm writing you this letter on a piece of my own clothing, using my own blood as ink. It's the same gown I had on when I met you in the palace garden, but it got torn on that dreadful night when I was trying to defend that precious jewel that belongs to Alfonso more than to me. Along with this letter I am sending you some strands of my own hair that were torn off during that terrible encounter with the king; not only that, but others were caught in the leafless tree outside the window as I scrambled my way out of that evil beast's clutches. And that is the very same Roderic in whose defense I now see you raising your sword. You will be defending his throne so you can help him keep the monarchy that he stole from your own father and so that he himself can use the very same hands to snatch away your own fiancée, a young maiden whom you claim to love. Has it escaped your notice that you are condemning her, her father, and not only her family but your own as well, to perdition? How can it be that you don't realize what Roderic has already done and what he proposes to do? So be aware then that he tried to ravish me and destroy my honor, using threats, fear, hope, and temptation in his efforts to show me how happy I would be if I did his will and how he would torment me if I did not. He paid no attention to my tears and showed not the slightest sympathy for my pleas. So I disobeyed him and preferred to suffer, all in the cause of my love for Alfonso and my abiding affection for him. We have not been apart very long, so perhaps you have forgotten the pledges you made on the banks of the river Tagus in Toledo when, rubbing your fingers against your hair, you pledged that, should you fail to keep your word, that hair could no longer stay on your head. So is this the way you keep that pledge? It's almost as though you've decided to kill me, my father, and the rest of my and your own families, as though you've made up your mind to support this tyrant's regime. If you can recall what I have just told you and the pledges that you made in the past, and decide that you should keep them, then abandon Roderic and his army. Either come to see me in the vineyard overlooking the two encampments, or join my father in the Arab army. However, if you have indeed decided to support this tyrant king but still have some vestige of your former love for Florinda, then do not let me die without seeing you once again, so I can explain to you how cold and unreasonable you have been, show you face to face just how much I disapprove of your actions, and glean from you a look that will help me forget all the misery I've gone through. Should you decide not to do even that, then I commit you to God's care until such time as we meet again in the next world, where Roderic will be able to testify on his own and your behalf. Farewell! Florinda.

One can only begin to imagine how Alfonso felt after reading Florinda's letter, particularly when he saw her hair, the hair of the girl whom he dearly loved and to whom he had dedicated his life. No sooner had he finished reading it than he had the feeling he had suddenly awakened from a long dream. Perhaps his true emotions had finally surfaced or else he had emerged from his trance. Now love took over, and that made him forget all about Oppas, his letter, his wisdom, and his courtesy. Love, after all, is a potent force that always prevails; it can overcome all kinds of authority, bring down monarchs, destroy commanders' swords, and confuse the minds of philosophers and sages.

For a few minutes Alfonso remained silent, as though he were totally distracted; all he could see before him was the image of Florinda in the purple gown she had been wearing the last time he had seen her, her golden hair contained within its snood. Now he was clutching pieces of both in his very own hand. He could remember the way they had scolded each other and how he had assured her that they would both be so happy once Roderic had been dethroned. He now felt so ashamed and flustered that he could almost hear Florinda's voice chiding him and see her actual tears.

Ya'qub was still standing in front of him. When he noticed how disturbed Alfonso was, he left the tent so that his master could be on his own. Once outside the tent, he encountered Sulayman, who was waiting anxiously. He asked Ya'qub how things had gone, and the latter closed his eyes as a way of showing that their plan seemed on the point of succeeding. While they were both standing there, they saw a horseman come rushing over with something in his hand. Ya'qub went over to ask him what he wanted. He was one of Oppas's retainers. When the two men met, they recognized each other. Ya'qub asked him what he wanted, and the man replied that he was bringing another letter from Oppas for Alfonso. Ya'qub sought his refuge in God from the impact of such a letter, for fear that its contents might well thwart their plan. With that in mind, he decided to use some underhanded methods.

"My master's changing his clothes at the moment," he told the man. "He can't receive anyone in the tent."

"I've been told to give him this letter at once," the man replied.

"Give it to me," Ya'qub told him. "I'm going back into the tent immediately."

The man handed over the letter and departed, having not the slightest doubt that he had fulfilled his mission. Ya'qub made it look as though he were going back inside the tent, but actually he went round the back and unsealed the letter. In Oppas's own handwriting, this is what it said:

Don't let the Jews deceive you with their trickery. Be stalwart in your defense of our nation, as I'm confident you will. Listen to what I have to say, for I am speaking in your father's stead.

When Ya'qub read this, the light in his eyes darkened, and he was amazed at how alert and sensitive Oppas could be. He realized that, if his plan did not work at this crucial moment, all his efforts and those of the Jewish community would go up in smoke. He called Sulayman over and told him about this latest letter. The two of them conferred and decided not to give it to Alfonso but instead to move ahead before the battle action started. Ya'qub entered the tent and found Alfonso sitting on a cushion, still deep in thought. He had not yet put his armor on, and his hair was still hanging down over his shoulders. When Ya'qub came in, he shook himself out of his reverie. He stood up, fully intending to tell Ya'qub about the contents of Florinda's letter, but shyness got the better of him.

"The messenger is still waiting outside," Ya'qub told him. "Julian has instructed him to return as soon as possible."

It occurred to Alfonso that he might ask the messenger something in person so as to put an end to this indecision once and for all.

"Tell him to come in," he instructed Ya'qub.

Ya'qub went out and brought Sulayman into the tent. Sulayman offered his greetings.

"Have you seen the person who wrote this letter?" Alfonso asked him.

"Yes, I have, my lord," he replied.

"Who is he and what do you know about him?"

Sulayman made a gesture toward Ya'qub, suggesting that there was something he did not wish to reveal with anyone else present. Alfonso signaled to Ya'qub to leave, so he did so. Sulayman now came over to Alfonso.

"Allow me, my lord," he told Alfonso, "to tell you everything I know completely frankly."

"Go ahead."

"I'm a friend of Count Julian, the governor of Sabta. He's charged me to escort his daughter Florinda from the monastery near Toledo where she has been staying. We reached here yesterday."

"Where is she now?" Alfonso asked.

"Very close to this encampment."

"Why didn't she join her father?"

Sulayman paused and gave the impression that there was something he did not wish to mention. Alfonso, needless to say, was all the more eager to hear what it was.

"Tell me everything you know," he said. "Don't hold anything back."

With tears in his eyes, Sulayman now looked directly at Alfonso.

"What can I tell you, my lord?" he said. "Florinda is now sadly weakened in spirit. Barely a day has gone by on this journey without my seeing her in tears. I thought that the reason was that she was missing her father. I told her that we would soon be with him, but that only made her cry even harder. When we drew close to the Arab encampment where her father was, she totally refused to go to see him; she almost fainted clear away. It was then that I learned from her aunt and other confidants that she was your fiancée. I heard her say that it was you she really wanted to see, even though you were on the field of battle. Never in my whole life have I witnessed such love. In order to meet you, she has rejected all thought of going to see her father. You should realize, my lord, that, while I've learned about this, no one else is aware of it. She handed me that letter with tears in her eyes, and made me promise to return as soon as possible with your response."

As Sulayman said this, his tone grew quiet as though he were about to cry himself.

Alfonso could not stop himself from crying as well. But just then he heard the beating of drums and the sound of trumpets. He realized that the battle was about to start. His heart pounding, he realized that he had to decide between the two sides. He busied himself putting on his armor and adjusting his clothing. He had decided to go along with his heart's passion and do as Florinda asked, but bashfulness prevented him from showing it.

Chapter 76

Love is Victorious

While Alfonso's mind was thus preoccupied, a man in clerical garb came hurrying into his tent, muttering all the way. When Alfonso looked up, it was to see Father Martin in his official multi-colored clerical robes and a pectoral cross hanging on his chest. He looked furious. Alfonso had no love for this priest, nor did he respect him in any way.

"How come you have entered my tent," Alfonso asked him when he saw the way he had barged his way in, "without informing my servant?"

"Which servant do you mean?" the priest stuttered in his normal fashion. "And since when did Father Martin need to ask permission before entering? Where's the letter your uncle sent you? Why are you still here and not on the battlefield? You're supposed to be commanding the army's left flank."

Alfonso decided that this was outrageous and made up his mind not to explain his reasons for delaying his arrival on the battlefield or tell the priest that in fact the recent letter had not even reached him.

"What has my presence on the battlefield to do with you?" he asked. "Or for that matter whether I've received letters from my uncle or anyone else?"

Father Martin was so furious that he could no longer control himself. "I'm heavily involved," he responded, "as you well know. If you won't acknowledge that in front of me, then maybe you'll do it in front of the king himself. He's the commander of this army and the commander in charge of the whole campaign."

Sulayman was still standing inside the tent in a spot from which he could observe Alfonso's expression. Every time the priest spoke, Sulayman made gestures of sheer derision and anger, and when Alfonso replied, Sulayman made very clear how much he approved of his dogged determination. As the conversation continued, his decision was only strengthened. Every time Father Martin referred to Roderic and his command of the army, Alfonso found himself becoming less and less hesitant about speaking his mind. Eventually Alfonso had had enough, left the tent, and hurried over to his horse. Once mounted, he seized the bit and turned toward the battlefield.

"Now you'll see who's really in command of this army," he said, "and what is the fate of tyrants. I was thinking of going by myself, but now my army will be going with me."

By now, the battle had already started. Arrows were flying hither and yon, swords were flashing through the air, and there was a huge din of shouting men, neighing horses, clinking bridles, rumbling wheels, and clashing sword blades. The king had placed himself in the midst of the army, surrounded by cavalry with his flags and banners. Oppas was on horseback, dashing among the various sections of the king's army; he had removed his beretta, so his hair hung loose over his shoulders and down his back. He was clasping the reins in his right hand and lifting a jewel-encrusted cross in his left as he urged the soldiers to stand firm and fight.

Once Alfonso had mounted his horse, he could see Oppas in the distance. He feared that his uncle might catch up with him before he changed sides and thwart his new purpose. Spurring his horse, he looked neither to left nor to right as he made for his own section of the army. Wimba and his colleague, the two junior commanders of the army after Alfonso, were waiting for him. He spoke to them and promised them that all would be well. He already knew, of course, that they would follow him and that they detested Roderic. They immediately followed his commands and gave orders to the army to quit the battle and take the entire Gothic contingent toward the Arab encampment. With that, the Gothic army was radically weakened, and its flanks were suddenly thrown into chaos.

Ever since the Gothic army had left Toledo for the south, Father Martin had been keeping a close eye on Oppas and intimating to Roderic his own doubts about the bishop's loyalty and intentions. When they had reached the plain of Jerez and the army had arrayed itself on the battlefield, he had noticed that Alfonso was slow to marshall his troops. He had then watched as one of Oppas's men had been given a letter to take to Alfonso's tent. Father Martin had then assumed the worst. He had rushed over to Roderic and shown him the messenger on his way to Alfonso. As we have just seen, he himself also hurried over to Alfonso's tent.

When Alfonso and Sulayman had rushed out, Father Martin had been left on his own inside the tent. He was furious at the way Alfonso had treated him with such obvious contempt. Looking around him, he noticed a piece of wrapped cloth and picked it up, assuming that it was Oppas's letter. But instead it turned out to be Florinda's letter; Alfonso had forgotten to take it because he was so furious and in such a hurry to leave. Now Father Martin was absolutely thrilled as he left the tent. He knew where Florinda was staying. Even so, he still believed, or rather he still wanted to believe, that Oppas had indeed written to Alfonso telling him to join the Arab army.

When the priest emerged from the tent, he noticed that Alfonso and his entire force were heading for the Arab encampment. Father Martin now rushed over to Roderic, who was still sitting on his throne in the midst of his retinue. When he looked over at Father Martin, he saw that he was pointing to Alfonso and his army. When Roderic saw that they were all heading for the Arab encampment, he was furious.

"What changed their minds?" he asked.

"Oppas's letter," Father Martin replied. "That's what changed their minds. I told you that we couldn't rely on his apparent loyalty. Have him arrested now and put in prison before he runs away as well or else encourages the rest of your army to do the same."

Roderic duly gave orders to the chief of his guards that Oppas should be arrested immediately. The chief rushed off with a troop of soldiers to execute the king's command.

Father Martin's fury was not calmed simply by having Oppas arrested. He wanted to take revenge on Alfonso as well. With that in mind, he exploited Roderic's fury by handing him Florinda's letter.

As he read it, his anger intensified because Florinda was accusing him of terrible things and encouraging others to do him harm. Once he had finished reading the letter, his entire beard was quivering and his hands were shaking in fury.

"Where's this vineyard," he asked Father Martin, "the one where this little whore is currently staying?"

The priest pointed to a particular spot. "I think that's it," he replied.

Roderic now ordered another troop of his cavalry to go and arrest everyone in the vineyard and bring them back, dead or alive.

Chapter 77

Florinda and Badr

When Sulayman had left Florinda that morning, she had stayed sitting by the window, watching the armies as they maneuvered and prepared for battle. She was obviously most concerned about the line of battle because that was where Alfonso was going to be. There's no need to describe how worried she was. Once she saw Alfonso's troops heading in the direction of the Arab encampment, she relaxed a little bit, assuming that things would soon be over. Her heart did a little dance for joy. Her aunt was standing beside her but she was very nearsighted, so Florinda had to tell her what was going on; then she, too, got excited. Ajilla and Chantilla were both stationed at the top of the hill overlooking the vineyard; they, too, were watching the battle unfold. When they saw the Gothic contingent under Alfonso join forces with the Arabs, they rushed up and told Florinda. They were all overjoyed and stood there talking about the things they had all seen during the battle that the others might have missed.

Just then the owner of the vineyard came rushing up with some of his sons and servants. They were running as fast as they could.

"Where's Sulayman the merchant?" he asked as soon as they reached the top. "He promised to protect us."

Florinda looked out of the window and noticed a troop of Gothic cavalry riding their horses through the grape arbors, trampling them down. Eventually they reached the storehouse, swords drawn. Once Florinda set eyes on them, she realized that they were Roderic's men. Her knees started to shake, and she shuddered all over.

"Ajilla, Chantilla!!" she yelled.

They had been rushing over to defend her even before they heard her shouts. They paid no attention to the superior numbers of the cavalry and were helped by the owner's sons and even his womenfolk. Women and children raised a hue and cry, while Florinda watched from the window with her aunt. She kept beating her breast and praying to God to save her. She besought Jesus the Savior and the Virgin Mary to rid her of this evil. Looking down at the wine store, she saw that both Ajilla and Chantilla had been killed, although they had managed to kill some of Roderic's cavalrymen first. She grieved for both men deeply, and yet at this point she had to think of herself first. There was no one else to come to her aid, only God. Kneeling in the middle of the storehouse, she uncovered her chest, loosened her hair, and stared up into the heavens.

"O God!" she prayed, slapping her cheeks and beating her chest, "You are the succor of the weak. O my God, You are the savior of the oppressed. Oh God, take pity on my youth and save me from these monsters, in memory of Your dear Son Jesus, who was crucified." Her voice was cracking because she was crying so hard, but she swallowed painfully and then started praying again. She paid no attention to the pounding of feet on the staircase leading up to her quarters. Oblivious to her surroundings, she concentrated her feelings, emotions, and thoughts entirely on God in heaven, completely sure that He would not abandon her. Her aunt was kneeling beside her, repeating the same prayers as her mistress intoned them.

Roderic's cavalry had killed Ajilla and Chantilla and some of the sheikh's sons as well. They climbed the stairs like ravenous wolves, with their commander—one of Roderic's courtiers—at the head. He had seen Florinda in Toledo on more than one occasion, but, when he saw her in this storehouse, he did not recognize her. The journeys she had been forced to undertake had completely changed her appearance, quite apart from the fact that, at this particular moment, she had untied her hair, uncovered her chest, and left her arms bare. Her cheeks were red from all the slapping, her eyes were also red from crying, and her eyelids were bathed in tears. Blood had stained her face and mingled with sweat that fell on to her chest, dampening her hair and chemise. When the cavalry commander went in and she paid him no attention whatsoever, he called out to her, but she still did not respond. He went over, grabbed her by the arm, and pulled her toward him. When she looked at him, she could see the sword in his other hand still dripping with blood. His fingernails were bloodstained as well. Once she saw that, she was even more frightened, but managed to control herself.

"What do you want?" she asked.

"We're going to take you and everyone here to King Roderic," he replied.

"No, no, no!" she yelled. "I won't go!"

"You can either go willingly," the man told her, "or else we'll take you by force. You can't escape. There's a whole troop of us."

So saying, he yelled out some orders to his men. They dragged her by the hand and led her outside. The old woman started shouting at them and asked them to show some mercy, but to no effect. They went back down the stairs and put her on one horse and her aunt on another, then led them both away. Florinda was still in the same state: hair loosened, bare-chested, red-eyed, and tearful. She kept asking God to come to her aid and defeat these dreadful tyrants. The cavalry ignored her cries and moans and simply continued descending the hill until they reached the battlefield. Florinda happened to spot Roderic in his procession. By now the fighting was fierce, and both armies were fully engaged in combat, both cavalry and infantry. Goths and Muslims were all mixed up in a single melée, although it was easy to spot the Muslims because of their white turbans. The Gothic army was considerably weakened, and Roderic had been forced to dismount and defend himself.

By this time, Florinda had given up all hope of being rescued. All she hoped was that one of the arrows raining down on them would hit her in the heart and save her from the sight of Roderic. Turning round, she noticed a Muslim soldier spinning around amid the chaos all around her. He was both fresh-faced and good-looking; but for his turban and clothes, she would have assumed he was a Goth. However, he had his turban firmly wrapped around his head. Sword drawn, he was ploughing his way relentlessly through the lines of the Gothic army. Looking over at Florinda, his eyes met hers, and she cried out for help in a language he did not understand. Even so, her gestures clearly showed what she wanted. From the very first glance he took the whole matter on himself and rushed over to defend her.

"Have no fear, my lovely," he said as he turned his horse toward her. "Badr has arrived. Don't be afraid."

Several Berber soldiers followed him, reciting the Koranic verse of unity, their swords drawn. Roderic's soldiers were not able to hold out against them for very long. When one of them realized they would not be able to complete their task, he rushed over to where Roderic was and asked him to help them. Roderic himself now came over, leaving his throne and riding on a horse weighed down with trappings; his crown, waistband, sword, and cloak, even his sandals, were all encrusted with jewels.[60] Even the horse's trappings were heavily decorated as well. It was a splendid and well-built stallion, but Badr's horse, like all Arab horses, was lighter and much more maneuverable.

Badr had by now managed to separate the troop of cavalry from Florinda, and she was almost free of them. Now Roderic arrived with all his heavy finery.

"There's the Gothic tyrant!" Florinda and her aunt both yelled out as soon as they set eyes on him.

Badr turned his horse toward Roderic and immediately recognized the king. They engaged in combat. As they parried and clashed, Badr was both fitter and more deft in his movements, but Roderic was also a renowned military commander. Florinda stayed there on her horse, watching every cut and thrust as the two men sparred with each other. She was holding her breath so as not to miss a single moment, realizing full well that the result would determine whether she was to live or die. Should Roderic be the loser, she felt she would be joining Badr in delivering the blow and might even raise her own hand to do it; whereas, if Badr should lose, she felt that she would lose as well. In fact, while she stayed glued to the spot, she felt she was participating in the fight with every sinew in her body. A moment later she saw Roderic gesture that the two of them should pause for a moment. Badr was eager to grab the king and haul him off to Tariq as a prisoner so that he could claim the credit for his capture. When he saw Roderic's signal, he gestured to him to go with him to the Muslim encampment. Roderic gestured that he would do so later. Badr took that to mean that he would do what he had to do before finally surrendering, and decided to let him do just that. In fact,

60 Al-Maqqari, *Nafh al-Tib*, Part I.

what Roderic had in mind was a trick that would enable him to flee, but Badr despised his foe and was keeping a close eye on him. Thus, when Roderic turned his horse back toward his own tent, Badr turned to his companions and told them in Berber to take Florinda back to his tent and chase after Roderic with him.

By now, the Goths had lost their will to fight. Once they saw their king running away, they all did the same. Badr was still pursuing Roderic, who was roaming around his encampment as though looking for something he had lost. Badr kept following him, amazed that the king should be behaving this way. Eventually they reached a tent from which a priest had emerged ready to get on his horse and run away as well.

"Father Martin!" Roderic called to him, whereupon the priest turned round and approached Roderic.

Roderic pointed his drawn sword at the priest.

"Your evil mind and stupidity are totally responsible for this disaster!" the king yelled, whereupon he aimed the sword at the priest's neck and cut him down, leaving him on the ground soaking in his own blood.

The king now steered his horse toward the valley, but Badr chased after him. Eventually they reached the riverbank, at which point it seemed that Roderic could no longer restrain his mount, so he let it dive into the water, where they both drowned. People say that he did that on purpose, preferring to die by drowning rather than be killed by one of his enemies.[61]

"The tyrant's dead," Badr proclaimed when he got back, "the tyrant's dead!"

The Arab army now took heart and invaded the enemy encampment. On that notable day, it was not even late afternoon by the time the Gothic encampment was completely cleared, save for those who had either been killed or taken prisoner. The Arabs managed to capture all the equipment, treasure, provisions, munitions, horses, pack animals, and whatever else there was.

---

61 Historians have no clear evidence as to how Roderic died. One suggestion is that he was drowned in the river.

During the battle, Tariq had been riding around on his horse, encouraging the Muslims to stand fast and fight the enemy. The relatively small size of his own forces compared with those of the Goths had not worried him in the slightest, and he was unaware of what Julian had written to Alfonso. But, as his speech before the battle had made clear, he was determined to fight this battle to the finish; in fact, he had already decided that he would do all that was necessary to conquer Spain, by burning the boats that had brought them across the Straits so that there could be no question of retreating in either his own mind or that of his men in the event the Goths should happen to win some battles. That is why any thought about the size of the Gothic army and the need to fight them did not unduly worry him. Courage and endurance were driving him and his men.

When he saw Alfonso and his troops joining his army, he gave thanks to God and grew even more confident of victory. He urged the Muslims to remain steadfast until such time as the Goths fled, as we have just seen. This battle was to be the final crushing blow to the Gothic monarchy, since their king and the cream of their gentry were all killed.

Chapter 78

Reproach

Once the fighting was over and the troops returned to their encampment, Tariq gave instructions for the booty, captives, and prisoners to be assembled in front of him, all in accordance with their usual custom after a victorious battle. They brought all the equipment, weapons, instruments, treasure, jewelry, and baubles that they had captured, most of it consisting of crosses and signet rings made of silver and gold, some embossed, others not. Some prisoners were in chains, others had their hands tied; some were fit and whole while others were wounded. Everything was gathered in one place, so much so that the spoils formed a gigantic pile in front of Tariq's tent. The prisoners were tied to each other either at the neck, hands, or feet, and Tariq's men kept bringing them in, either in groups or one by one.

The army commanders gathered in front of Tariq's tent and sat themselves down on a large rug where the booty was piled high. Tariq sat right in the middle, with Count Julian to his right and Prince Alfonso to his left. The major commanders were arrayed in front of him, Badr among them. Alfonso had met Julian as soon as he had joined up with the Arab armies, and they had talked for a few moments about the kingdom and the question of Oppas. They both mentioned Florinda as well and the fact that she would be staying at the vineyard storehouse until such time as they sent someone to fetch her. They both decided to send for her the next morning, after the booty and spoils had been distributed. Ever since the battle had ended, Alfonso had been looking carefully at the prisoners in case he spotted Oppas among them, but he did not expect to see the bishop because he assumed that his uncle would prefer death to being taken prisoner.

Once everyone was gathered, Tariq told a senior commander to divide the booty into fifths as was their custom. One fifth would go to the treasury, and the rest would be divided among the tribes in accordance with their numbers. As he gave those instructions, his expression was a picture of pride. Julian and Alfonso, meanwhile, were both wondering what might have happened to Oppas: had he been killed or taken prisoner or had he escaped? They both doubted that he would ever have been captured, but just at that moment a group of soldiers appeared, pulling behind them a tall man with long hair that reached his shoulders and down his back. When they reached Tariq's tent, one of them approached the commander.

"We found this prisoner in chains at the Gothic camp," one of them told Tariq, "so we've untied him and brought him here."

"Bring him over," Tariq said.

Oppas came over. He still looked exactly the same way as he had during the battle, hair loose, a cross on his chest and another in his hand. When Alfonso saw him, he stood up and went over to him. Kneeling in front of the bishop, he seized his hands and starting kissing them, tears falling silently as he did so. Julian did the same thing, although his delight at the victory was heavily tempered by his shame at the way he had betrayed the Gothic cause. He could not help feeling utterly depressed, so he bent over the bishop's hands and started kissing them. Embracing Oppas, he invited him to take a seat. Tariq, Badr, and the other Arab commanders were all watching this new arrival, his imposing and august demeanor only enhanced by his long hair.

Oppas stared unconcernedly at the people all around him. When Julian asked him to sit down, he ignored him and stayed right where he was, staring at everyone. If Alfonso had been able to look closely at Oppas's eyes, he would have seen that they were gleaming. It would never have even occurred to him that they might be gleaming with tears because he fervently believed that nothing in nature could overwhelm Oppas. An intelligent man who can control his emotions and harness them to his will won't let any issue affect him. For such a person, there is nothing in life that can cause either sorrow or gladness; after all, life is merely a waft of breeze in mankind's existence, so why bother with its incidentals? Emotions make a person subject to both joy and sorrow. So let us not blame Oppas if he was in tears as he saw the Gothic kingdom in Spain disappearing as the direct result of the bad policies of a single ruler in spite of all the hopes and expectations he had had of avoiding such an outcome. Just when he thought he had managed to achieve his goal, all his efforts had come to naught.

Even so, these initial thoughts had soon turned into a different set of emotions. Thus it was that, when Julian invited him to sit down, he refused.

"So, Julian," he said after a moment's pause, speaking in a loud voice coarsened by what he was feeling, "are you now inviting me to sit down in a place you consider your own home, when on this very day you have lost it forever? You, Julian, have sold it at the cheapest rate imaginable, claiming as you did so that your motive was taking revenge on a man whose weakness touched upon your sense of honor. You, your family, and the rest of the soldiers of Gothic Spain have been driven to lose not only themselves but also their wealth and lands. Even your own daughter, in defense of whose honor you have committed this foul treachery, is now a prisoner in the hands of a man who does not belong to your community of faith, nation, or language."

As Oppas spoke, everyone remained silent, even the Arabs. They had no idea of what he was saying but certainly felt a sense of respect for his voice and his demeanor. Julian was so ashamed that he almost melted away, but when he heard Florinda's name mentioned and that she had been taken prisoner, he suddenly came to himself with a start, and so did Alfonso. They were not surprised that Oppas had such information nor were they willing to dismiss it because they knew that the bishop never spoke frivolously.

"Where is she now?" they asked in unison.

Oppas now looked straight at Alfonso.

"Your fiancée is now lost forever," Oppas told him. "What you've done is something not even Roderic ever did. You've betrayed your country and family, and now you've lost them all. Assuming that you did it to take revenge on someone who infringed your sense of honor, then what kind of punishment do you deserve now when you've left Gothic honor, property, and spirits as victims of death and spoliation? Pass judgment on yourself!"

All Alfonso could do was to burst into tears. For his part, Julian was crushed by Oppas's words, especially now he had heard that his daughter was lost. He dearly wanted to ask for more details, but he decided to say nothing.

Tariq and Badr had been listening to Oppas and were deeply impressed even though they could not understand what he was saying. Tariq turned to the people around him and asked for someone to translate. He noticed Sulayman the merchant, who realized what Tariq wanted before being asked. He came over and explained what Oppas had been saying, anticipating that Tariq would be furious. However, once Tariq had understood, he was even more impressed with the bishop and spoke to him via Sulayman's translation.

"God bless you for an intelligent and courageous man!" Tariq said. "I am amazed that the Gothic army should have been defeated when they not only had superior numbers and equipment but also an intelligent man such as you in their midst."

"There's no cause for surpise, young man," Oppas replied. "States are just like people; they all have their allotted span. Once their time is up, no stratagems can keep them in place. Even so, I expected the time span of this dynasty to be longer than this. The end has been accelerated by the weakness of the monarch and the corruption of evil men. It is God's will."

"If, indeed, it is God's will, as you say," Tariq told the bishop, "then it should not trouble you that it is now been wrested from Gothic control. Its entry into Arab hands should be a cause for happiness, since the Spanish people can now live under our protection. We will fend off their enemies and guarantee their security. All it will cost them is a minimal payment of poll tax. Provided that is paid, they will all have complete safety as regards honor, spirit, and property."

So saying, he took Oppas by the hand and led him away.

"Come to the tent," he said, "while the commanders finish apportioning the booty."

Oppas, Julian, Alfonso, and Badr, accompanied by both Sulayman and Ya'qub, now entered Tariq's tent. It was huge, and Tariq took a seat in the middle. Oppas sat to his right, Julian and Alfonso to his left, and

Badr sat further away to one side, still wearing his fighting garments along with his sword and shield. Hardly had Julian sat down before he forgot his sense of shame in the presence of Oppas. He asked again about Florinda.

"I heard you mention that Florinda had been taken prisoner," he said to Oppas. "Do you really mean that?"

"When did Oppas ever talk in vain?" the bishop replied.

Julian was now even more curious and concerned. He wanted to know more, but Alfonso got ahead of him.

"How can that be?" he asked. "Who took her prisoner?"

"I don't know the man's name," Oppas replied, "but I could see her while I was being kept a prisoner in the tent. Through a gap, I could see her there with her hair loose, begging the birds in the sky and the beasts of the field to save her from Roderic, who had sent a troop of cavalry to bring her to him. An Arab horseman came up, but he wasn't a Berber. He was wearing a white turban. He rescued her and then chased after Roderic; I have no idea where he went. But he ordered his men to take her and bring her to this encampment. She's certainly a prisoner and now belongs to whomever took her prisoner."

"Would you recognize the man if you saw him again?" Julian asked. "It seems that whoever it was brought her here and kept her hidden from Tariq, because I haven't spotted her among the prisoners."

"I think I'd recognize him," Oppas replied. "He's different from other soldiers; he has a light complexion and blond hair."

When Julian heard that, he thought immediately of Badr. He looked over at Badr, who was sitting just a few feet away listening to the conversation but not understanding because he did not know Gothic. But even if he had known that his prisoner was Julian's daughter, it would not have bothered him; Julian had already aroused his anger by refusing to allow him to take the vineyard owner's daughter on the night when they had reached Jerez. Julian was always very moody because of something that had happened to him some ten years earlier, so he tended to treat people grudgingly. He found life difficult to cope with and would fly into a temper very quickly. His companions disliked the way he dealt with them, particularly Badr, because of the large difference in their ages.

When Julian looked over at Badr, the younger man was fiddling with his sword strap; he was thinking about Florinda because he had found her very attractive. Julian noticed that Badr was paying no attention, so he turned to Tariq, gave him a summary of what Oppas had told him, and then suggested that it was, in fact, Badr who had taken her prisoner. He asked Tariq to get her back for him. Tariq now turned to Badr.

"Badr," he said.

Badr had heard Julian talking to Tariq and understood the gist of what he was saying full well. When he heard Tariq talking to him, he decided to remain seated.

"Yes?" he said.

Now Tariq was extremely fond of Badr; he loved him, spoiled him, and treated him as a father would a son or an elder brother a younger one. When he realized that Badr's response was so noncommittal, he smiled.

"I see you're still sitting down," he said. "Didn't you hear me call?"

"Yes, I heard you," Badr replied, still fiddling with his sword strap, "and I replied."

"Come over here," Tariq said. "I've a question for you."

"What's that?" Badr asked as he stood up. "Ask away, and demand anything you like, except for my prisoner. She belongs to me now, and there's no need for a lot of chatter about it. "

So saying, he adjusted his turban as though he were about to leave.

Tariq laughed so loud, you could see his molars. "I don't know why you're getting so angry," Tariq said. "We haven't talked about anything yet. Listen to what we have to say, then speak your mind."

"Go ahead," Badr replied. "I'm listening."

"Tell me how you came across this prisoner."

Chapter 79

Sword Fight

Badr now gave them a short account, finishing up with Roderic's escape. He told them how the king had killed Father Martin and then drowned in the river. Neither Alfonso nor Oppas understood what he was saying, so they got together and asked Sulayman to interpret for them. When he reached the point where Roderic killed Father Martin, Oppas thought to himself that Roderic's was the only hand sanctioned to do so. Once Badr had finished, Tariq spoke to him.

"You're obviously very fond of this prisoner of yours," he said, "but you're apparently unaware of the fact that she's Julian's daughter."

"True enough," Badr replied, "I didn't know that, but it doesn't change my intentions in any way."

So saying, he turned away to go back to his seat. Tariq yelled at him, seriously this time.

"How can you not change your intentions, when Count Julian here is the one who has allowed us to score this great triumph? But for him, we would never have invaded this country. Is it fitting now for us to wrong his daughter, his only daughter? Give her back to him, and you can choose any other prisoners from this peninsula and its plentiful booty."

"I don't want anything else," Badr replied. "She's part of my spoils in war. Yesterday it was Julian who stopped me taking my first spoils because she wasn't actually captured in battle. But what about this girl? Didn't I capture her on the very field of battle? Wasn't it for her sake that I took on the king of the Goths? I killed him, and that led to the defeat of his army. Now you object to my keeping a girl I captured, when I've left you to distribute all the other booty as you see fit?"

Tariq was still trying to convince him to change his mind. "If your intention is to get your own back on Count Julian by taking revenge," he told Badr, "then choose some other way of doing it. My dear brother, you are well aware that doing this contravenes all rules of companionship and correct behavior. What will Muslims have to say when they learn that the count played an important role in this conquest, but then hear that we took his daughter prisoner? Please behave in a way that is more in line with your noble character. Do it out of respect for me and the rights of brotherhood."

Badr was a decent man. He did not want to commit such a dastardly act, but he had fallen in love with the girl the minute he first set eyes on her. The fact that he had worn himself out rescuing her had only served to increase his infatuation. Whenever anyone devotes great efforts to protecting a person or object, he develops a great affection for it; he is loath to see it taken away from him. Badr looked down for a moment, but, when he looked up again, there was a smile on his face.

"You're right, my lord," he said. "It would be an act of betrayal for me to take this girl as a prisoner. But I've fallen in love with her, and I can't let her go. So ask Count Julian to marry her to me in accordance with God's due practice. Then there won't be any reason to complain."

Tariq now looked at Julian as though to ask his opinion.

"She's already engaged, and this man is her fiancé," he replied, pointing at Alfonso.

"I don't care," Badr replied. "Engagements can easily be broken off."

Julian now became angry and lost his temper.

"This talk has gone on for long enough," he said. "My daughter is engaged, and this is her fiancé. Even if she were not engaged, you would have no chance with her, and that's it!"

Badr leapt to his feet, his hand on his sword handle.

"She's my prisoner," he said. "I captured her during the battle and used this sword to do it. I will not give her up for anyone; I don't care if it's the caliph himself. Let anyone who wants to try use his sword just as I used mine."

Sulayman was still translating what was going on for Oppas and Alfonso. When it reached the point of a challenge, Alfonso stood up, hand on sword.

"I'm the person who should take on this young man," he said. "We're both suitors. Whoever wins will get the girl."

But Julian stood up, too, and restrained Alfonso.

"No, Alfonso," he said, "I'm the one who should do it, not you. If I kill this youth, I'll be giving him the punishment he deserves. If he kills me, then my death will be better for me than yet another disaster, worse even than the first. I cannot bear the thought of having to bear them both."

As he spoke, he moved forward, sword in hand. Badr was ahead of him and drew his own sword as well. Tariq yelled out, but Badr paid no attention. Oppas yelled out, too, but Julian did not obey. By now all rational thought was gone, and anger had taken over. Each one of them swore that they would not give way till one of them was dead. A huge din now enveloped the tent, while Sulayman and Ya'qub stayed to one side.

Badr made the first thrust and delivered a mighty blow that would have certainly killed Julian if it had not been for one of the tent poles. The sword stuck in the pole and would not budge. Badr's hand suffered a jolt because the blow was so hard, but he could not dislodge the sword from the pole. Julian now took advantage of his predicament and pounced on the young man to put an end to the fight. But then he noticed that Sulayman had got there first and put himself between the two of them.

"Stop now, Count Julian," he said, grabbing his arm, "stop in Thomas's name."

Hardly had Sulayman pronounced that name than Julian threw his sword to the ground and started weeping. Everyone was astonished, not least Badr. They all turned and looked at Sulayman, as though asking for an explanation. He signaled to everyone to calm down. Everyone stood up. Sulayman went over to Julian, took his hand, and tried to calm him down, crying all the while.

"Why did you have to remind me of that tragedy, Sulayman?" Julian asked.

"Had you forgotten?" Sulayman said.

"Of course not," Julian replied. "But I haven't heard that particular name for years. If you hadn't said it just then, I would certainly have ended that boy's life and rid people of his impudence."

"If you knew him," Sulayman said meaningfully, "you would certainly not want to be rid of him."

"Why should I be bothered about knowing him?" Julian asked. "His impudence and stupidity give clear enough evidence of his origins."

"Don't insult him so much," Sulayman replied. "Take a good look at his face. You'll find yourself remembering a beloved person, someone you thought you'd lost forever. But in fact he's right in front of you."

Chapter 80

Revealing the Final Secret

Julian did not understand what he meant. By now he had sat down; in place of anger, there was now sorrow. Oppas, Tariq, and Alfonso were still standing up, utterly amazed by what they had just witnessed. They were all waiting to hear what Sulayman would have to say. When Julian heard what Sulayman had referred to, he took a good look at him to see if he was joking or serious. He found that his expression could hardly have been more serious. However, before he could say anything, Sulayman himself stood up, turned to the people present, and signaled to them all to be seated so he could tell them all something he wanted them to hear. They all did so, apart, that is, from Badr, who seized the opportunity to go out and get another sword in preparation for renewing his fight with Julian. Sulayman sat down as well.

"Listen as I reveal a secret to you," he said. "I have kept it for many, many years. Therein lies a lesson for everyone."

He started telling his story in Gothic then translated it into Arabic.

"As you are already aware, my lord Metropolitan," he said, addressing Oppas, "the Jewish people in Spain have suffered a good deal of oppression and mistreatment at the hands of the Gothic rulers; eventually they were given the choice of either converting to Christianity or else leaving the country.[62] Some left, others pretended to convert and stayed in the country while making every effort to bring down the government. I'll not hide the fact that I myself am one of those phony converts. All the years I spent with Count Julian, he assumed that I was a Christian, whereas in fact I still adhered to the faith of my ancestors. I believe that

---

62 Dozy, Part I.

the metropolitan also knows that Ya'qub over there is a Jewish leader and one of the wealthiest members of our community. He, too, has pretended to be a convert and has managed to infiltrate himself into service at the royal court ever since the time of the late king Witiza. He made all kinds of efforts to put an end to the oppression of the Jewish people, and he would certainly have succeeded, had not Witiza's reign been brought to an abrupt end.

When Roderic took over as king, things went back to the way they had been in the past. We Jews regularly held secret meetings and spent our funds on resistance to this tyrannical regime and the destruction of its means of support. We have spared no effort in our attempts to frustrate the government and all those who support it, governors, generals, and others. However, we obviously could not do that openly, so we worked in secret—and now I get to the core of my story. Once I had pretended to be a convert, I had the chance to travel abroad. Some ten years ago I visited Sabta, got to know Count Julian, and spared no effort to gain his confidence. Having done so, I used to visit his house often, just like one of the family. He had two children: a daughter named Florinda and a son named Thomas. It so happened that, at that precise moment, the government renewed its oppressive tactics against the Jews. We received secret instructions to take revenge on the Goths in any way possible. I decided to deprive the count of something of immense value to him, his only son. I did not allow myself to actually kill him, but I conspired to snatch him away and take him with me on one of my journeys to the Berber tribes. There I sold him to one of the tribal marabouts[63] for a paltry sum. I did not tell the man where I had obtained the boy. He bought him from me and then gave him to Ziyad, Tariq's father, who brought him up like one of his own children. So the young man grew up without knowing his own father. I was the only person who knew who he was. They named him Badr[64] because his complexion was so light. He is that young man who has been right in front of you here. Now that Count Julian has revolted against the Gothic regime and allowed their enemies to triumph in this battle, he is one of our allies. As a result, this secret had to be revealed..."

---

63 A Muslim spritual leader or holy man, especially in North Africa. *Translator's Note*

64 The literal translation of Badr is "full moon". *Translators' Note*

As Sulayman was talking, everyone was staring in disbelief, especially Julian himself, who could not tell if he was dreaming or not. His heart pounding, he kept looking for Badr around the tent. By now the sun had set, and the inside of the tent was getting dark. At this point, Tariq felt as though a cloud had been cleared from his eyes—now that he knew the boy's origins.

"Badr!" he called.

No one answered for the moment, but then the tent flap opened and Badr came in with another sword.

When Sulayman saw him, he leapt to his feet, not knowing exactly what to say.

"Thomas, Thomas," he yelled as he rushed over toward the boy.

When Badr spotted him rushing toward him, he drew back with his hand grasping the sword as though he were about to strike him or use the sword against him.

Sulayman stood in front of him.

"Come over here, Badr," he told the boy, "and kiss Count Julian's hand. He will kiss you back. He is your father!"

Badr was stunned and assumed that Sulayman was joking at his expense. But then Tariq came over as well.

"Praise be to God!" he said. "You've finally found your father. Ever since we've known you, we've been wondering who he was…"

"Count Julian is my father," Badr asked, "and Florinda's my sister? How can I possibly be related to them?"

All the while, Julian was standing in front of Badr, looking carefully at him in the twilight. When they brought Julian a lamp, he took it and started examining Badr's facial features carefully. It did not take long for him to recognize the similarities to the image that was still imprinted in his mind. He felt a surge of affection, grabbed Badr, hugged him to his chest and started embracing him, smelling his scent, and weeping tears of sheer joy. Everyone else just stood there, deeply moved by this extraordinary scene. It took a while for Badr to realize that he was not dreaming. Kissing his father's hand, he just stood there as though he had been paralyzed.

As minutes passed by, everyone inside the tent commented on the extraordinary turn of events. They praised God for saving Badr from his own father's sword. Sulayman was the one to be thanked for that. Now Oppas, who was still in the same state as when he had brought in— head uncovered and hair loose—spoke to Tariq.

"Would my lord Tariq—whom God may preserve—please give instructions for our daughter, Florinda, to be brought here so that she may meet her family?"

"Where is she, Badr?" Tariq asked.

"In my tent," he replied.

Tariq gave orders for her to be brought to his tent.

When Florinda had arrived at Badr's tent, she had had time to adjust her clothing. She was expecting them to take her to her father's tent. When they dithered, she specifically asked the guards to take her there, but they did not understand what she wanted. Even so, they were able to make her understand that she could not leave the tent, so she stayed there with her aunt until evening, at which point Sulayman arrived. When she saw him, she welcomed him with a smile.

"Where's my father?" she asked. "Where's Alfonso?"

"Your father's longing to see you," he replied with a laugh. "You'll be seeing him very soon. But from now on you'll have to forget about Alfonso; the Arab cavalier who rescued you from Roderic's clutches will accept nothing less than having you become his bride..."

Florinda was stunned.

"Did my father agree to that?" she asked.

"What was he supposed to do?"

"And what about Alfonso? I'm not going to accept anyone else... Sulayman, it looks as though you're teasing me!"

"Come with me," Sulayman told her, "and you'll see for yourself how important this young man is to your father."

Florinda left the tent with her aunt and Sulayman, and they all headed for Tariq's tent. Sulayman went in and gestured to them not to say a word. When Florinda entered the tent, she was so shocked that it even overcame her delight at seeing her father again. Sulayman went ahead of her, seized Badr by the hand, and brought him over to her.

"Kiss Florinda, Badr," he told the young man.

Florinda recoiled, but her father told her to kiss him.

Once she heard her father saying that, implying that he had accepted Badr as her husband, she turned away and started crying.

"No, no," she said, "I have no need of that!"

Julian now went over and hugged his daughter with his right hand. She kissed his hand, and he kissed her. With his left hand, he hugged Badr and kissed him, too.

"Kiss him, Florinda," her father said. "He's your brother, Thomas, whom we lost over ten years ago!"

When she was younger, Florinda had heard that she had had a brother but that he had been lost; they had given up all hope of finding him alive. When her father told her that Badr was in fact her brother, she took a good look at him although she did not recognize him at all. She still felt too shy to actually kiss him. At this point, Oppas stood up.

"Florinda!" he shouted.

She was surprised because she had never expected to hear that special voice here. She turned round, spotted Oppas, and rushed over to him. Bending over his hand, she kissed it. The expression in her eyes spoke volumes, although she could not think of anything to say...

Oppas gave her his blessing.

"We thank God for rescuing you and rediscovering your long-lost brother. We praise him, too, for bringing Alfonso and you together again and saving you from the snares of evil."

"Uncle," said Alfonso, echoing what Oppas had just said, "it's you alone we have to thank for her rescue. You have blessed us and brought us God's bountiful goodness."

With that, his voice choked up.

"If only I'd been able to achieve my goals," said Oppas with a sigh. "But if I'd done so, Badr would never have met his father and sister, nor would you have found your fiancée again. Man is forever striving along one path, and God has other plans in mind. This is God's will, and all we can do is to thank Him for what has come to pass."

Florinda's aged aunt was standing there. When she heard that they had found Thomas and showed her where he was, she went over and hugged him to her bosom. She started kissing him and smelling his scent till he almost suffocated. After greeting Julian and Alfonso, she seized Oppas's hand and kissed it.

"There's one thing more that needs to happen," she said, "in order for our happiness to be complete. You're the only one who can bring it about."

"I think you mean Florinda's marriage to Alfonso," the bishop replied. "I think that I'm the one to marry them because I was responsible for the engagement in the first place. We'll have the ceremony tomorrow evening."

She could not object.

Tariq now got to his feet.

"I'm delighted," he said, "that all this has happened on the day of our great victory. From now on, you're all under my personal protection. You may reside wherever you wish, safe, sound, and duly respected, not only yourselves but also those who seek your protection."

Then they all spent some time talking about a variety of issues, but Florinda's eyes were glued to those of Alfonso; we need not even wonder what their eyes were telling each other. By now, much of the night had already passed.

"It's time for bed," said Julian. "After all we've been through today, we need some rest."

So saying, he left the tent, followed by Oppas, Alfonso, Florinda, and Badr. Julian showed them all where they could sleep. At this moment, Alfonso remembered Ya'qub and started looking for him. He could not find him and assumed that he must have gone to sleep in another tent.

Chapter 81

The End of the Conquest

Everyone was so affected by all the events and surprises of the previous day that few, I suspect, got much sleep that night. Next morning, Oppas wanted to survey the battlefield and go through the two encampments to learn how many grandees had been killed and how many had managed to escape. He went with Julian, Badr, and Alfonso, and they all saw dead bodies piled on all sides. They recognized several commanders, among them Kumis; that made them particularly sad. When they passed by the king's tent, they saw Father Martin's body spread-eagle on the ground. Oppas did not even want to look at it. Once they had returned from this tour of the battlefield, Oppas asked Tariq's permission to remove the bodies for a funeral followed by burial.

Tariq agreed, and so the bodies of the commanders and Father Martin were carried away, prayed over, then buried. When Florinda saw them burying the dead, she went over to Oppas and told him about the deaths of both Ajilla and Chantilla and asked him to pray for them as well and bury them. He did so, bitterly regretting their deaths. Along with them he buried the children of the sheikh who owned the vineyard. When Florinda told him how the sheikh and his sons had defended her, he entrusted them all to the benevolence of Tariq.

Once the sun had set, Alfonso prepared himself for his marriage to Florinda in Julian's tent. They celebrated the event with a very simple liturgy. Everyone was so happy with the reunion of the two lovers that they all smiled, except for Oppas, who as usual remained silent, feeling neither joy nor sorrow. Once the marriage ceremony was concluded, Oppas asked them where they would prefer to live in the future.

"Wherever you wish," they both said.

"No," Oppas replied. "Leave me to my own devices."

"How can we do that?" they asked. "You're our counselor and adviser."

"If I'd been that," Oppas replied, "I would have been able to help you. But now, let me spend the rest of my life in prayer and worship, far removed from this world. I've seen quite enough of its evils. Now that this battle is over, should I expect to see anything that would not make me even more unhappy and regretful? As it is, I can't undertake any of those things that my conscience tells me I should do and necessity urges me to do. It would be better for me to spend the rest of my days on earth somewhere where I don't have to see other human beings. None of you can dissuade me from this."

There was only one other person who could try to dissuade Oppas, and he echoed the bishop's statement in front of everyone. "And where am I supposed to go?" he asked.

Alfonso thought it was Ya'qub, but the dress looked unfamiliar. However, Oppas knew.

"This is Ya'qub," he said, "and he's fulfilled his vow. He's trimmed his beard and washed."

Alfonso now recalled that his uncle had said something about this when they met in Toledo. He now looked at Ya'qub and saw that he was well attired; he had trimmed his beard and was wearing a Jewish rabbi's garments.

"What's this all about, Ya'qub?" he asked.

"It's time for me to fulfill my vow and cast off humiliation's noose. As a result of this conquest, people are free to follow their own religious faith. Through God's good grace, I am a Jew by race and religion. I want to go back to my faith, pray in my own synagogue, and read my own scripture."

When night was over and morning came, they all looked for Oppas but could not locate him either in his tent or anywhere else in the encampment. No one could find any trace of him thereafter. They all realized that he had indeed gone away to live the life of a hermit.

Alfonso and Julian stayed on as aides to Tariq and his army till the whole of Spain was conquered. After this major battle, the only place where they encountered any real opposition was in Astigi. After the battle in Jerez, they had made for Astigi immediately and fought a fierce battle. Once Jerez was defeated, people were in a panic and fled to Toledo. Julian now suggested to Tariq that he split up his armies and head for various Spanish cities, since people had already left them and headed for the capital city. So Tariq sent one force to Cordoba, another to Granada, another to Malaga, and still another to Murcia. With the major part of his army, he himself headed for Toledo, but they found it empty as well because everyone had fled to a city over the mountains. The army that went to Cordoba was shown a gap in the wall by a shepherd, and they were thus able to enter the city and capture it easily. Murcia was conquered in battle, as were other cities. When Tariq saw that the city of Toledo was empty, he brought in a lot of Jews and left some of his own men behind with them. That done, he proceeded to complete the conquest of Spain, as is recounted in detail in history books.

The End

The Conquest of Andalusia

Afterword

Roger Allen

This translation of Jurji Zaidan's novel, *Fath al-Andalus*, first published in serial form in his own journal, *Al-Hilal*, and subsequently in book form in 1903, is part of a larger project devoted to a reconsideration of this important figure in the nineteenth century Arab cultural revival known as *al-nahda*. Within that larger movement, he was to play a major role in the development of journalism, in the penning of histories of the Arabic language, its literary heritage, and Islamic history; and, as exemplified by this particular work, in the early development of the novel genre in Arabic. Here is not the place to examine all those roles,[65] but, in the context of any discussion of his status as a novelist, what is significant is the sheer breadth of his interests and learning. In his novels, as in his multiple other writings, his primary role was that of a polymathic educator, one who wished to exploit the newly available publication media to the fullest extent as a means of forging a new sense of pride in and identity with the heritage of the Arab-Islamic past.

Within the context of any study of historical approaches to the development of the novel genre in Arabic, the central role that Jurji Zaidan played in the early phases of that lengthy process clearly needs to be revisited and indeed revised, all as part of a widespread scholarly reevaluation of the cultural movement in the nineteenth century that

---

65 For accounts of Jurji Zaidan's biography, see Thomas Philipp, *The Autobiography of Jurji Zaidan*, Boulder, Colorado: Lynne Rienner Publishers, 1990; and Walid Hamarneh, "Jurji Zaidan," in *Essays in Arabic Literary Biography 1850-1950*, ed. Roger Allen, Wiesbaden: Harrassowitz Verlag, 2010, pp. 382-92.

has been underway for the past decade or so.[66] Previous surveys of the period and its movements, which have tended to rely heavily on the Egyptian cultural milieu to provide the developmental model—that indeed being the milieu within which Zaidan was to function for much of his professional career in spite of his Lebanese origins—have identified Muhammad Husayn Haykal's 1913 novel, *Zaynab*, as the first "real" Arabic novel or the first "artistic" Arabic novel, thus consigning Zaidan's novelistic output, not to mention earlier narratives by Fransis Marrash, Salim al-Bustani, and Mahmud Tahir Haqqi, just to provide three examples, to some other category.[67] What seems most noteworthy about these verdicts is that the developmental model being adopted is based almost exclusively on the European novelistic tradition as precedent, something that can perhaps be seen at its most obvious in Egyptian Fabian journalist Salama Musa's advice to the young Naguib Mahfouz in the 1930s that he read John Drinkwater's survey volume, *An Outline of Literature*, in order to get some idea of what the novel genre's primary generic characteristics were.

However, as we look back from the perspective of the twenty-first century and especially from the post-June 1967 War era, we can suggest that, if such a model of the Arabic novel's development had a certain validity up to a particular point in the process, more recent trends in novel-writing and criticism—say since the 1970s—have been far more cognizant of indigenous narrative genres and styles and indeed have had to reflect the considerable variety and particularity (to use a term much favored by more recent commentators on the Arabic novel) of today's expanded publication markets across the breadth of the Arabic-speaking world. Part of that process has suggested, or indeed demanded, that certain trends in the earliest phases of the emergence of modern Arabic narratives—reflected perhaps in such works as Ahmad Faris al-Shidyaq's *Al-Saq 'Ala al-Saq Fi-ma Huwa al-Far-yaq* (1855) and Muhammad al-Muwaylihī's *Hadith 'Isa ibn Hisham* (1907)—need to be reassessed, and

---

66 See, for example, Stephen Sheehi, *Foundations of Modern Arab Identity*, Gainesville: University Press of Florida, 2004; and Samah Selim, "Fiction and Cultural Identitites," *Middle Eastern Literatures,* Vol. 13 n. 2 (August 2010): 191-201.

67 Fransis Marrash, *Ghabat al-Haqq* (1865); Salim al-Bustani, *Huyam fi Jinan al-Sham* (1870), among other works, and Mahmud Tahir Haqqi, *'Adhra Dinshaway* (1906).

that linkages to the Arabic narrative heritage need to be placed alongside those other connections to European traditions that have up till now occupied center stage in discussions of the genre's developmental process. Explorations of newspaper archives and family records are providing contemporary scholars with evidence of a wide variety of publication outlets—daily, weekly, and monthly, not to mention magazines specifically devoted to the publication of serialized novels. Within such a context, Zaidan's journal, *al-Hilal*, still in publication in Cairo today, and his list of twenty-two novels clearly make him an important figure in this process of reassessment, one that will not completely replace one version of development with another but rather will suggest the need for an adjustment of the balance between two cultural forces, the one imported, the other indigenous.

Those who have analyzed the early history of the Arabic novel and emphasized the significance of Haykal's *Zaynab* have described Zaidan's novels—when they have done so—as being historical novels or educational novels, implying perhaps that in some way or other the novels of a Sir Walter Scott or even Charles Dickens are not "real" novels in the way that those of, say, the Brontes or Thackeray are. The majority of Zaidan's novels are indeed historical and have clearly educational aspects, but a starting point in any analysis of them must surely be that they are indeed novels and therefore at least precedents to the publication of *Zaynab*. So what precisely are some of the features of these narratives of Zaidan that participate in the generic definitions of the novel genre and indeed recommend their translated versions to an anglophone readership of fictional works?

Zaidan's novels (with one exception, his first novel, *Jihad al-muhibbin*, 1893) are indeed historical, a term by which is implied that each one is placed within a particular context of time and place that allow for the development of a narrative depicting an important period within the history of Islam and the Arabic-speaking peoples. Many locations within the broad expanse of the Islamic world and time frames within its lengthy history are included: to provide a few examples, from the Mesopotamia of ninth-century Baghdad and the 'Abbasi caliphate in *Al-Amin wal-Ma'mun* (1907), to the Crusades and Saladin in *Salāh al-din al-Ayyubi* (1913), to eighteenth-century Egypt in the period preceding the 1798 Napoleonic invasion in *Istibdad al-Mamalik* (Mamluk Tyranny, 1893), and to pre-710 Visigothic Spain in the current novel, *Fath al-*

Andalus aw Tariq ibn Ziyad (*The Conquest of Andalusia or Tariq ibn Ziyad*). In many of the novels, including this one, Zaidan lists his source texts in the introductory materials; additionally, references to those sources are cited in footnotes throughout the original Arabic text, and such references have been retained in this translation. Thus, even though Zaidan is creating works of historical fiction, his educational motives are made clear through the placement of each novel within a framework that is based on actual historical accounts—which are themselves, of course, constructed narratives with their own conceptions of the relative roles of accuracy and opinion.

In the case of *The Conquest of Andalusia*, the reader is introduced to Visigothic Spain in the period immediately preceding the Muslim invasion of 710 AD (91 AH).[68] The period is one in which the Arian beliefs of the Visigothic dynasty have been challenged and eventually replaced, at least at the center of authority, the city of Toledo, by Roman Catholicism.[69] The Spanish Catholic bishops have conspired to depose the Visigothic King Witiza and replace him with a monarch of their own choosing, Roderic. The deposed king's brother, Oppas, remains as metropolitan bishop of the land, but is clearly a controversial figure, as the narrative of the novel is to make abundantly clear. In a cruel gesture, the new king has kept the former heir-apparent, Alfonso, Witiza's son, as a retainer at the palace, and has to tolerate the continued presence of the metropolitan bishop, Alfonso's uncle, as senior figure in the Spanish church hierarchy, in spite of the latter's obvious dislike of the way that

---

68 Indeed, we might note with regard to Zaidan's choice of title that the actual narrative postpones that crucial event—the Muslim invasion—until the latter part of the work, giving much more prominence to the politics and intrigues of the Visigothic dynasty, its ruling classes, and the fraught relationship between church and state. Without wishing to downplay the role of Tariq ibn Ziyad and his forces in bringing about this profound transformation in European history, we might suggest that a title such as "The Fall of Visigothic Spain" would serve as a better reflection of the contents of Zaidan's narrative, whether as title or subtitle.

69 Arianism is named for Arius (d. 336), a church leader of Alexandria who opposed the linkages implicit in the doctrine of the Trinity, choosing to regard Jesus as a perfect human being separate from the divine essence of God. The primary agenda of the Council of Nicaea (325 AD) was to refute Arian doctrine by linking the Father and Son in their divinity. The result was what is now known, and regularly used by Christians, as the Nicene Creed.

the king and the Catholic bishops have dethroned his brother. As if those historical facts are not enough to provide the novel with an atmosphere of political tension and intrigue, the bishop has also arranged the engagement of Alfonso to Florinda, the beautiful and devout daughter of Julian, the governor of the Spanish garrison at Sabta on the North African coast. Within the context of this complex web of relationships that the historical sources provide, Zaidan is thus able to give his readers ample detail about Visigothic history, Christian rituals and beliefs, attitudes of the populace toward the ruling elite, and, in particular, the role of the Jewish community of Spain—through an elaborate system of covert cells—in bringing about the downfall of the dynasty that has been systematically oppressing them. The novel opens on Christmas Day in the royal capital of Toledo, and the ceremonial aspects of that festival— the royal procession from the palace and the ceremonies at the cathedral, are recounted in detail, as are many other rituals of the court. It ends with the aftermath of the great battle of Guadalete in 711 AD (92 AH), at which the outnumbered forces of Tariq ibn Ziyad have defeated King Roderic's army and the king himself has died.

In his excellent study devoted to Zaidan's works (see footnote 65 above), Walid Hamarneh points out that a prominent feature of the narrative of Zaidan's historical novels is the inclusion in the plot of a local love story. Whereas in the case of many of the novels that love story is a creative insertion into the context of the historical events involved, in this novel the two lovers are already principal players in the historical action itself. It is Roderic's unbridled passion for Florinda and his assault on her person that arouses the fury of her fiancé's uncle, Bishop Oppas, and, even more so, of her father in Africa, an outrage that persuades him to join forces with the Muslim army that is about to cross the Straits. Florinda's fate, coupled to that of Bishop Oppas, who has been imprisoned by Roderic, are both key factors in the tangled series of negotiations that precede the final battle and are only fully resolved in its aftermath.

Zaidan's clear educational purpose in his historical fiction manifests itself in this particular novel in a number of ways. Prime amongst them is the mode of narration. In terms originally coined by the British novelist E.M. Forster, this narrator "tells" rather than "shows." Events are duly narrated; informational details are provided, where necessary, about ceremonies, protocols, and rituals; and the motivations and emotions of characters are described and often commented on, the comments frequently taking the form of gnomic or moralizing judgments. In a word, the narrator of this novel is omniscient, and the narrative is, in Mikhail Bakhtin's terminology, monologic. The reader, thereby, not only follows the course of the events and the role that the various characters play in them, but in the process is given a good deal of information and counsel about history, religion, and human behavior. Among the more striking aspects of the context provided by this novel is the belief by many of the characters that the advent of Islam to Spain will radically improve the lives of the majority of its inhabitants who have suffered so badly under Visigoth rule, or at least during the latter phases of that dynasty.

These narrative features are further enhanced by another aspect of the novel's overall structure, one that is an anticipated consequence of its original mode of publication, namely its serialized form. Since the historical framework and the identity of the principal characters are already established, Zaidan does not have to suffer in the way that a serializing novelist such as Charles Dickens did at the hands of his readership. Not only that, but, since Zaidan was the owner of the journal, *al-Hilal*, in which the episodes were being published, he was presumably not subject to the same pressures of deadlines and monetary rewards established by someone else. As it is, every episode of the original publication, and, in its current printed form, every chapter in the novel, is assigned a title with the obvious aim—somewhat similar to the opening strategies connected with the short-story genre—of enticing the reader's expectations. As the action of the narrative moves from the capital city of Toledo to Sabta in North Africa and to Astigi in southern Spain, to which Alfonso and his troops are dispatched by the king, so does the serialized narrative follow each subplot through a sequence of chapters, which often conclude with a narrator's statement of closure and shift of venue. For a while, we stay with Alfonso, then we move to Florinda and her confrontation with the king, then we linger with Bishop Oppas as he faces an ecclesiastical trial followed by a period of virtual incarceration. Each character strand is pursued for several chapters, and it is only when the Visigothic and Muslim armies confront each other toward the conclusion of the novel that all the strands come together and personal problems are resolved. Florinda and Alfonso are reunited, Julian discovers a long-lost son, and Oppas is allowed to retire to a monastery. A happy ending, one might suggest, although we are left to assume that the villain of the piece, King Roderic, has met his just deserts.

The Conquest of Andalusia provides its readers with an excellent example of the traditional historical novel, providing as it does a vivid portrait of a country on the eve of a major cultural and social transformation, one that in subsequent centuries would have an enormous and often unappreciated impact not only within its own borders but also far beyond. In addition to that, the translator of the novel will conclude by suggesting that, like its Scottish analogue with Robert Louis Stevenson, this novel is also a thoroughly enjoyable read, a verdict that seems to be confirmed by the continuing popularity of Zaidan's novels well over a century after their initial publication.

I noted earlier that the bulk of this novel by Zaidan is actually set in the period before the Muslim invasion of Spain. For that reason, the majority of the names included in the text are non-Arab—for example, Alfonso, Roderic, Oppas, and Florinda. I have therefore chosen not to include any of the symbols (macrons and diacritical dots) that would normally accompany a text that includes Arabic names. Thus, Tariq ibn Ziyad is printed that way, rather than as Tāriq ibn Ziyād.

Also as noted in the text, Jurji Zaidan uses the Arabic term barbari to describe the indigenous peoples of North Africa. We have translated it as Berber. More recently, however, that term has come to be regarded with disfavor by the people whom it describes, the preferred term being the one by which they describe themselves: Amazigh (plural: Imazighen).

The Conquest of Andalusia

Study Guide

Roger Allen

1. Who was Jurji Zaidan?

Jurji Zaidan was a famous Arab writer who was born and grew up in Lebanon and lived in Egypt. He was born in 1861 in Beirut, where, as a teenager, he helped his father run a small restaurant. When he was nineteen years old, Zaidan enrolled in the medical school at what was then the Syrian Protestant College, now the American University of Beirut. However, after taking part in a student strike, he decided to leave the university. He soon left his native Lebanon and moved to Cairo, Egypt. Once settled there, Zaidan began a long career as a writer and journalist. In 1892, he established a magazine called *Al-Hilal* (The Crescent Moon), which is being published to this day. He wrote twenty-two novels, all of which were published in serialized form in that magazine. *The Conquest of Andalusia* (that being the name of one of the southern provinces of Spain, which was adopted by the Muslims as the name for the Iberian Peninsula as a whole) is one of them. In addition to the novels, he also published books and wrote articles in his magazine on a large number of topics: the history of Islamic civilization, the history and development of languages, as well as political, social, educational, and ethical issues. He thus played a very important role in making readers of Arabic more aware of the important events in their history and in developing a sense of national identity. He died in 1914.

2. What is a historical novel?

A historical novel is a kind of fiction that makes use of important events from history and people who took part in them in order to provide readers with a vivid portrayal of previous eras in the life of their national community. Among prominent writers of historical novels are Sir Walter Scott (d. 1832), who, among other novels, wrote *Ivanhoe* (set in twelfth-century England) and *Rob Roy* (set in Scotland just before the Jacobite rising in the eighteenth century); the Russian author Leo Tolstoy (d. 1910), whose enormous novel *War and Peace* describes Russian society before and during Napoleon's invasion in 1812; and the American writer James Fenimore Cooper (d. 1851), whose *The Last of the Mohicans* portrays the role of native Americans during the 1757 war in the North American colonies. This type of novel often provides the reader with a sense of what it was like to live in the historical period and region in question, but it also brings the events to life by revealing through conversations how the people involved in those events interact with each other and share their views and emotions. In Zaidan's case, the novels include a love story in order to show how ordinary people manage to respond to the important events going on around them. In *The Conquest of Andalusia*, the two lovers are actually important participants in the events leading up to the Muslim invasion of Spain in 710 AD: Alfonso, the son of the deposed king of Spain, and Florinda, the daughter of the governor of Sabta, a city on the coast of North Africa.

3. What is the early history of the Arabic novel?

Like most new kinds of literature that appeared in the Arabic-speaking world during the nineteenth and into the twentieth century, the novel's development involved a combination of imported examples translated into Arabic from Western literature and revived and adapted examples of types of narrative from the pre-modern heritage. Among the first European works to be translated into Arabic were Alexandre Dumas's famous novel, *The Count of Monte Cristo*, which served as a model and precedent for the appearance of a number of serialized works, including, for example, those of Salim al-Bustani published in his family's journal, *al-Jinan*. Alongside these translations of European works and imitations of them, there were other narratives that revived earlier types and styles of Arabic story writing, such as Ahmad Faris al-Shidyaq's *Al-Saq 'Ala al-Saq* (One Leg Over Another, 1855) and Muhammad al-Muwaylihi's *Hadith 'Isa ibn Hisham* ('Isa Hisham's Tale, 1907). The novels that Zaidan wrote and published were a very important part of the developmental process through which the novel was accepted into Middle Eastern culture as a form of narrative that could express the hopes and aspirations of people in quest of national identity. In the first three decades of the twentieth century, these different strands were gradually fused together into a form of narrative writing that was to see its acceptance into Arabic culture crowned by the work of Naguib Mahfouz, the great Egyptian novelist and winner of the Nobel Prize in 1988.

4. What historical period does *The Conquest of Andalusia* cover?

By 710 AD, the date of the Muslim invasion of Spain, the Muslim community was not yet a century old. The Prophet Muhammad had emigrated from Mecca to Medina in 622 AD, that emigration (*hijra*) marking the beginning of the Islamic calendar—AH 1; he died ten years later (632 AD). Since those earliest times, the Islamic faith had spread rapidly to both east and west: Syria, Iraq, and Egypt first, but then east toward India and west along the northern shores of Africa.

In the case of Africa, the Umayyad caliphate, now centered in Damascus, had dispatched a general, Musa ibn Nusayr, at the head of the Muslim army that had moved rapidly to the west, converting many of the peoples in its path. Among those people were the Berbers, the indigenous tribes of the regions that the army was passing through. Many Berbers converted to Islam and joined the forces in their push to the west. As Zaidan shows in this novel, one of those converts was Tariq ibn Ziyad, a renowned warrior and leader, who was to be trusted by Musa ibn Nusayr with leading the Muslim forces across the Straits at the western end of the Mediterranean and invading the Iberian Peninsula.

The Conquest of Andalusia is set during the period immediately before the Muslim invasion. Starting on Christmas Day, with all its official ceremonies in the capital city and royal residence of Toledo, the novel follows the events and intrigues that lead up to the Muslim invasion under the leadership of Tariq ibn Ziyad and the eventual defeat of King Roderic's army at the Battle of Guadalete in 711 or 712 AD.

5. What kind of social, political, and religious picture does Zaidan present of Spain before the Muslim conquest?

For several centuries before the Muslim invasion of 710 AD (91 AH), the Iberian Peninsula—now Spain and Portugal—had been ruled by a dynasty of Visigoths, a tribe whose origins lay in Northern Europe. Originally followers of the early Christian doctrine known as Arianism, the Goths adopted Roman Catholicism as their official faith at the end of the sixth century (although some members of the ruling family continued to practice their Arian beliefs). During this time period, the Jewish communities in the peninsula were subjected to harsh treatment by the ruling authorities, with demands that they convert to the Roman Catholic version of Christianity. The church and its authorities exerted increasing power from the capital city of Toledo, and in 710 AD, they appear to have helped engineer a coup in which the Visigoth king, Witiza, was dethroned and replaced by Roderic—the king during the events recounted in this novel. It should be noted, however, that the historical record is not clear about the precise circumstances involved.

6. Who are the novel's main characters?

Alfonso is the son of the deposed king, Witiza. He is engaged to Florinda, the beautiful daughter of Count Julian, the governor of the North African province of Sabta. In a cruel gesture, Alfonso has been kept at court as a retainer by the new king to keep track of all his comings and goings.

Florinda, Count Julian's daughter, is engaged to Alfonso, but is the target of the lustful desires of King Roderic. When the novel opens, she has recently been moved into quarters within the king's palace in Toledo. She is saved from his advances through the intervention of Metropolitan Bishop Oppas, who is Alfonso's uncle and has supervised the engagement of the young couple.

King Roderic is the king of Spain, who has been installed as monarch after the previous king, Witiza, had been dethroned in a move approved and perhaps orchestrated by the Catholic bishops. In Zaidan's novel, he is portrayed as impulsive and tyrannical. He develops a passion for Florinda, and his conduct toward her leads to a confrontation with Oppas, the metropolitan bishop. It is because of the king's conduct toward Florinda that her father, Count Julian, sides with the Muslim invaders in order to get rid of Roderic.

Metropolitan Bishop Oppas, the brother of the deposed king, Witiza, and thus uncle of Alfonso, is the senior ecclesiastical figure in Spain during King Roderic's reign. But he is obviously bitterly opposed to not only the method used in his brother's dethronement but also the cruel, tyrannical, and corrupt methods that Roderic is using to maintain his authority as king. In spite of his opposition to Roderic, Oppas remains intensely loyal to Visigothic Spain as the Muslim invasion of the country threatens to overthrow the Christian monarchy that he has known throughout his life.

Father Martin, the thoroughly evil and duplicitous Catholic priest and counselor to King Roderic, is clearly more interested in preserving his own position of influence with the king than he is with upholding the moral and spiritual doctrines of the Christian church to whose clergy he belongs.

Count Julian is the father of Florinda and governor of the North African province of Sabta. Once he hears about the way in which King Roderic has attempted to force himself upon Florinda, his daughter, he joins the forces of Tariq ibn Ziyad and guides the Muslim forces through southern Spain after they have crossed the Straits that have since become known as the Straits of Gibraltar—Gibraltar meaning literally "Tariq's mountain"—in Arabic, Jabal Tariq.

Ya'qub, Alfonso's faithful and reliable retainer, turns out to be a major figure in the secret Jewish community, which for many years had been organizing and collecting money with a view to bringing about a change in the ruling system in Spain and thus their own status within the society. In the novel, Ya'qub and his Jewish colleague, the much-traveled Sulayman, are portrayed as playing a major role in the negotiations that take place before the final and crucial battle.

7. Why were the smaller Arab armies successful in their invasion of Andalusia?

Accounts of the crucial battle of Guadalete in which the forces of Tariq ibn Ziyad defeated the much larger army of King Roderic were all written some time after the event. They are, therefore, not all that precise; indeed, it is not even known what the exact date or year of the battle was. With regard to the reasons for the defeat of King Roderic's army, history makes clear that there was widespread discontent with his tyrannical rule among the people of Spain, whereas, as Zaidan notes in his novel, the Muslim invaders were not only battle-experienced but also had no choice but to engage in fierce combat since any backward retreat would be cut off by the sea that they had just crossed. The actual sequence of events that took place during the battle is not known, but Zaidan describes a crucial moment in the battle when Alfonso, who is commander of a regiment that has already been sent south to the city of Astigi to put down a local rebellion against the king, receives a letter from his beloved Florinda in which she tells him about the treatment she has received from King Roderic. At that point he decides that during the battle he will abandon the Spanish king's ranks and lead his entire regiment over to the Muslim side. The mere sight of such a movement and the inevitable impact it had on the Spanish army's strategy are shown to be deeply disillusioning to King Roderic's forces and mark a crucial turning point in the battle.

As the invasion of Andalusia proceeded, the Muslim armies were clearly aided in their progress through the country both by the general discontent that the populace felt toward the monarchy ruling in Toledo and by the strong support and monetary assistance of the Jewish communities not only in Spain but across the Muslim world as well. These communities, as Zaidan shows in the novel, regarded life under Muslim rule as being potentially far more tolerant than it was under the rule of the Visigothic dynasty.

8. How did the Jewish community help the Arab invasion? Why was it in their interest to do so?

Zaidan's novel introduces its readers (through the character of Ya'qub, Alfonso's chamberlain) to the existence of a number of highly secretive Jewish communities, not only in the Iberian Peninsula itself, but in other regions of the Islamic world in which Jewish communities existed. While Alfonso is residing in the southern city of Astigi (to which he has been sent as commander of a regiment so that King Roderic may be free to seduce Florinda, Alfonso's fiancée), Ya'qub takes him into a subterranean network of tunnels that eventually lead to a meeting room where the local Jewish community gathers in secret. There, Alfonso learns of the existence of a number of such Jewish communities, all of which were established in great secrecy because of the way the Visigothic kingdom had been persecuting Jews, demanding, at the insistence of the now-powerful Catholic church in the country, that Jews convert to Christianity. Zaidan's novel shows clearly that, in the eyes of Jewish people, the religious freedoms that existed within the regions where Islam was the predominant faith were considerably more favorable than the intolerance and persecution practiced by the oppressive regime in Toledo. Tariq ibn Ziyad's invading army was thus viewed as a means of bringing about religious tolerance and a more just society in which to live and flourish. Later historical sources confirm for us that such was, in fact, to be the case in Andalusia for several centuries after the invasion of 710 AD.

OTHER RESOURCES

Philipp Thomas, *Gurji Zaidan. His Life and Thought*. Wiesbaden, Germany: Steiner Verlag, 1979.

Zaidan Jurji, *The Autobiography of Jurji Zaidan*, edited and translated by Thomas Philip, Washington, DC: Three Continents Press, 1990.

Cities of Light: The Rise and Fall of Islamic Spain a PBS documentary about the history of Muslim Spain (Al-Andalus), Gardner Films (www. islamicspain.tv). The DVD can be ordered at 1-800-PLAYPBS, $24.95.

Thomas Philipp, *Jurji Zaidan's Secular Analysis of History and Language as Foundations of Arab Nationalism*, (Forthcoming).